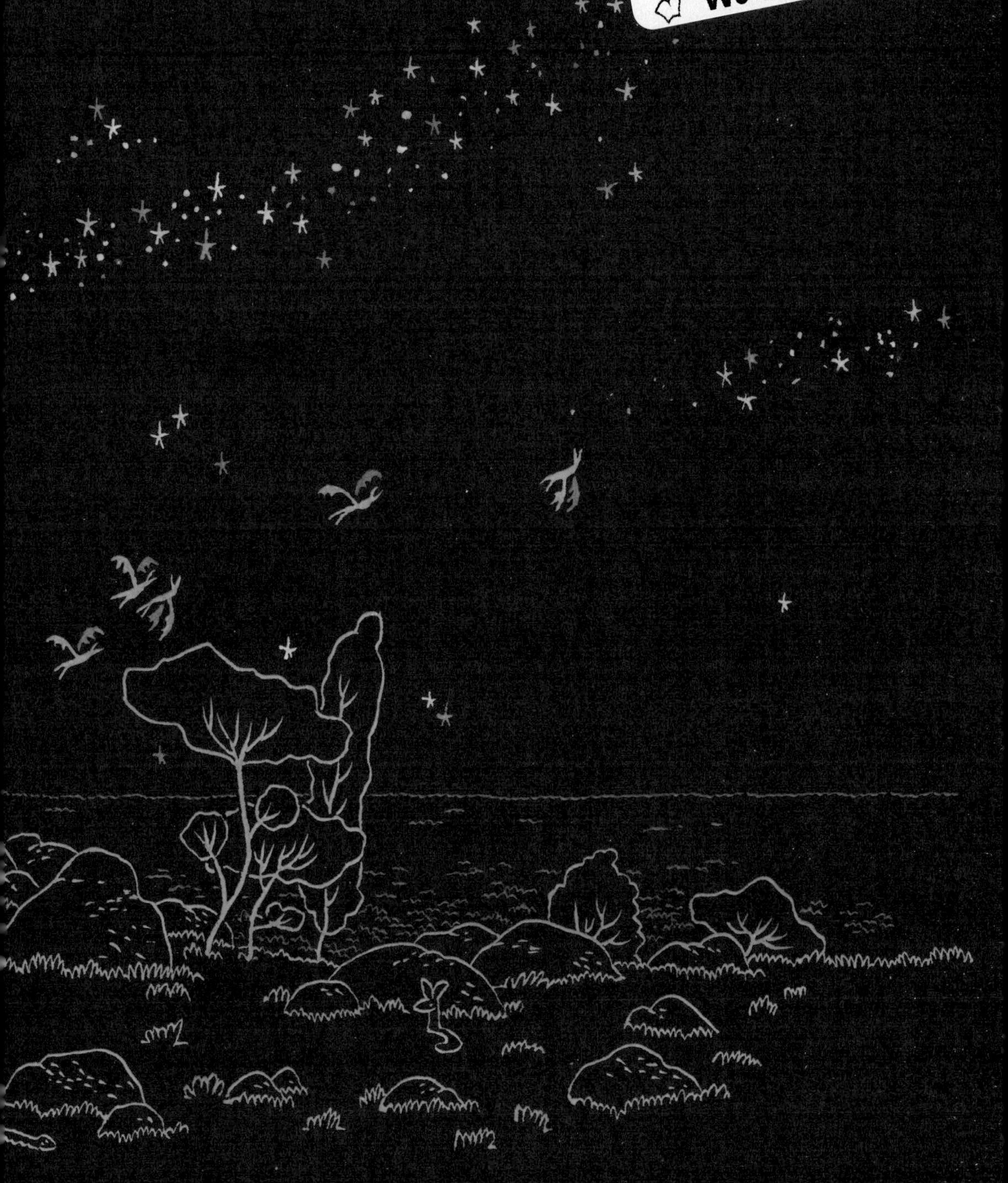

Ralph Azham

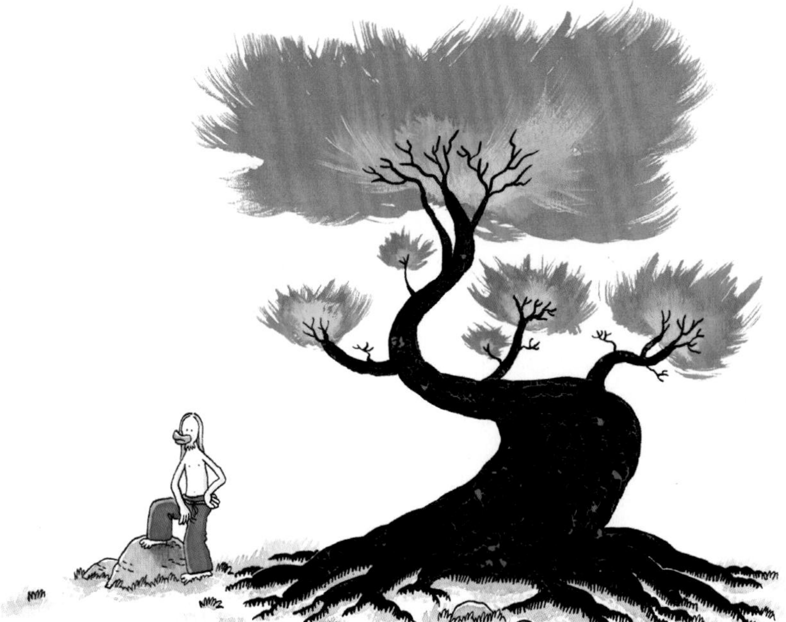

SUPER GENIUS
New York

Ralph Azham

Originally published by Éditions Dupuis RALPH AZHAM 1—*Est-ce qu'on ment aux gens qu'on aime?*, RALPH AZHAM 2—*La mort au début du chemin*, RALPH AZHAM 3—*Noirs sont les étoiles*

Super Genius is an imprint of Papercutz.

Story and Art: Lewis Trondheim
Color: Brigitte Findakly

JayJay Jackson — Production
Kim Thompson, Joe Johnson — Translation
Emory Liu, Nikki FoxRobot, and Wilson Ramos Jr — Lettering
Spenser Nellis — Marketing Coordinator
Jordan Hillman — Editorial Intern
Jeff Whitman — Managing Editor
Jim Salicrup
Editor-in-Chief

Special thanks to Gary Groth and Anton Heully

HC ISBN: 978-1-5458-0879-5
PB ISBN: 978-1-5458-0880-1

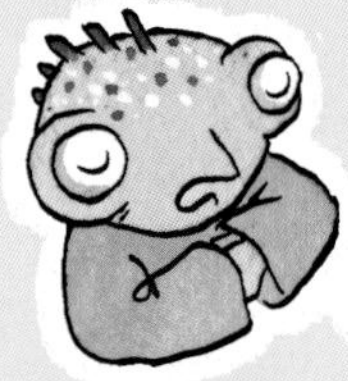

Go to www.supergeniuscomics.com for information about other Super Genius titles.

SUPER GENIUS

Printed in China
April 2022

Super Genius books may be purchased for business or promotional use. For information on bulk purchases please contact Macmillan Corporate and Premium Sales Department at (800) 221-7945 x5442.

Distributed by Macmillan
First Super Genius Printing

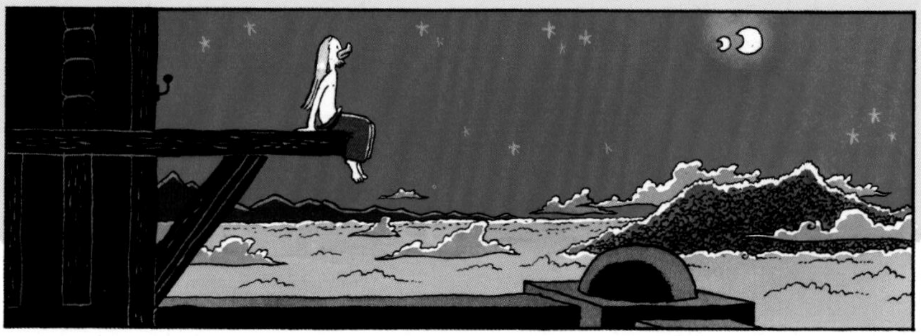

TABLE OF CONTENTS

Ralph Azham

1

Why Would You Lie to Someone You Love?

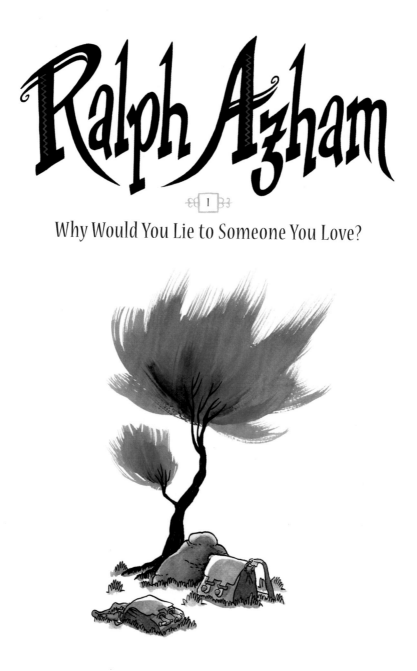

Story and Art: Lewis Trondheim
Colors: Brigitte Findakly
Translation: Kim Thompson
Lettering: Emory Liu

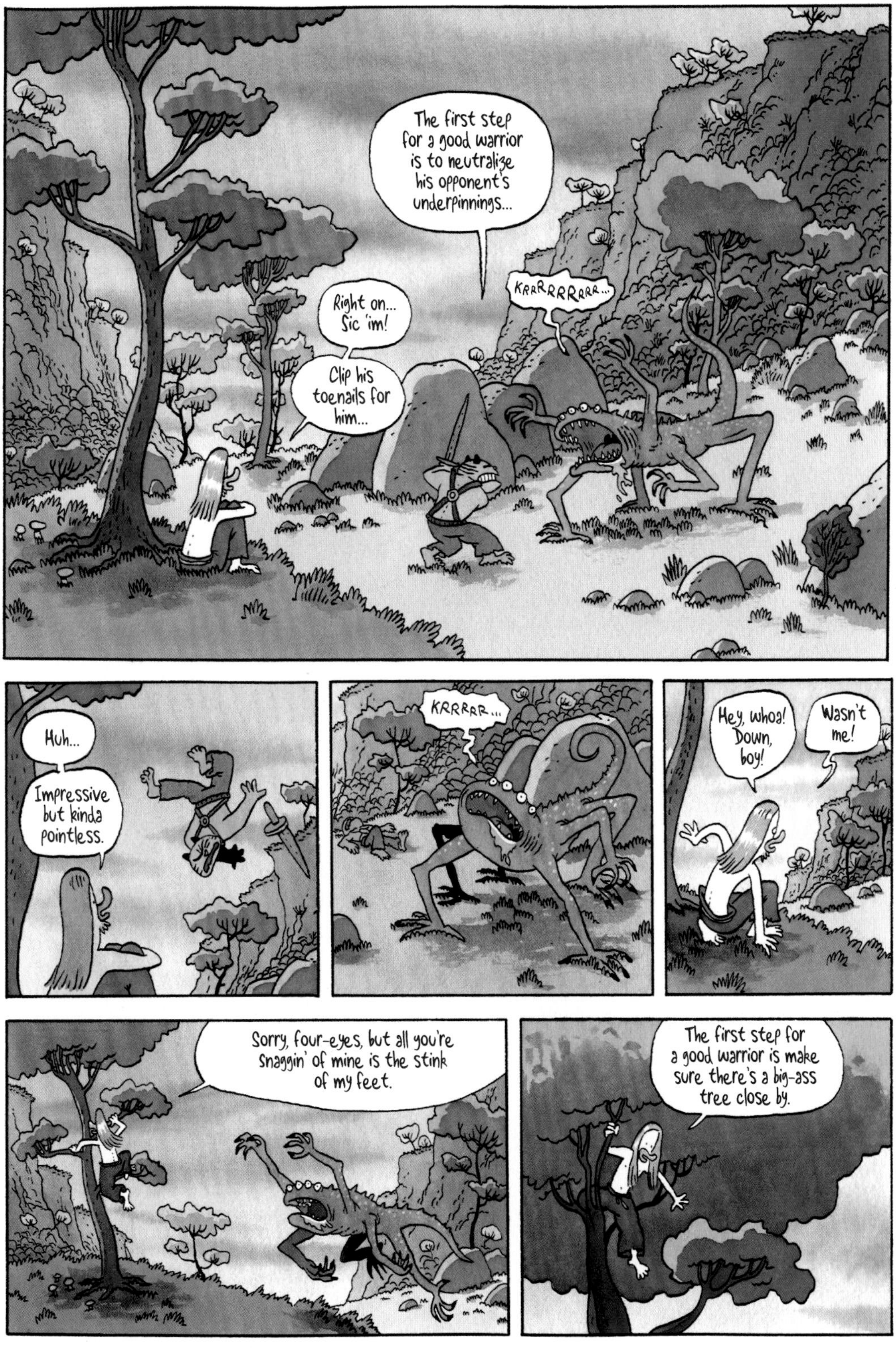

The first step for a good warrior is to neutralize his opponent's underpinnings...
Right on... Sic 'im!
Clip his toenails for him...
KRRRRRRRRR...
Huh...
Impressive but kinda pointless.
KRRRRR...
Hey, whoa! Down, boy!
Wasn't me!
Sorry, four-eyes, but all you're snaggin' of mine is the stink of my feet.
The first step for a good warrior is make sure there's a big-ass tree close by.

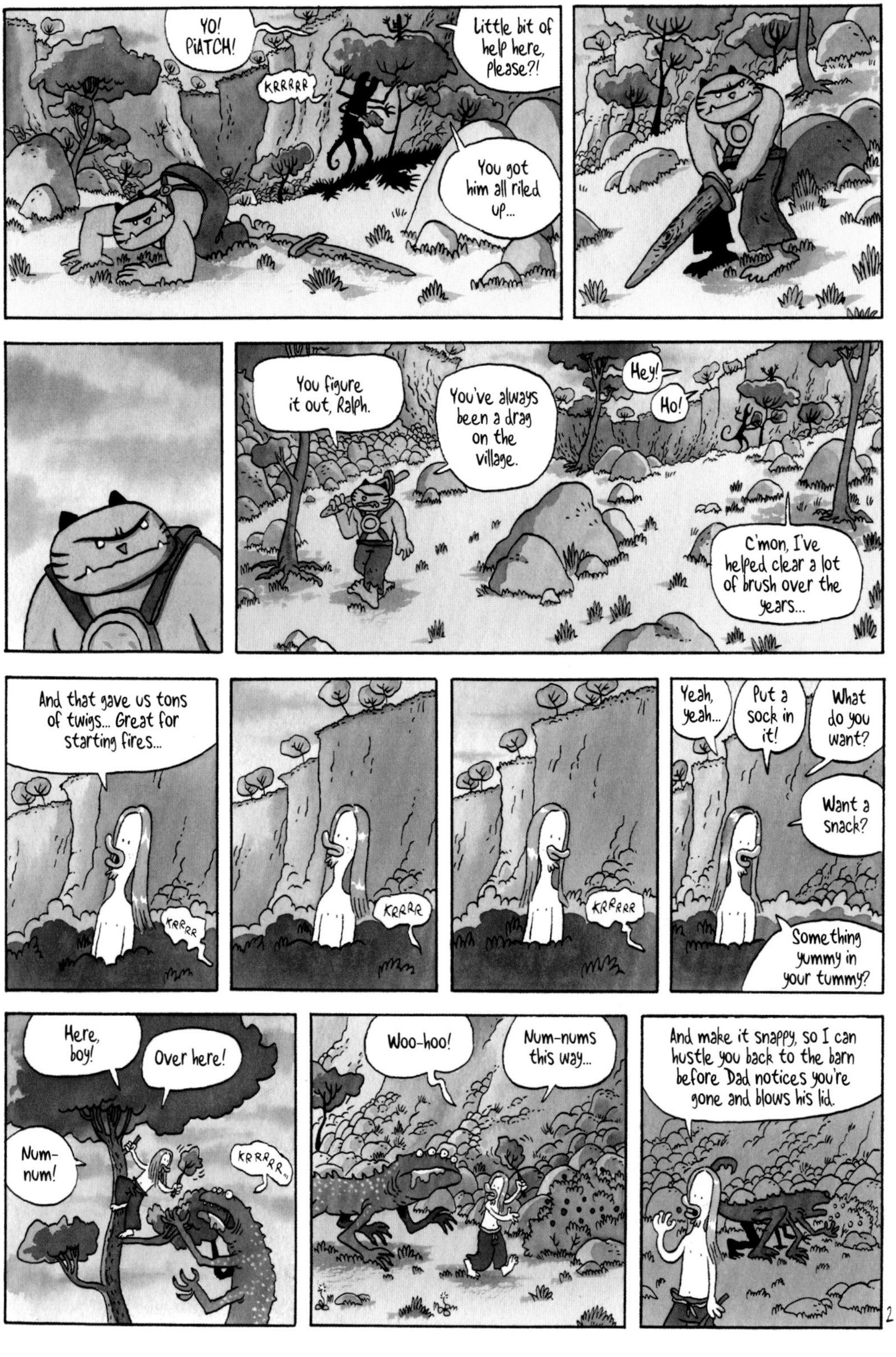
YO! PIATCH!
KRRRRR
Little bit of help here, please?!
You got him all riled up...
You figure it out, Ralph.
You've always been a drag on the village.
Hey!
Ho!
C'mon, I've helped clear a lot of brush over the years...
And that gave us tons of twigs... Great for starting fires...
KRRRR
KRRRR
KRRRRR
Yeah, yeah...
Put a sock in it!
What do you want?
Want a snack?
Something yummy in your tummy?
Here, boy!
Over here!
Num-num!
KRRRRR...
Woo-hoo!
Num-nums this way...
And make it snappy, so I can hustle you back to the barn before Dad notices you're gone and blows his lid.
2

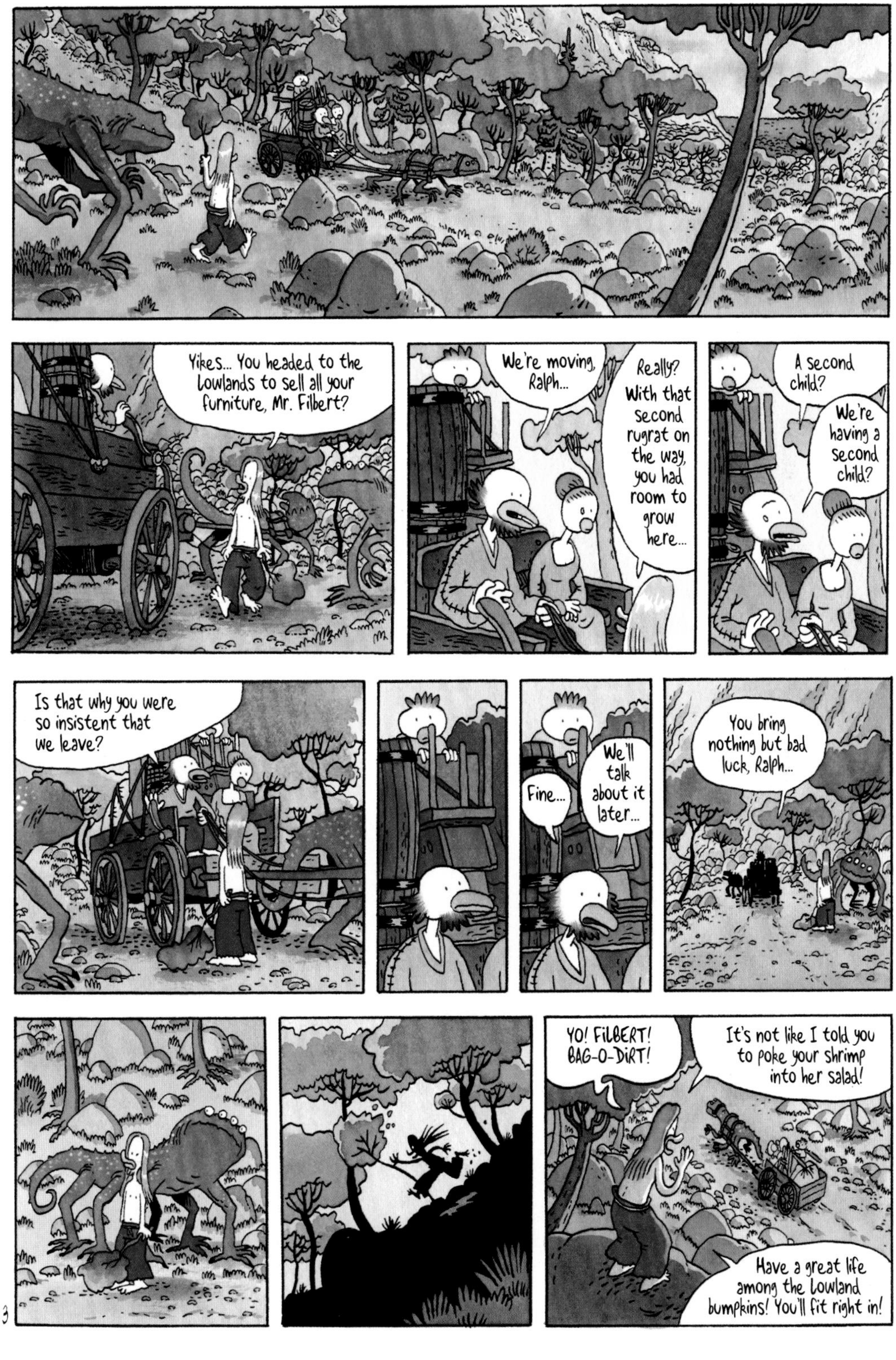
Yikes... You headed to the Lowlands to sell all your furniture, Mr. Filbert?
We're moving, Ralph...
Really? With that second rugrat on the way, you had room to grow here...
A second child?
We're having a second child?
Is that why you were so insistent that we leave?
Fine...
We'll talk about it later...
You bring nothing but bad luck, Ralph...
YO! FILBERT! BAG-O-DIRT!
It's not like I told you to poke your shrimp into her salad!
Have a great life among the Lowland bumpkins! You'll fit right in!
3

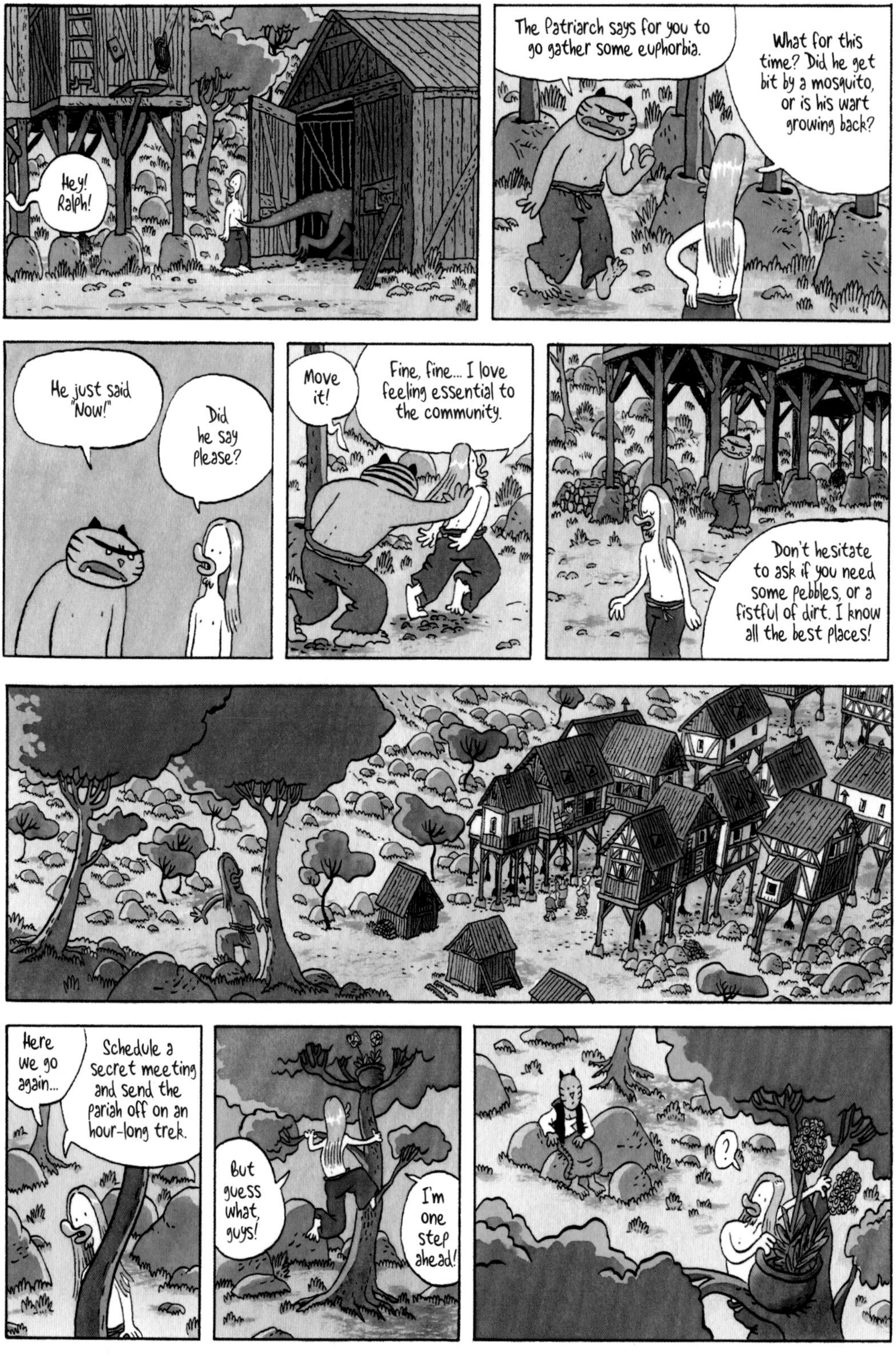
Hey! Ralph!
The Patriarch says for you to go gather some euphorbia.
What for this time? Did he get bit by a mosquito, or is his wart growing back?
He just said "Now!"
Did he say please?
Move it!
Fine, fine... I love feeling essential to the community.
Don't hesitate to ask if you need some pebbles, or a fistful of dirt. I know all the best places!
Here we go again...
Schedule a secret meeting and send the pariah off on an hour-long trek.
But guess what, guys!
I'm one step ahead!
?
4

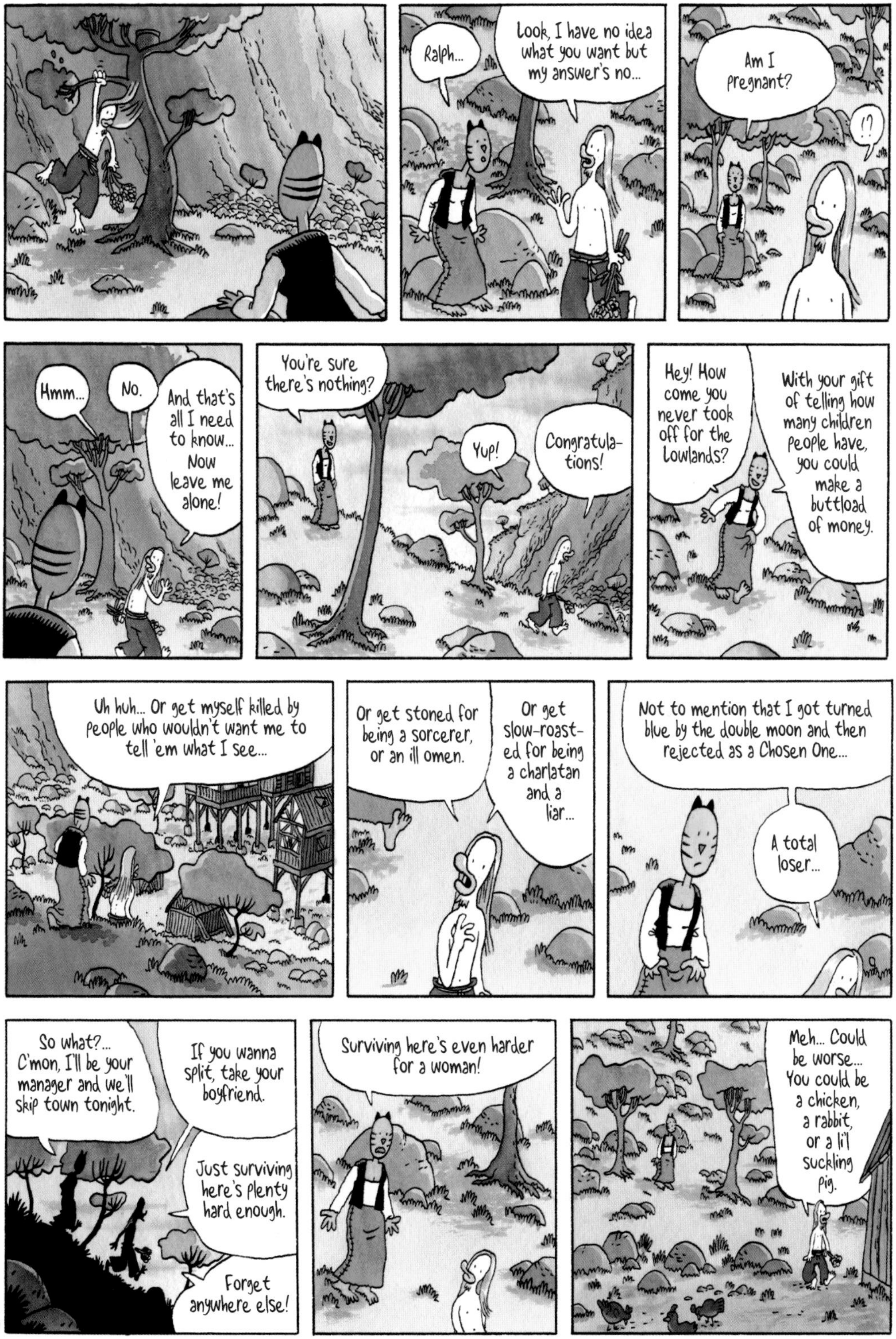
Ralph...
Look, I have no idea what you want but my answer's no...
Am I pregnant?
!?
Hmm...
No.
And that's all I need to know... Now leave me alone!
You're sure there's nothing?
Yup!
Congratula-tions!
Hey! How come you never took off for the Lowlands?
With your gift of telling how many children people have, you could make a buttload of money.
Uh huh... Or get myself killed by people who wouldn't want me to tell 'em what I see...
Or get stoned for being a sorcerer, or an ill omen.
Or get slow-roast-ed for being a charlatan and a liar...
Not to mention that I got turned blue by the double moon and then rejected as a Chosen One...
A total loser...
So what?... C'mon, I'll be your manager and we'll skip town tonight.
If you wanna split, take your boyfriend.
Just surviving here's plenty hard enough.
Forget anywhere else!
Surviving here's even harder for a woman!
Meh... Could be worse... You could be a chicken, a rabbit, or a li'l suckling pig.

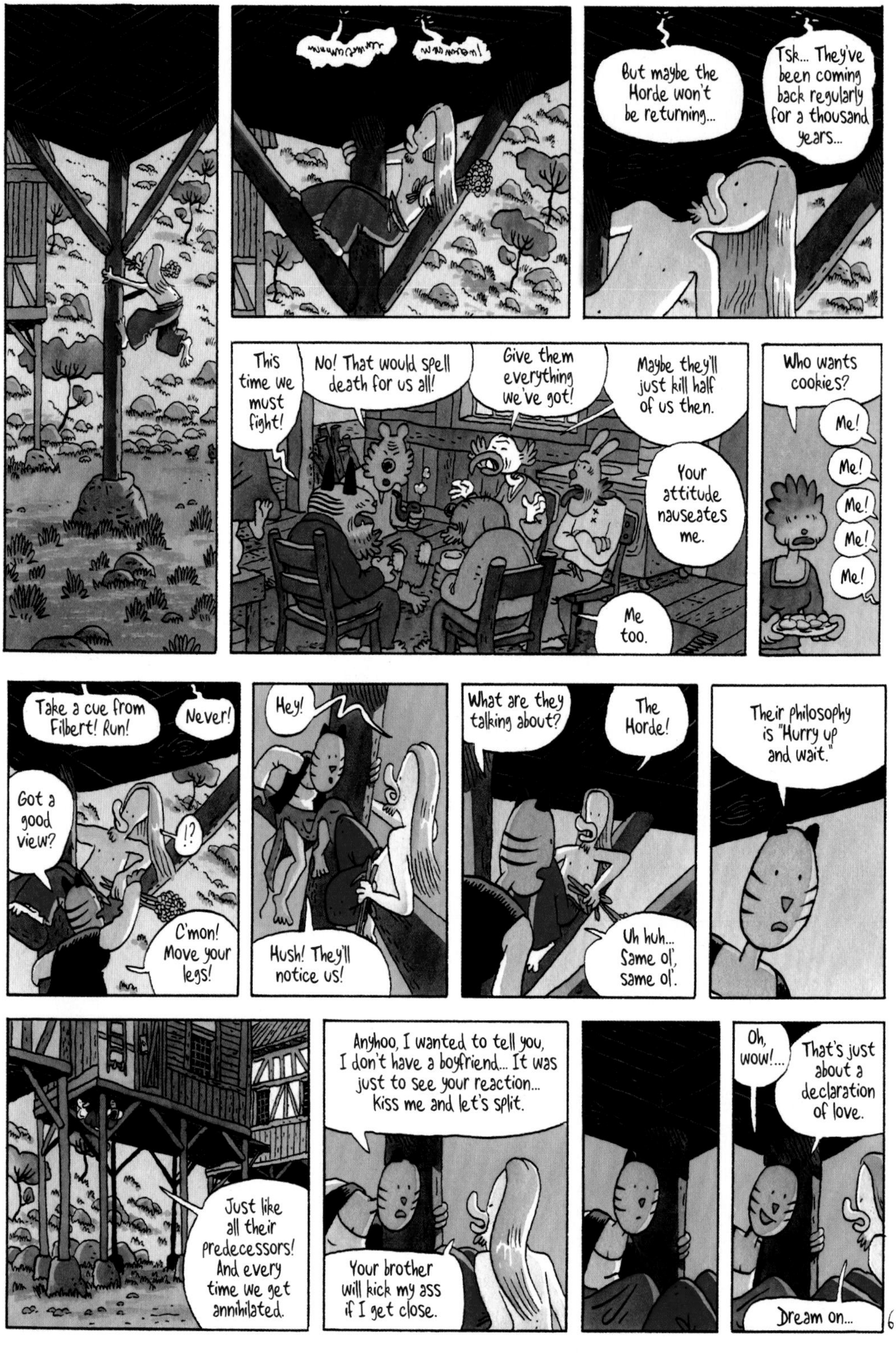

But maybe the Horde won't be returning...
Tsk... They've been coming back regularly for a thousand years...
This time we must fight!
No! That would spell death for us all!
Give them everything we've got!
Maybe they'll just kill half of us then.
Your attitude nauseates me.
Me too.
Who wants cookies?
Me!
Me!
Me!
Me!
Me!
Take a cue from Filbert! Run!
Never!
Got a good view?
!?
C'mon! Move your legs!
Hey!
Hush! They'll notice us!
What are they talking about?
The Horde!
Uh huh... Same ol', same ol'.
Their philosophy is "Hurry up and wait."
Just like all their predecessors! And every time we get annihilated.
Anyhoo, I wanted to tell you, I don't have a boyfriend... It was just to see your reaction... Kiss me and let's split.
Your brother will kick my ass if I get close.
Oh, wow!...
That's just about a declaration of love.
Dream on...
6

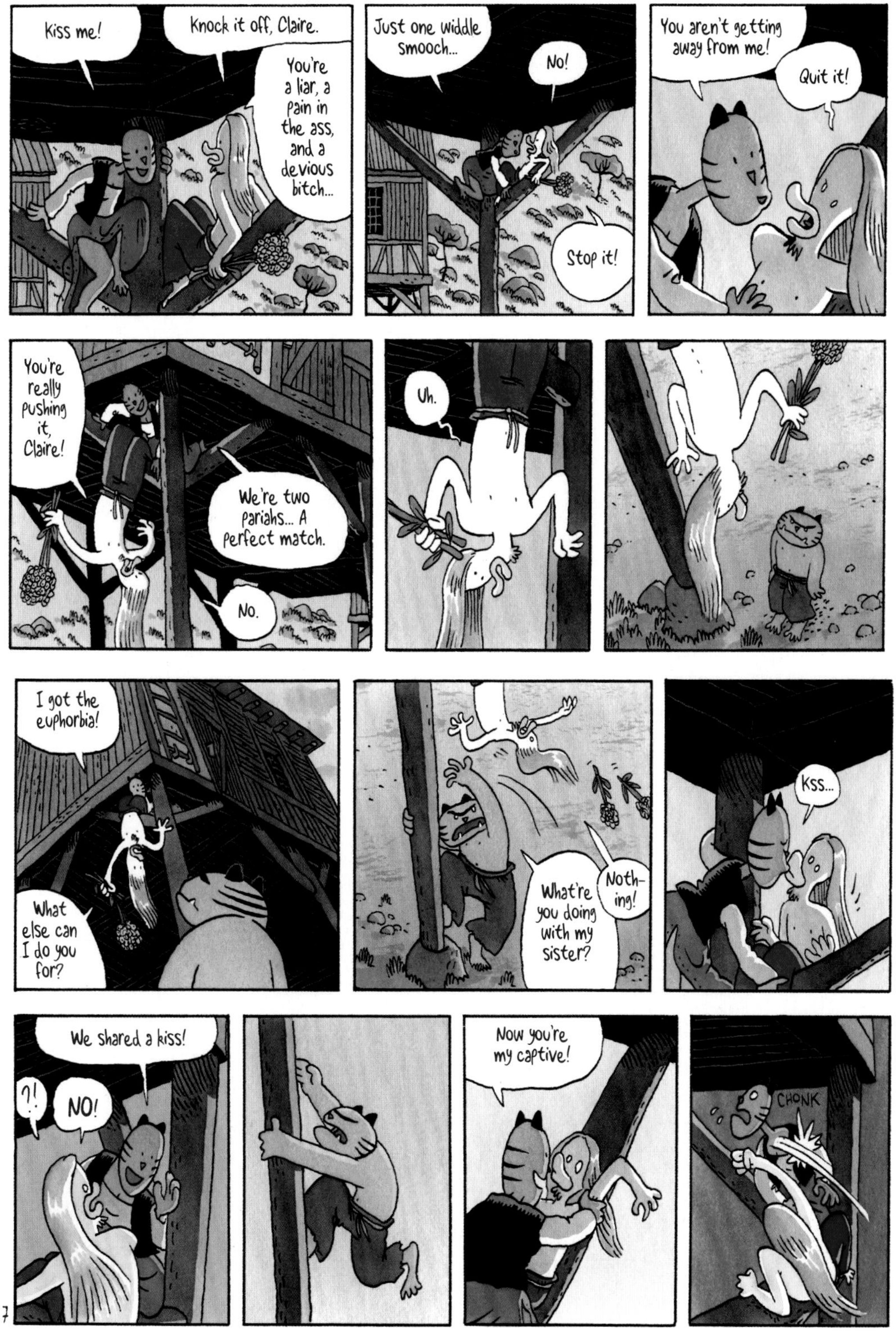

Kiss me!
Knock it off, Claire.
You're a liar, a pain in the ass, and a devious bitch...
Just one widdle smooch...
No!
Stop it!
You aren't getting away from me!
Quit it!
You're really pushing it, Claire!
We're two pariahs... A perfect match.
No.
Uh.
I got the euphorbia!
What else can I do you for?
What're you doing with my sister?
Noth-ing!
Kss...
We shared a kiss!
?!
NO!
Now you're my captive!
CHONK

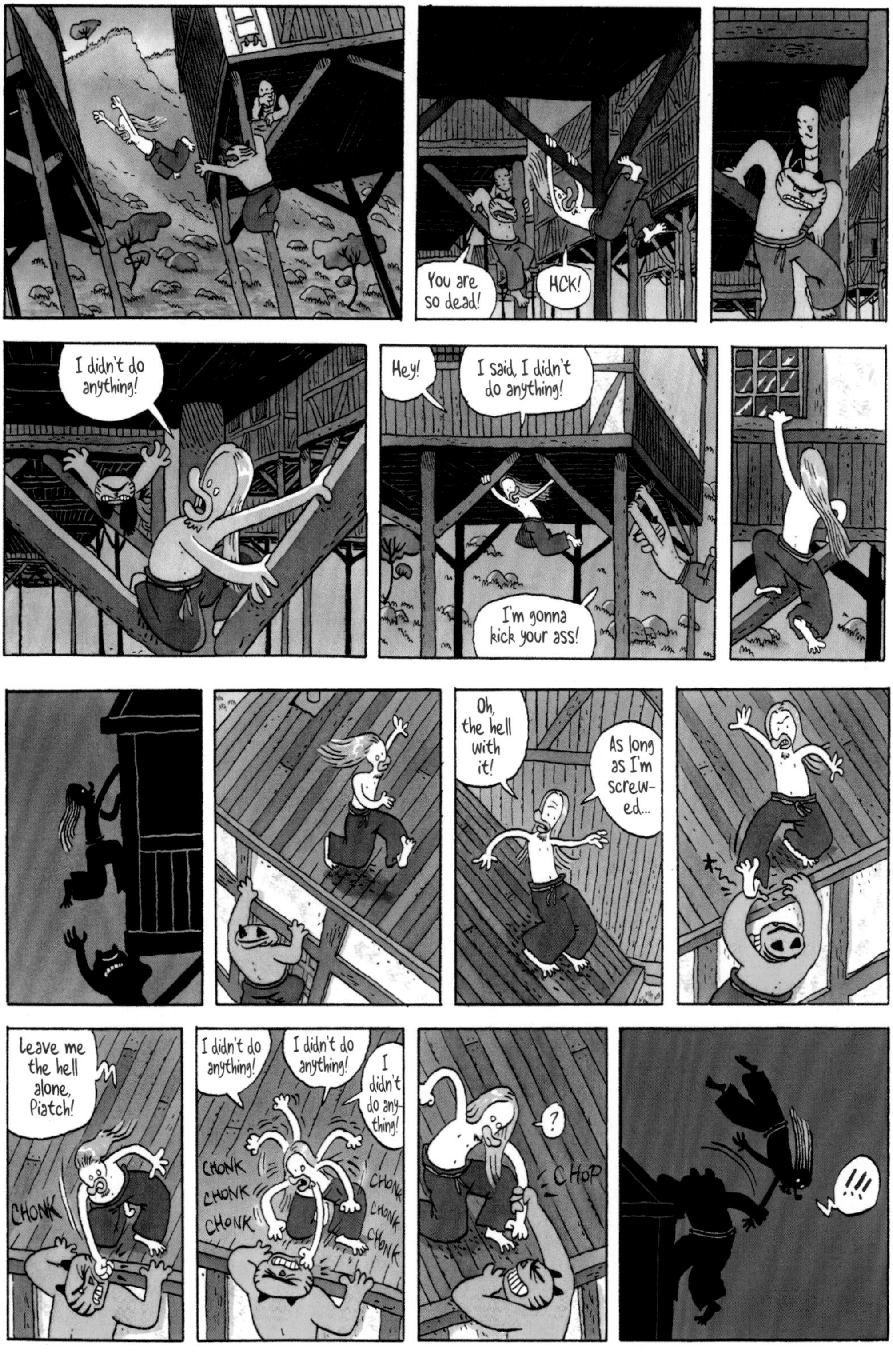
You are so dead!
HCK!
I didn't do anything!
Hey!
I said, I didn't do anything!
I'm gonna kick your ass!
Oh, the hell with it!
As long as I'm screw-ed...
Leave me the hell alone, Piatch!
CHONK
I didn't do anything!
I didn't do anything!
I didn't do any-thing!
CHONK
CHONK
CHONK
CHONK
CHONK
CHONK
?
CHOP
!!!

8

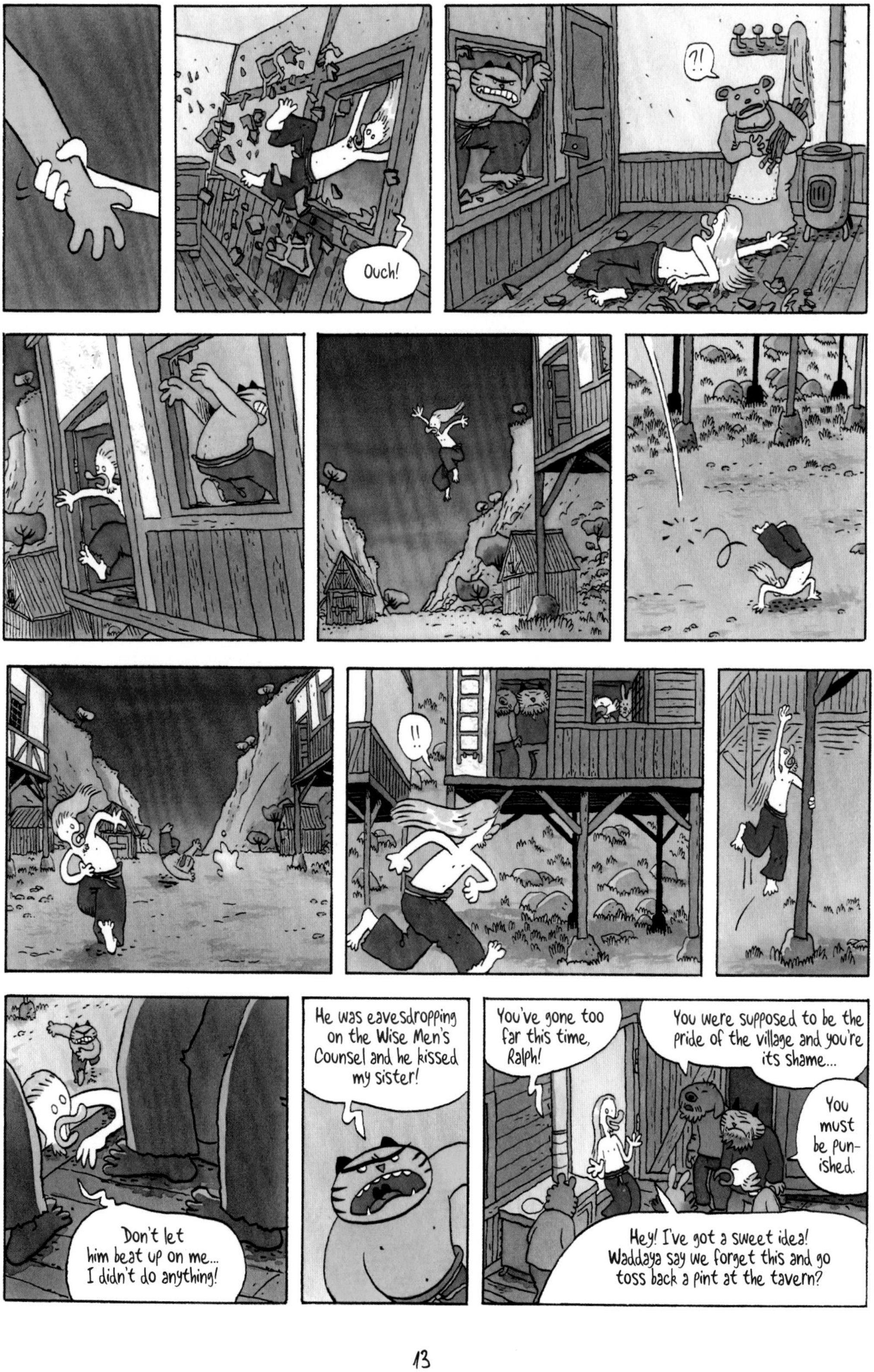
Ouch!
?!
!!
Don't let him beat up on me... I didn't do anything!
He was eavesdropping on the Wise Men's Counsel and he kissed my sister!
You've gone too far this time, Ralph!
You were supposed to be the pride of the village and you're its shame...
You must be pun-ished.
Hey! I've got a sweet idea! Waddaya say we forget this and go toss back a pint at the tavern?

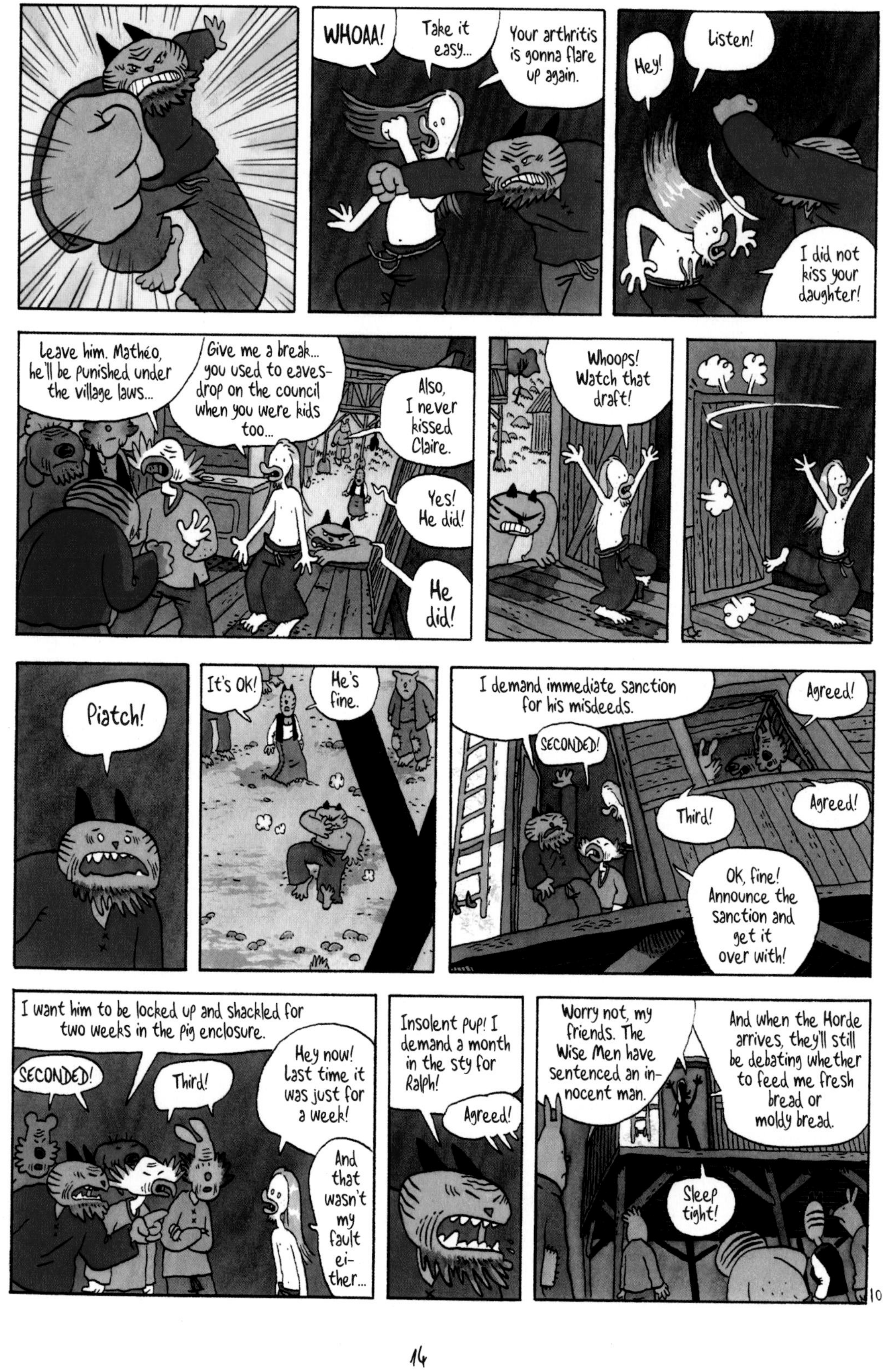
WHOAA!
Take it easy...
Your arthritis is gonna flare up again.
Hey!
Listen!
I did not kiss your daughter!
Leave him. Mathéo, he'll be punished under the village laws...
Give me a break... you used to eaves-drop on the council when you were kids too...
Also, I never kissed Claire.
Yes! He did!
He did!
Whoops! Watch that draft!
Piatch!
It's OK!
He's fine.
I demand immediate sanction for his misdeeds.
SECONDED!
Agreed!
Third!
Agreed!
Ok, fine! Announce the sanction and get it over with!
I want him to be locked up and shackled for two weeks in the pig enclosure.
SECONDED!
Third!
Hey now! Last time it was just for a week!
And that wasn't my fault ei-ther...
Insolent pup! I demand a month in the sty for Ralph!
Agreed!
Worry not, my friends. The Wise Men have sentenced an in-nocent man.
And when the Horde arrives, they'll still be debating whether to feed me fresh bread or moldy bread.
Sleep tight!
10

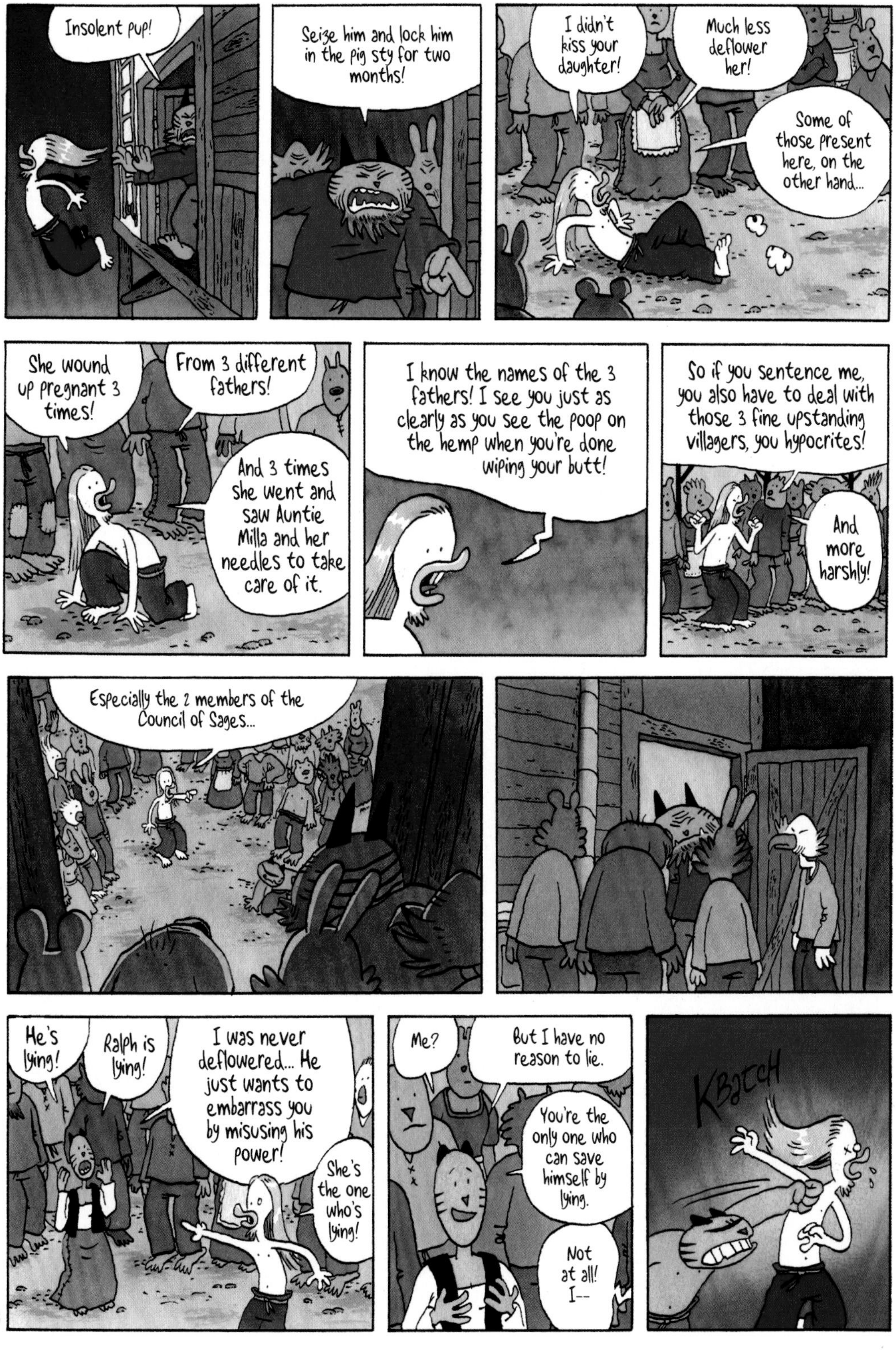

Insolent pup!
Seize him and lock him in the pig sty for two months!
I didn't kiss your daughter!
Much less deflower her!
Some of those present here, on the other hand...
She wound up pregnant 3 times!
From 3 different fathers!
And 3 times she went and saw Auntie Milla and her needles to take care of it.
I know the names of the 3 fathers! I see you just as clearly as you see the poop on the hemp when you're done wiping your butt!
So if you sentence me, you also have to deal with those 3 fine upstanding villagers, you hypocrites!
And more harshly!
Especially the 2 members of the Council of Sages...
He's lying!
Ralph is lying!
I was never deflowered... He just wants to embarrass you by misusing his power!
She's the one who's lying!
Me?
But I have no reason to lie.
You're the only one who can save himself by lying.
Not at all! I--
KRATCH

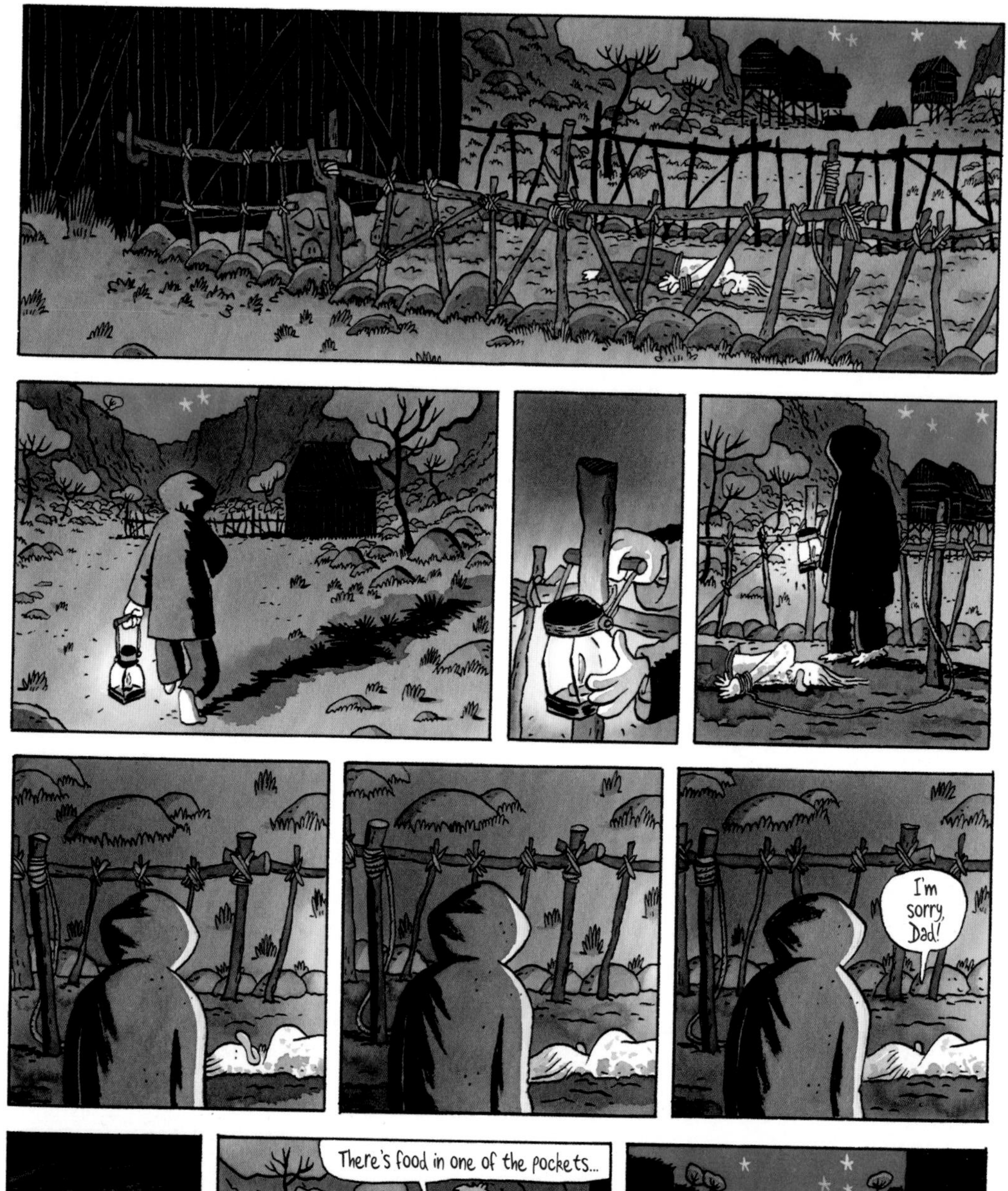

I'm sorry, Dad!
There's food in one of the pockets...
And a knife in the other...
12

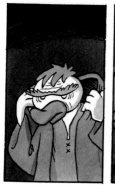

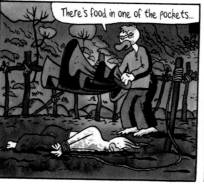

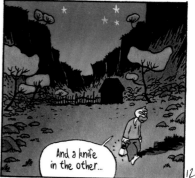

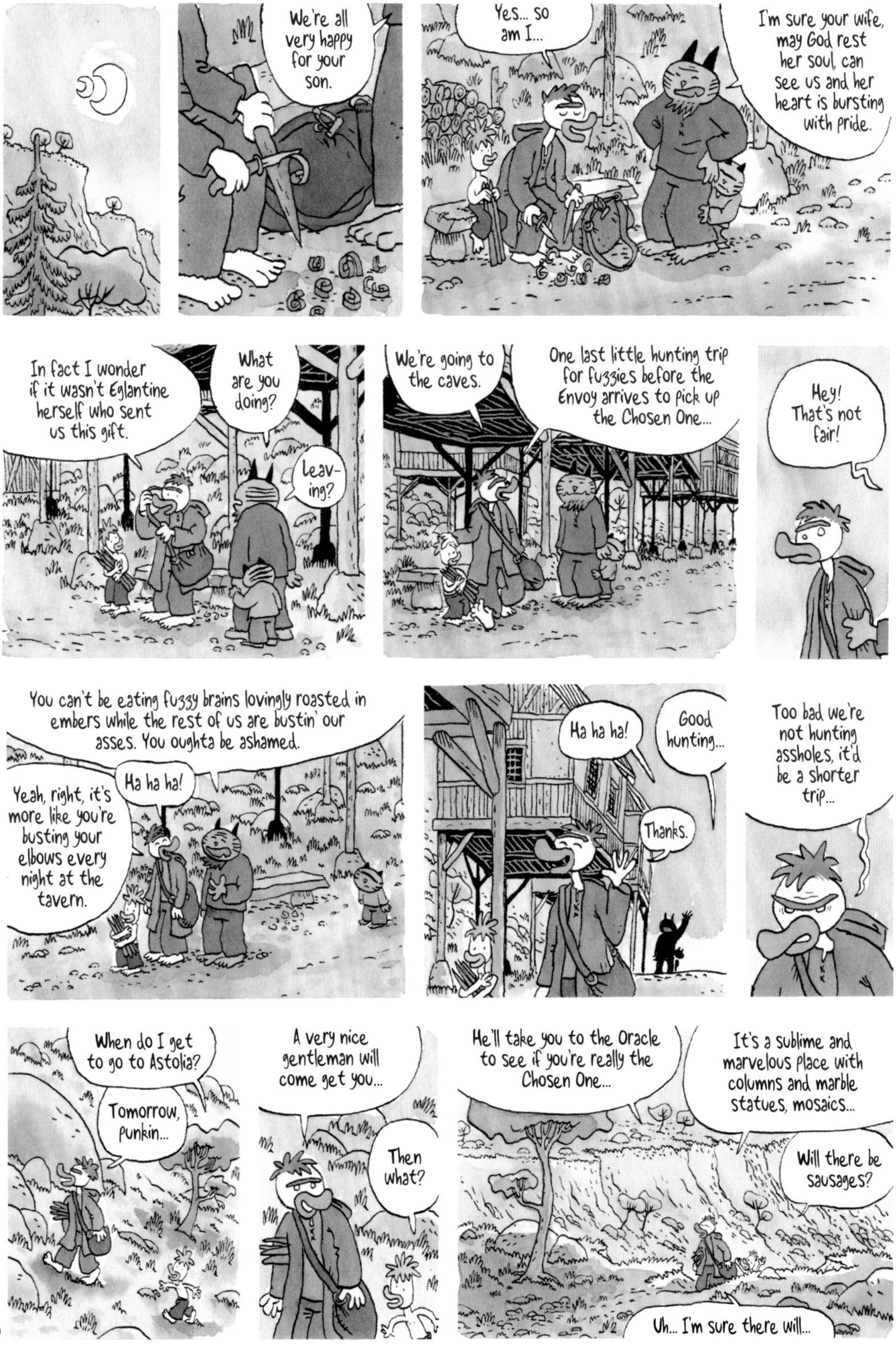
We're all very happy for your son.
Yes... so am I...
I'm sure your wife, may God rest her soul, can see us and her heart is bursting with pride.
In fact I wonder if it wasn't Eglantine herself who sent us this gift.
What are you doing?
Leav-ing?
We're going to the caves.
One last little hunting trip for fuzzies before the Envoy arrives to pick up the Chosen One...
Hey! That's not fair!
You can't be eating fuzzy brains lovingly roasted in embers while the rest of us are bustin' our asses. You oughta be ashamed.
Ha ha ha!
Yeah, right, it's more like you're busting your elbows every night at the tavern.
Ha ha ha!
Good hunting...
Thanks.
Too bad we're not hunting assholes, it'd be a shorter trip...
When do I get to go to Astolia?
Tomorrow, punkin...
A very nice gentleman will come get you...
Then what?
He'll take you to the Oracle to see if you're really the Chosen One...
It's a sublime and marvelous place with columns and marble statues, mosaics...
Will there be sausages?
Uh... I'm sure there will...
13

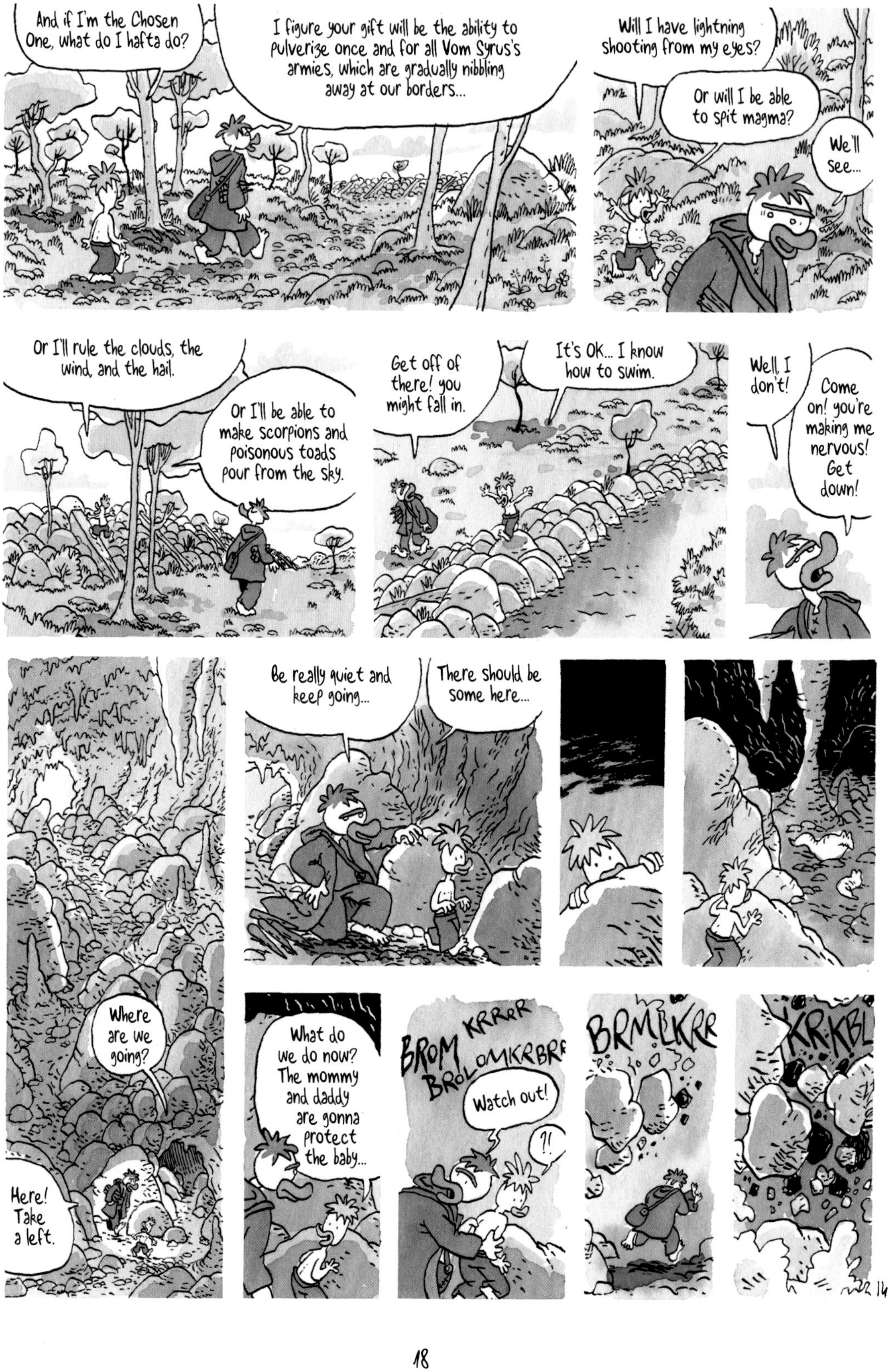
And if I'm the Chosen One, what do I hafta do?
I figure your gift will be the ability to pulverize once and for all Vom Syrus's armies, which are gradually nibbling away at our borders...
Will I have lightning shooting from my eyes?
Or will I be able to spit magma?
We'll see...
Or I'll rule the clouds, the wind, and the hail.
Or I'll be able to make scorpions and poisonous toads pour from the sky.
Get off of there! you might fall in.
It's OK... I know how to swim.
Well, I don't!
Come on! you're making me nervous! Get down!
Where are we going?
Here! Take a left.
Be really quiet and keep going...
There should be some here...
What do we do now? The mommy and daddy are gonna protect the baby...
BROM KRRRR
BROLOMKRBRR
Watch out!
?!
BRMLKRR
KR-KBL

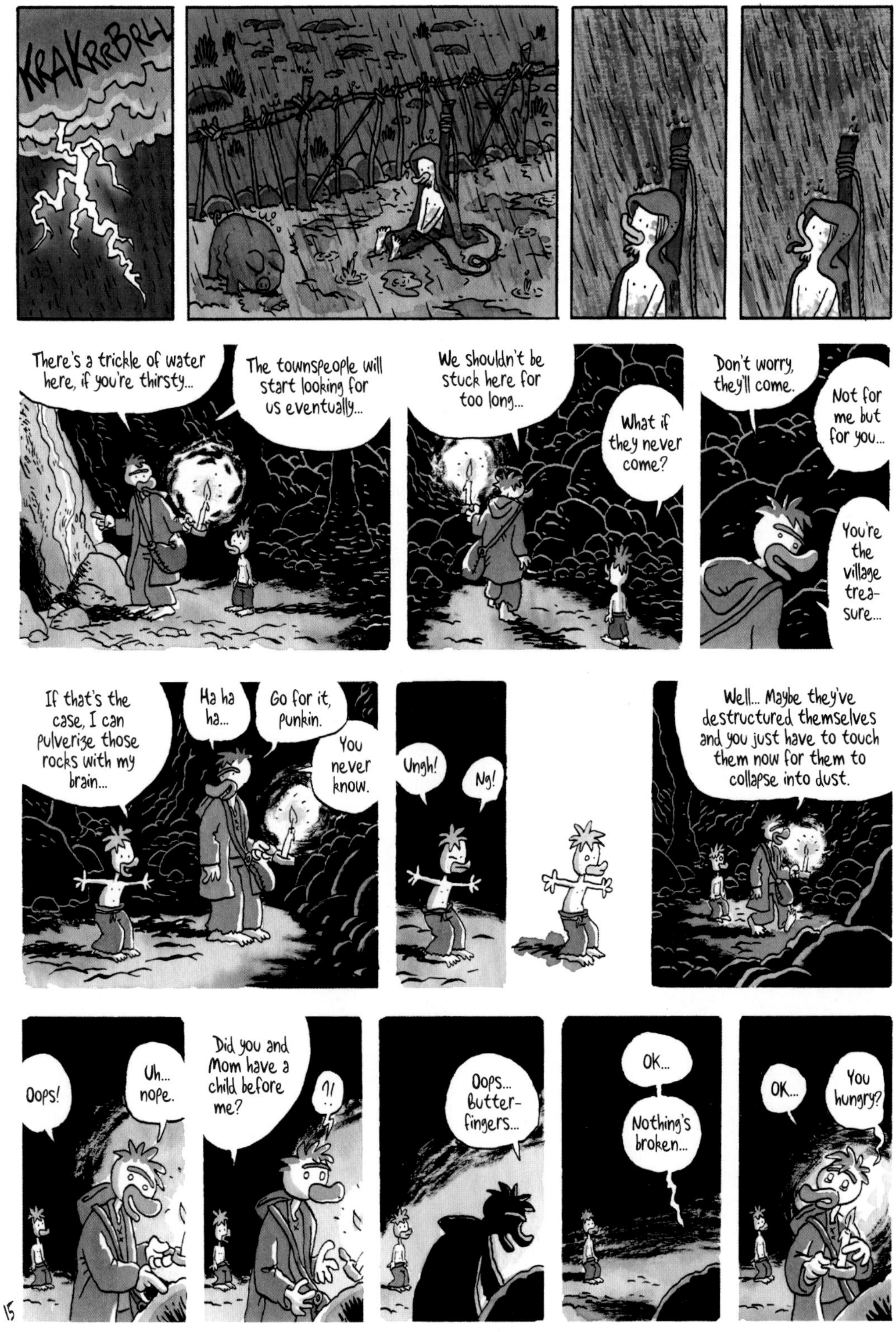
KRAKRRBRLL
There's a trickle of water here, if you're thirsty...
The townspeople will start looking for us eventually...
We shouldn't be stuck here for too long...
What if they never come?
Don't worry, they'll come.
Not for me but for you...
You're the village trea-sure...
If that's the case, I can pulverize those rocks with my brain...
Ha ha ha...
Go for it, punkin.
You never know.
Ungh!
Ng!
Well... Maybe they've destructured themselves and you just have to touch them now for them to collapse into dust.
Oops!
Uh... nope.
Did you and Mom have a child before me?
?!
Oops... Butter-fingers...
OK...
Nothing's broken...
OK...
You hungry?
15

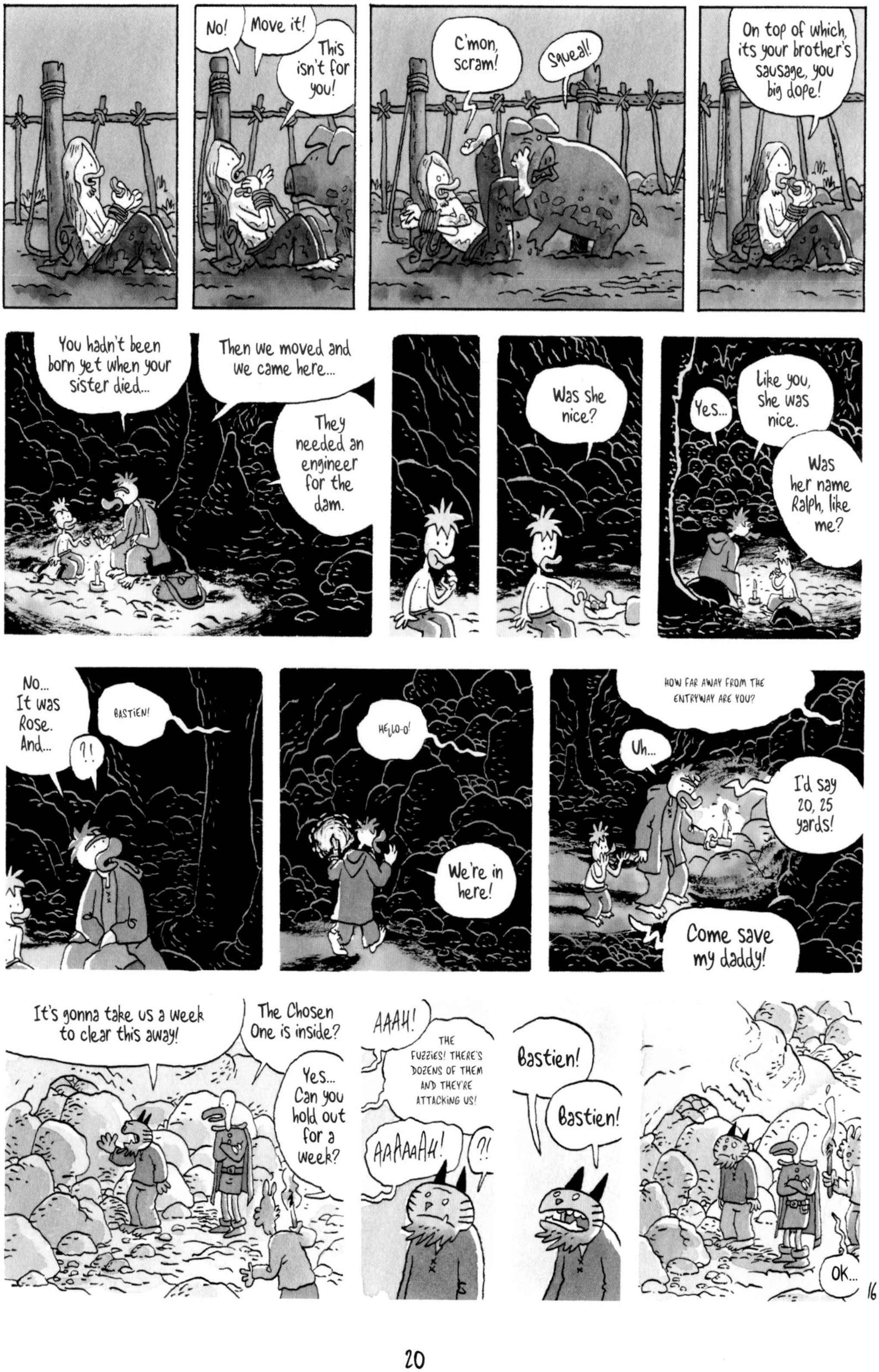
No!
Move it!
This isn't for you!
C'mon, scram!
Squeal!
On top of which, its your brother's sausage, you big dope!
You hadn't been born yet when your sister died...
Then we moved and we came here...
They needed an engineer for the dam.
Was she nice?
Yes...
Like you, she was nice.
Was her name Ralph, like me?
No... It was Rose. And...
BASTIEN!
?!
HELLO-O!
We're in here!
HOW FAR AWAY FROM THE ENTRYWAY ARE YOU?
Uh...
I'd say 20, 25 yards!
Come save my daddy!
It's gonna take us a week to clear this away!
The Chosen One is inside?
Yes... Can you hold out for a week?
AAAH!
THE FUZZIES! THERE'S DOZENS OF THEM AND THEY'RE ATTACKING US!
AAAAAAH!
?!
Bastien!
Bastien!
OK...
16

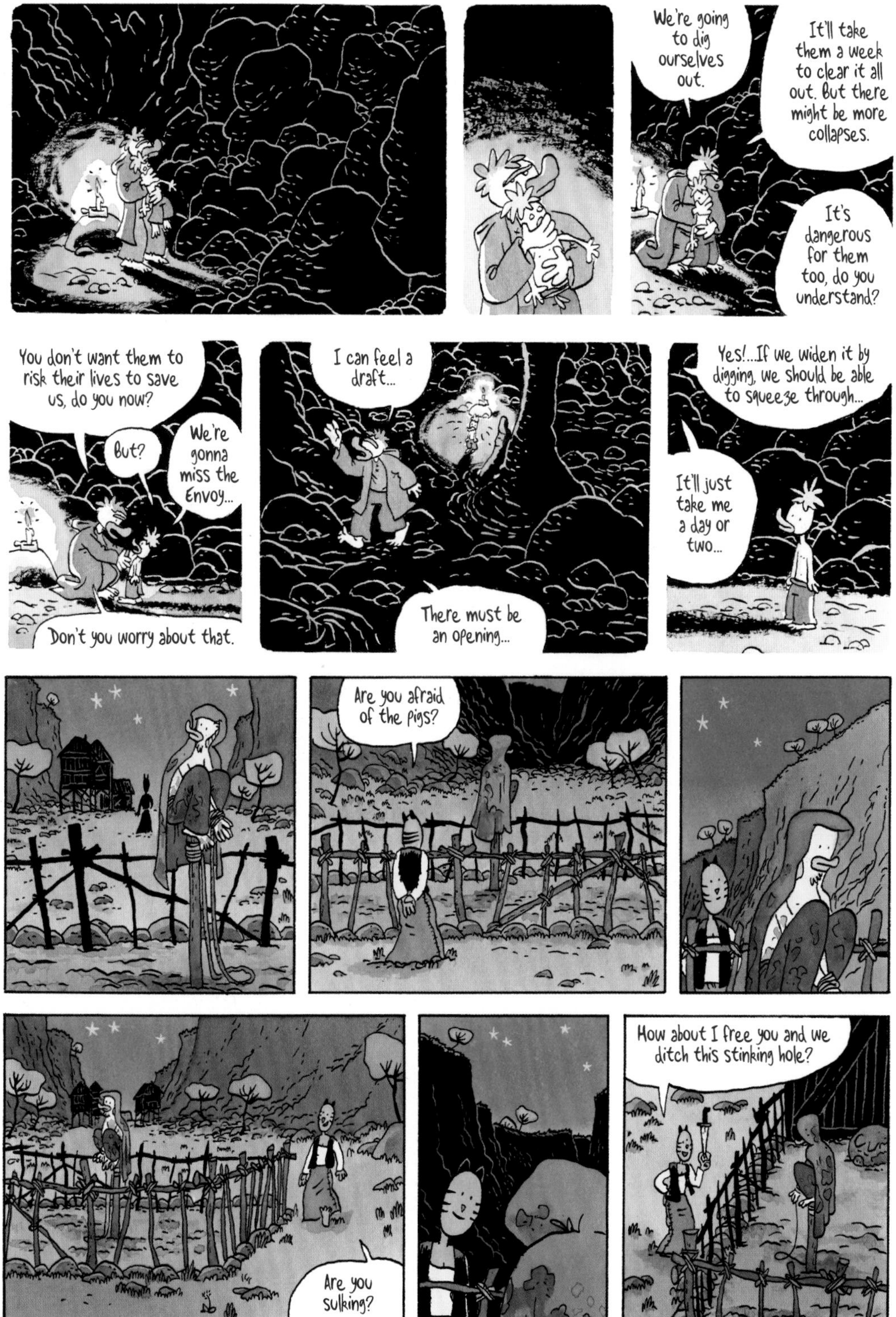
We're going to dig ourselves out.
It'll take them a week to clear it all out. But there might be more collapses.
It's dangerous for them too, do you understand?
You don't want them to risk their lives to save us, do you now?
But?
We're gonna miss the Envoy...
Don't you worry about that.
I can feel a draft...
There must be an opening...
Yes!...If we widen it by digging, we should be able to squeeze through...
It'll just take me a day or two...
Are you afraid of the pigs?
Are you sulking?
How about I free you and we ditch this stinking hole?

17

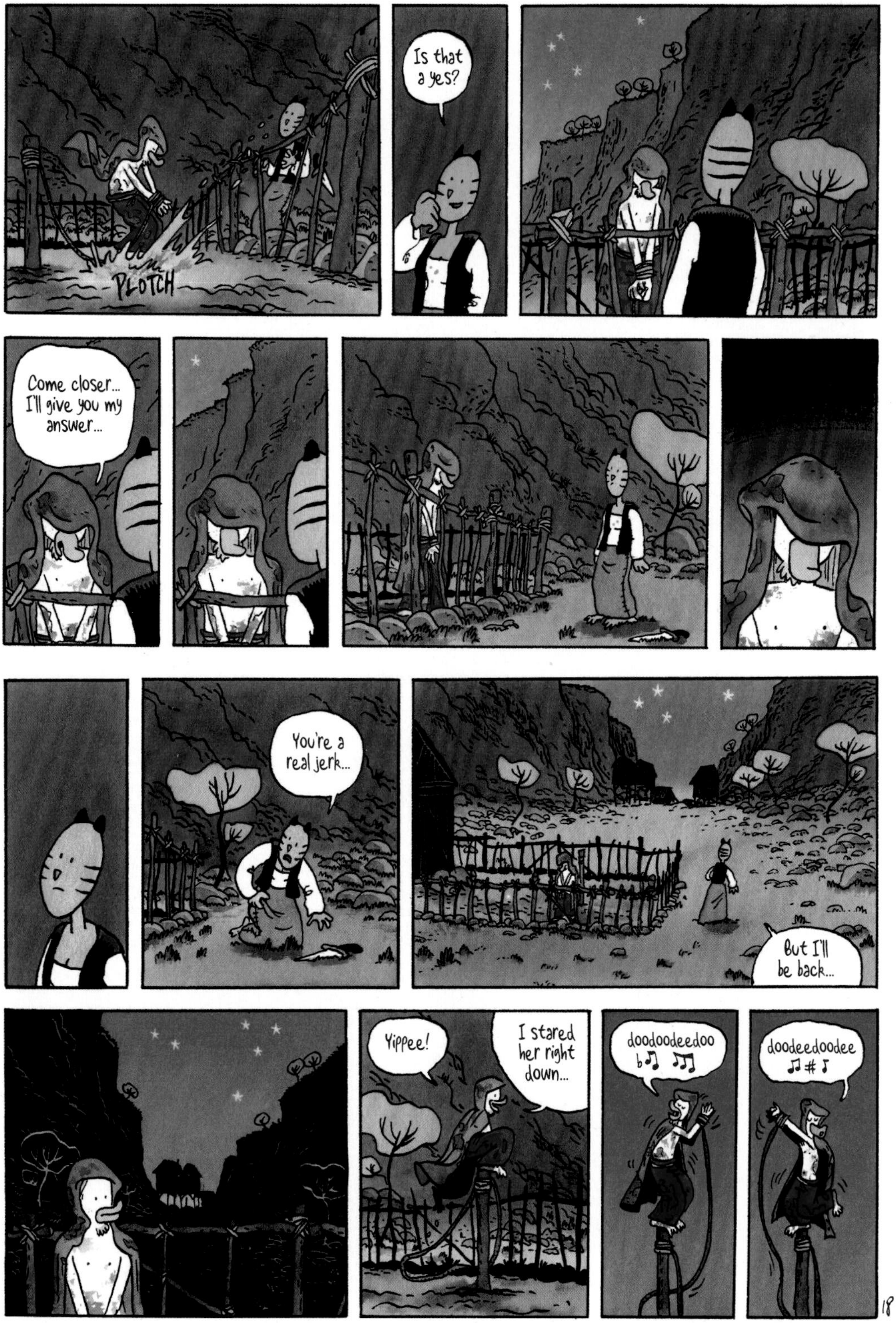
PLOTCH
Is that a yes?
Come closer... I'll give you my answer...
You're a real jerk...
But I'll be back...
Yippee!
I stared her right down...
doodoodeedoo
doodeedoodee
18

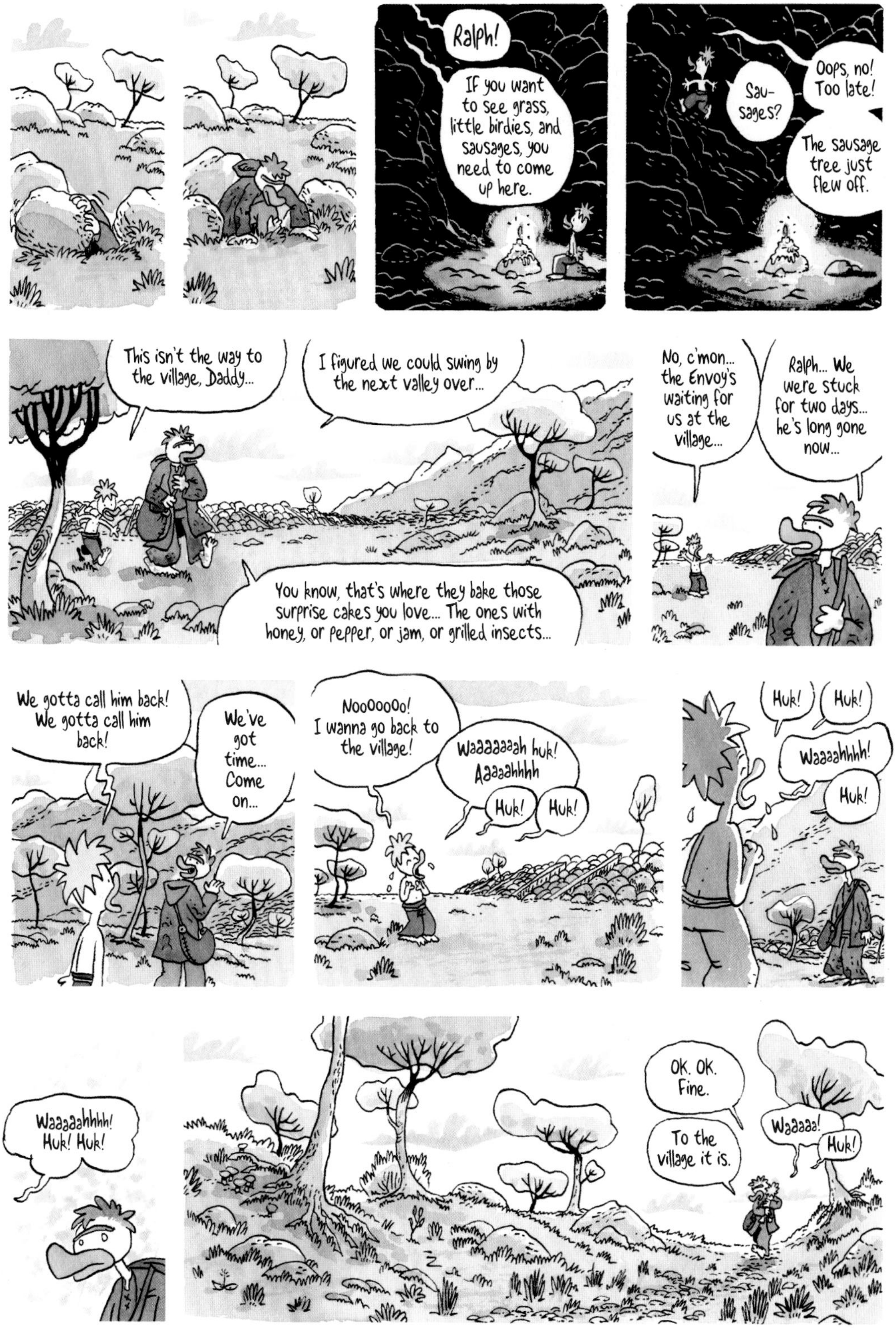
Ralph!
If you want to see grass, little birdies, and sausages, you need to come up here.
Sau-sages?
Oops, no! Too late!
The sausage tree just flew off.
This isn't the way to the village, Daddy...
I figured we could swing by the next valley over...
You know, that's where they bake those surprise cakes you love... The ones with honey, or pepper, or jam, or grilled insects...
No, c'mon... the Envoy's waiting for us at the village...
Ralph... We were stuck for two days... he's long gone now...
We gotta call him back! We gotta call him back!
We've got time... Come on...
Noooooo! I wanna go back to the village!
Waaaaaaah huk! Aaaaahhhh
Huk!
Huk!
Huk!
Huk!
Waaaahhhh!
Huk!
Waaaahhhh! Huk! Huk!
OK. OK. Fine.
To the village it is.
Waaaa!
Huk!

19

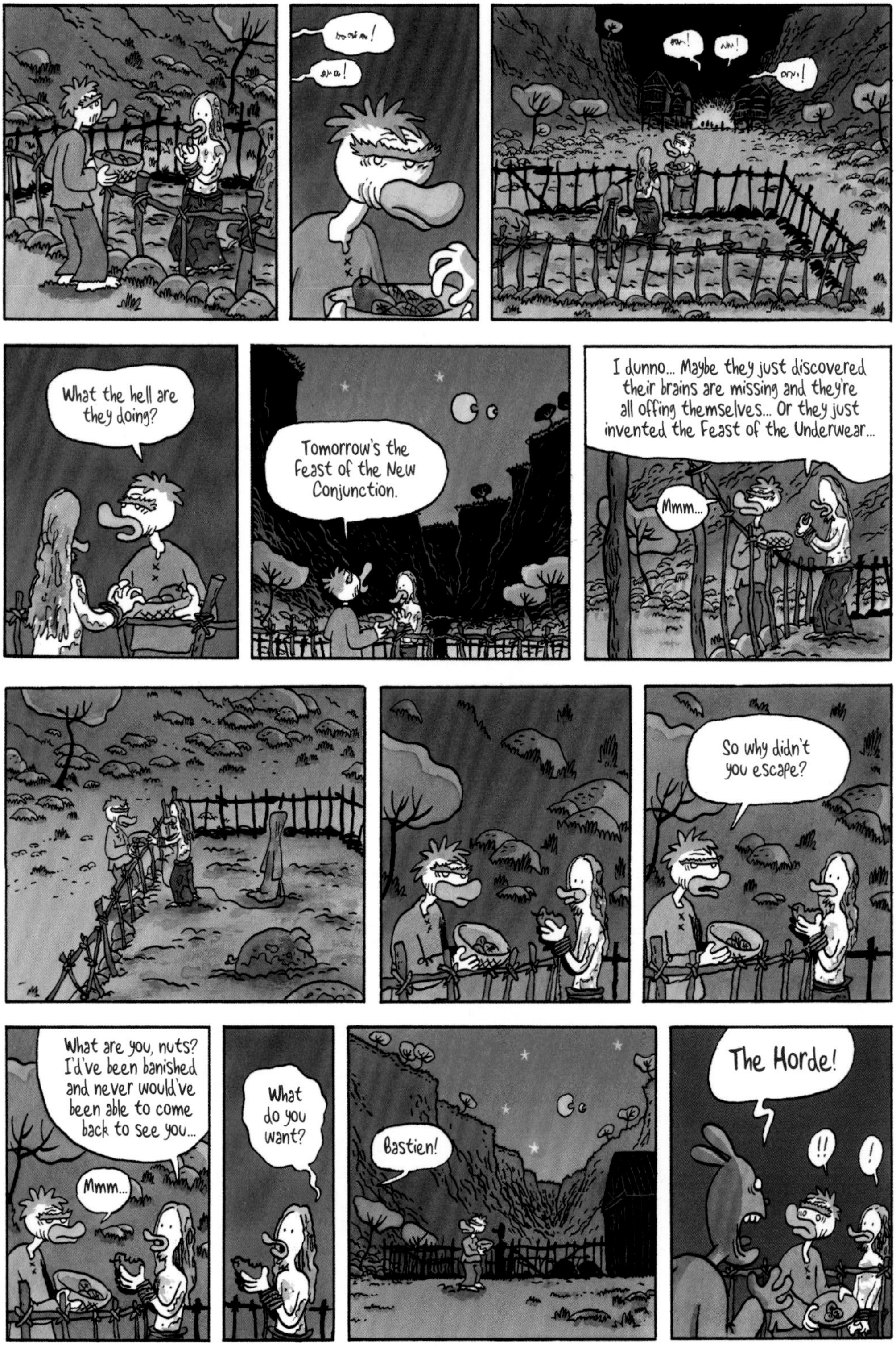
What the hell are they doing?
Tomorrow's the Feast of the New Conjunction.
I dunno... Maybe they just discovered their brains are missing and they're all offing themselves... Or they just invented the Feast of the Underwear...
Mmm...
So why didn't you escape?
What are you, nuts? I'd've been banished and never would've been able to come back to see you...
Mmm...
What do you want?
Bastien!
The Horde!
!!
!

20

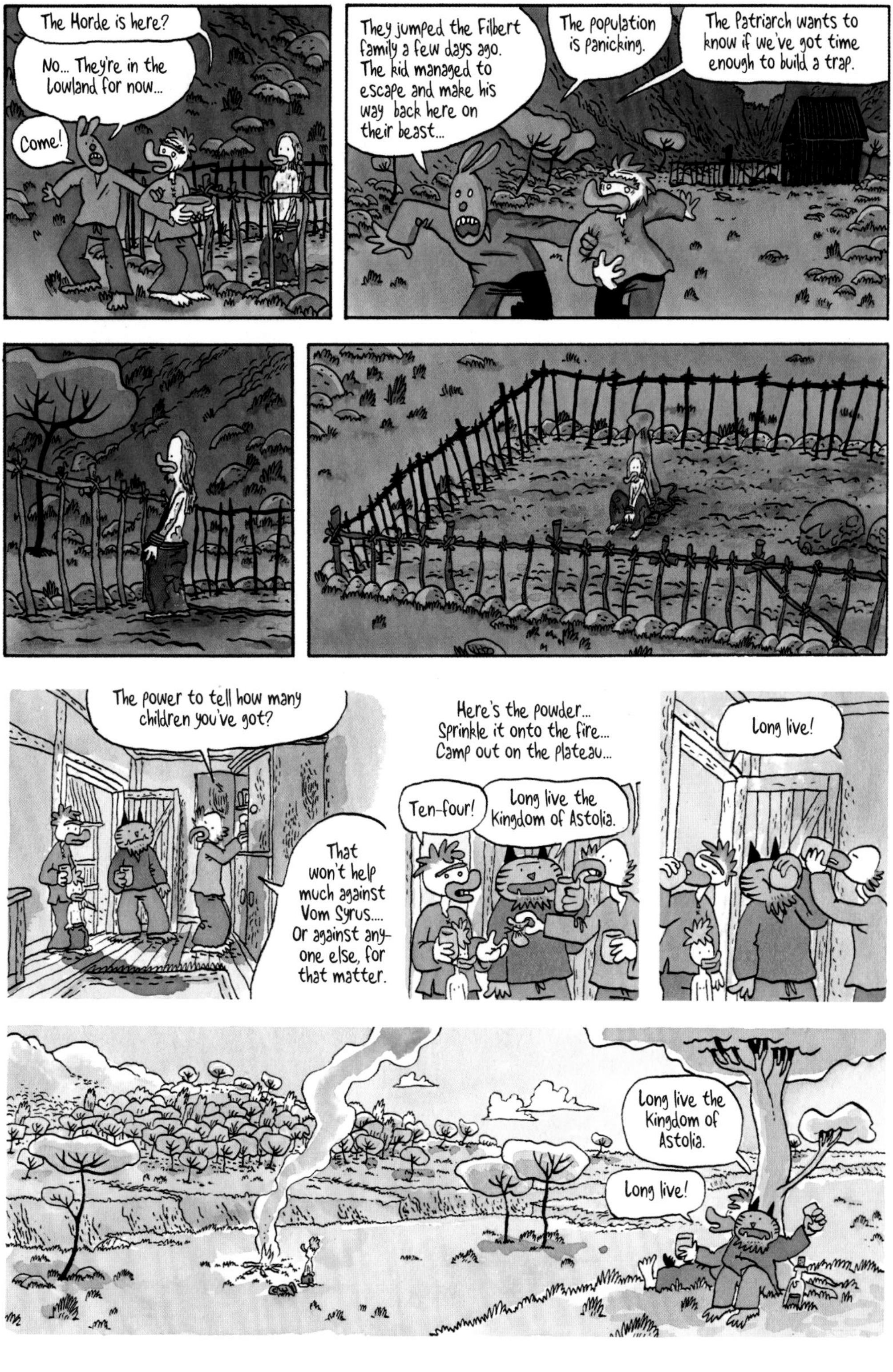
The Horde is here?
No... They're in the Lowland for now...
Come!
They jumped the Filbert family a few days ago. The kid managed to escape and make his way back here on their beast...
The population is panicking.
The Patriarch wants to know if we've got time enough to build a trap.
The power to tell how many children you've got?
That won't help much against Vom Syrus.... Or against anyone else, for that matter.
Here's the powder... Sprinkle it onto the fire... Camp out on the plateau...
Ten-four!
Long live the Kingdom of Astolia.
Long live!
Long live the Kingdom of Astolia.
Long live!

21

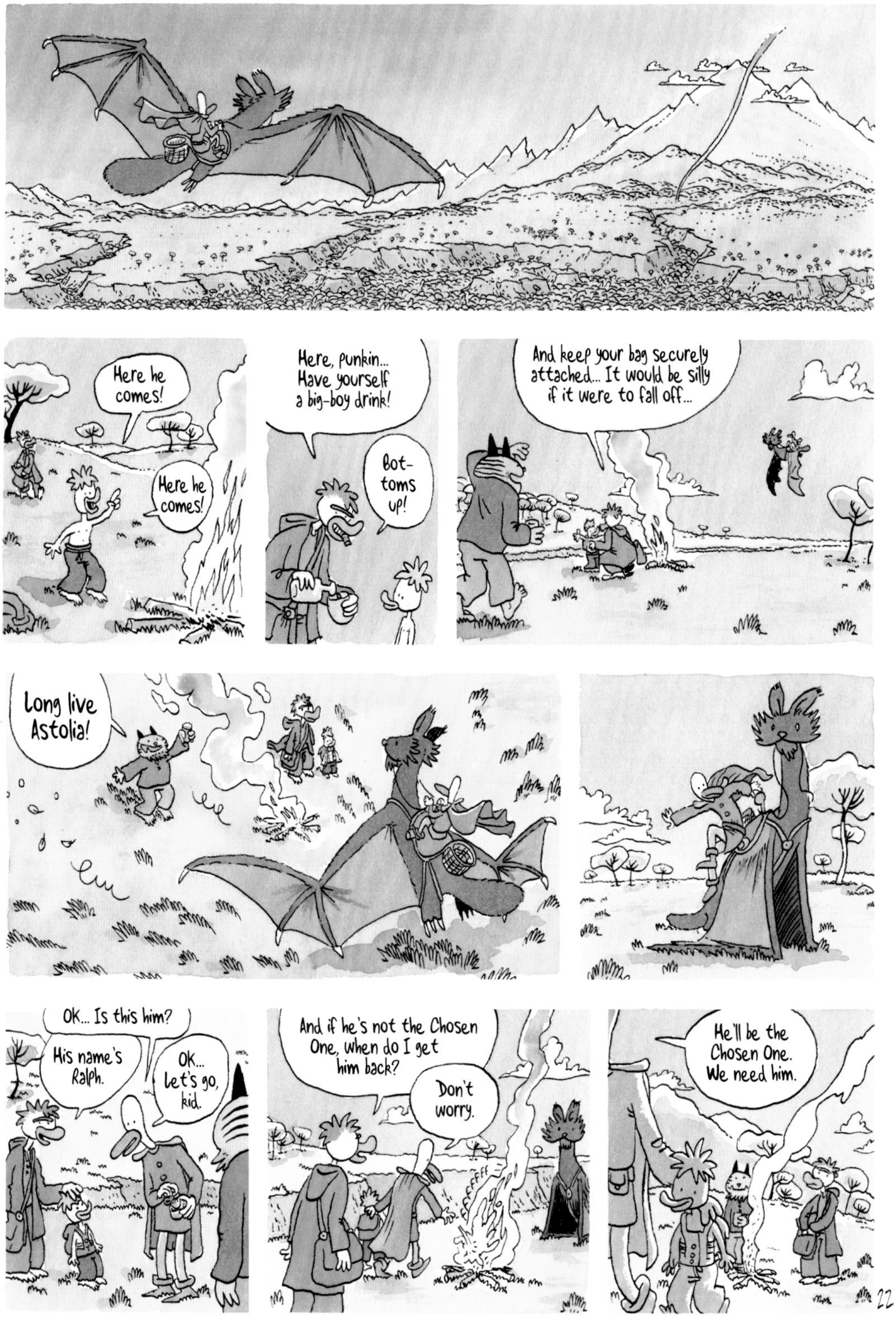
Here he comes!
Here he comes!
Here, punkin... Have yourself a big-boy drink!
Bot-toms up!
And keep your bag securely attached... It would be silly if it were to fall off...
Long live Astolia!
OK... Is this him?
His name's Ralph.
OK... Let's go, kid.
And if he's not the Chosen One, when do I get him back?
Don't worry.
FFFFFF
He'll be the Chosen One. We need him.
22

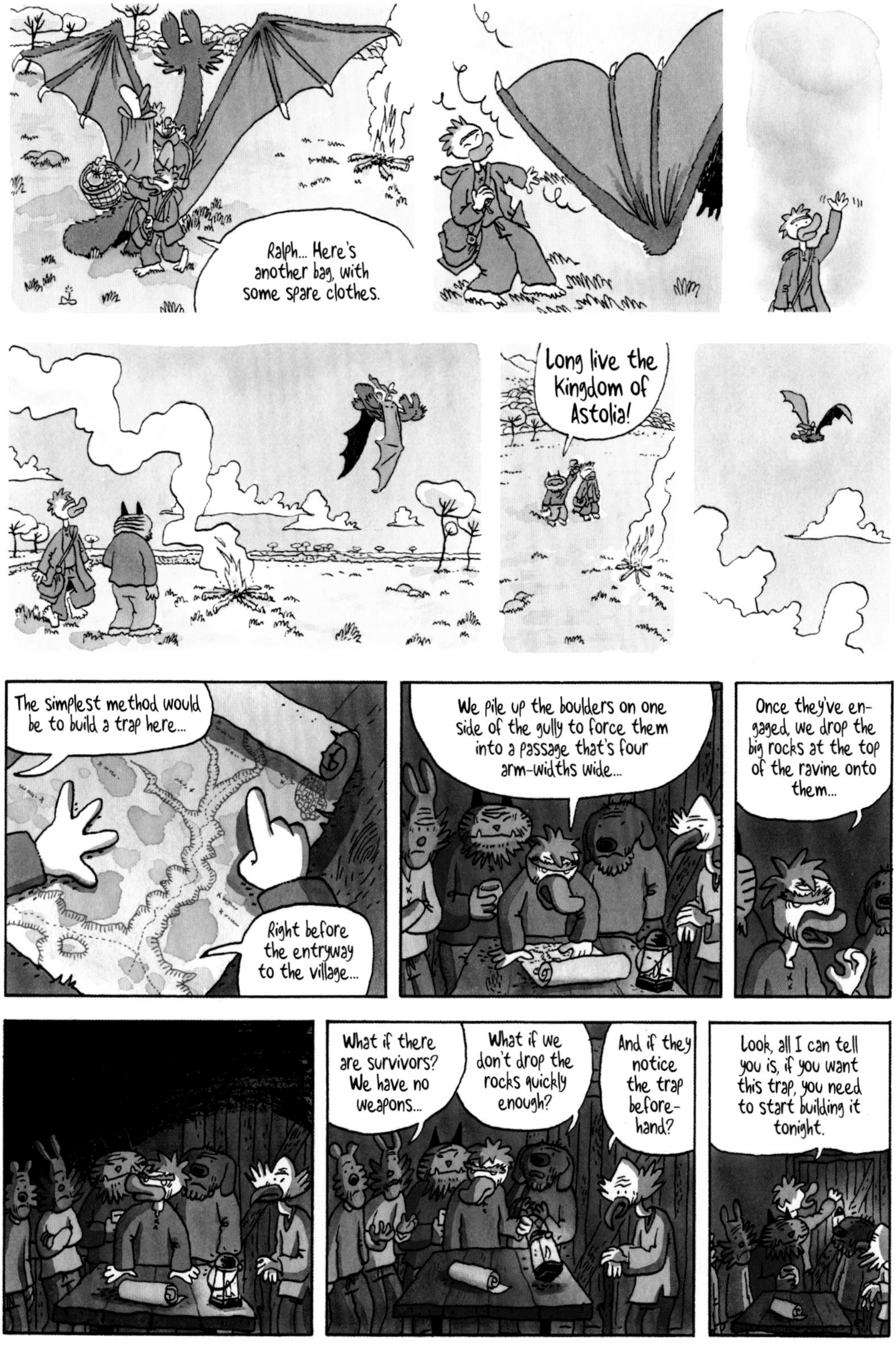

Ralph... Here's another bag, with some spare clothes.
Long live the Kingdom of Astolia!
The simplest method would be to build a trap here...
Right before the entryway to the village...
We pile up the boulders on one side of the gully to force them into a passage that's four arm-widths wide...
Once they've engaged, we drop the big rocks at the top of the ravine onto them...
What if there are survivors? We have no weapons...
What if we don't drop the rocks quickly enough?
And if they notice the trap beforehand?
Look, all I can tell you is, if you want this trap, you need to start building it tonight.
23

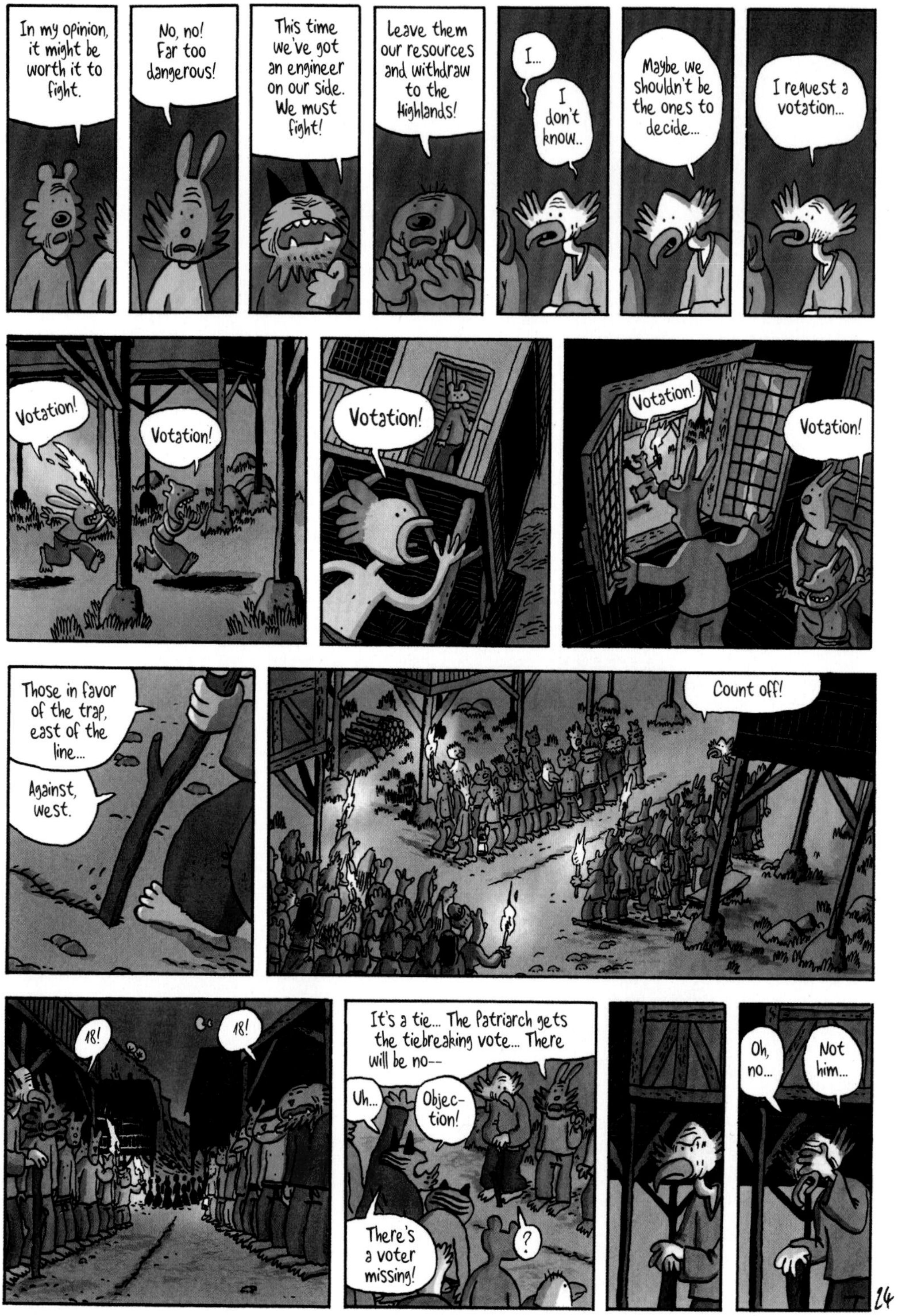
In my opinion, it might be worth it to fight.
No, no! Far too dangerous!
This time we've got an engineer on our side. We must fight!
Leave them our resources and withdraw to the Highlands!
I...
I don't know..
Maybe we shouldn't be the ones to decide...
I request a votation...
Votation!
Votation!
Votation!
Votation!
Votation!
Those in favor of the trap, east of the line...
Against, west.
Count off!
18!
18!
It's a tie... The Patriarch gets the tiebreaking vote... There will be no--
Uh...
Objec-tion!
There's a voter missing!
?
Oh, no...
Not him...
24

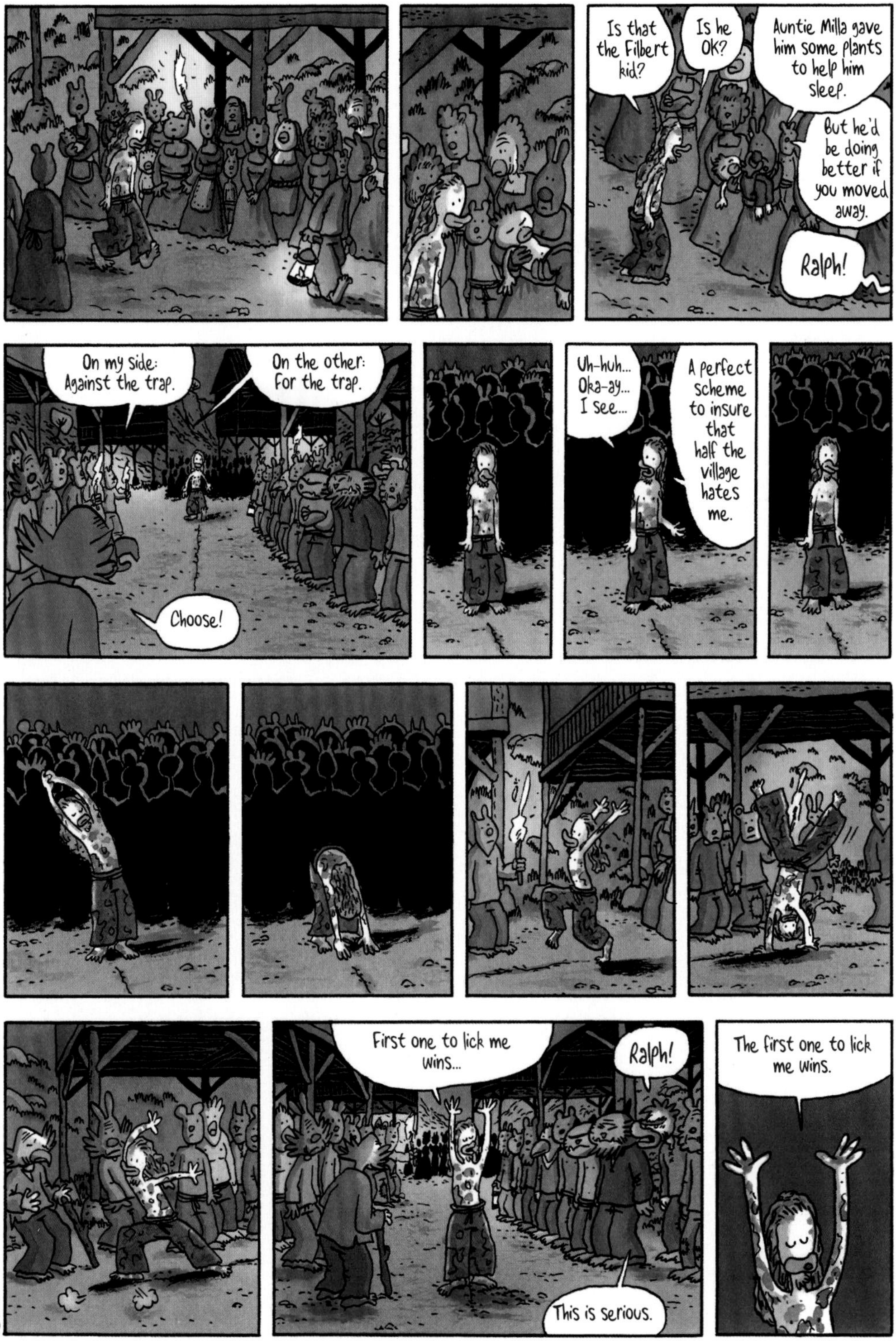
Is that the Filbert kid?
Is he OK?
Auntie Milla gave him some plants to help him sleep.
But he'd be doing better if you moved away.
Ralph!
On my side: Against the trap.
On the other: For the trap.
Choose!
Uh-huh... Oka-ay... I see...
A perfect scheme to insure that half the village hates me.
First one to lick me wins...
Ralph!
This is serious.
The first one to lick me wins.

25

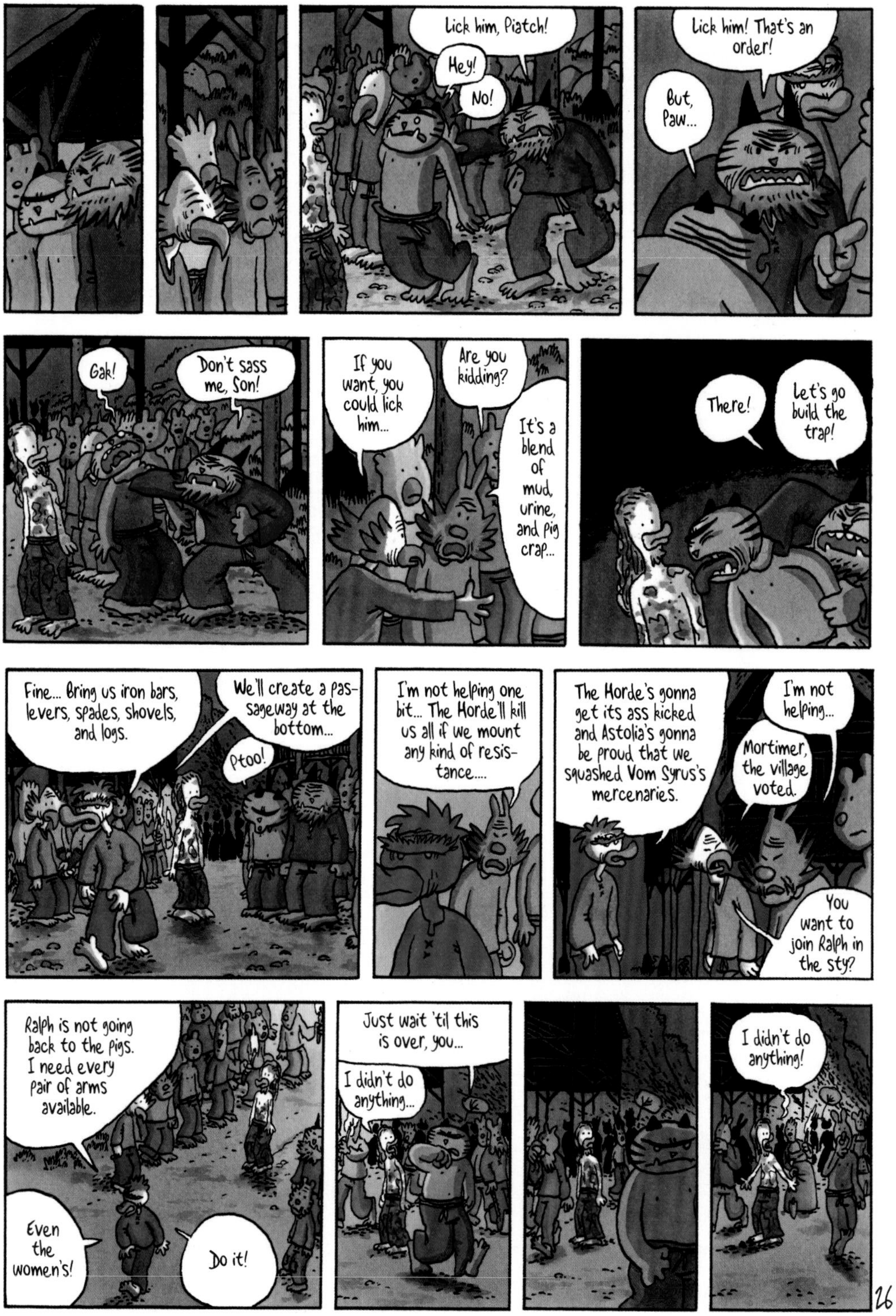
Lick him, Piatch!
Hey!
No!
Lick him! That's an order!
But, Paw...
Gak!
Don't sass me, Son!
If you want, you could lick him...
Are you kidding?
It's a blend of mud, urine, and pig crap...
There!
Let's go build the trap!
Fine... Bring us iron bars, levers, spades, shovels, and logs.
We'll create a passageway at the bottom...
Ptoo!
I'm not helping one bit... The Horde'll kill us all if we mount any kind of resistance....
The Horde's gonna get its ass kicked and Astolia's gonna be proud that we squashed Vom Syrus's mercenaries.
I'm not helping...
Mortimer, the village voted.
You want to join Ralph in the sty?
Ralph is not going back to the pigs. I need every pair of arms available.
Even the women's!
Do it!
Just wait 'til this is over, you...
I didn't do anything...
I didn't do anything!
26

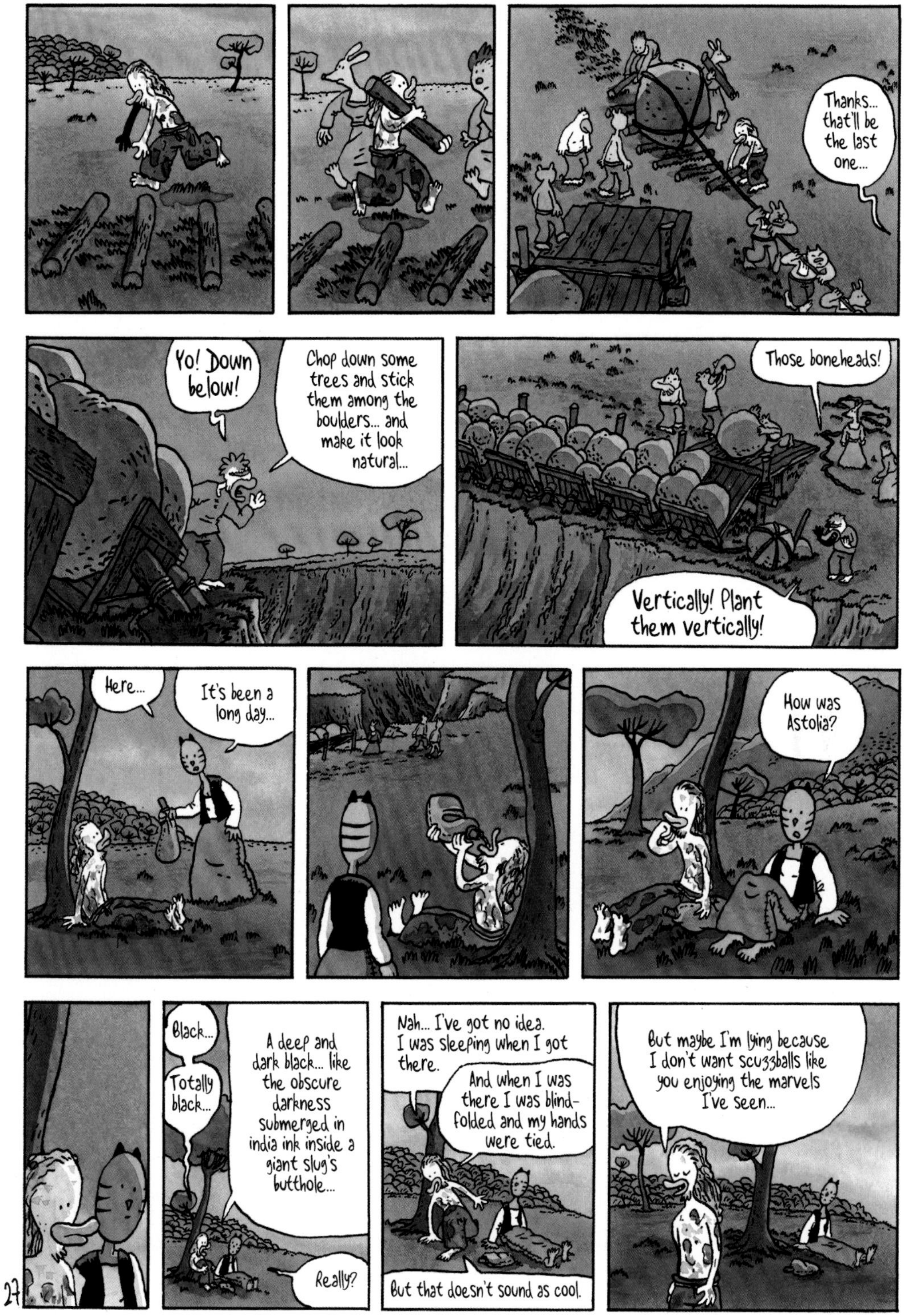
Thanks... that'll be the last one...
Yo! Down below!
Chop down some trees and stick them among the boulders... and make it look natural...
Those boneheads!
Vertically! Plant them vertically!
Here...
It's been a long day...
How was Astolia?
27
Black...
Totally black...
A deep and dark black... like the obscure darkness submerged in india ink inside a giant slug's butthole...
Really?
Nah... I've got no idea. I was sleeping when I got there.
And when I was there I was blind-folded and my hands were tied.
But that doesn't sound as cool.
But maybe I'm lying because I don't want scuzzballs like you enjoying the marvels I've seen...

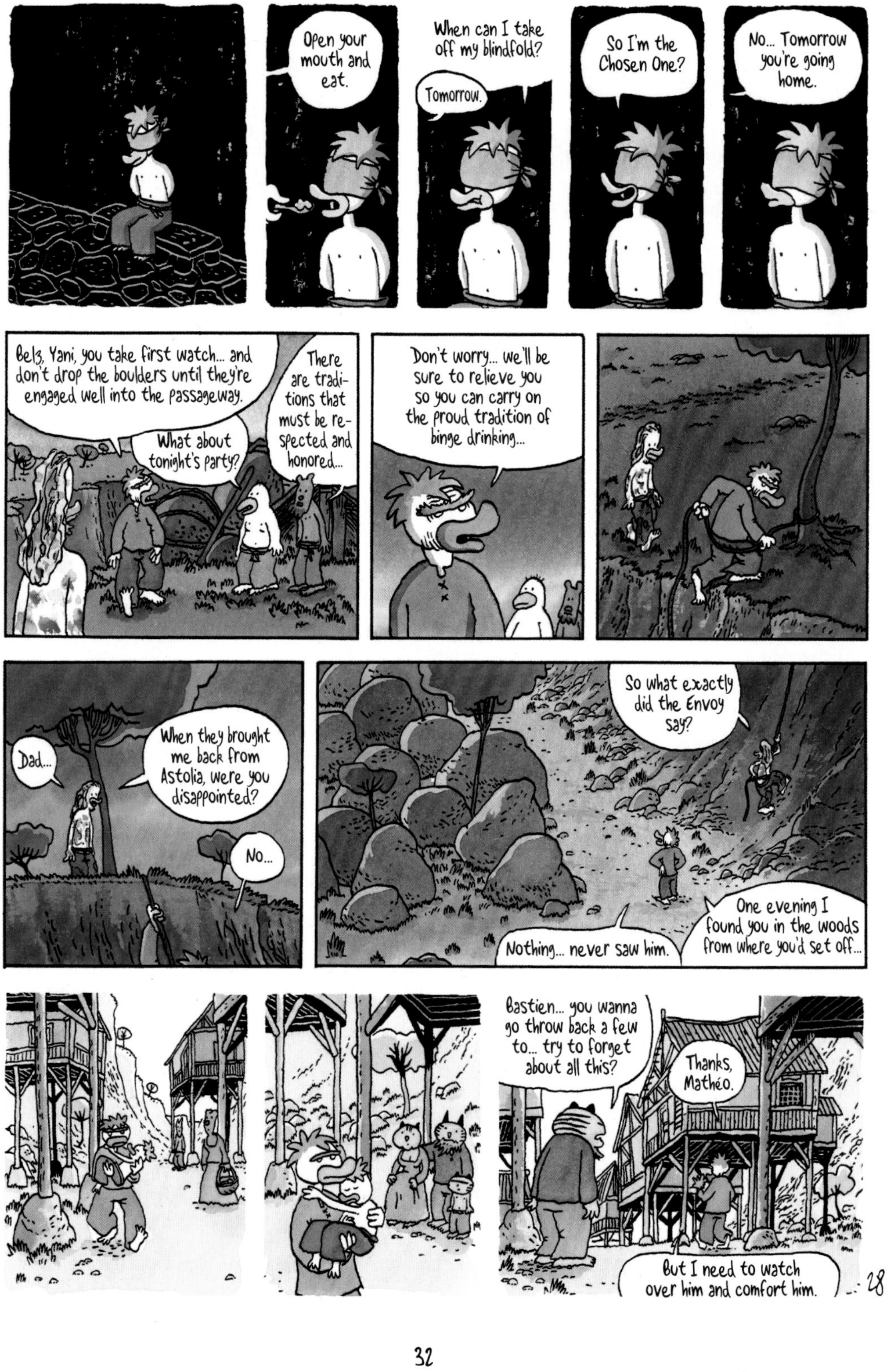
Open your mouth and eat.
When can I take off my blindfold?
Tomorrow.
So I'm the Chosen One?
No... Tomorrow you're going home.
Belz, Yani, you take first watch... and don't drop the boulders until they're engaged well into the passageway.
What about tonight's party?
There are traditions that must be respected and honored...
Don't worry... we'll be sure to relieve you so you can carry on the proud tradition of binge drinking...
Dad...
When they brought me back from Astolia, were you disappointed?
No...
So what exactly did the Envoy say?
Nothing... never saw him.
One evening I found you in the woods from where you'd set off...
Bastien... you wanna go throw back a few to... try to forget about all this?
Thanks, Mathéo.
But I need to watch over him and comfort him.
28

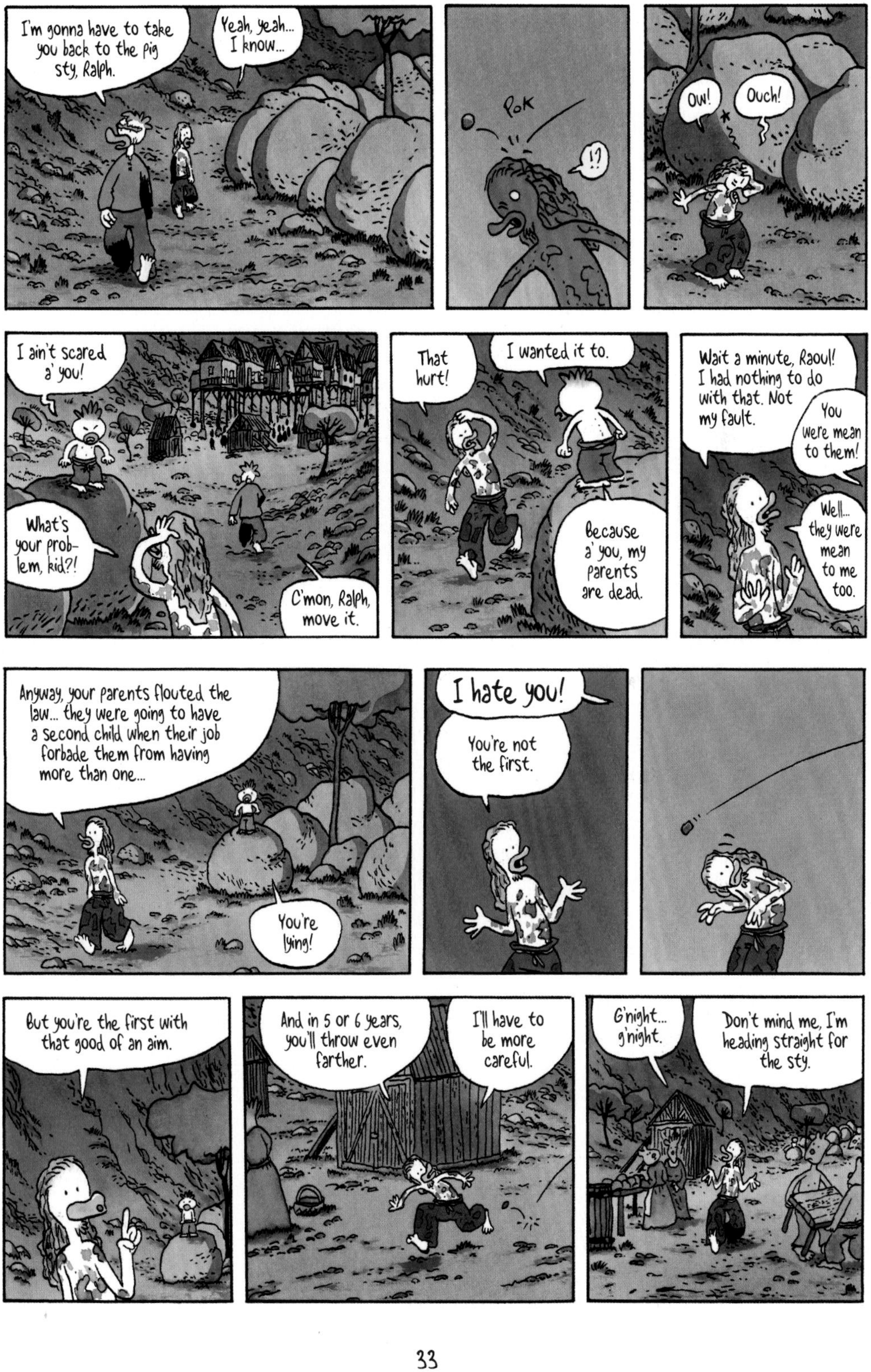
I'm gonna have to take you back to the pig sty, Ralph.
Yeah, yeah... I know...
POK
!?
Ow!
Ouch!
I ain't scared a' you!
What's your prob-lem, kid?!
C'mon, Ralph, move it.
That hurt!
I wanted it to.
Because a' you, my parents are dead.
Wait a minute, Raoul! I had nothing to do with that. Not my fault.
You were mean to them!
Well... they were mean to me too.
Anyway, your parents flouted the law... they were going to have a second child when their job forbade them from having more than one...
You're lying!
I hate you!
You're not the first.
But you're the first with that good of an aim.
And in 5 or 6 years, you'll throw even farther.
I'll have to be more careful.
G'night... g'night.
Don't mind me, I'm heading straight for the sty.

29

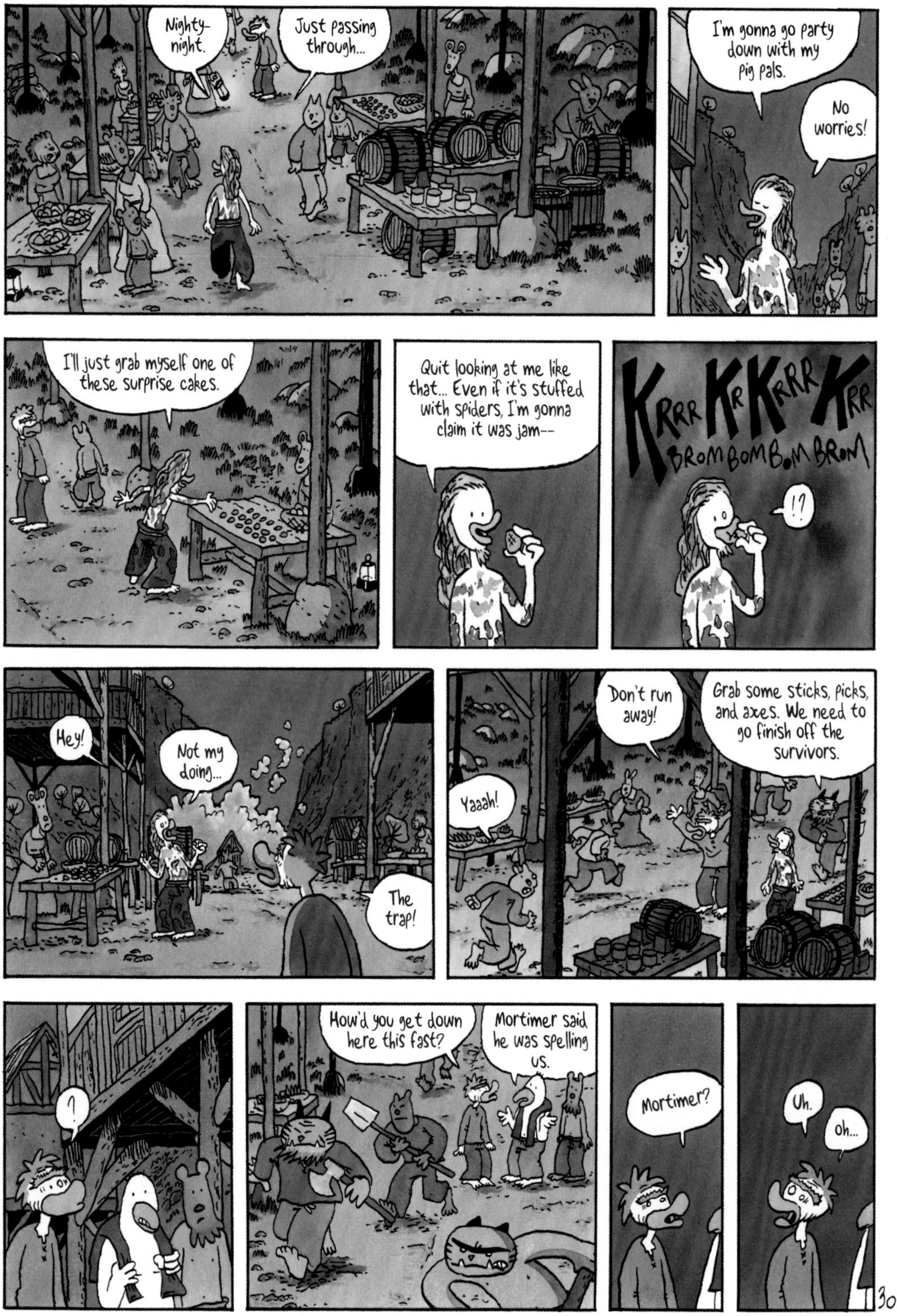
Nighty-night.
Just passing through...
I'm gonna go party down with my pig pals.
No worries!
I'll just grab myself one of these surprise cakes.
Quit looking at me like that... Even if it's stuffed with spiders, I'm gonna claim it was jam--
KRRR KR KRRR KRR
BROM BOM BOM BROM
!?
Hey!
Not my doing...
The trap!
Don't run away!
Grab some sticks, picks, and axes. We need to go finish off the survivors.
Yaaah!
?
How'd you get down here this fast?
Mortimer said he was spelling us.
Mortimer?
Uh.
oh...
30

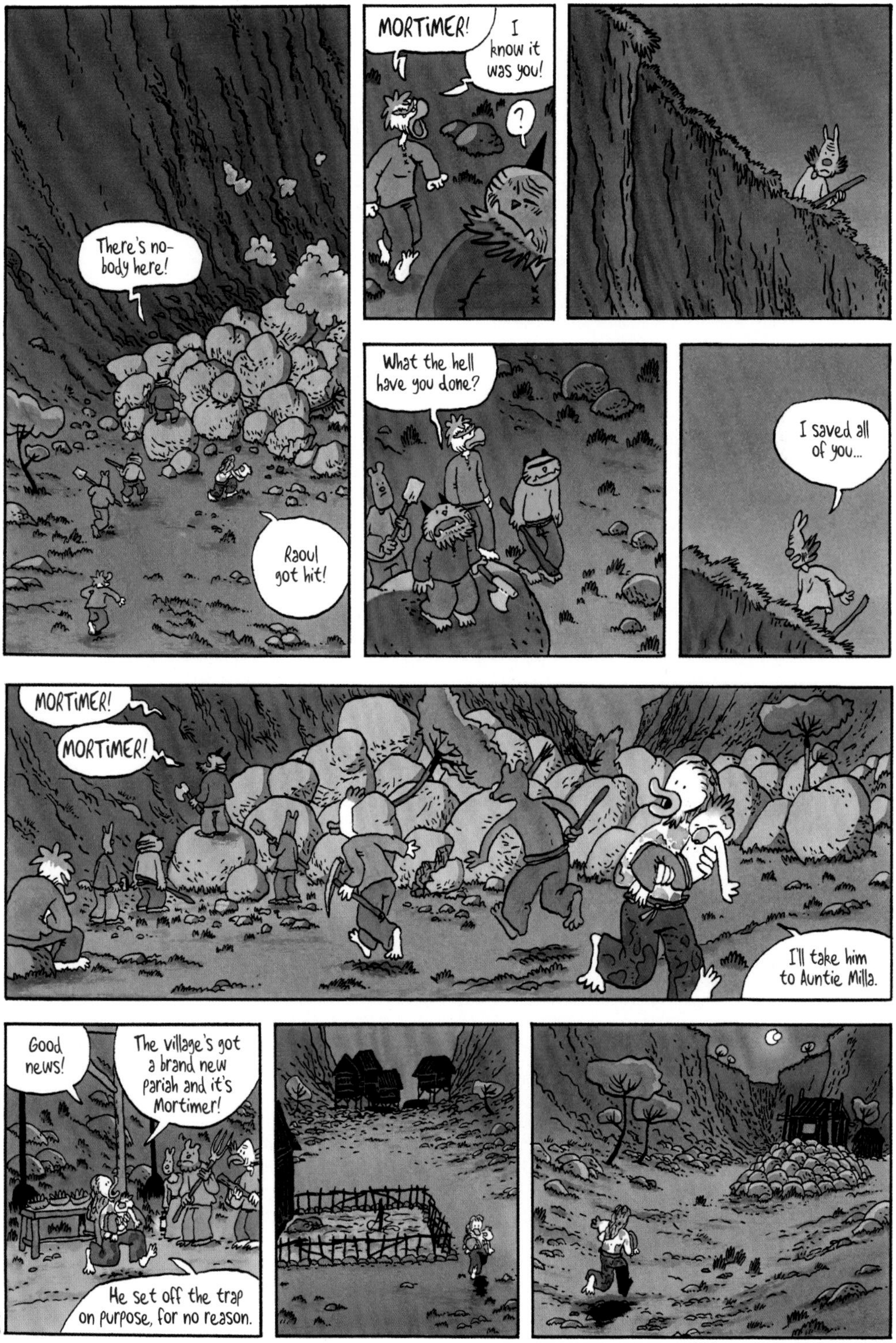
There's no-body here!
Raoul got hit!
MORTIMER!
I know it was you!
?
What the hell have you done?
I saved all of you...
MORTIMER!
MORTIMER!
I'll take him to Auntie Milla.
Good news!
The village's got a brand new pariah and it's Mortimer!
He set off the trap on purpose, for no reason.

31

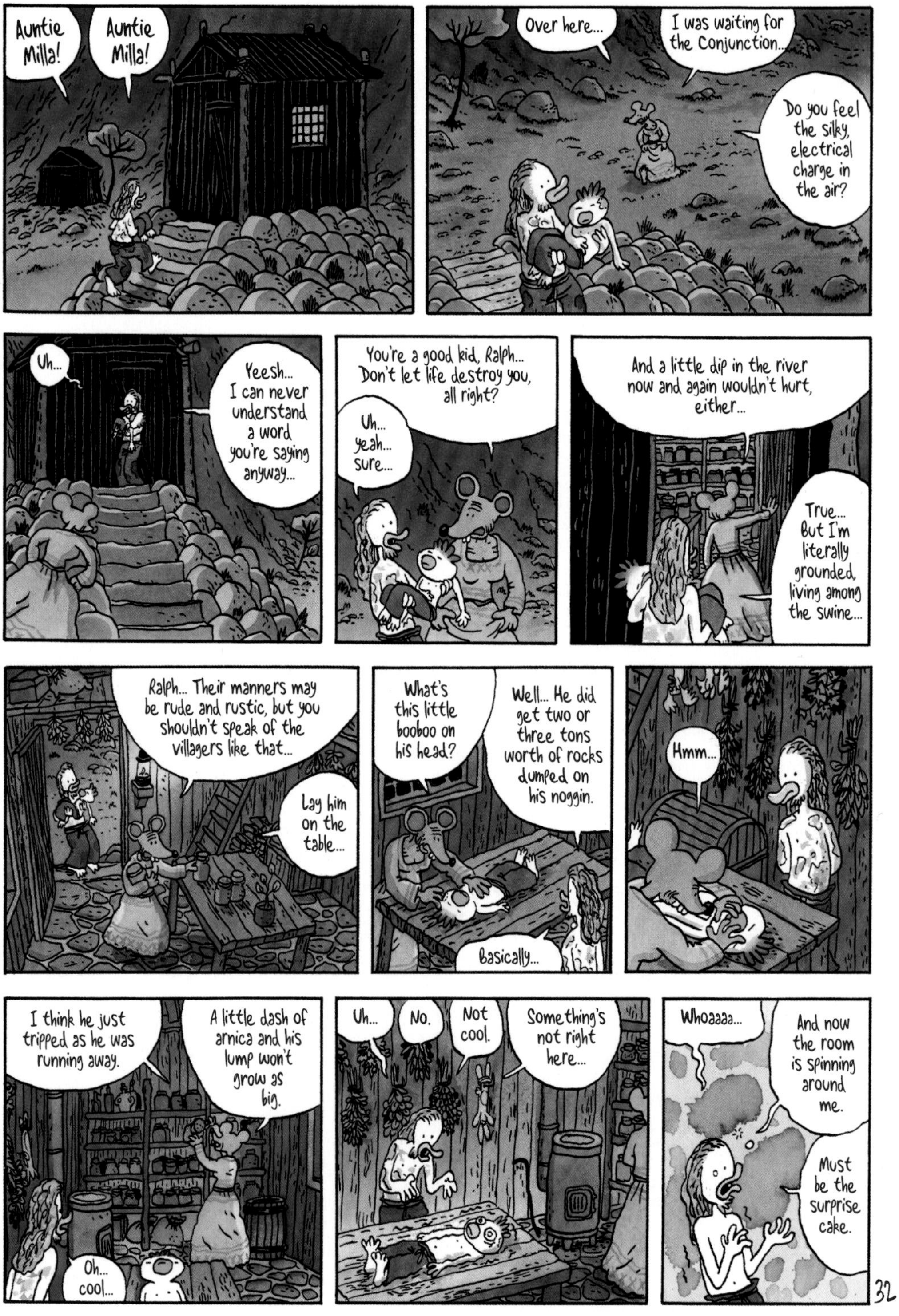
Auntie Milla!
Auntie Milla!
Over here...
I was waiting for the Conjunction...
Do you feel the silky, electrical charge in the air?
Uh...
Yeesh... I can never understand a word you're saying anyway...
You're a good kid, Ralph... Don't let life destroy you, all right?
Uh... yeah... sure...
And a little dip in the river now and again wouldn't hurt, either...
True... But I'm literally grounded, living among the swine...
Ralph... Their manners may be rude and rustic, but you shouldn't speak of the villagers like that...
Lay him on the table...
What's this little booboo on his head?
Well... He did get two or three tons worth of rocks dumped on his noggin.
Basically...
Hmm...
I think he just tripped as he was running away.
A little dash of arnica and his lump won't grow as big.
Oh... cool...
Uh...
No.
Not cool.
Something's not right here...
Whoaaaa...
And now the room is spinning around me.
Must be the surprise cake.
32

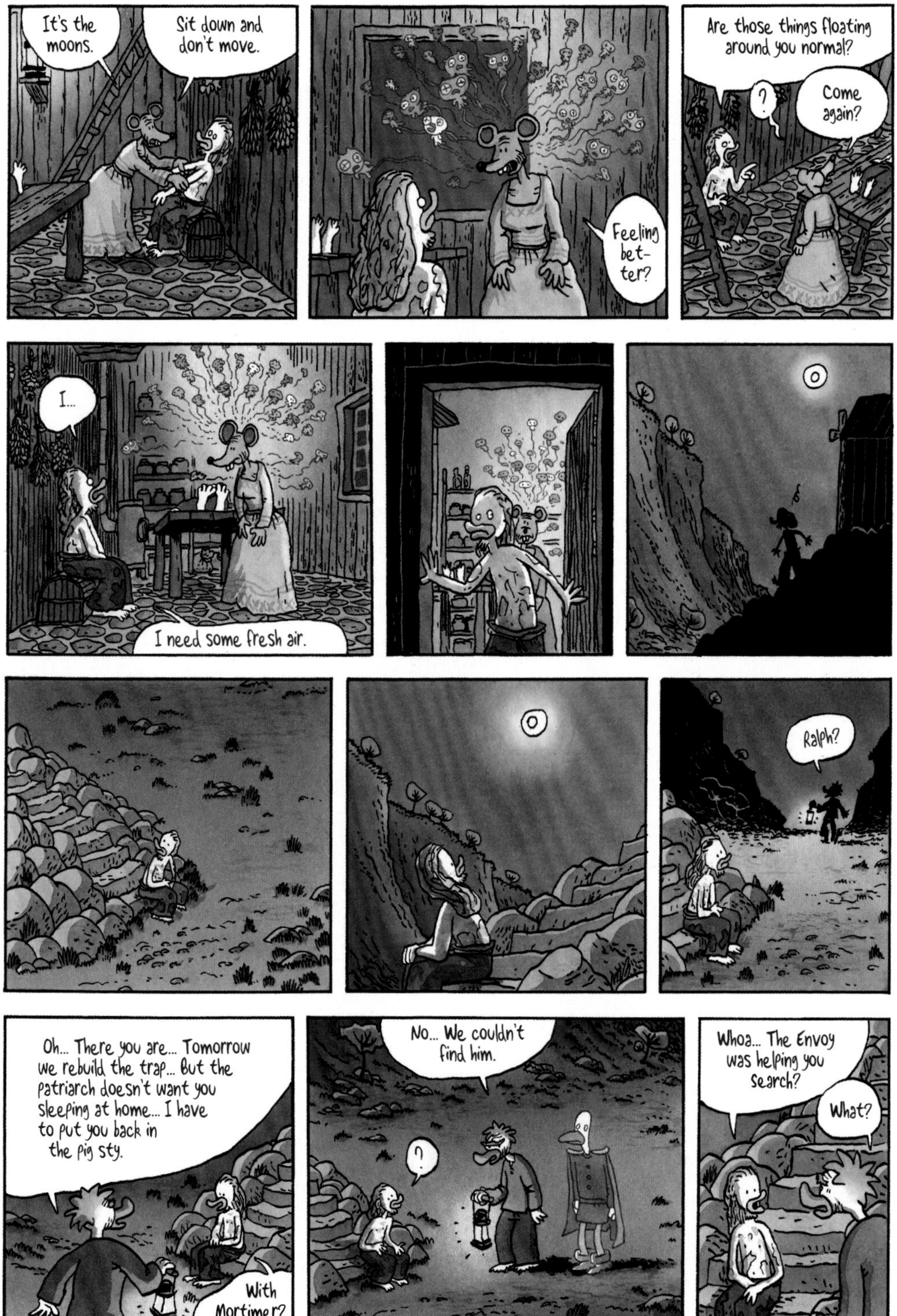
It's the moons.
Sit down and don't move.
Feeling bet-ter?
Are those things floating around you normal?
?
Come again?
I...
I need some fresh air.
Ralph?
Oh... There you are... Tomorrow we rebuild the trap... But the patriarch doesn't want you sleeping at home... I have to put you back in the pig sty.
With Mortimer?
No... We couldn't find him.
?
Whoa... The Envoy was helping you search?
What?
33

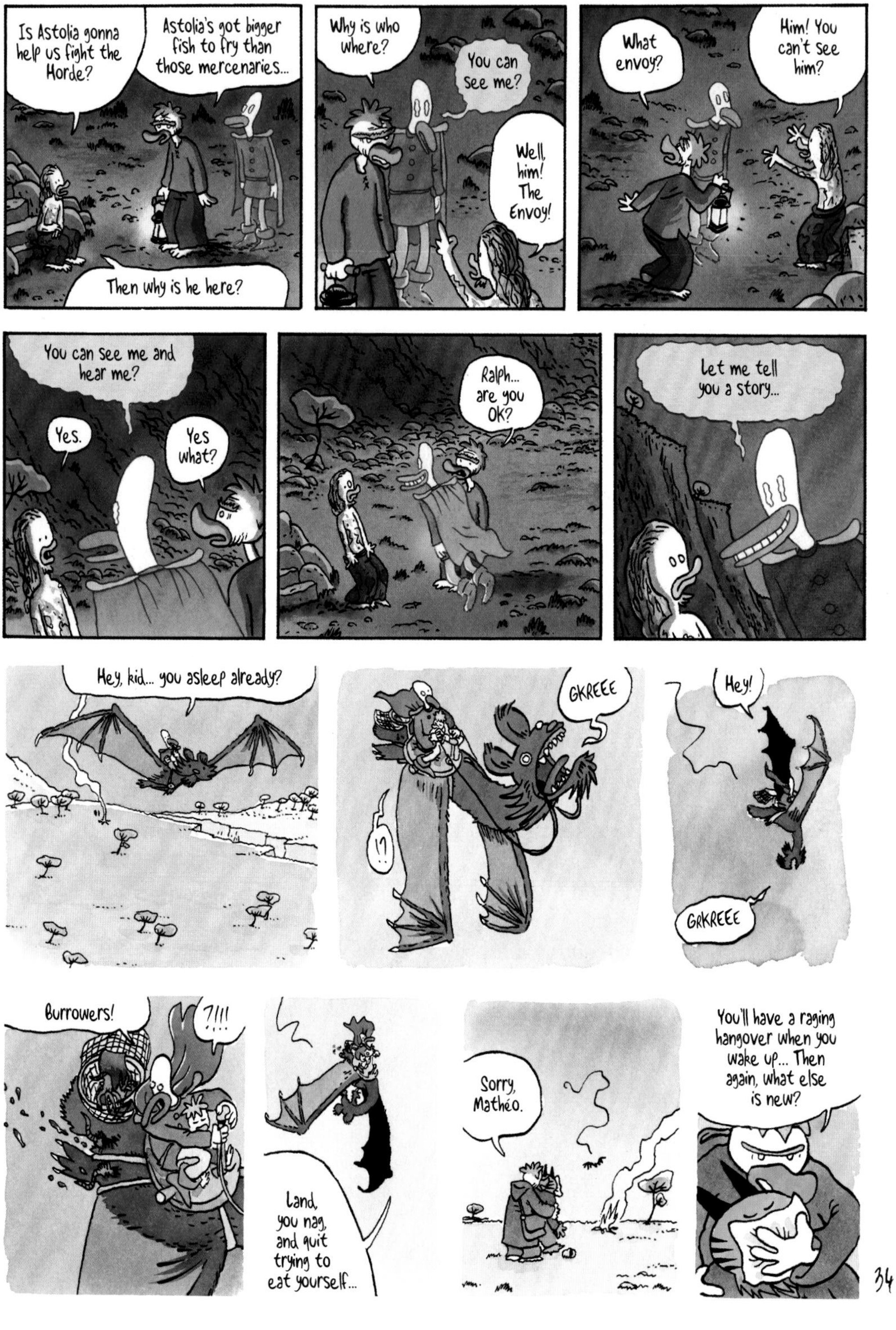

Is Astolia gonna help us fight the Horde?
Astolia's got bigger fish to fry than those mercenaries...
Then why is he here?
Why is who where?
You can see me?
Well, him! The Envoy!
What envoy?
Him! You can't see him?
You can see me and hear me?
Yes.
Yes what?
Ralph... are you OK?
Let me tell you a story...
Hey, kid... you asleep already?
GKREEE
!?
Hey!
GRKREEE
Burrowers!
?!!!
Land, you nag, and quit trying to eat yourself...
Sorry, Mathéo.
You'll have a raging hangover when you wake up... Then again, what else is new?
34

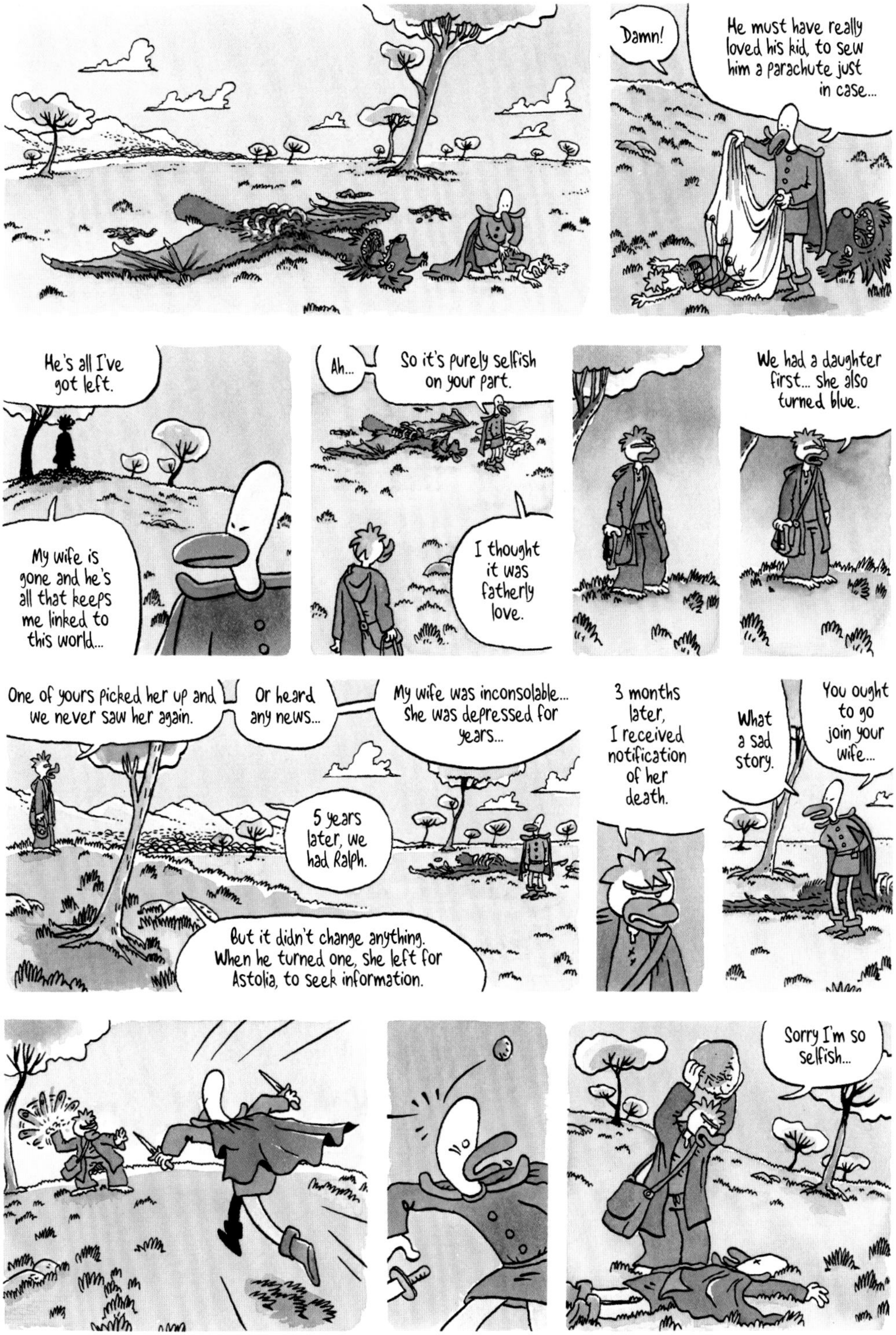

Damn!
He must have really loved his kid, to sew him a parachute just in case...
He's all I've got left.
My wife is gone and he's all that keeps me linked to this world...
Ah...
So it's purely selfish on your part.
I thought it was fatherly love.
We had a daughter first... she also turned blue.
One of yours picked her up and we never saw her again.
Or heard any news...
My wife was inconsolable... she was depressed for years...
5 years later, we had Ralph.
But it didn't change anything. When he turned one, she left for Astolia, to seek information.
3 months later, I received notification of her death.
What a sad story.
You ought to go join your wife...
Sorry I'm so selfish...

35

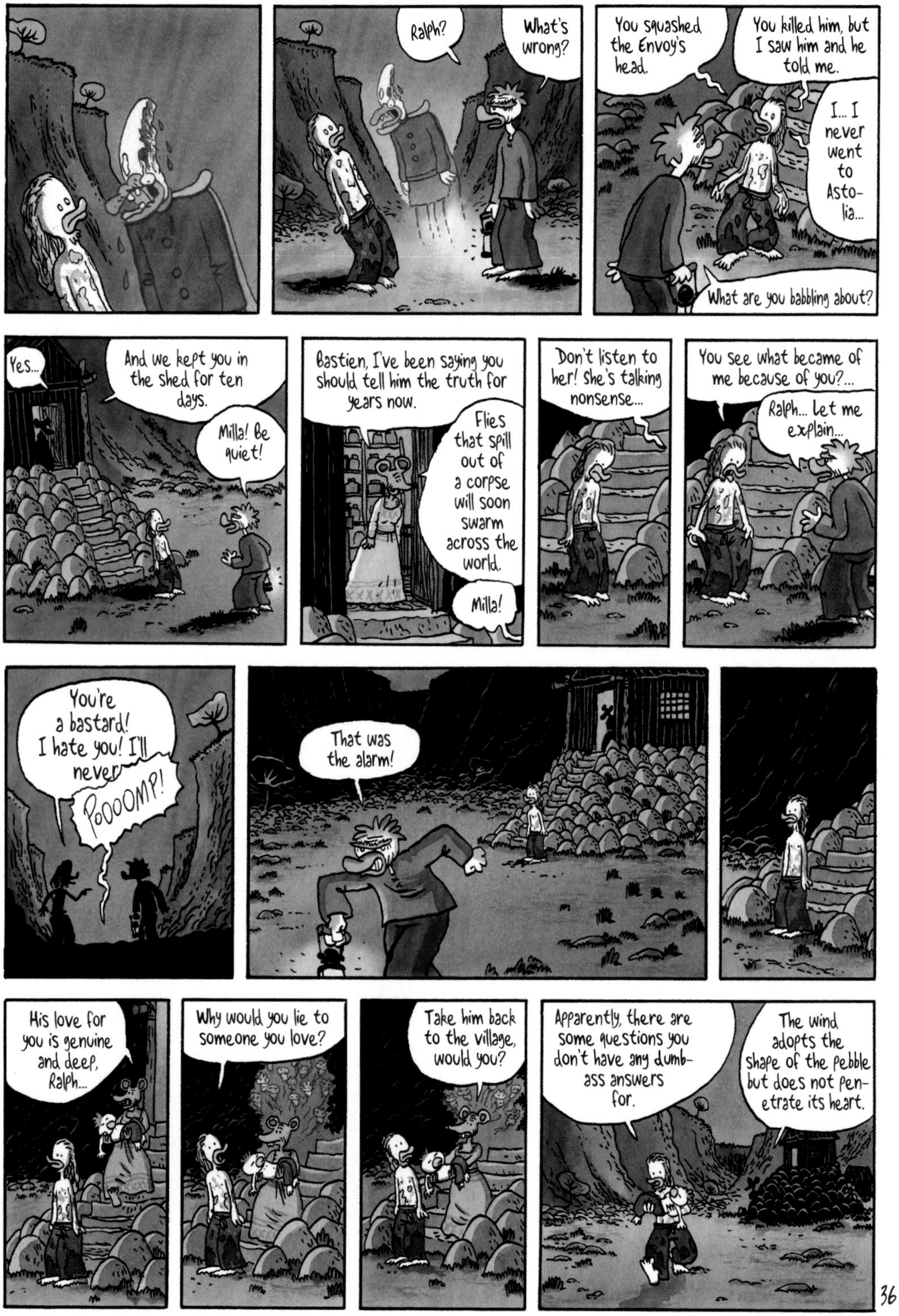
Ralph?
What's wrong?
You squashed the Envoy's head.
You killed him, but I saw him and he told me.
I... I never went to Asto-lia...
What are you babbling about?
Yes...
And we kept you in the shed for ten days.
Milla! Be quiet!
Bastien, I've been saying you should tell him the truth for years now.
Flies that spill out of a corpse will soon swarm across the world.
Milla!
Don't listen to her! She's talking nonsense...
You see what became of me because of you?...
Ralph... Let me explain...
You're a bastard! I hate you! I'll never
POOOOMP!
That was the alarm!
His love for you is genuine and deep, Ralph...
Why would you lie to someone you love?
Take him back to the village, would you?
Apparently, there are some questions you don't have any dumb-ass answers for.
The wind adopts the shape of the pebble but does not pen-etrate its heart.
36

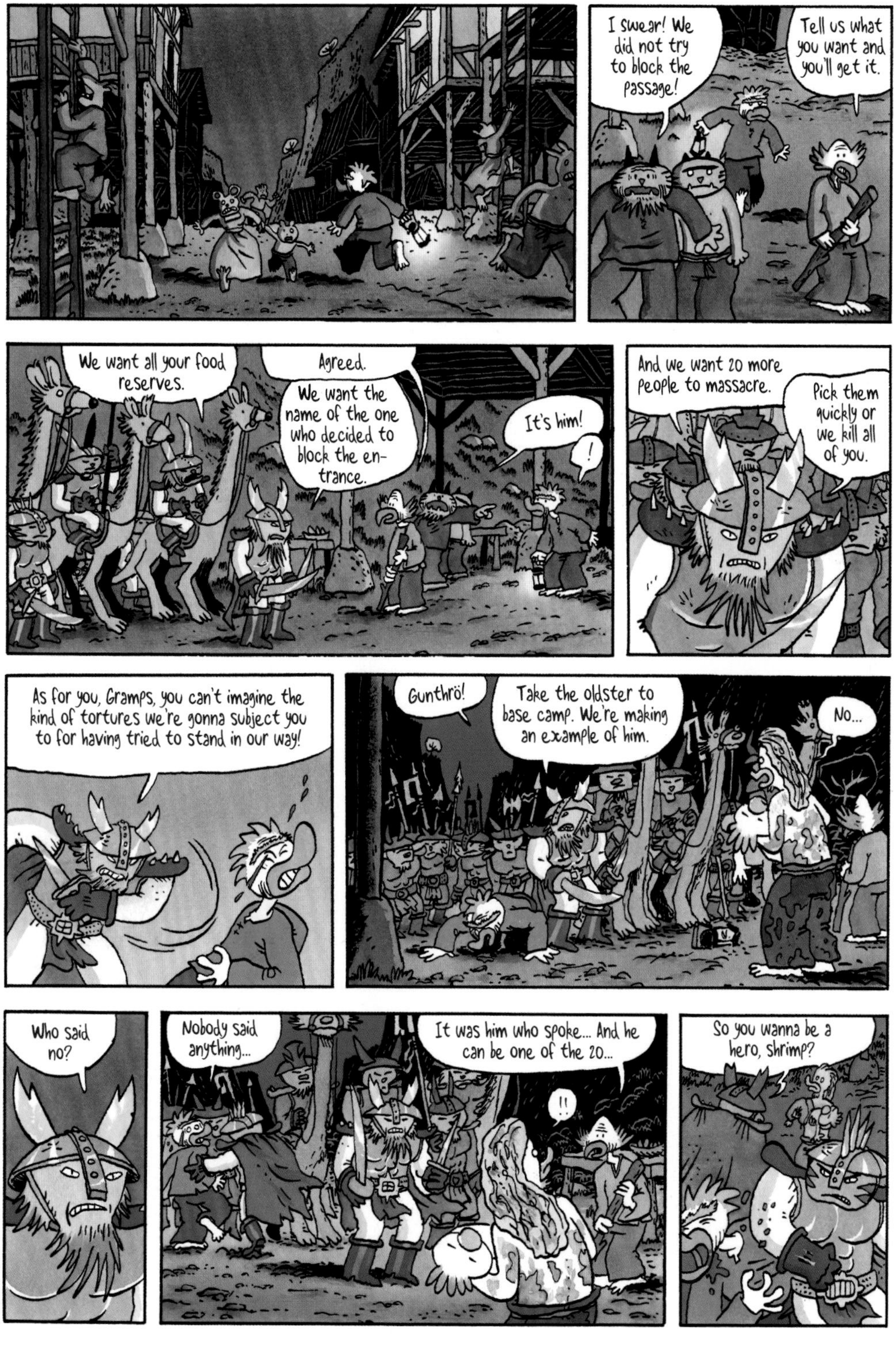
I swear! We did not try to block the passage!
Tell us what you want and you'll get it.
We want all your food reserves.
Agreed.
We want the name of the one who decided to block the entrance.
It's him!
!
And we want 20 more people to massacre.
Pick them quickly or we kill all of you.
As for you, Gramps, you can't imagine the kind of tortures we're gonna subject you to for having tried to stand in our way!
Gunthrö!
Take the oldster to base camp. We're making an example of him.
No...
Who said no?
Nobody said anything...
It was him who spoke... And he can be one of the 20...
!!
So you wanna be a hero, shrimp?
37

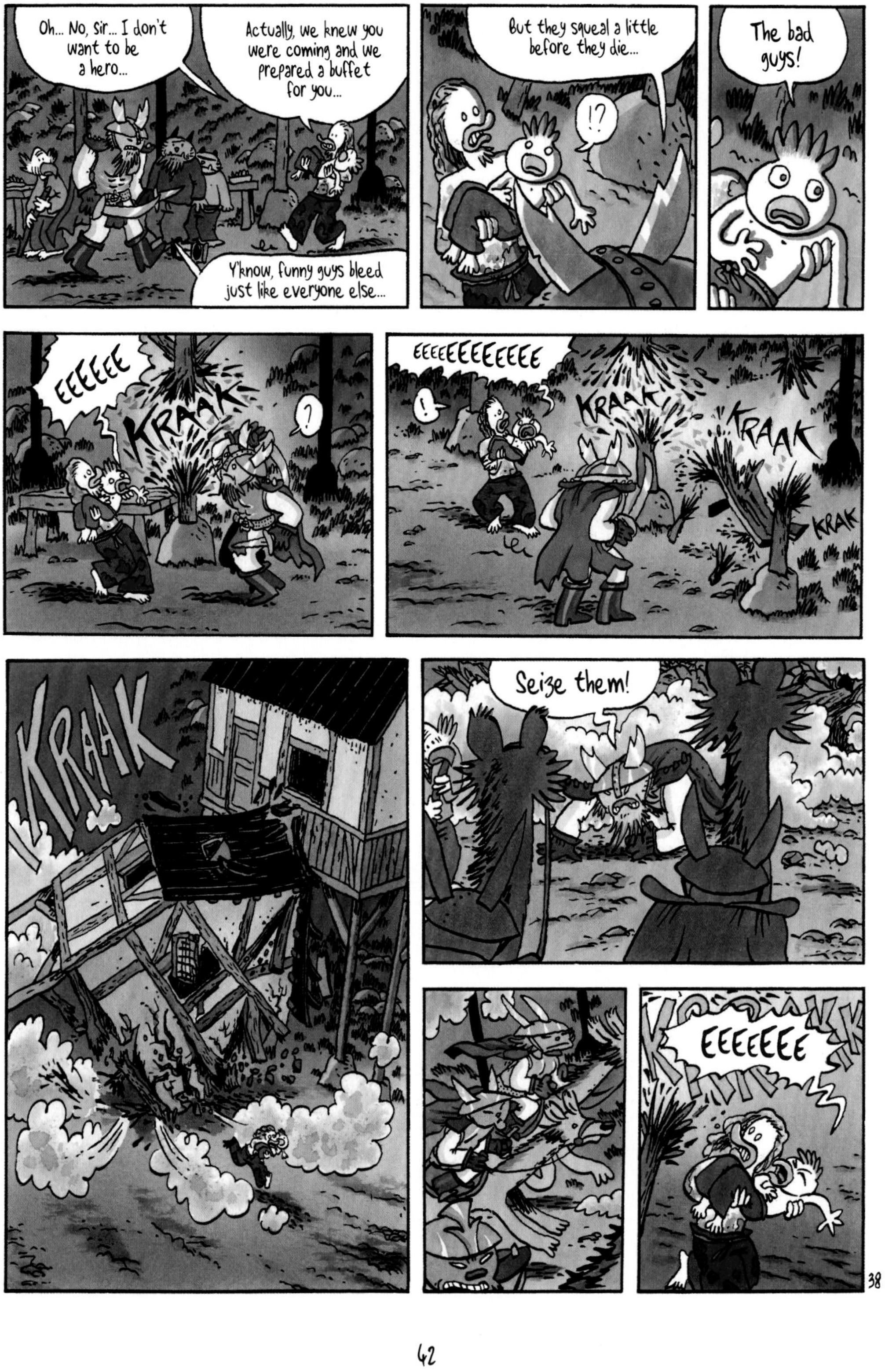
Oh... No, sir... I don't want to be a hero...
Actually, we knew you were coming and we prepared a buffet for you...
Y'know, funny guys bleed just like everyone else...
But they squeal a little before they die...
!?
The bad guys!
EEEEEE
KRAAK
?
EEEEEEEEEEEE
!
KRAAK
KRAAK
KRAK
KRAAK
Seize them!
EEEEEEE

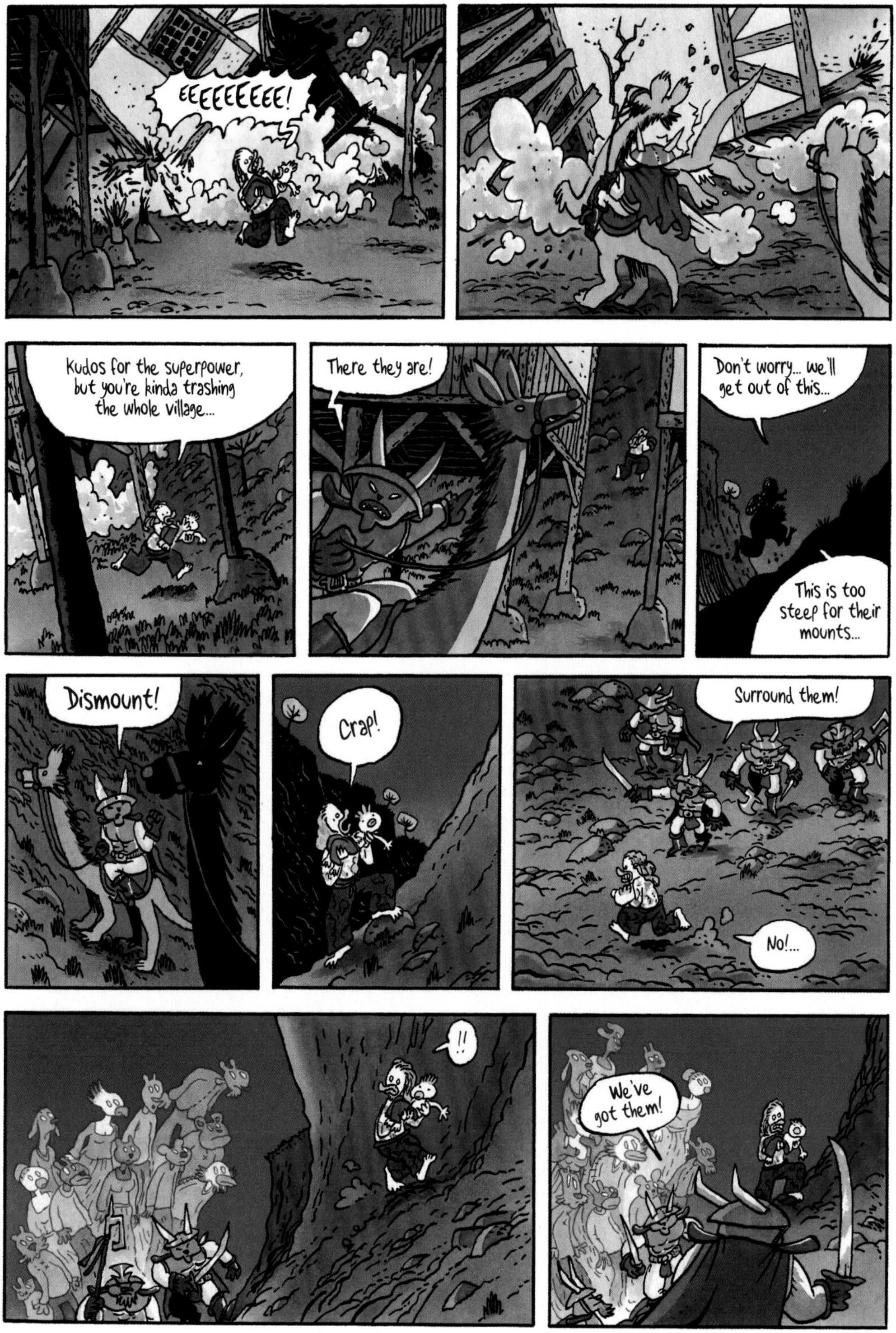

EEEEEEEEE!
Kudos for the superpower, but you're kinda trashing the whole village...
There they are!
Don't worry... we'll get out of this...
This is too steep for their mounts...
Dismount!
Crap!
Surround them!
No!...
!!
We've got them!

39

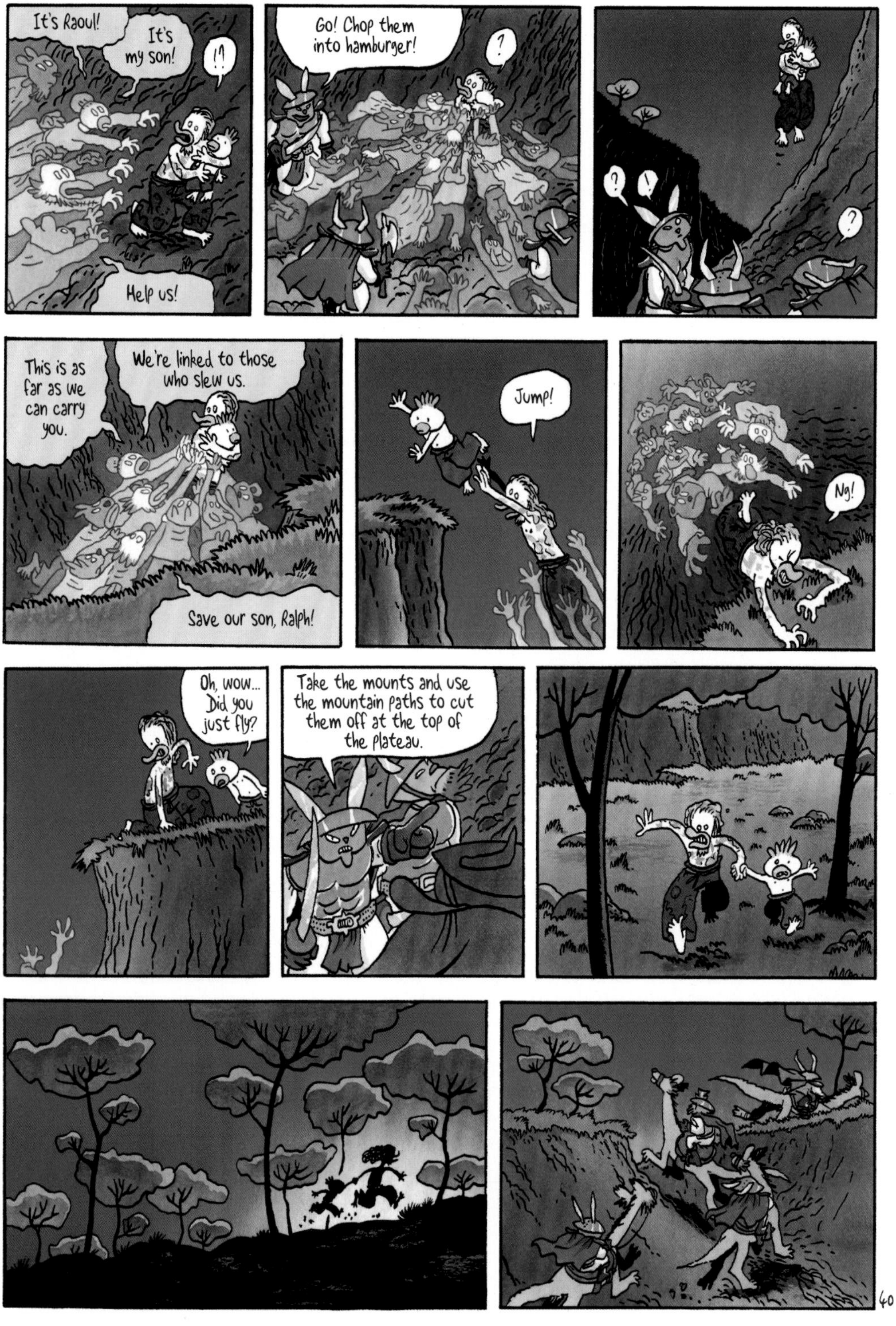
It's Raoul!
It's my son!
!?
Help us!
Go! Chop them into hamburger!
?
?
!
?
This is as far as we can carry you.
We're linked to those who slew us.
Save our son, Ralph!
Jump!
Ng!
Oh, wow... Did you just fly?
Take the mounts and use the mountain paths to cut them off at the top of the plateau.
40

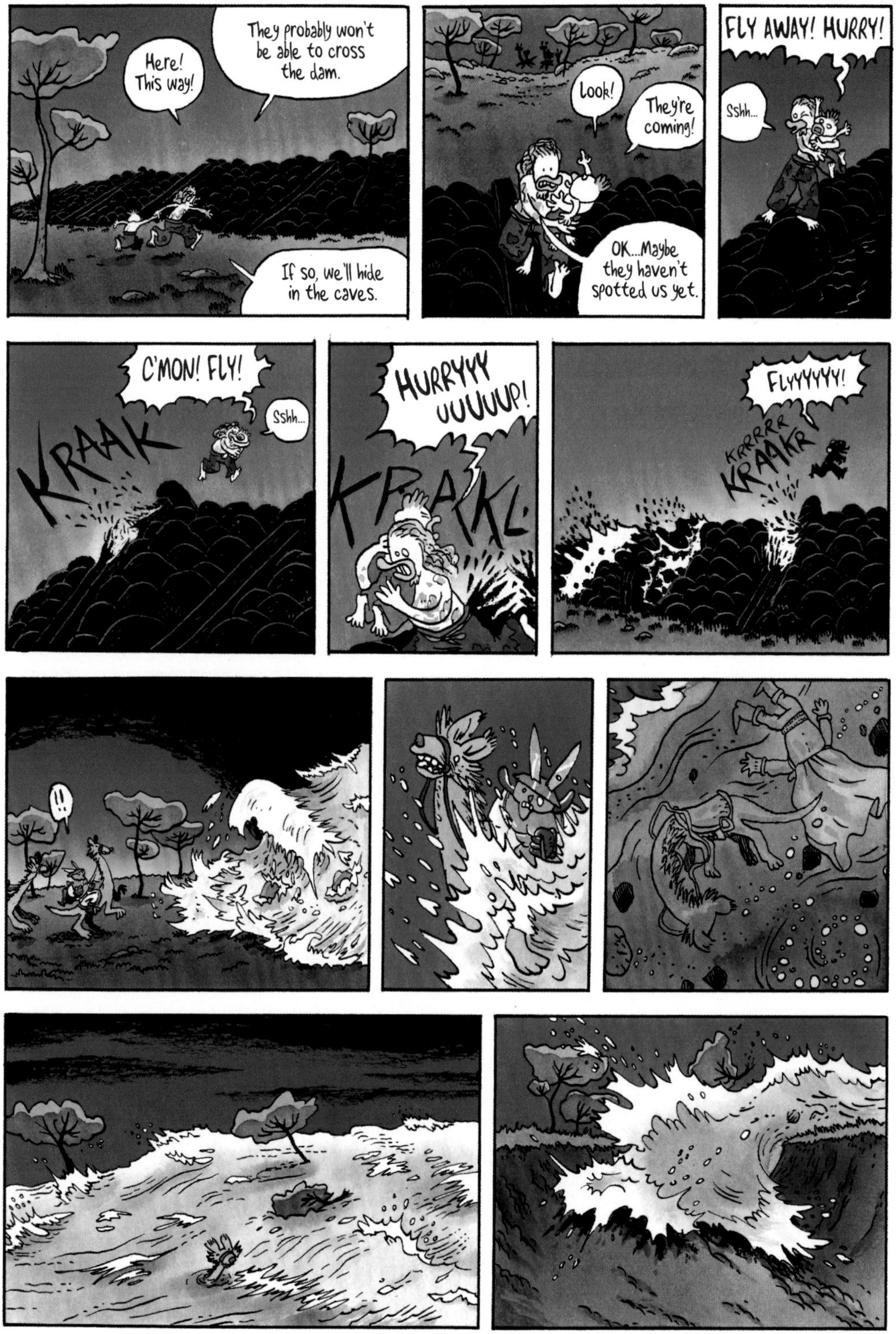
Here! This way!
They probably won't be able to cross the dam.
If so, we'll hide in the caves.
Look!
They're coming!
OK...Maybe they haven't spotted us yet.
FLY AWAY! HURRY!
Sshh...
C'MON! FLY!
Sshh...
KRAAK
HURRYYY UUUUUP!
KRAKL
FLYYYYYY!
KRRRRR
KRAAKR
!!

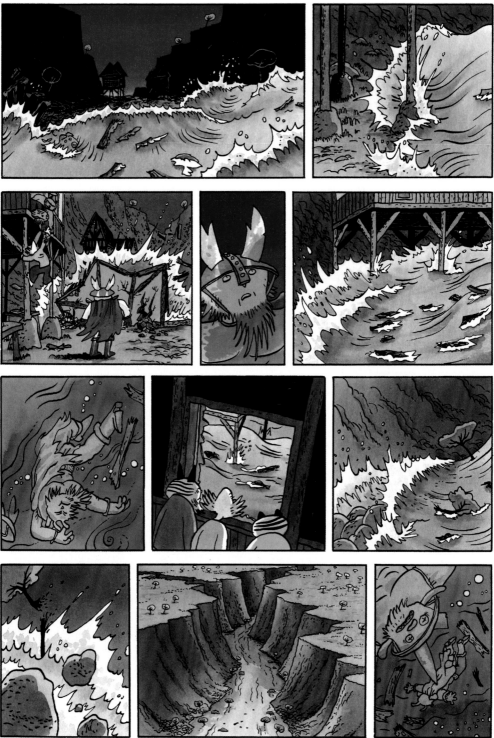

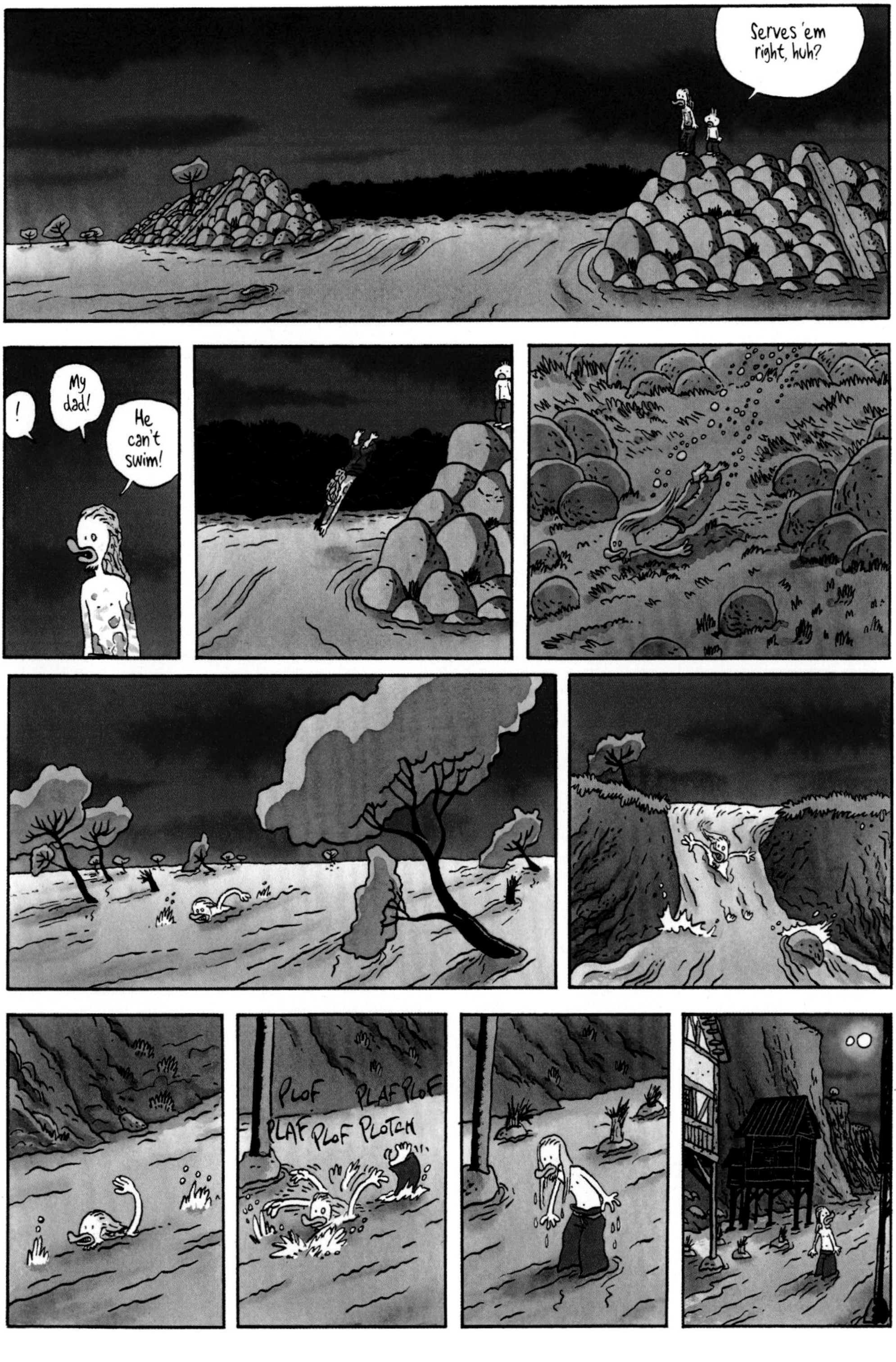
Serves 'em right, huh?
!
My dad!
He can't swim!
PLOF
PLAF PLOF
PLAF PLOF PLOTCH

43

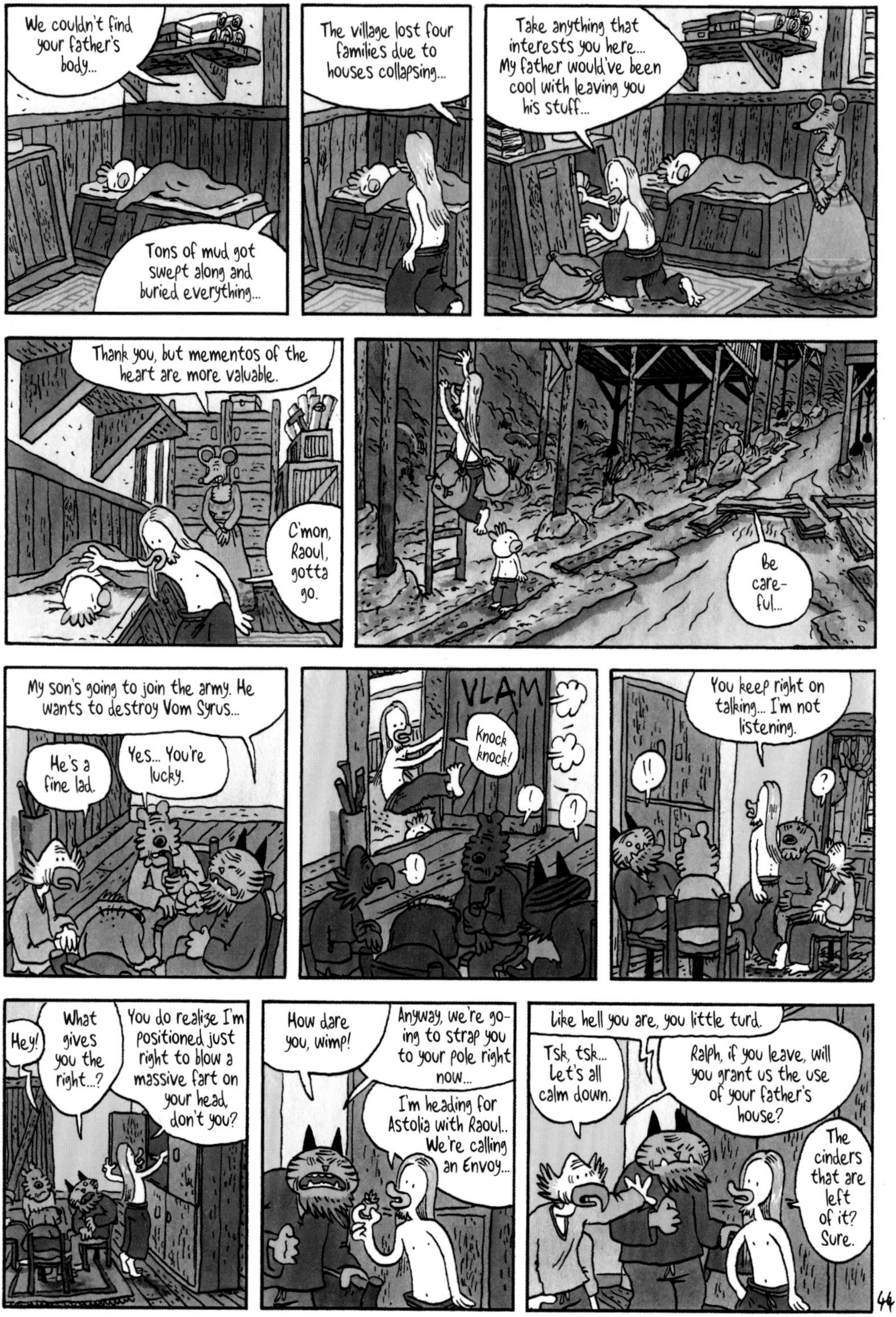
We couldn't find your father's body...
Tons of mud got swept along and buried everything...
The village lost four families due to houses collapsing...
Take anything that interests you here... My father would've been cool with leaving you his stuff...
Thank you, but mementos of the heart are more valuable.
C'mon, Raoul, gotta go.
Be care-ful...
My son's going to join the army. He wants to destroy Vom Syrus...
He's a fine lad.
Yes... You're lucky.
VLAM
Knock knock!
!
?
!
You keep right on talking... I'm not listening.
!!
?
Hey!
What gives you the right...?
You do realize I'm positioned just right to blow a massive fart on your head, don't you?
How dare you, wimp!
Anyway, we're go-ing to strap you to your pole right now...
I'm heading for Astolia with Raoul.. We're calling an Envoy...
Like hell you are, you little turd.
Tsk, tsk... Let's all calm down.
Ralph, if you leave, will you grant us the use of your father's house?
The cinders that are left of it? Sure.
44

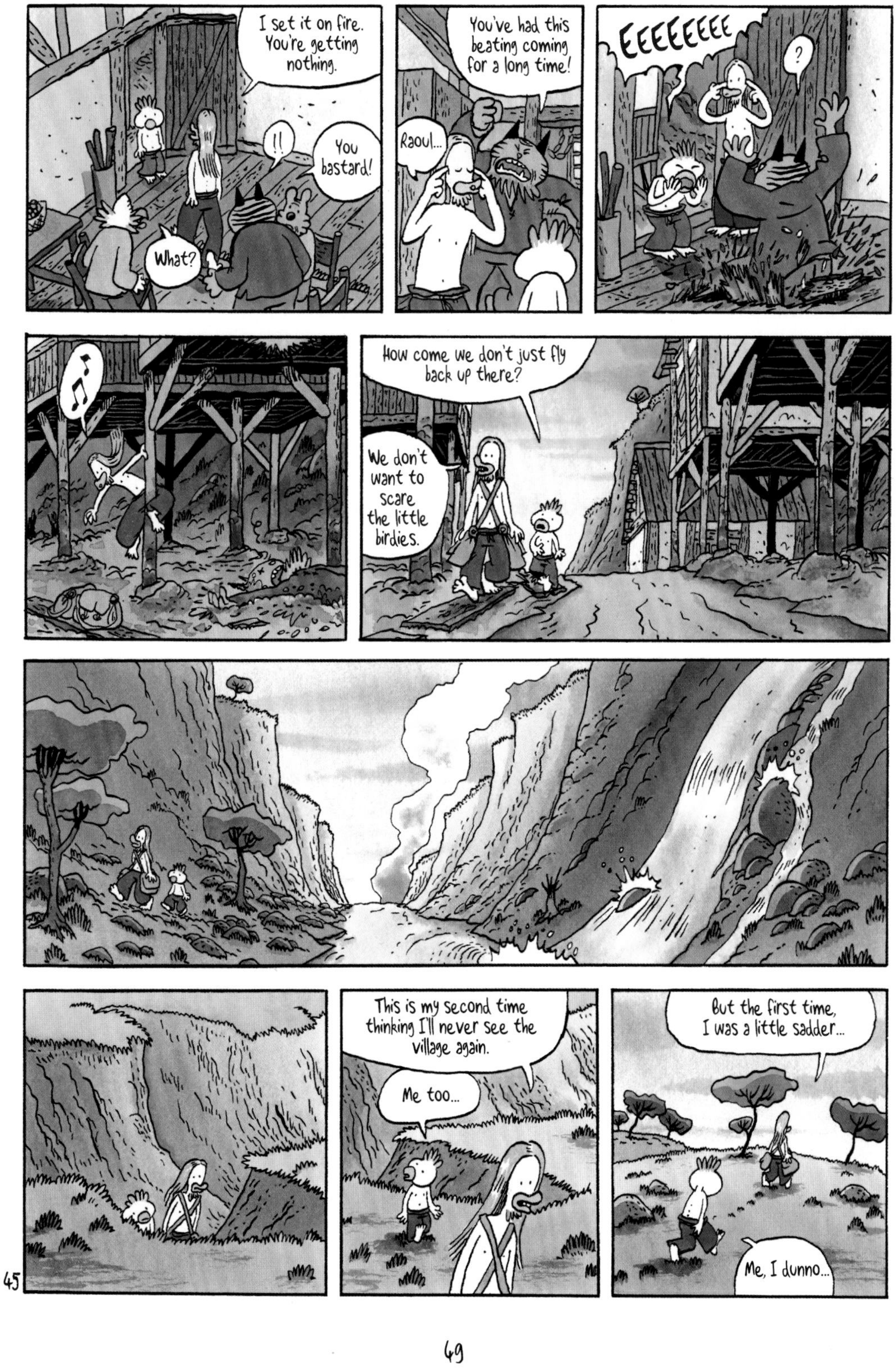
I set it on fire. You're getting nothing.
!!
You bastard!
What?
You've had this beating coming for a long time!
Raoul...
EEEEEEEE
?
How come we don't just fly back up there?
We don't want to scare the little birdies.
This is my second time thinking I'll never see the village again.
Me too...
But the first time, I was a little sadder...
Me, I dunno...

45

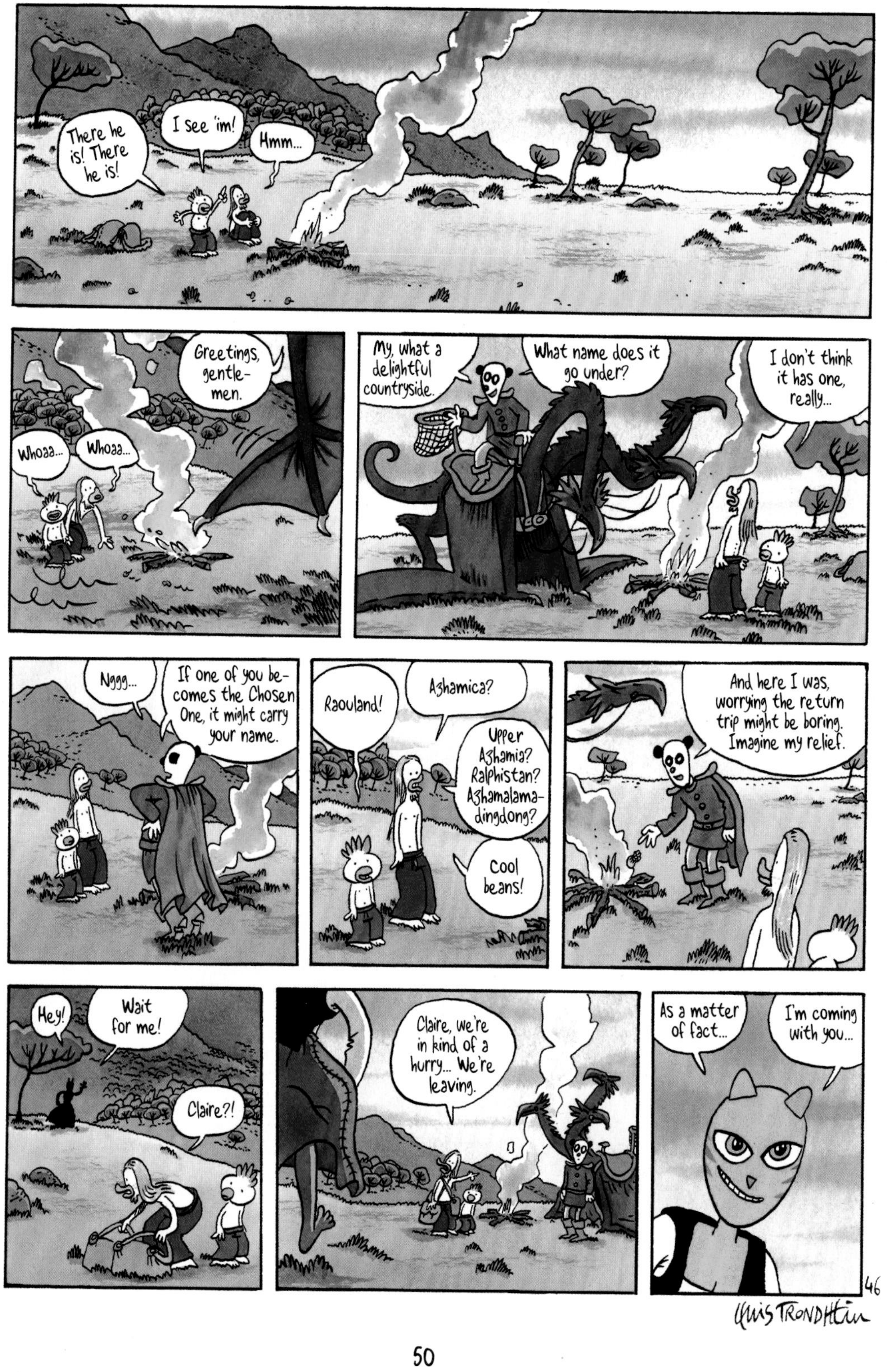
There he is! There he is!
I see 'im!
Hmm...
Greetings, gentle-men.
Whoaa...
Whoaa...
My, what a delightful countryside.
What name does it go under?
I don't think it has one, really...
Nggg...
If one of you be-comes the Chosen One, it might carry your name.
Raouland!
Azhamica?
Upper Azhamia? Ralphistan? Azhamalama-dingdong?
Cool beans!
And here I was, worrying the return trip might be boring. Imagine my relief.
Hey!
Wait for me!
Claire?!
Claire, we're in kind of a hurry... We're leaving.
As a matter of fact...
I'm coming with you...
46

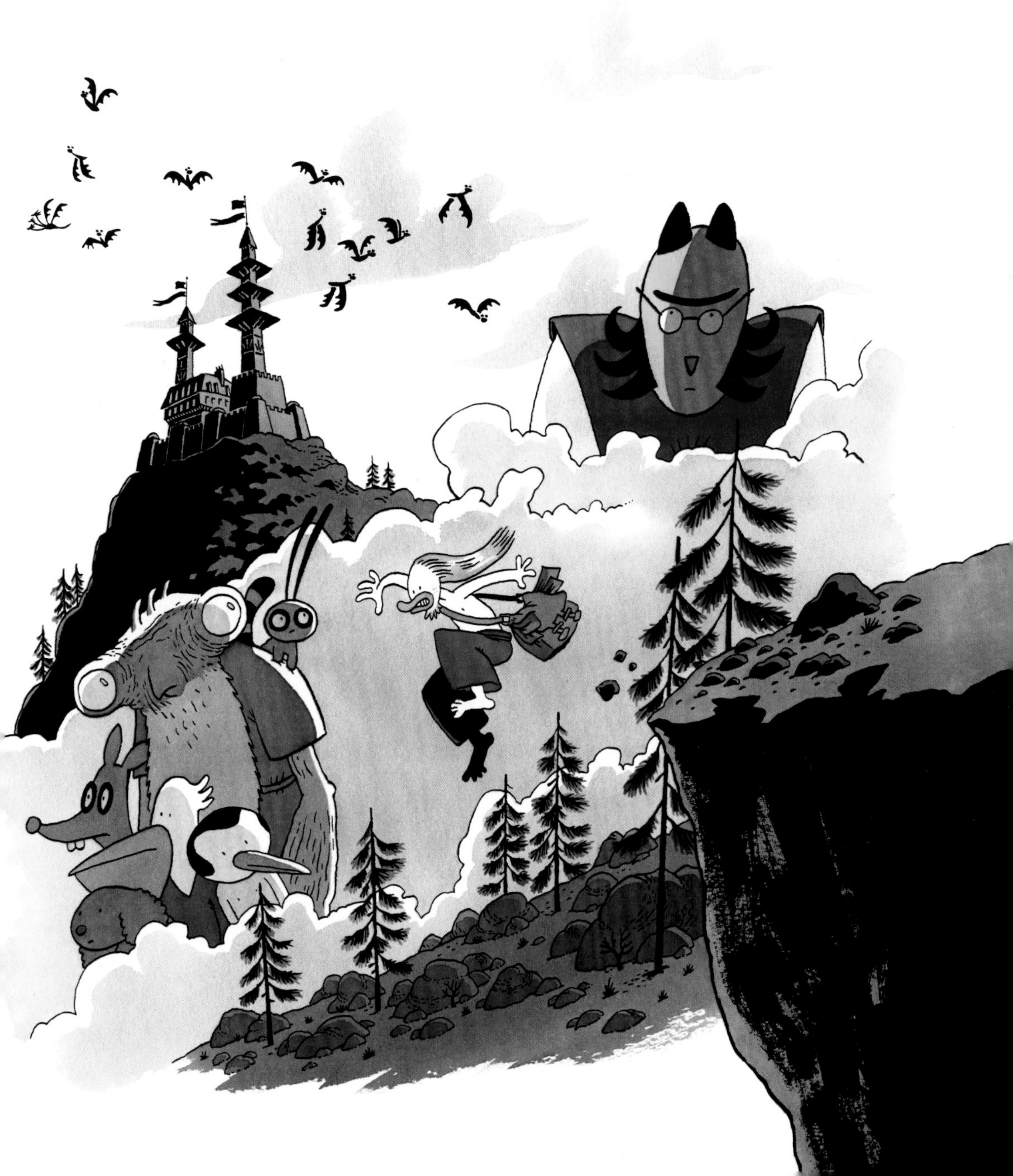

Ralph Azham

2

Death at the Beginning of the Road

Story and Art: Lewis Trondheim
Colors: Brigitte Findakly
Translation: Joe Johnson
Lettering: Nikki FoxRobot

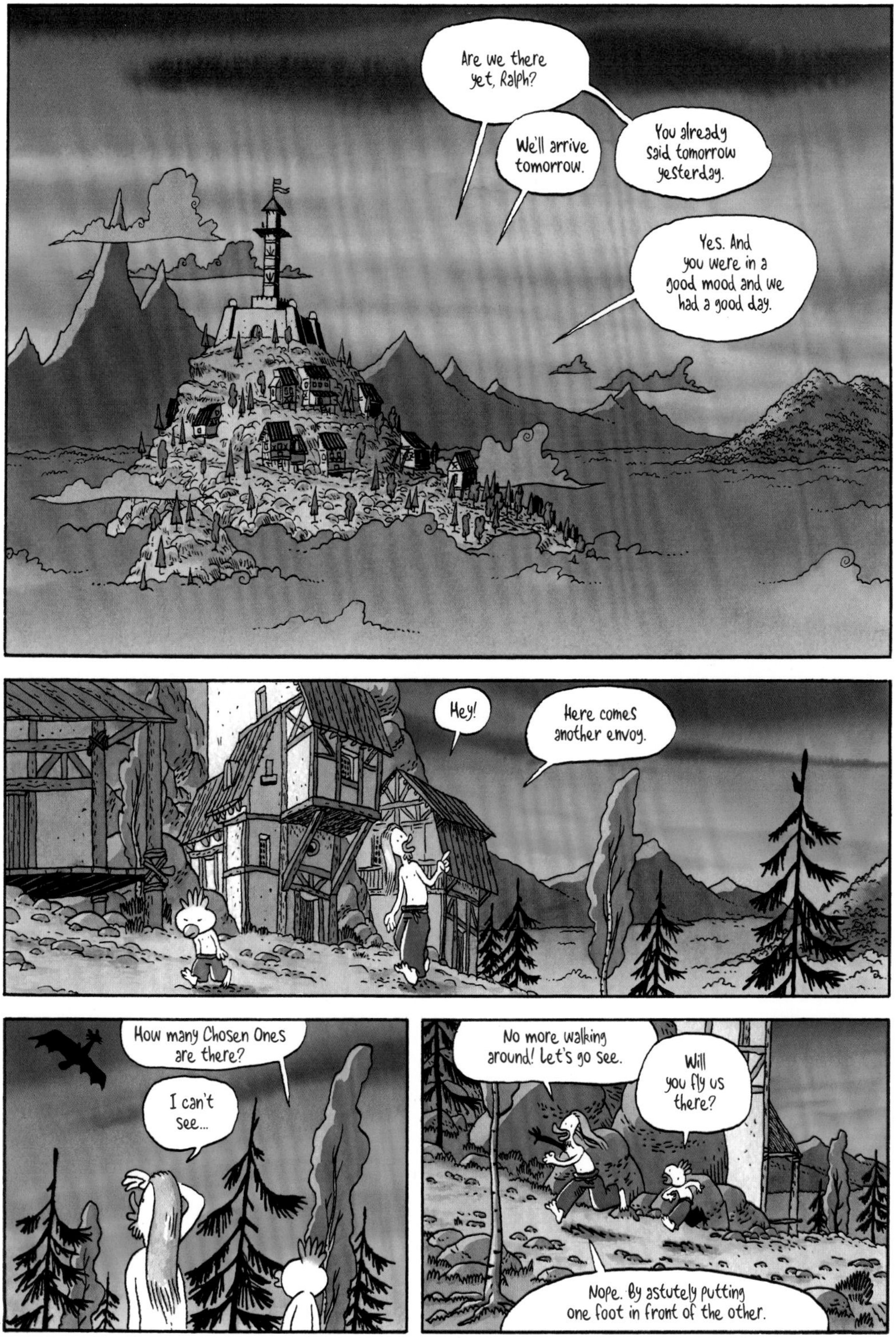

Are we there yet, Ralph?
We'll arrive tomorrow.
You already said tomorrow yesterday.
Yes. And you were in a good mood and we had a good day.
Hey!
Here comes another envoy.
How many Chosen Ones are there?
I can't see...
No more walking around! Let's go see.
Will you fly us there?
Nope. By astutely putting one foot in front of the other.

47

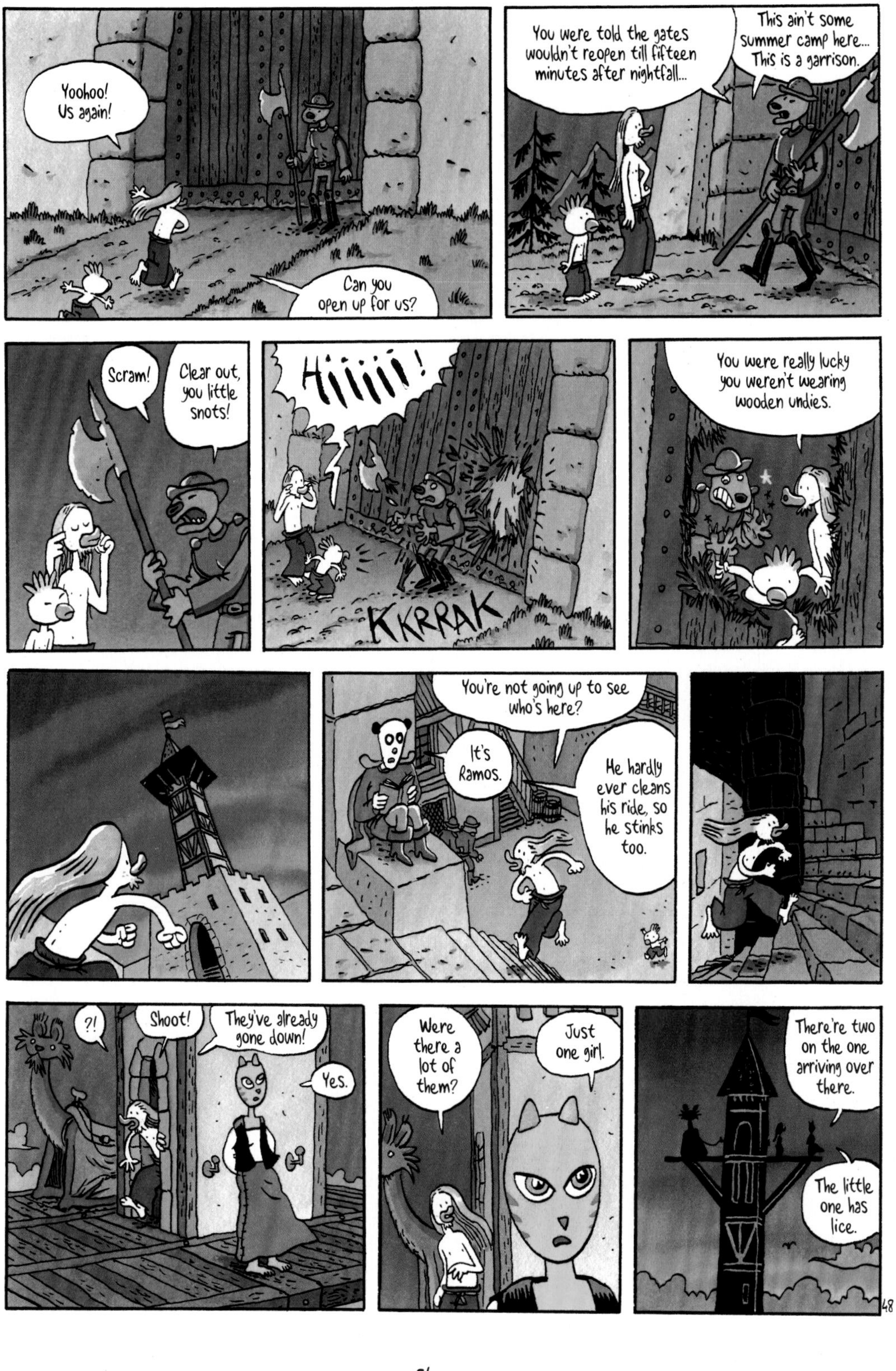
Yoohoo!
Us again!
Can you open up for us?
You were told the gates wouldn't reopen till fifteen minutes after nightfall...
This ain't some summer camp here... This is a garrison.
Scram!
Clear out, you little snots!
Hiiiii!
KKRRAK
You were really lucky you weren't wearing wooden undies.
You're not going up to see who's here?
It's Ramos.
He hardly ever cleans his ride, so he stinks too.
?!
Shoot!
They've already gone down!
Yes.
Were there a lot of them?
Just one girl.
There're two on the one arriving over there.
The little one has lice.
48

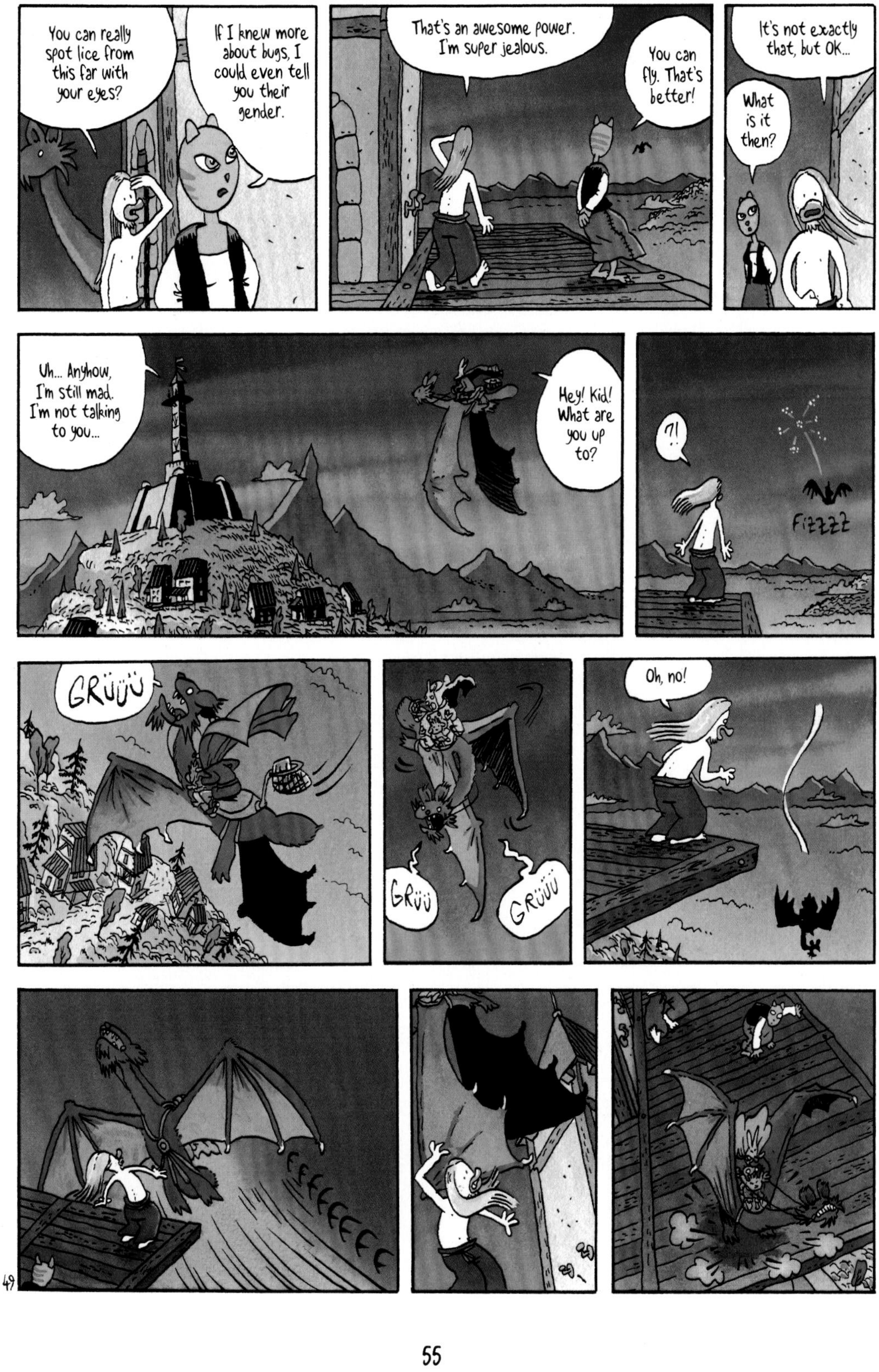
You can really spot lice from this far with your eyes?
If I knew more about bugs, I could even tell you their gender.
That's an awesome power. I'm super jealous.
You can fly. That's better!
It's not exactly that, but OK...
What is it then?
Uh... Anyhow, I'm still mad. I'm not talking to you...
Hey! Kid! What are you up to?
?!
FIZZZZ
GRÜÜÜ
GRÜÜ
GRÜÜÜ
Oh, no!
FFFFFFFF

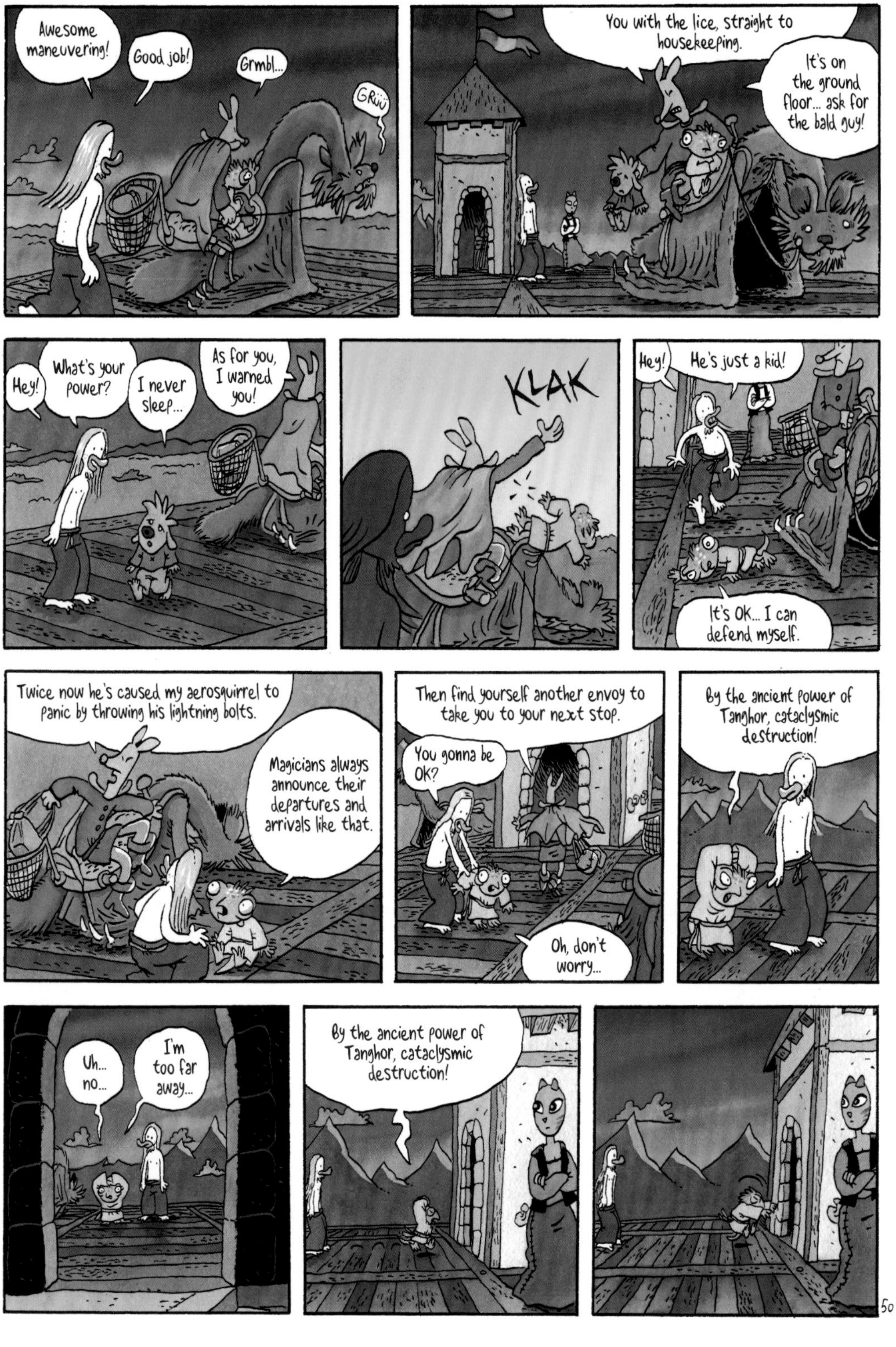
Awesome maneuvering!
Good job!
Grmbl...
GRüü
You with the lice, straight to housekeeping.
It's on the ground floor... ask for the bald guy!
Hey!
What's your power?
I never sleep...
As for you, I warned you!
KLAK
Hey!
He's just a kid!
It's OK... I can defend myself.
Twice now he's caused my aerosquirrel to panic by throwing his lightning bolts.
Magicians always announce their departures and arrivals like that.
Then find yourself another envoy to take you to your next stop.
You gonna be OK?
Oh, don't worry...
By the ancient power of Tanghor, cataclysmic destruction!
Uh... no...
I'm too far away...
By the ancient power of Tanghor, cataclysmic destruction!
50

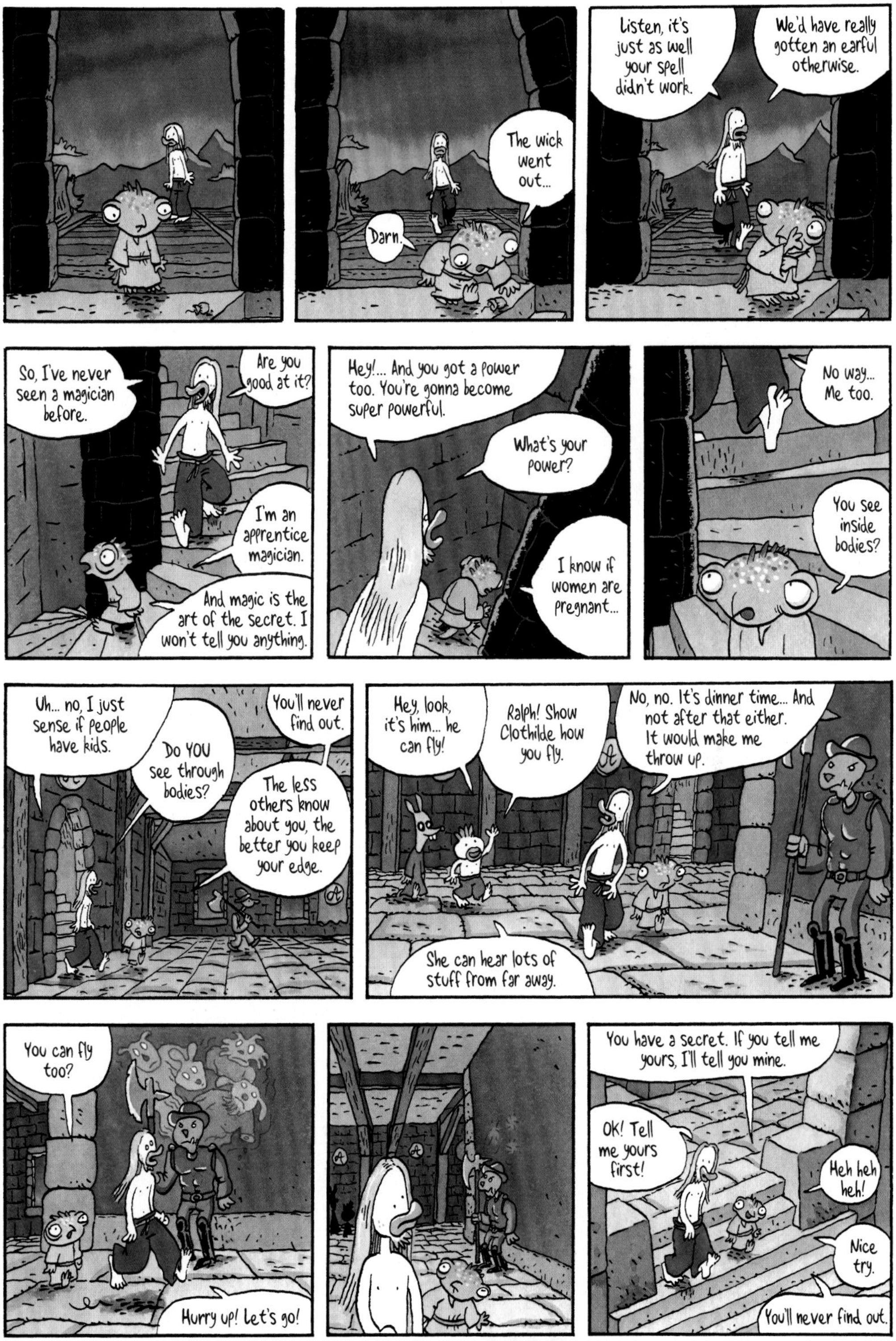
The wick went out...
Darn.
Listen, it's just as well your spell didn't work.
We'd have really gotten an earful otherwise.
So, I've never seen a magician before.
Are you good at it?
I'm an apprentice magician.
And magic is the art of the secret. I won't tell you anything.
Hey!... And you got a power too. You're gonna become super powerful.
What's your power?
I know if women are pregnant...
No way... Me too.
You see inside bodies?
Uh... no, I just sense if people have kids.
Do YOU see through bodies?
You'll never find out.
The less others know about you, the better you keep your edge.
Hey, look, it's him... he can fly!
Ralph! Show Clothilde how you fly.
No, no. It's dinner time... And not after that either. It would make me throw up.
She can hear lots of stuff from far away.
You can fly too?
Hurry up! Let's go!
You have a secret. If you tell me yours, I'll tell you mine.
OK! Tell me yours first!
Heh heh heh!
Nice try.
You'll never find out.

51

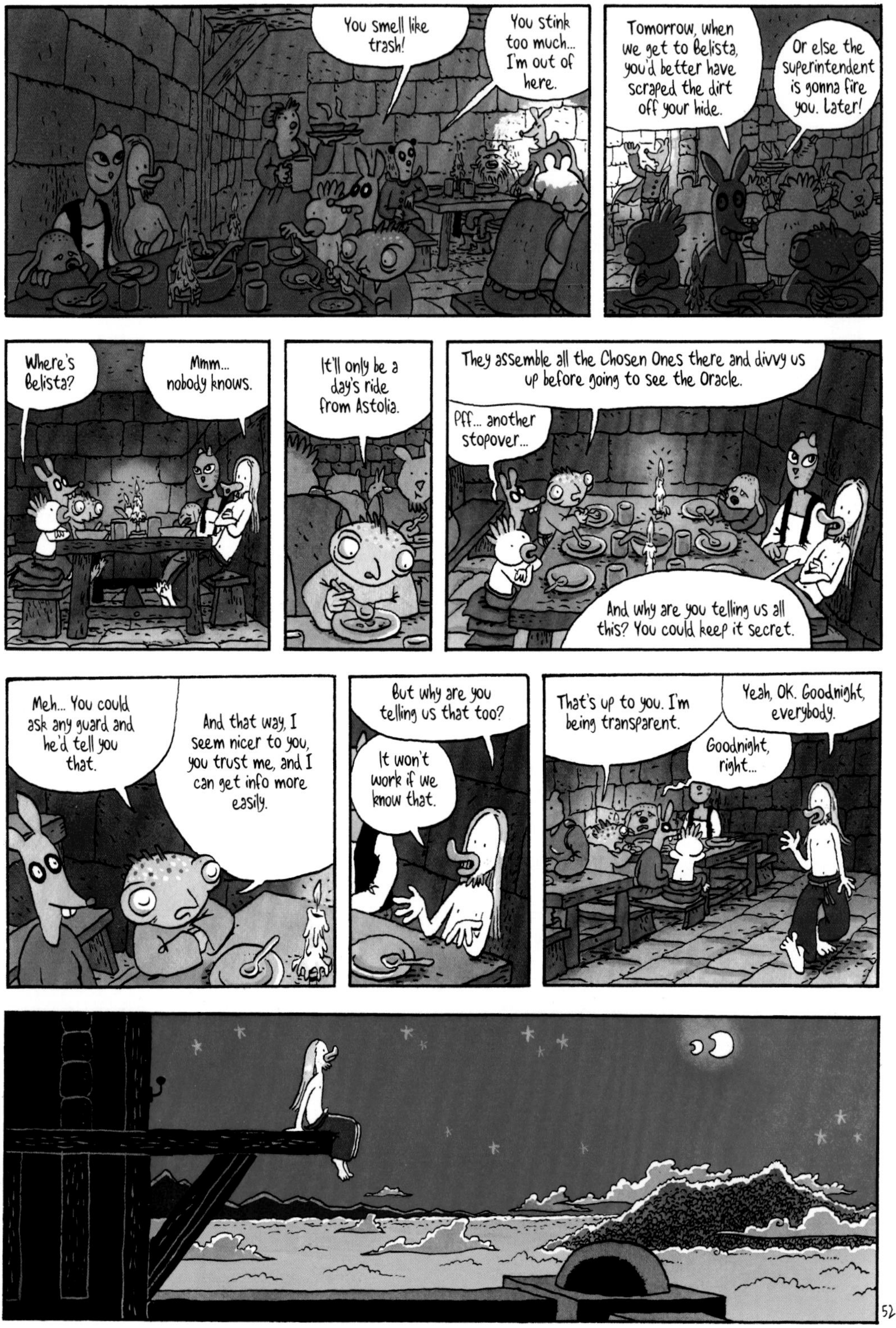
You smell like trash!
You stink too much... I'm out of here.
Tomorrow, when we get to Belista, you'd better have scraped the dirt off your hide.
Or else the superintendent is gonna fire you. Later!
Where's Belista?
Mmm... nobody knows.
It'll only be a day's ride from Astolia.
They assemble all the Chosen Ones there and divvy us up before going to see the Oracle.
Pff... another stopover...
And why are you telling us all this? You could keep it secret.
Meh... You could ask any guard and he'd tell you that.
And that way, I seem nicer to you, you trust me, and I can get info more easily.
But why are you telling us that too?
It won't work if we know that.
That's up to you. I'm being transparent.
Goodnight, right...
Yeah, OK. Goodnight, everybody.
52

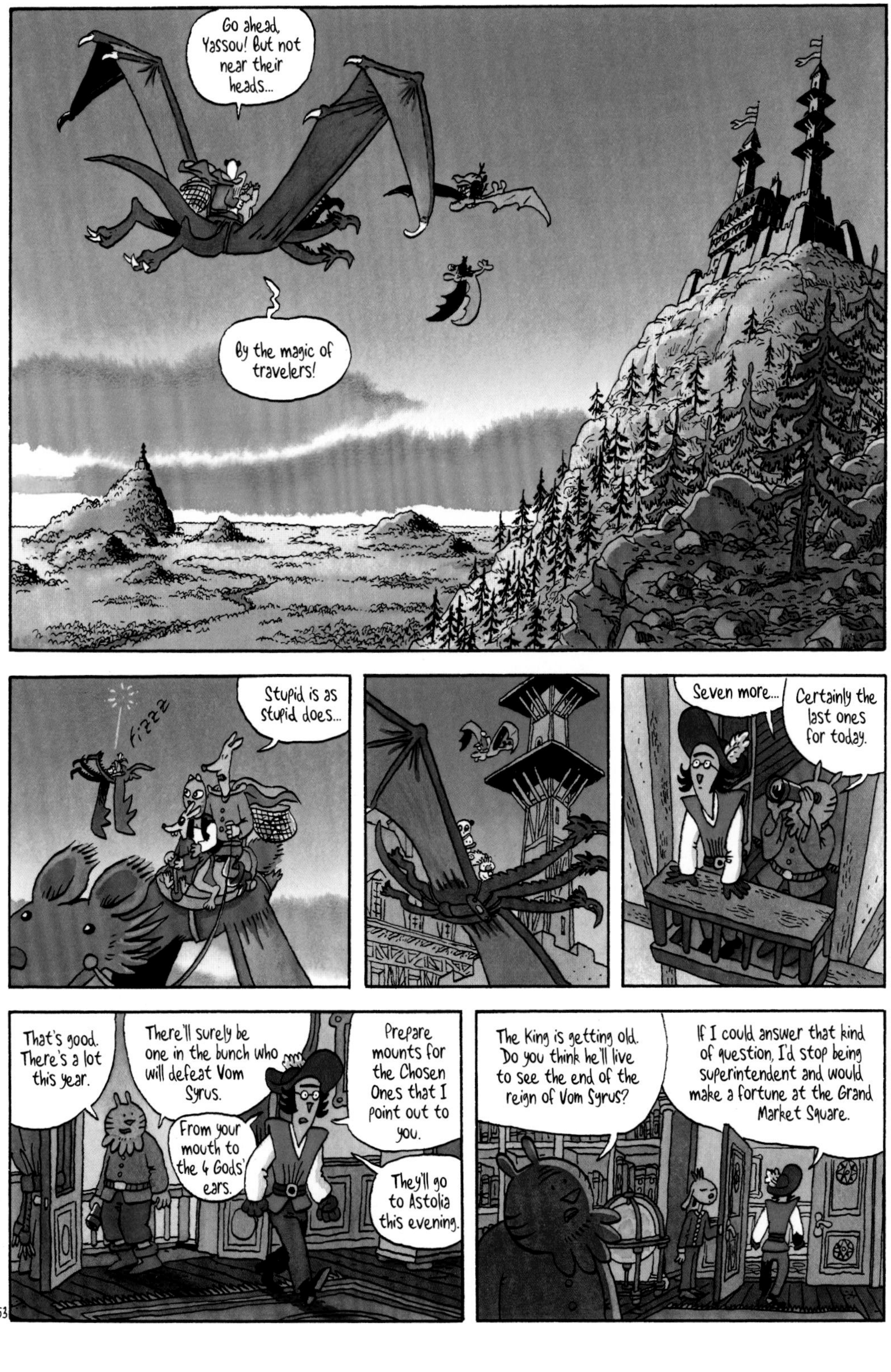
Go ahead, Yassou! But not near their heads...
By the magic of travelers!
FIZZZ
Stupid is as stupid does...
Seven more...
Certainly the last ones for today.
That's good. There's a lot this year.
There'll surely be one in the bunch who will defeat Vom Syrus.
From your mouth to the 4 Gods' ears.
Prepare mounts for the Chosen Ones that I point out to you.
They'll go to Astolia this evening.
The King is getting old. Do you think he'll live to see the end of the reign of Vom Syrus?
If I could answer that kind of question, I'd stop being superintendent and would make a fortune at the Grand Market Square.

53

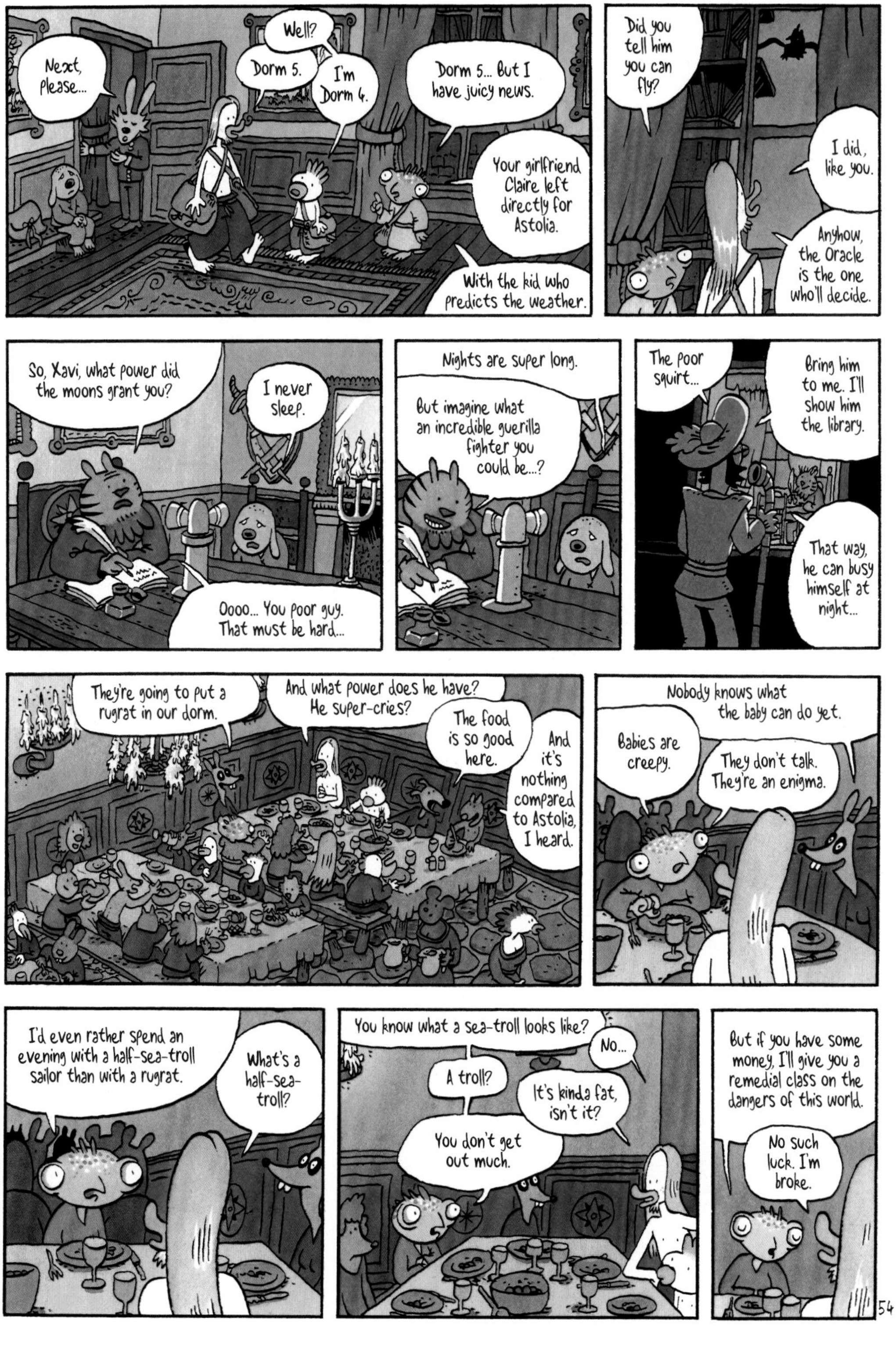
Next, please...
Well?
Dorm 5.
I'm Dorm 4.
Dorm 5... But I have juicy news.
Your girlfriend Claire left directly for Astolia.
With the kid who predicts the weather.
Did you tell him you can fly?
I did, like you.
Anyhow, the Oracle is the one who'll decide.
So, Xavi, what power did the moons grant you?
I never sleep.
Oooo... You poor guy. That must be hard...
Nights are super long.
But imagine what an incredible guerilla fighter you could be...?
The poor squirt...
Bring him to me. I'll show him the library.
That way, he can busy himself at night...
They're going to put a rugrat in our dorm.
And what power does he have? He super-cries?
The food is so good here.
And it's nothing compared to Astolia, I heard.
Nobody knows what the baby can do yet.
Babies are creepy.
They don't talk. They're an enigma.
I'd even rather spend an evening with a half-sea-troll sailor than with a rugrat.
What's a half-sea-troll?
You know what a sea-troll looks like?
No...
A troll?
It's kinda fat, isn't it?
You don't get out much.
But if you have some money, I'll give you a remedial class on the dangers of this world.
No such luck. I'm broke.
54

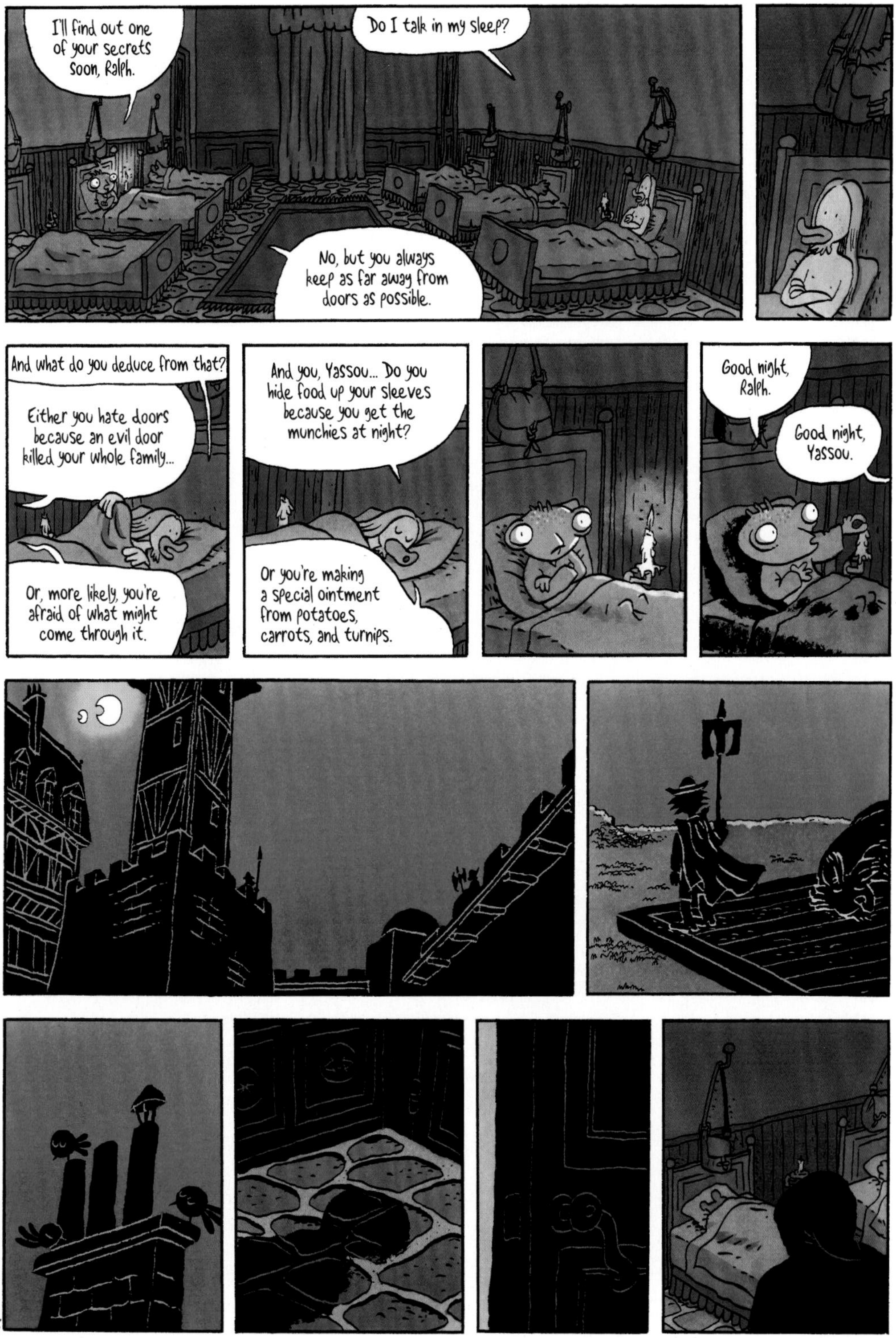
I'll find out one of your secrets soon, Ralph.
Do I talk in my sleep?
No, but you always keep as far away from doors as possible.
And what do you deduce from that?
Either you hate doors because an evil door killed your whole family...
Or, more likely, you're afraid of what might come through it.
And you, Yassou... Do you hide food up your sleeves because you get the munchies at night?
Or you're making a special ointment from potatoes, carrots, and turnips.
Good night, Ralph.
Good night, Yassou.

55

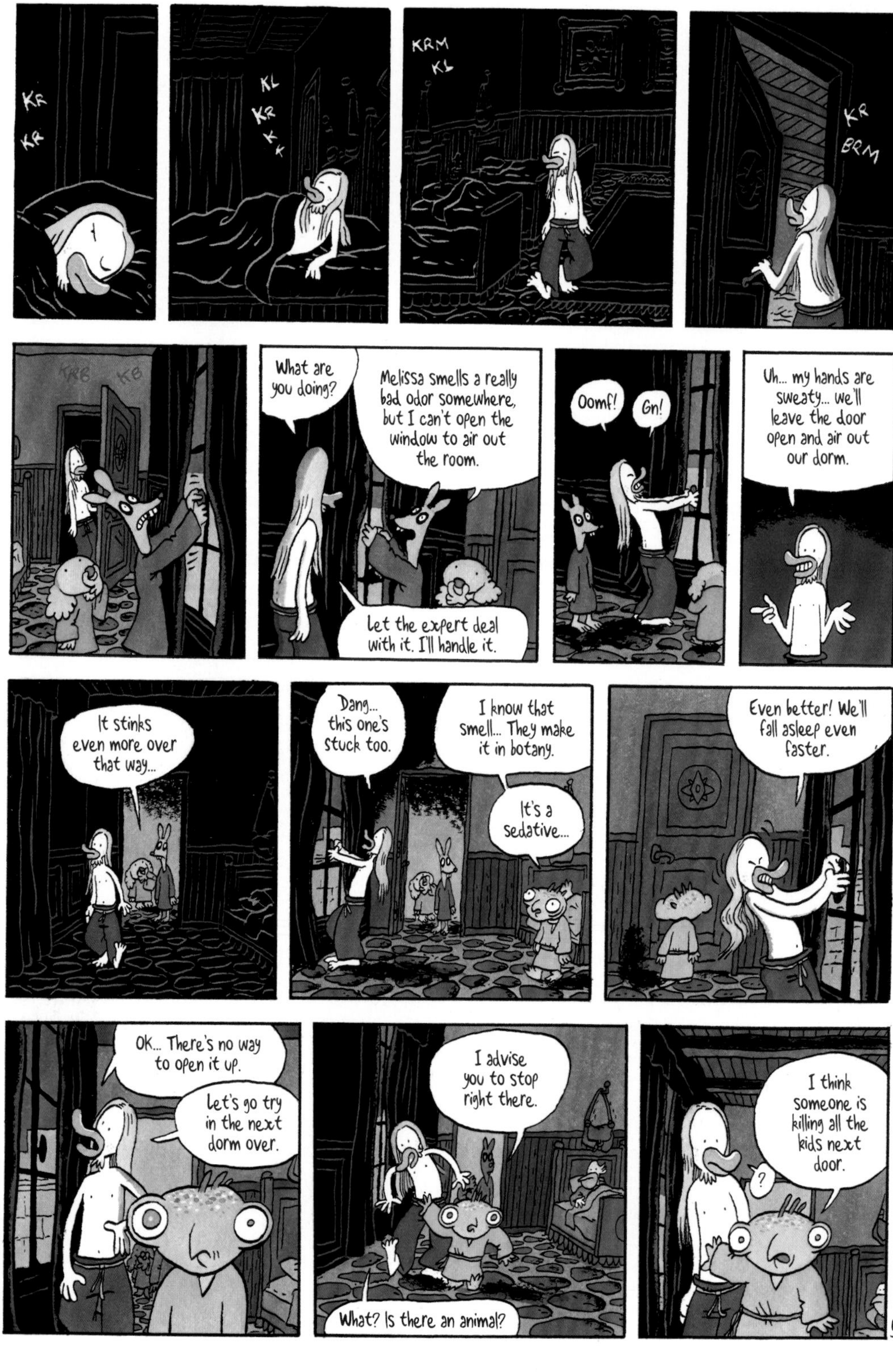
KR
KR
KL
KR
KK
KRM
KL
KR
BRM
KRB KB
What are you doing?
Melissa smells a really bad odor somewhere, but I can't open the window to air out the room.
Let the expert deal with it. I'll handle it.
Oomf!
Gn!
Uh... my hands are sweaty... we'll leave the door open and air out our dorm.
It stinks even more over that way...
Dang... this one's stuck too.
I know that smell... They make it in botany.
It's a sedative...
Even better! We'll fall asleep even faster.
OK... There's no way to open it up.
Let's go try in the next dorm over.
I advise you to stop right there.
What? Is there an animal?
I think someone is killing all the kids next door.
?

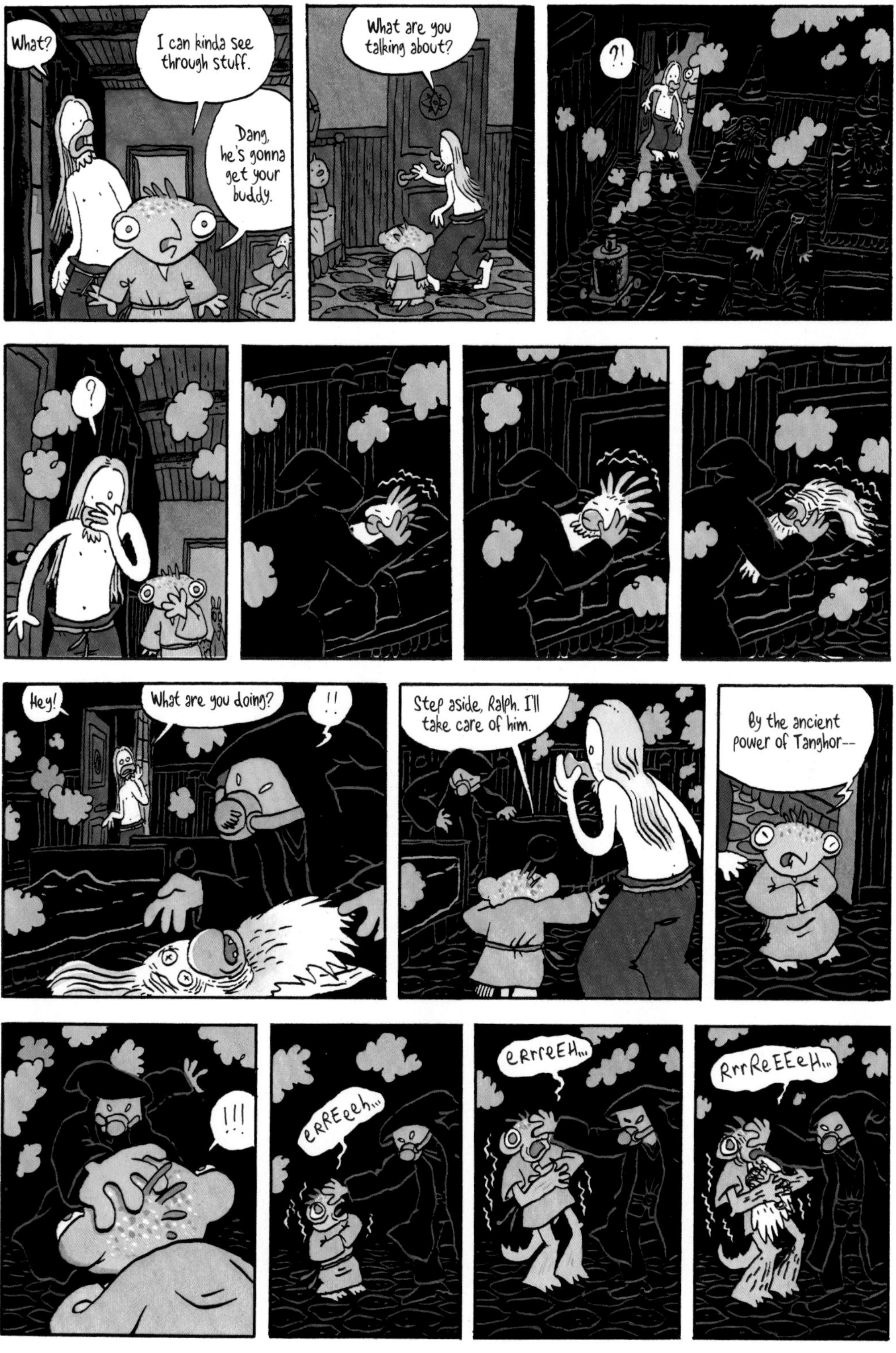
What?
I can kinda see through stuff.
Dang, he's gonna get your buddy.
What are you talking about?
?!
?
Hey!
What are you doing?
!!
Step aside, Ralph. I'll take care of him.
By the ancient power of Tanghor--
!!!
eRREeeh...
eRrreEH...
RrrReEEeH...

57

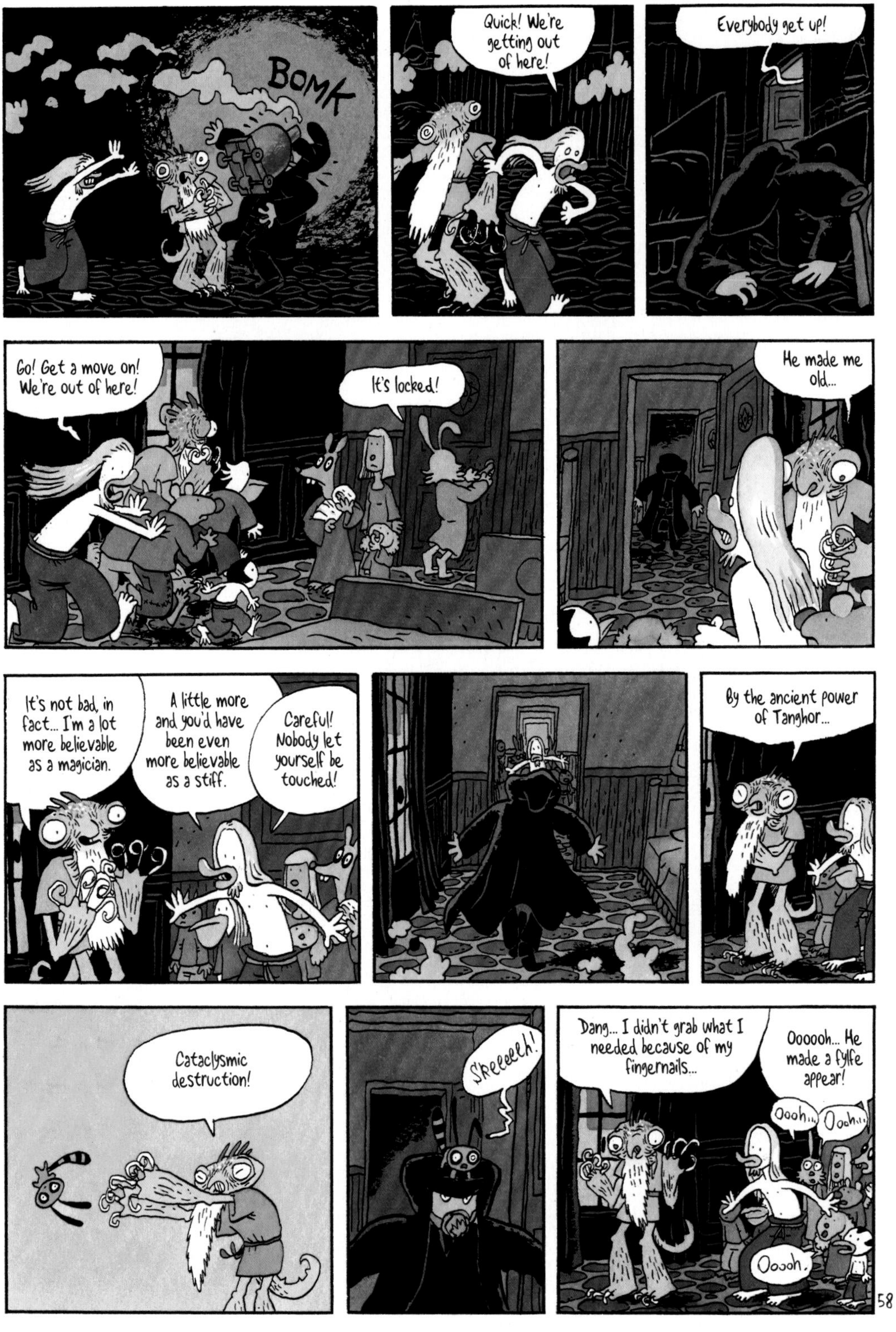

BOMK
Quick! We're getting out of here!
Everybody get up!
Go! Get a move on! We're out of here!
It's locked!
He made me old...
It's not bad, in fact... I'm a lot more believable as a magician.
A little more and you'd have been even more believable as a stiff.
Careful! Nobody let yourself be touched!
By the ancient power of Tanghor...
Cataclysmic destruction!
Skreeeeh!
Dang... I didn't grab what I needed because of my fingernails...
Oooooh... He made a fylfe appear!
Oooh...
Oooh...
Ooooh.
58

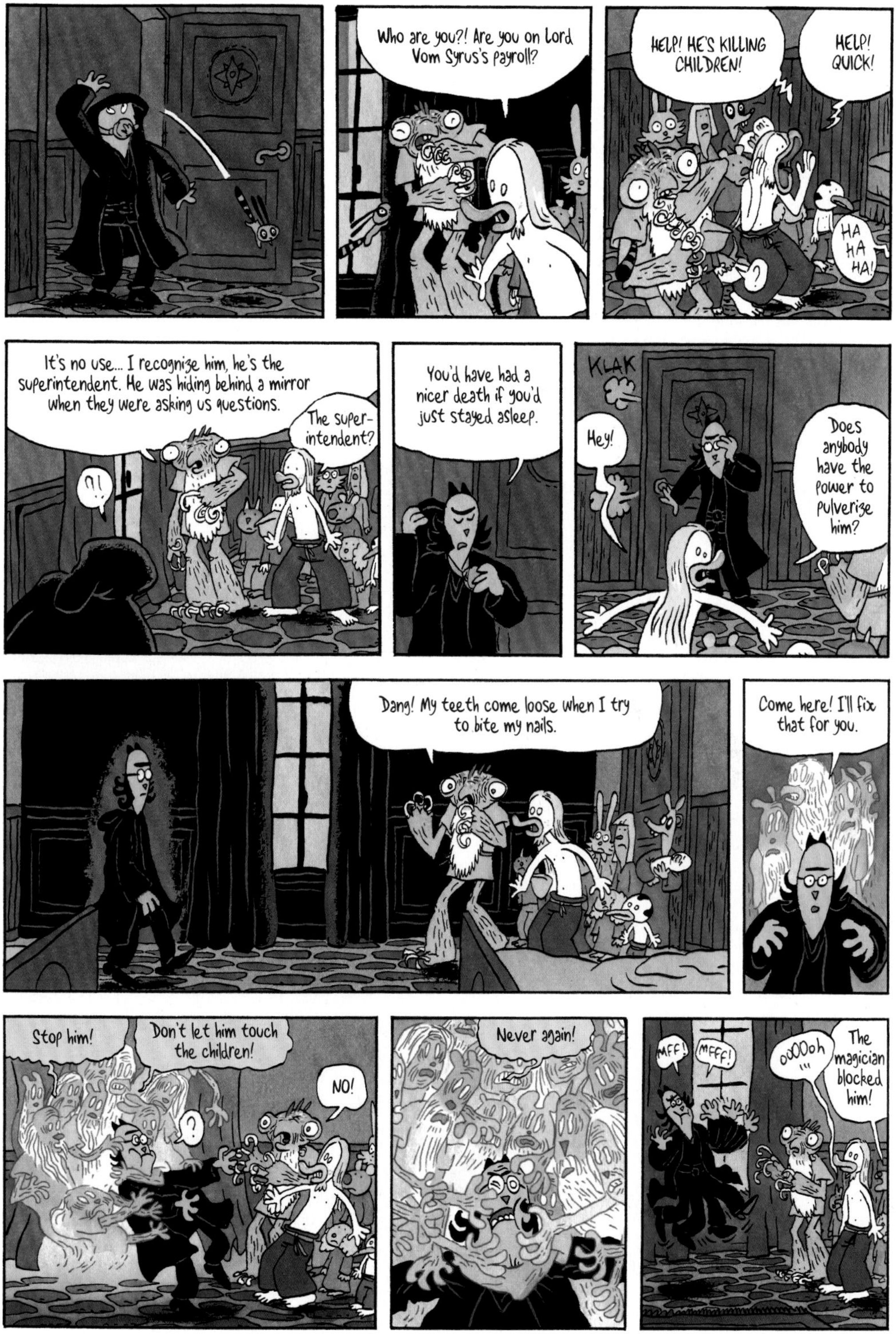
Who are you?! Are you on Lord Vom Syrus's payroll?
HELP! HE'S KILLING CHILDREN!
HELP! QUICK!
HA HA HA!
It's no use... I recognize him, he's the superintendent. He was hiding behind a mirror when they were asking us questions.
?!
The super-intendent?
You'd have had a nicer death if you'd just stayed asleep.
KLAK
Hey!
Does anybody have the power to pulverize him?
Dang! My teeth come loose when I try to bite my nails.
Come here! I'll fix that for you.
Stop him!
Don't let him touch the children!
?
NO!
Never again!
MFF!
MFFF!
oOOOh
The magician blocked him!
59

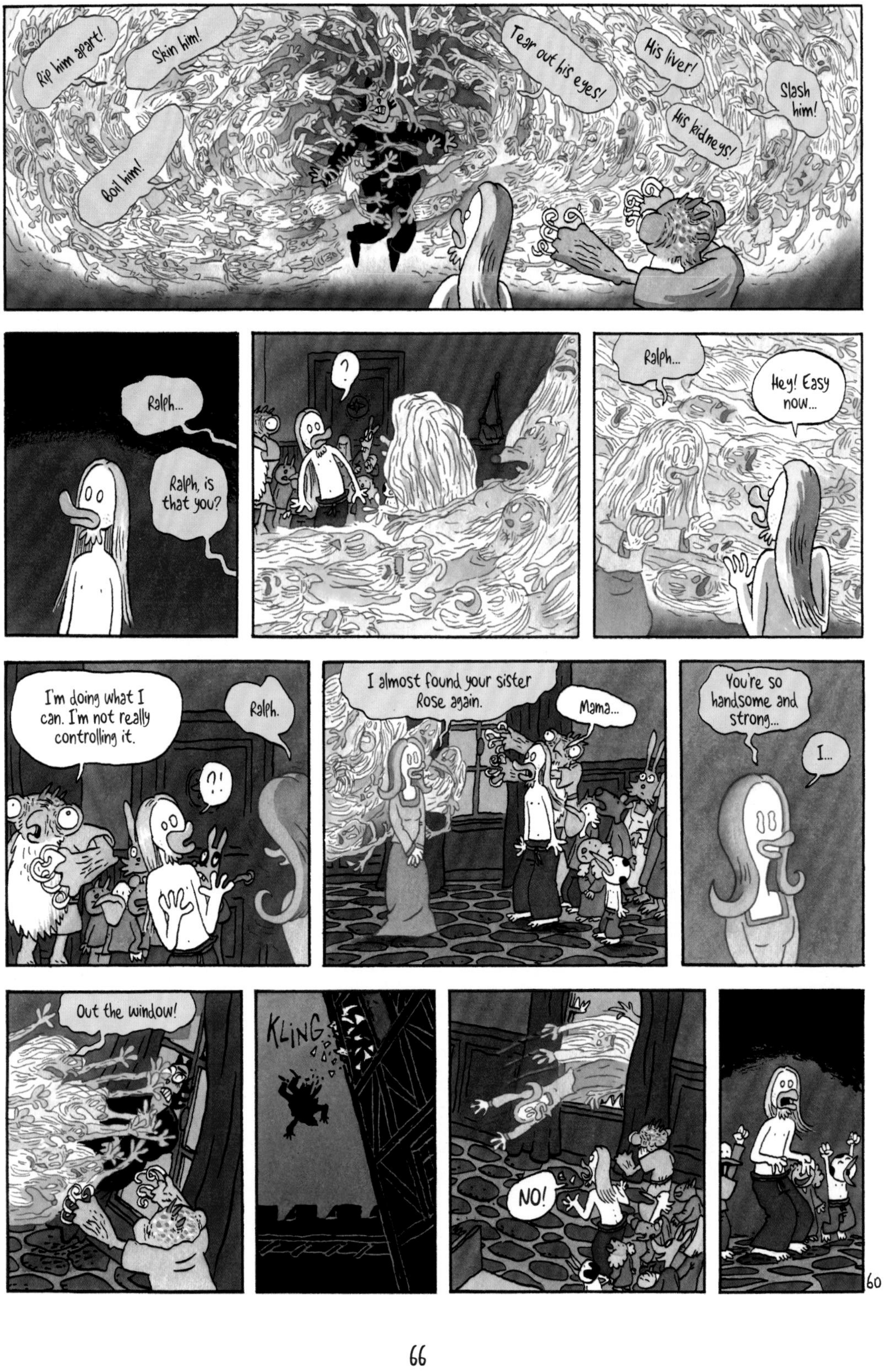
Rip him apart!
Skin him!
Boil him!
Tear out his eyes!
His liver!
His kidneys!
Slash him!
Ralph...
Ralph, is that you?
?
Ralph...
Hey! Easy now...
I'm doing what I can. I'm not really controlling it.
Ralph.
?!
I almost found your sister Rose again.
Mama...
You're so handsome and strong...
I...
Out the window!
KLING
NO!

60

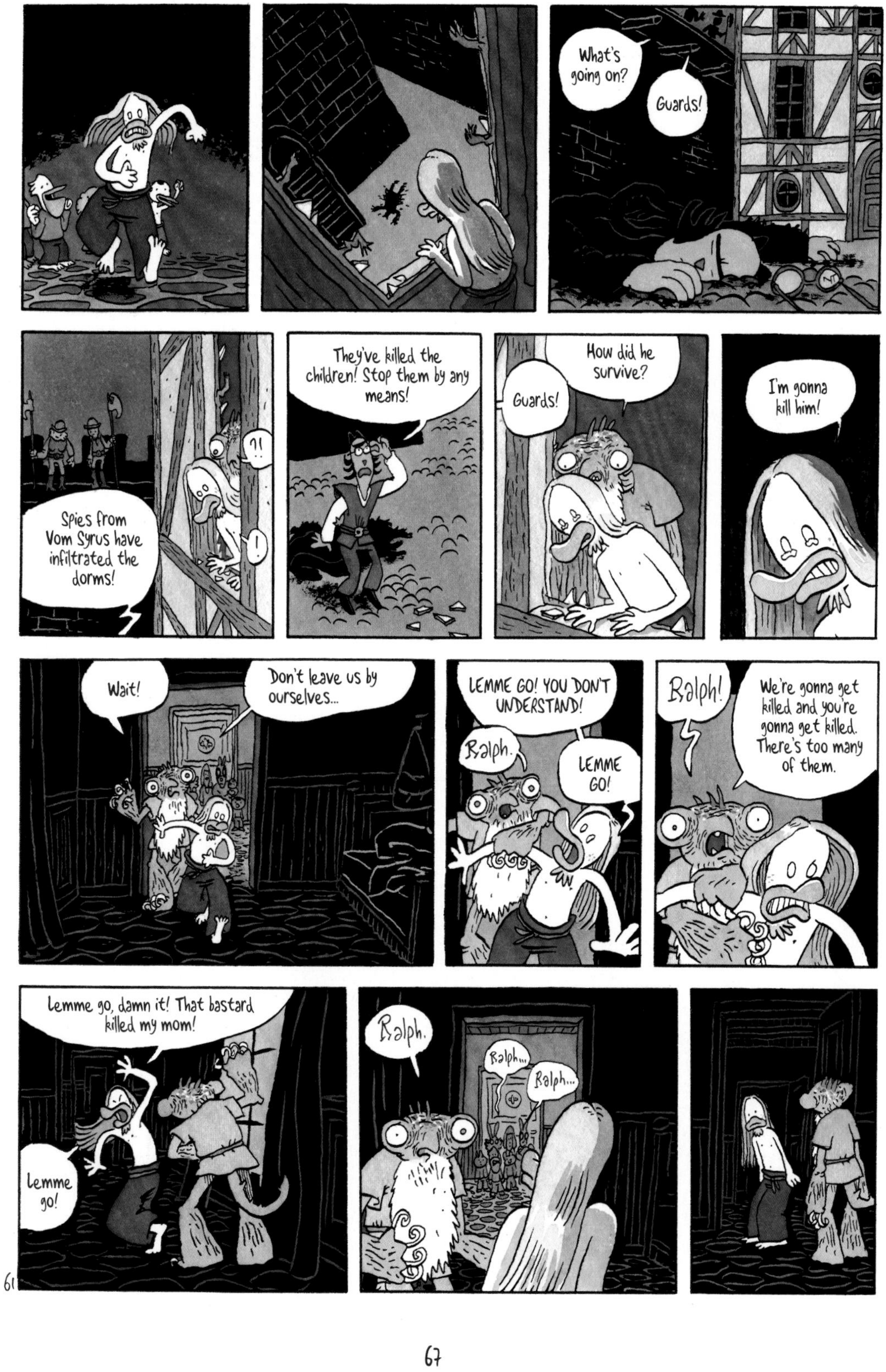
What's going on?
Guards!
Spies from Vom Syrus have infiltrated the dorms!
?!
!
They've killed the children! Stop them by any means!
How did he survive?
Guards!
I'm gonna kill him!
Wait!
Don't leave us by ourselves...
LEMME GO! YOU DON'T UNDERSTAND!
Ralph.
LEMME GO!
Ralph!
We're gonna get killed and you're gonna get killed. There's too many of them.
Lemme go, damn it! That bastard killed my mom!
Lemme go!
Ralph.
Ralph...
Ralph...

61

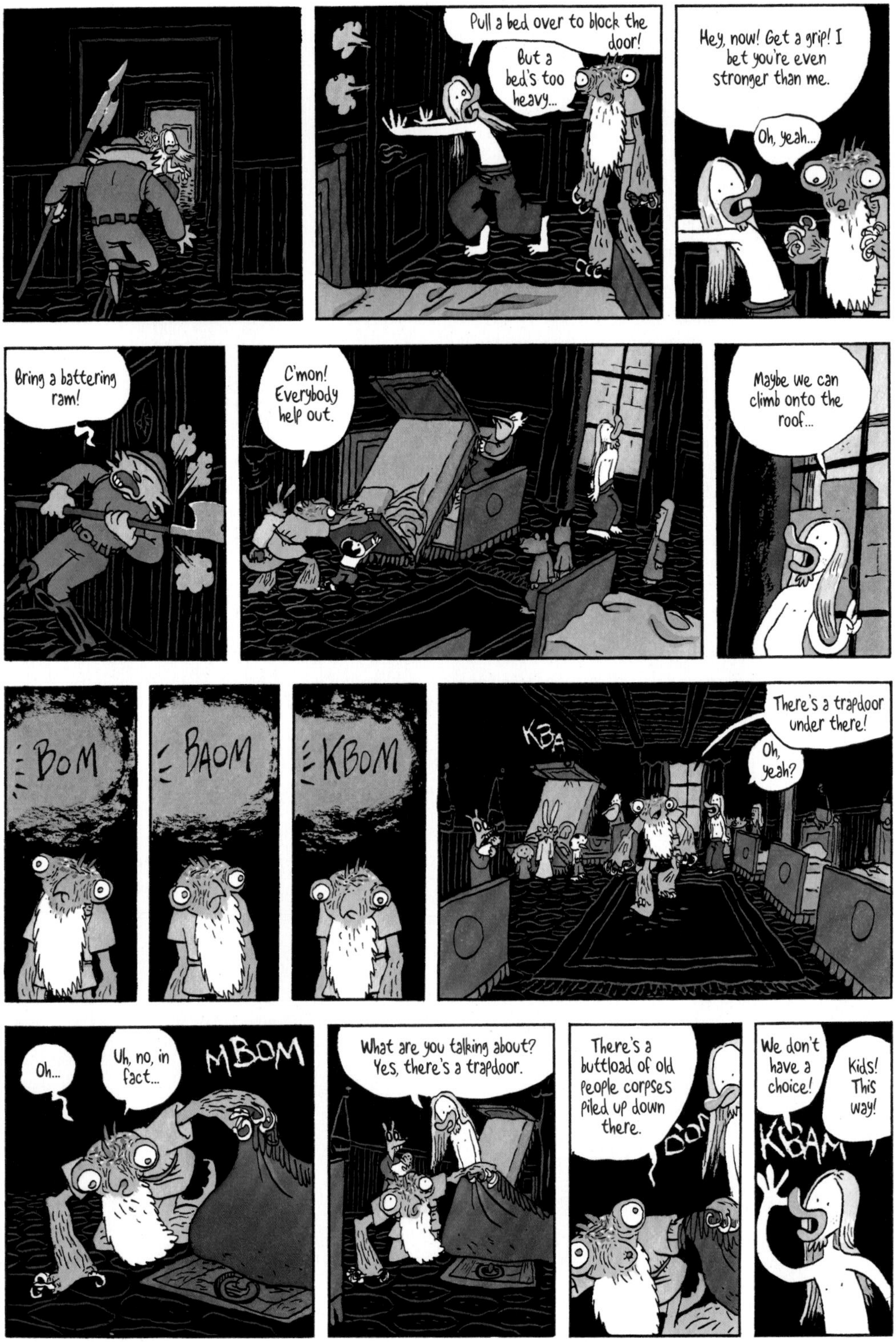
Pull a bed over to block the door!
But a bed's too heavy...
Hey, now! Get a grip! I bet you're even stronger than me.
Oh, yeah...
Bring a battering ram!
C'mon! Everybody help out.
Maybe we can climb onto the roof...
BOM
BAOM
KBOM
KBA
There's a trapdoor under there!
Oh, yeah?
Oh...
Uh, no, in fact...
MBOM
What are you talking about? Yes, there's a trapdoor.
There's a buttload of old people corpses piled up down there.
DOM
We don't have a choice!
Kids! This way!
KBAM

62

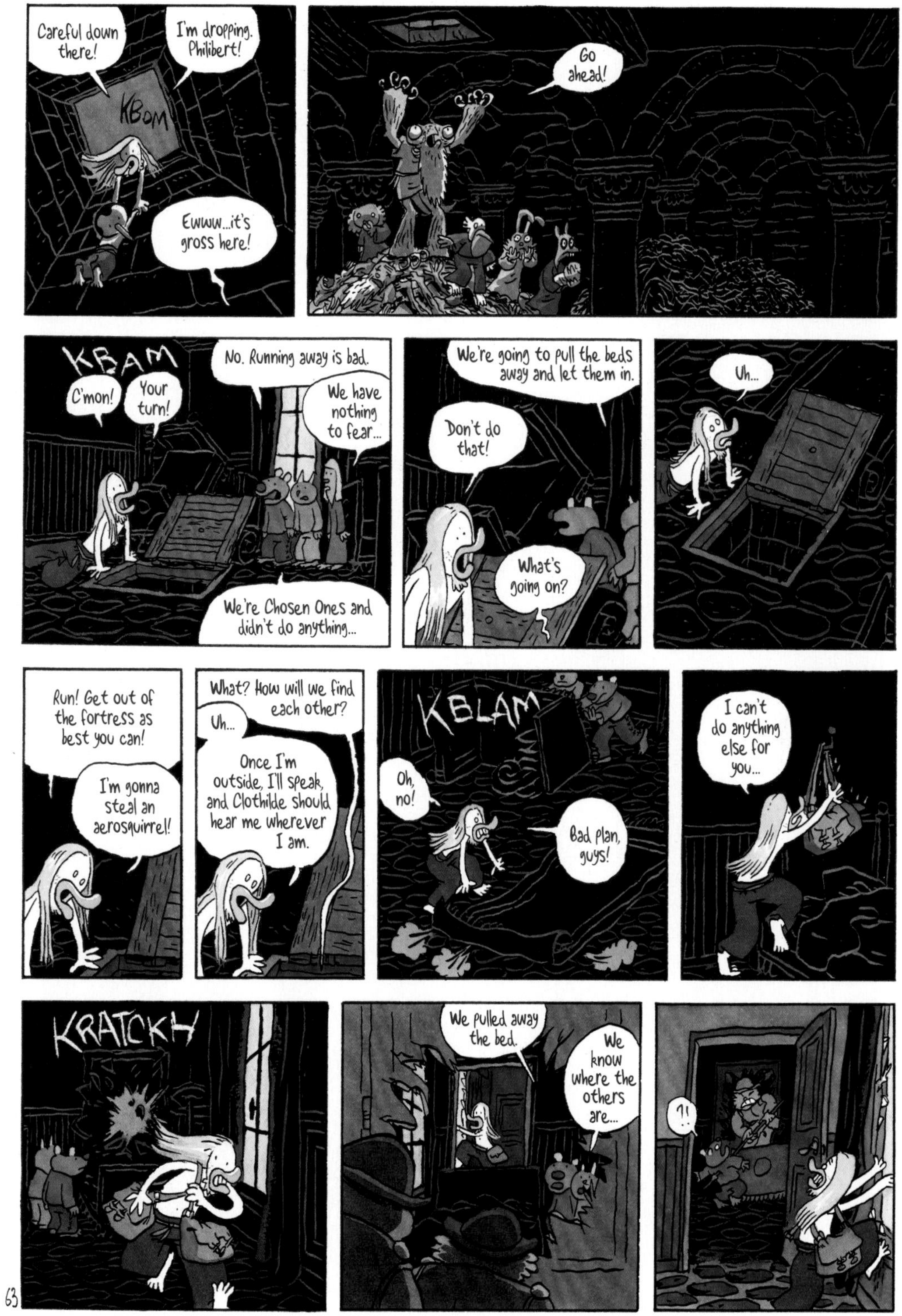
Careful down there!
I'm dropping. Philibert!
KBOM
Ewww...it's gross here!
Go ahead!
KBAM
C'mon!
Your turn!
No. Running away is bad.
We have nothing to fear...
We're Chosen Ones and didn't do anything...
We're going to pull the beds away and let them in.
Don't do that!
What's going on?
Uh...
Run! Get out of the fortress as best you can!
I'm gonna steal an aerosquirrel!
What? How will we find each other?
Uh...
Once I'm outside, I'll speak, and Clothilde should hear me wherever I am.
KBLAM
Oh, no!
Bad plan, guys!
I can't do anything else for you...
KRATCKH
63
We pulled away the bed.
We know where the others are...
?!

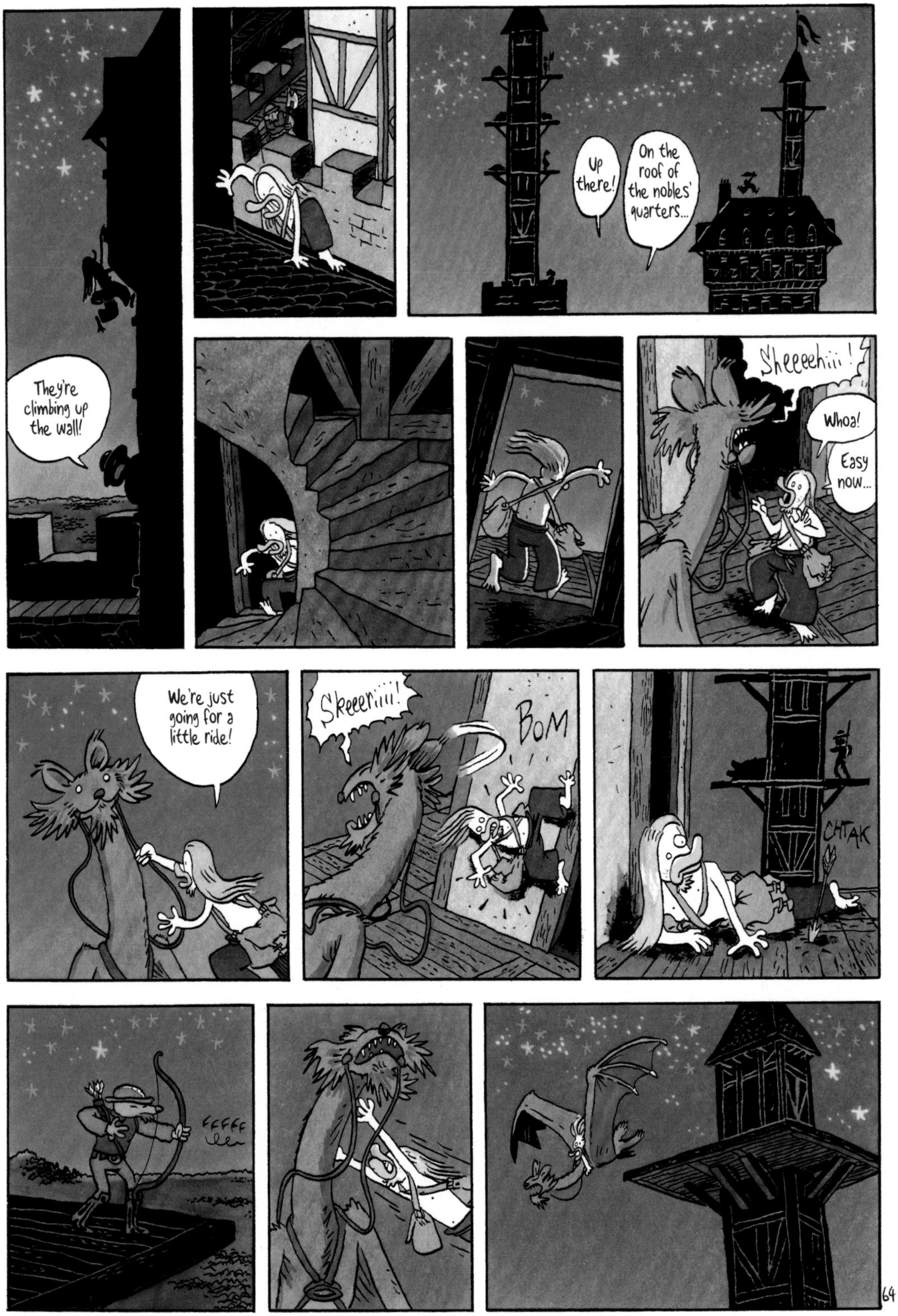
They're climbing up the wall!
Up there!
On the roof of the nobles' quarters...
Sheeeehiiii!
Whoa!
Easy now...
We're just going for a little ride!
Skeeeriiii!
BOM
CHTAK
FFFFF
64

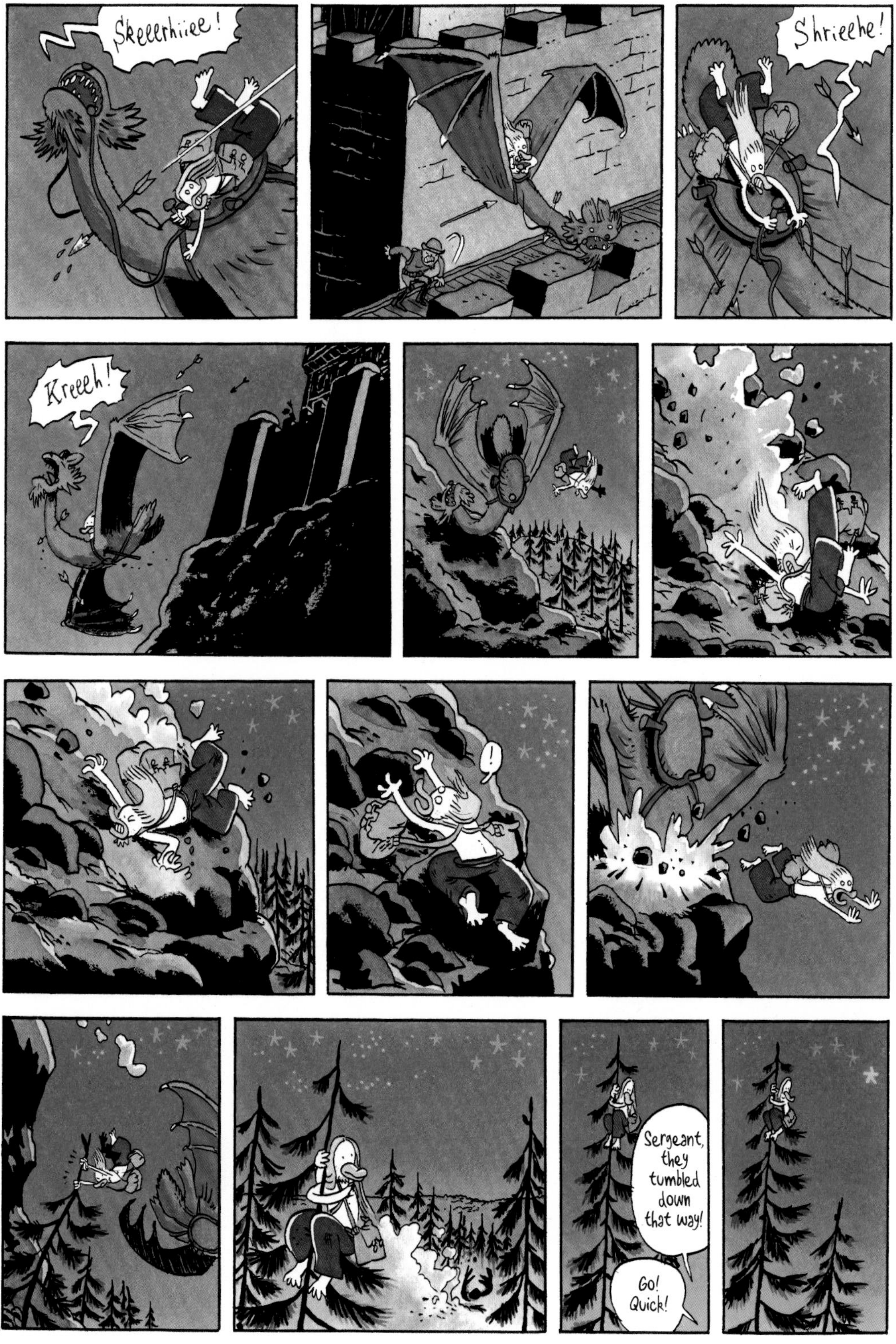
Skeeerhiiee!
Shrieehe!
Kreeeh!
!
Sergeant, they tumbled down that way!
Go! Quick!

65

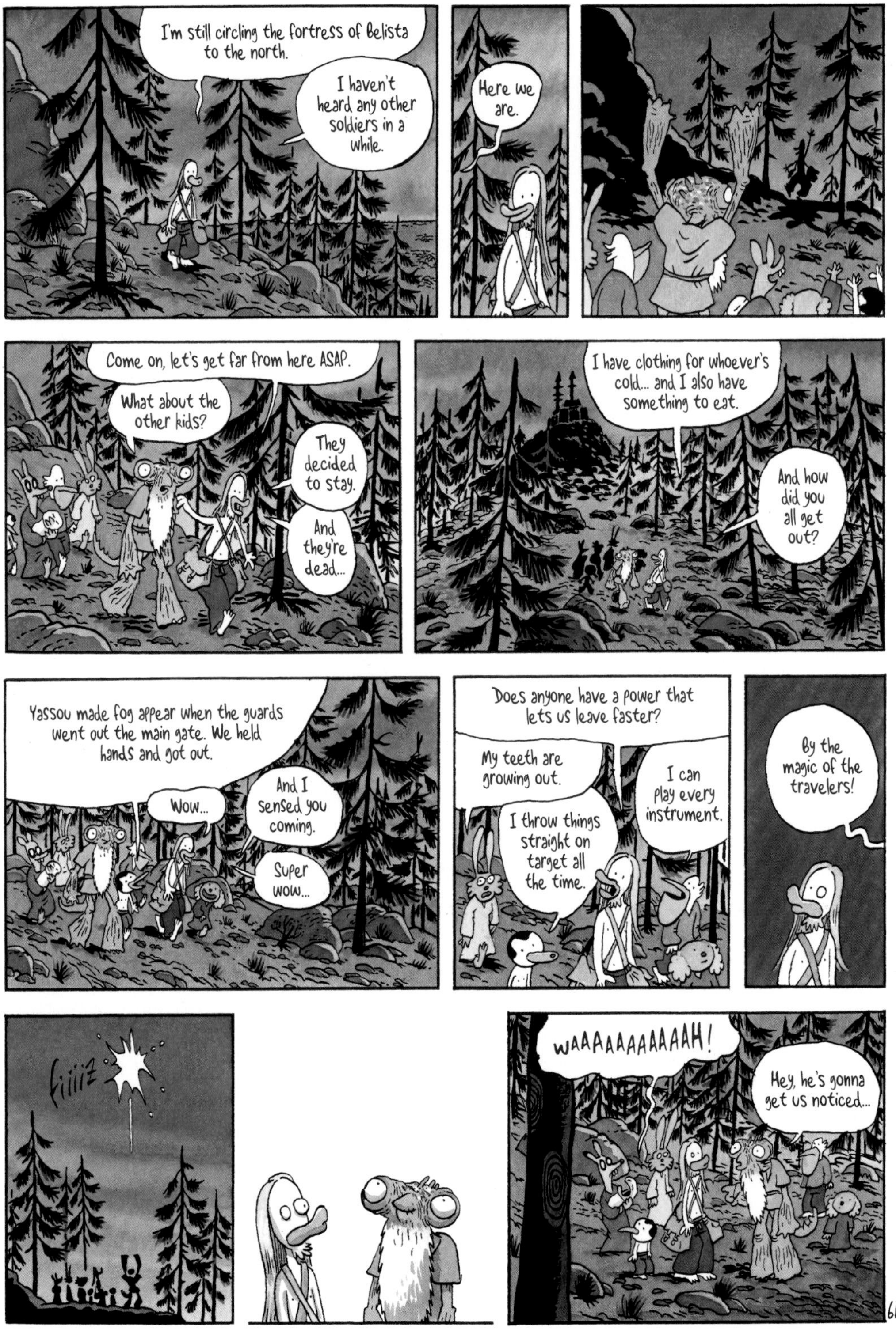
I'm still circling the fortress of Belista to the north.
I haven't heard any other soldiers in a while.
Here we are.
Come on, let's get far from here ASAP.
What about the other kids?
They decided to stay.
And they're dead...
I have clothing for whoever's cold... and I also have something to eat.
And how did you all get out?
Yassou made fog appear when the guards went out the main gate. We held hands and got out.
Wow...
And I sensed you coming.
Super wow...
Does anyone have a power that lets us leave faster?
My teeth are growing out.
I throw things straight on target all the time.
I can play every instrument.
By the magic of the travelers!
fiiiiz
WAAAAAAAAAAH!
Hey, he's gonna get us noticed...
66

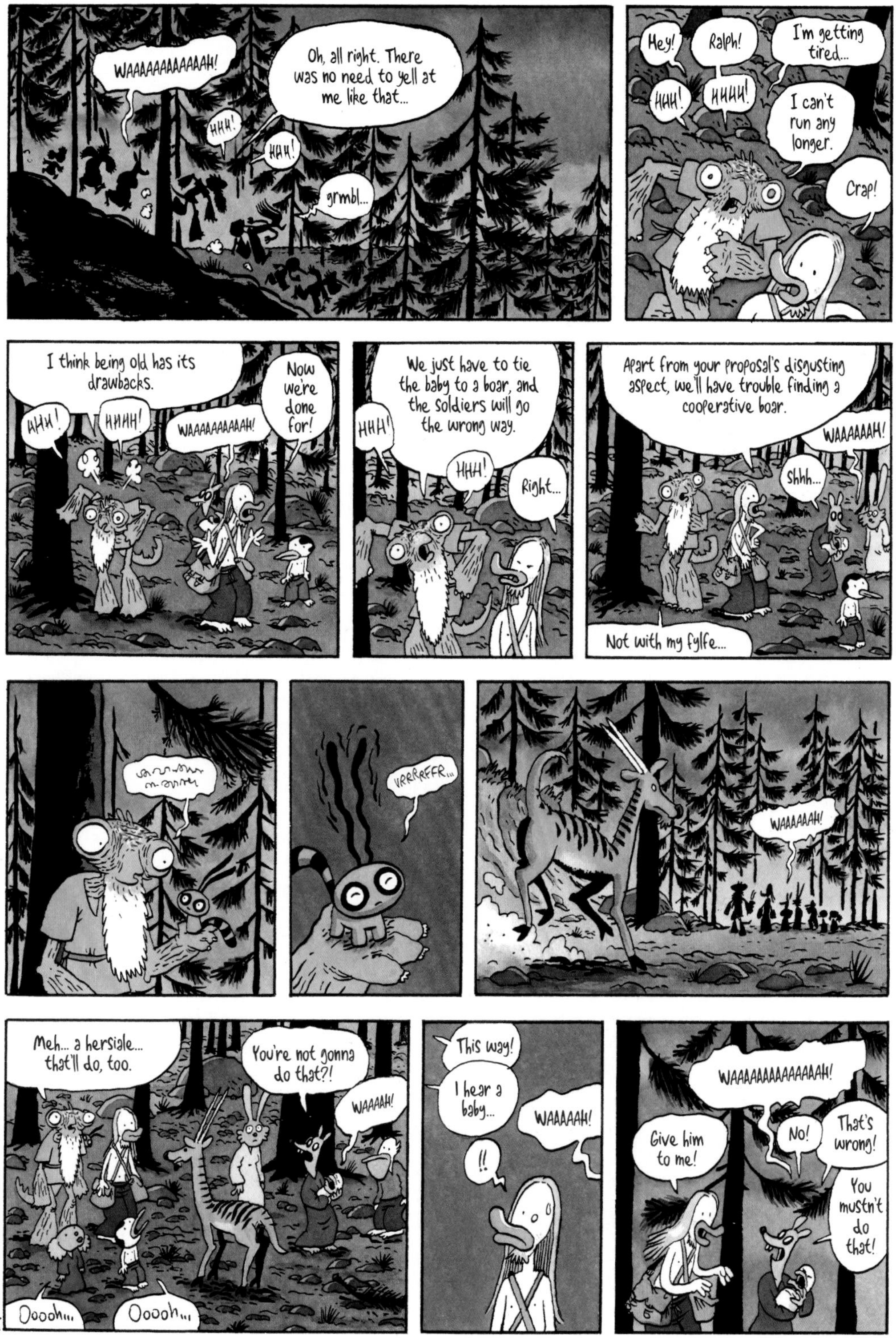
WAAAAAAAAAAAAH!
Oh, all right. There was no need to yell at me like that...
HHH!
HHH!
grmbl...
Hey!
Ralph!
I'm getting tired...
HHH!
HHHH!
I can't run any longer.
Crap!
I think being old has its drawbacks.
AHH!
HHHH!
WAAAAAAAAAAH!
Now we're done for!
We just have to tie the baby to a boar, and the soldiers will go the wrong way.
HHH!
HHH!
Right...
Apart from your proposal's disgusting aspect, we'll have trouble finding a cooperative boar.
WAAAAAAH!
Shhh...
Not with my fylfe...
VRRRAFFR...
WAAAAAAH!
Meh... a hersiale... that'll do, too.
You're not gonna do that?!
WAAAAH!
Ooooh...
Ooooh...
This way!
I hear a baby...
WAAAAAH!
!!
WAAAAAAAAAAAAAAH!
Give him to me!
No!
That's wrong!
You mustn't do that!

67

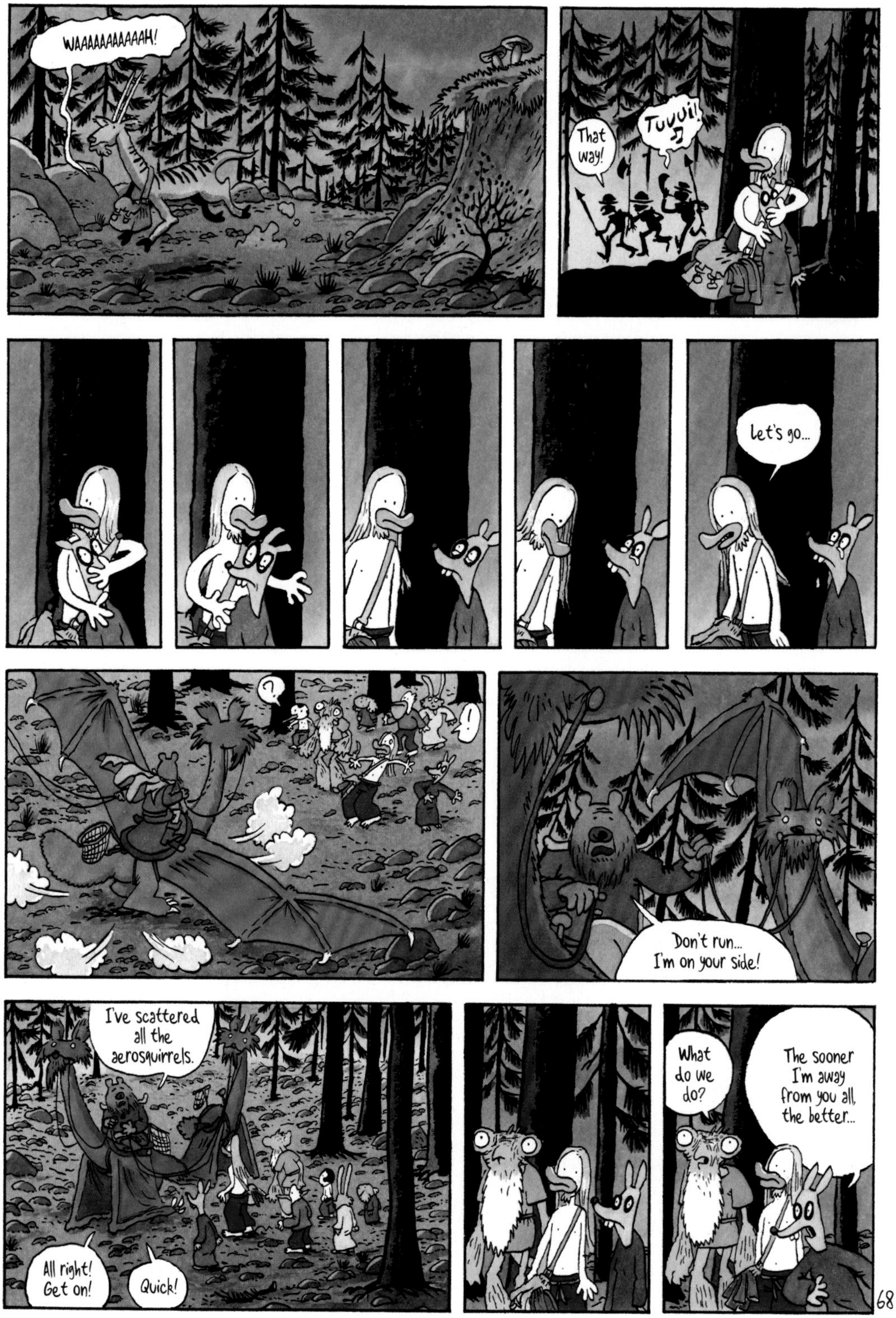
WAAAAAAAAAAAH!
That way!
Tuuui!
Let's go...
Don't run... I'm on your side!
I've scattered all the aerosquirrels.
All right! Get on!
Quick!
What do we do?
The sooner I'm away from you all, the better...
68

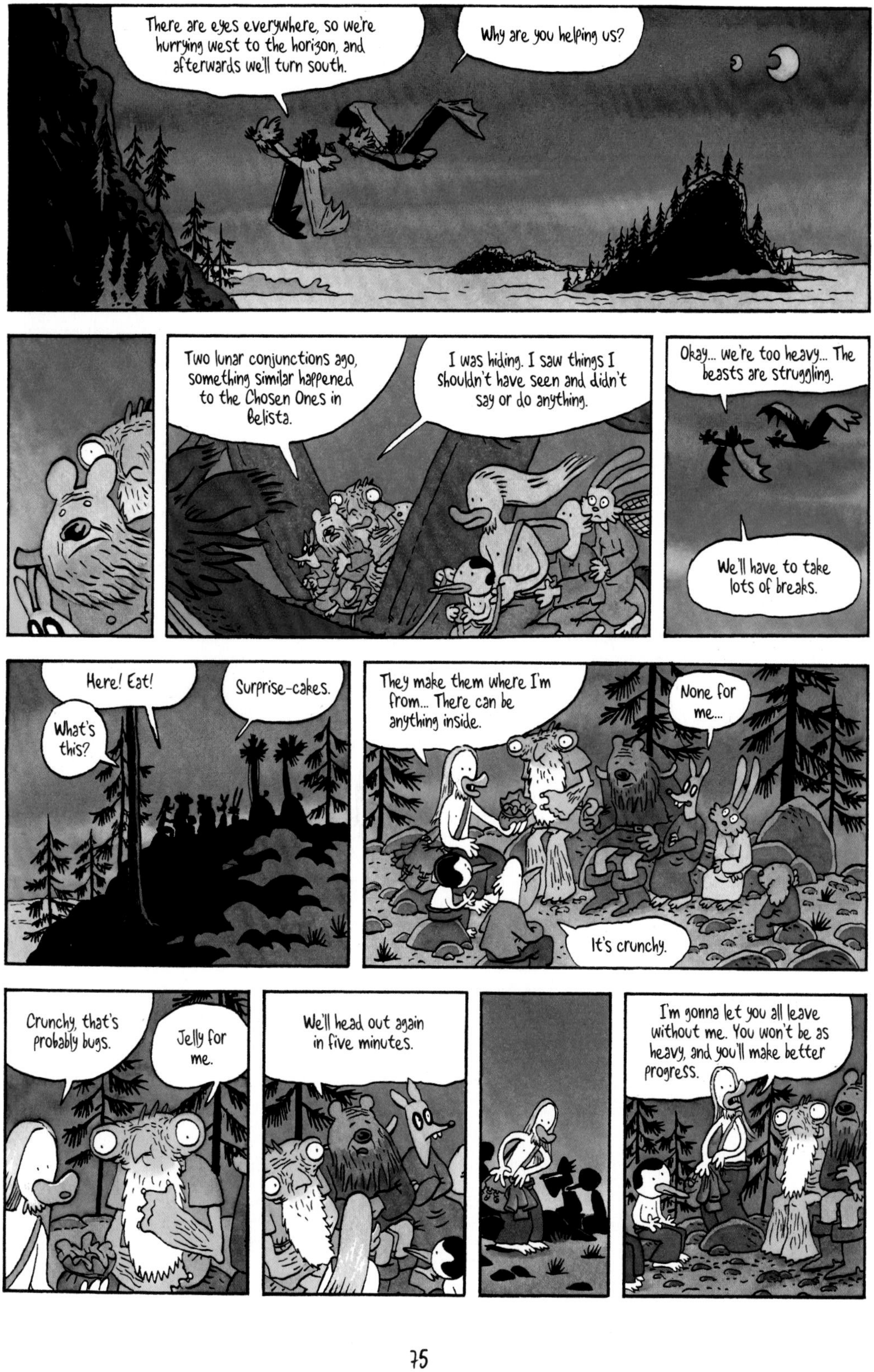
There are eyes everywhere, so we're hurrying west to the horizon, and afterwards we'll turn south.
Why are you helping us?
Two lunar conjunctions ago, something similar happened to the Chosen Ones in Belista.
I was hiding. I saw things I shouldn't have seen and didn't say or do anything.
Okay... we're too heavy... The beasts are struggling.
We'll have to take lots of breaks.
Here! Eat!
What's this?
Surprise-cakes.
They make them where I'm from... There can be anything inside.
None for me...
It's crunchy.
Crunchy, that's probably bugs.
Jelly for me.
We'll head out again in five minutes.
I'm gonna let you all leave without me. You won't be as heavy, and you'll make better progress.
69

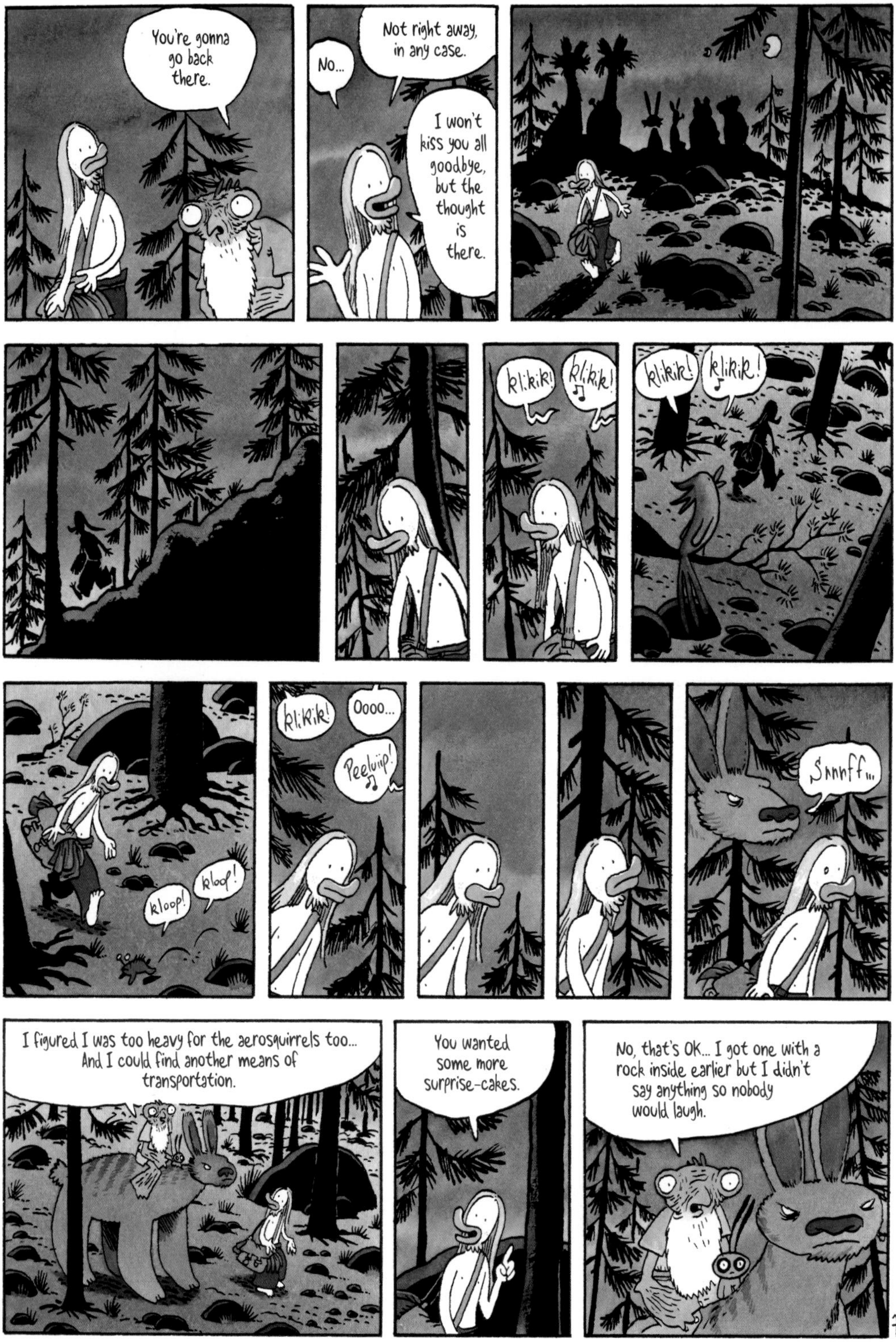
You're gonna go back there.
No...
Not right away, in any case.
I won't kiss you all goodbye, but the thought is there.
klikik!
klikik!
klikik!
klikik!
kloop!
kloop!
klikik!
Oooo...
Peeluiip!
Snnnff...
I figured I was too heavy for the aerosquirrels too... And I could find another means of transportation.
You wanted some more surprise-cakes.
No, that's OK... I got one with a rock inside earlier but I didn't say anything so nobody would laugh.
70

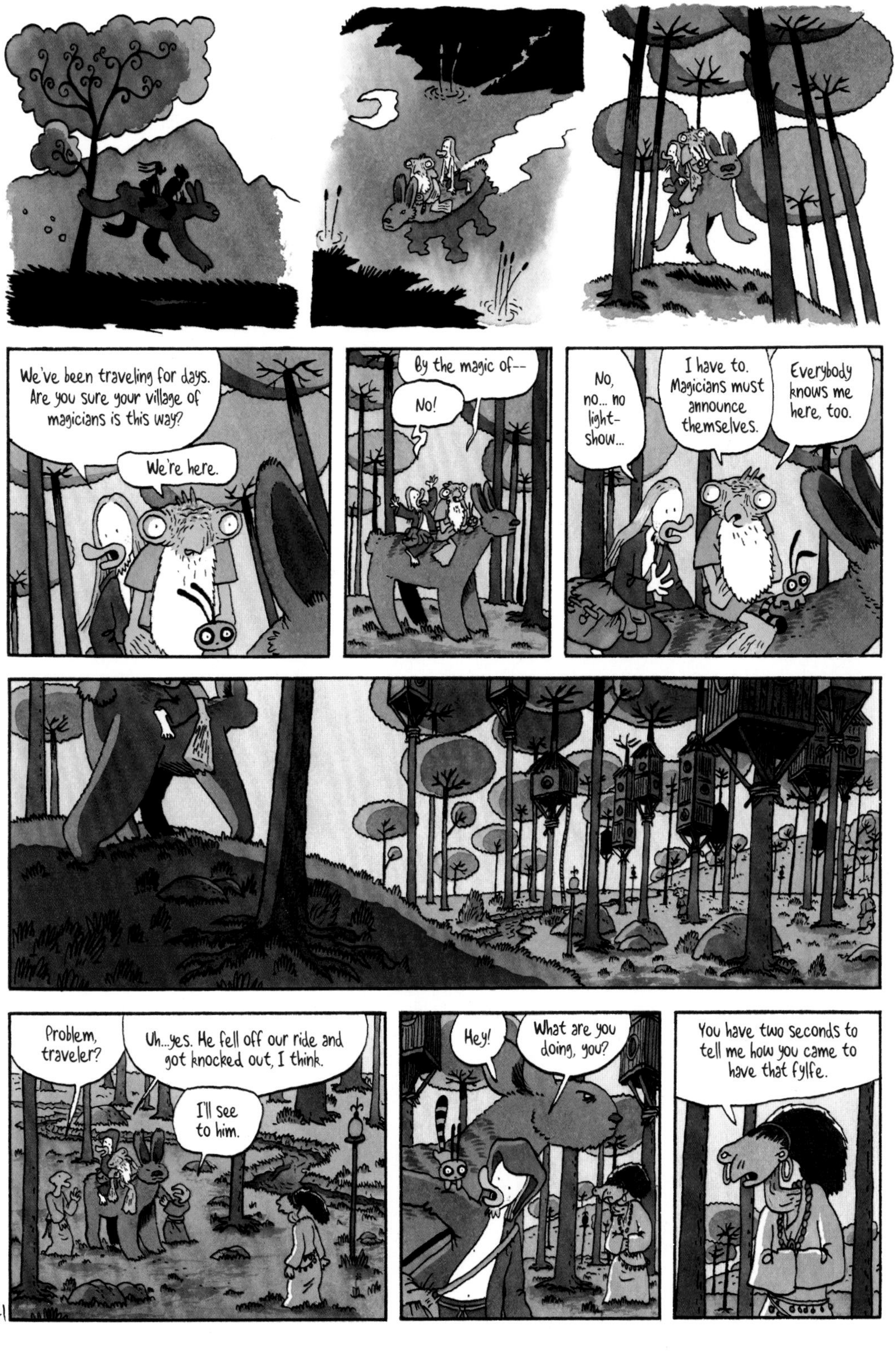

We've been traveling for days. Are you sure your village of magicians is this way?
We're here.
By the magic of--
No!
No, no... no light-show...
I have to. Magicians must announce themselves.
Everybody knows me here, too.
Problem, traveler?
Uh...yes. He fell off our ride and got knocked out, I think.
I'll see to him.
71
Hey!
What are you doing, you?
You have two seconds to tell me how you came to have that fylfe.

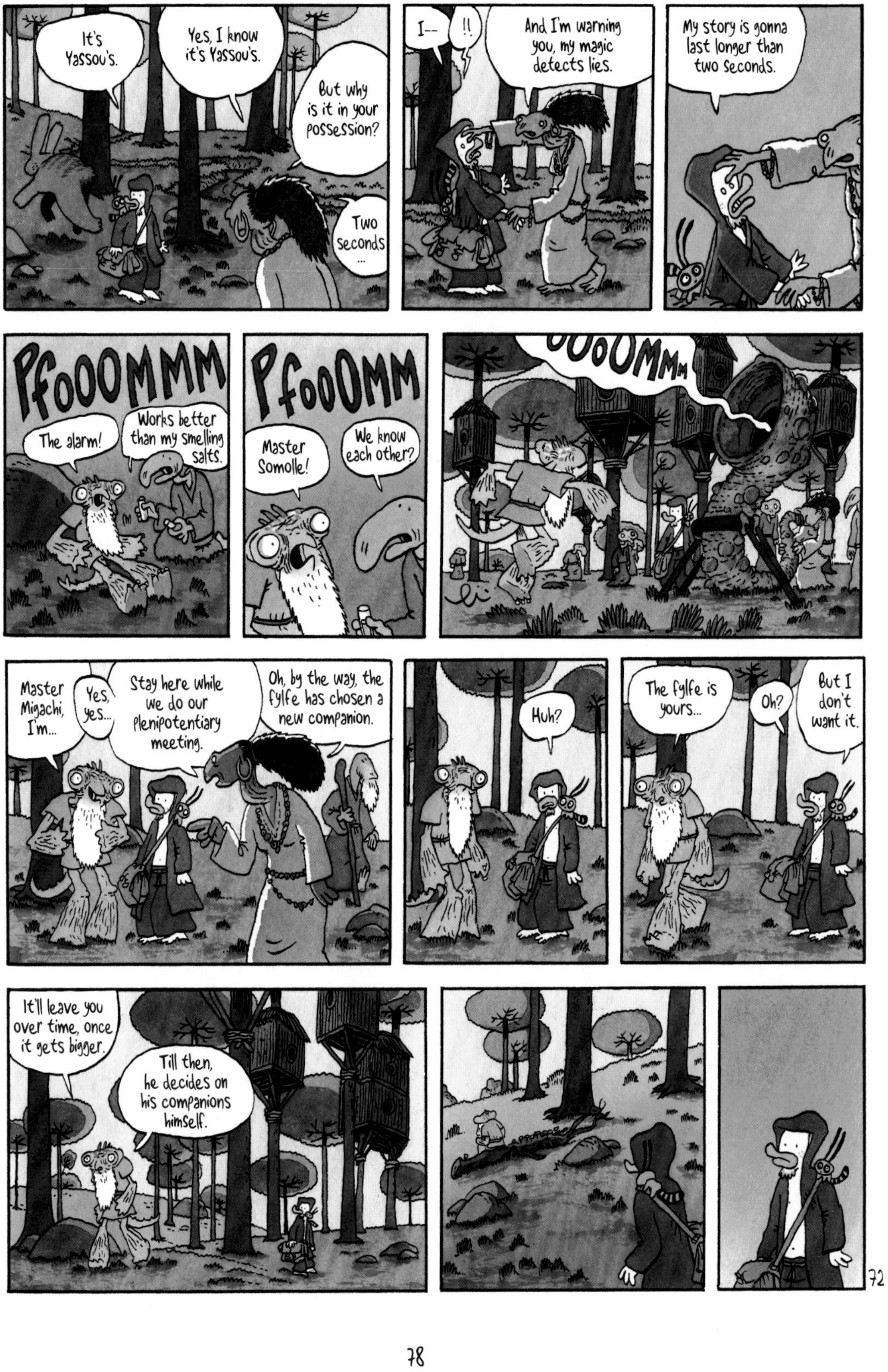
It's Yassou's.
Yes, I know it's Yassou's.
But why is it in your possession?
Two seconds ...
I--
!!
And I'm warning you, my magic detects lies.
My story is gonna last longer than two seconds.
PfOOOMMM
The alarm!
Works better than my smelling salts.
PfooOMM
Master Somolle!
We know each other?
OOOOOMMM
Master Migachi, I'm...
Yes, yes...
Stay here while we do our Plenipotentiary meeting.
Oh, by the way, the fylfe has chosen a new companion.
Huh?
The fylfe is yours...
Oh?
But I don't want it.
It'll leave you over time, once it gets bigger.
Till then, he decides on his companions himself.
72

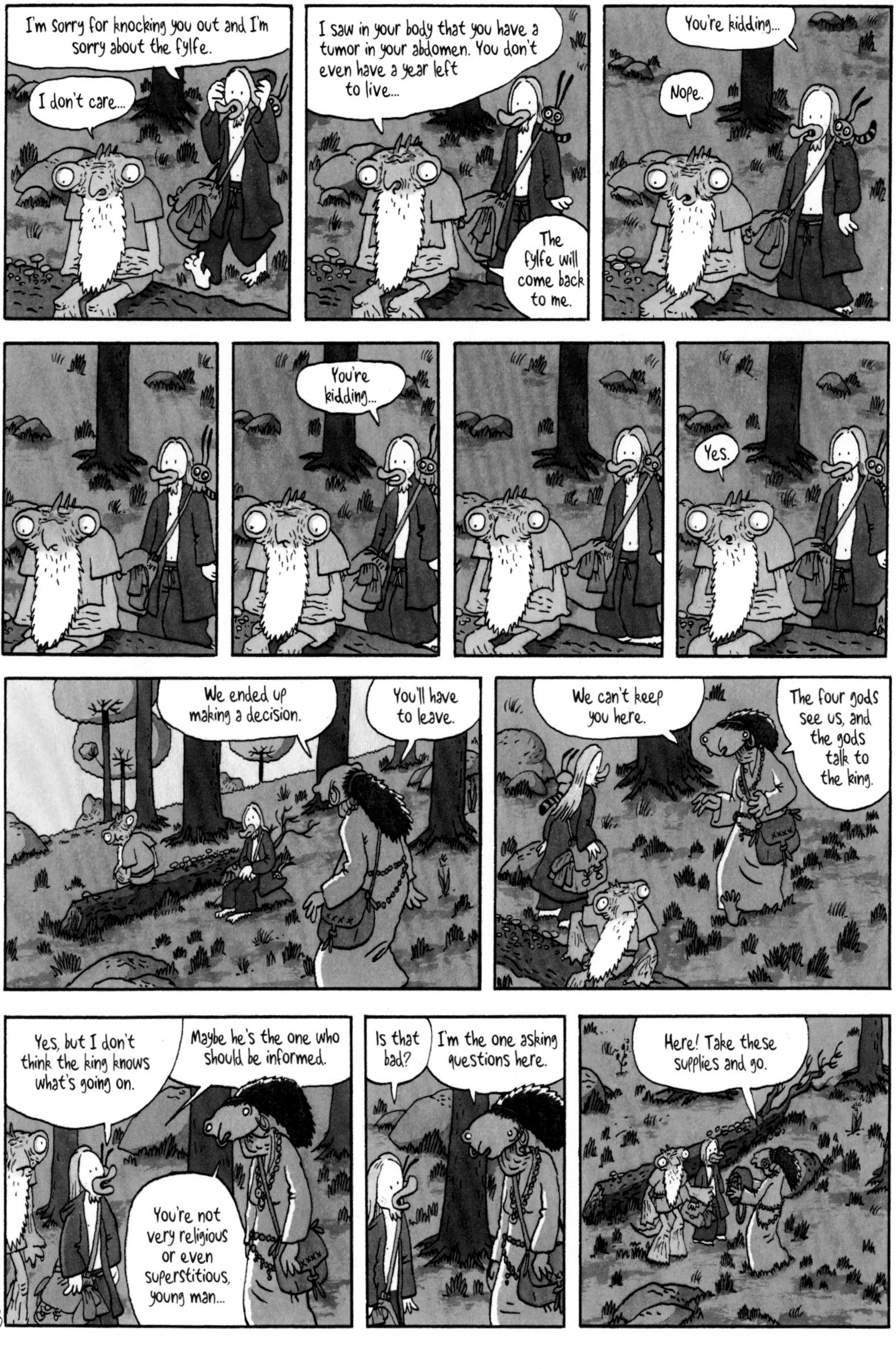
I'm sorry for knocking you out and I'm sorry about the fylfe.
I don't care...
I saw in your body that you have a tumor in your abdomen. You don't even have a year left to live...
The fylfe will come back to me.
You're kidding...
Nope.
You're kidding...
Yes.
We ended up making a decision.
You'll have to leave.
We can't keep you here.
The four gods see us, and the gods talk to the king.
Yes, but I don't think the king knows what's going on.
Maybe he's the one who should be informed.
You're not very religious or even superstitious, young man...
Is that bad?
I'm the one asking questions here.
Here! Take these supplies and go.

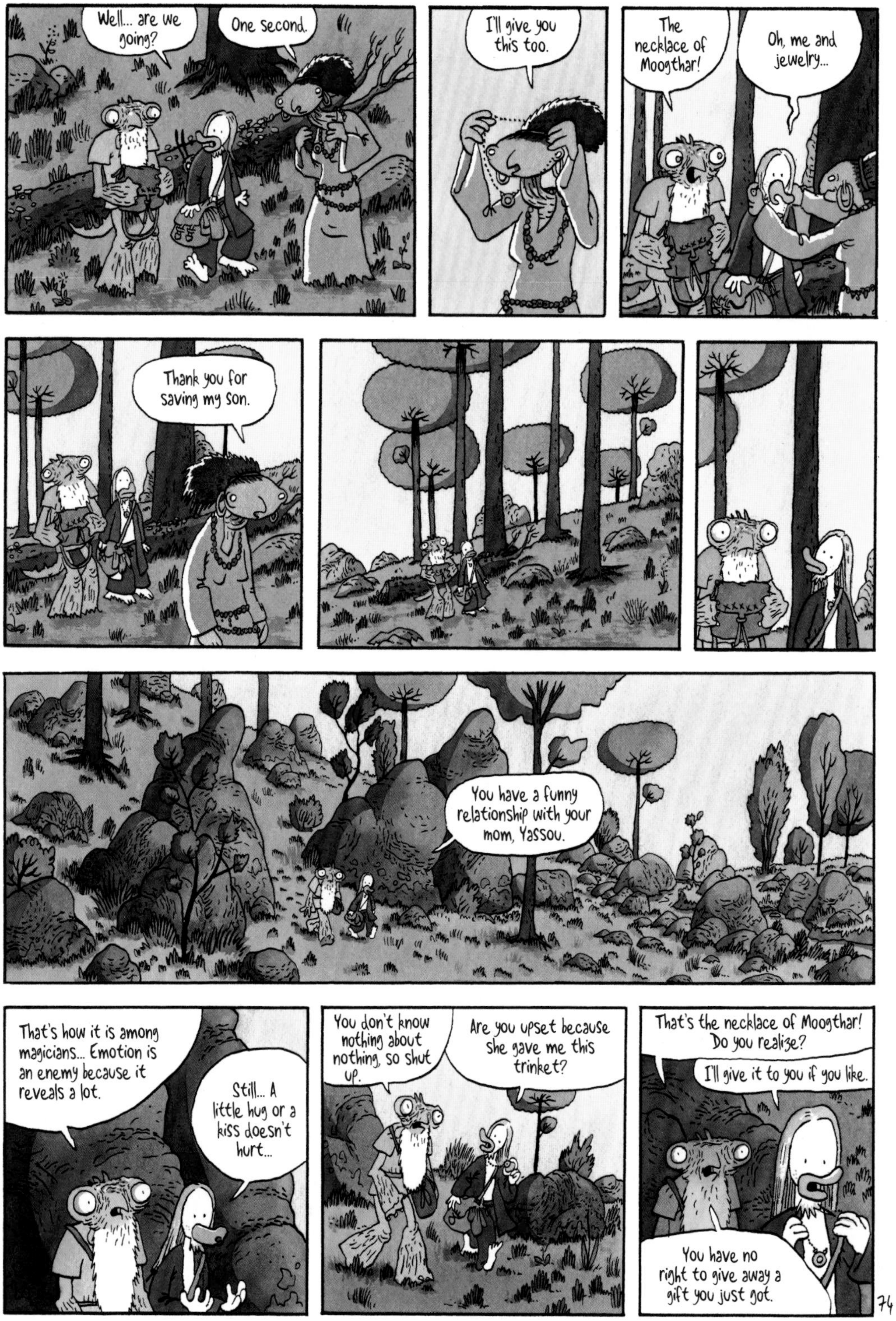
Well... are we going?
One second.
I'll give you this too.
The necklace of Moogthar!
Oh, me and jewelry...
Thank you for saving my son.
You have a funny relationship with your mom, Yassou.
That's how it is among magicians... Emotion is an enemy because it reveals a lot.
Still... A little hug or a kiss doesn't hurt...
You don't know nothing about nothing, so shut up.
Are you upset because she gave me this trinket?
That's the necklace of Moogthar! Do you realize?
I'll give it to you if you like.
You have no right to give away a gift you just got.
74

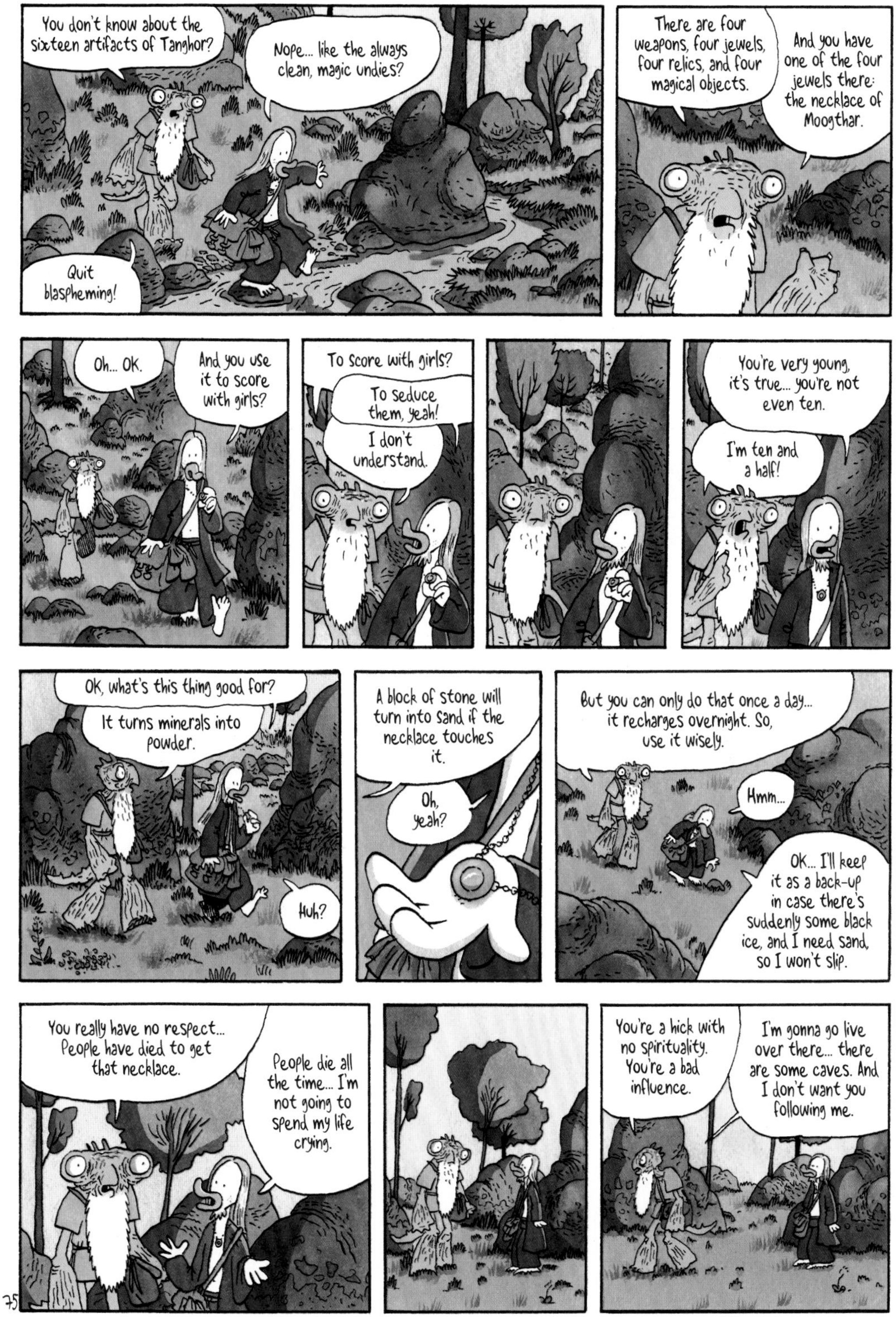
You don't know about the sixteen artifacts of Tanghor?
Nope... like the always clean, magic undies?
Quit blaspheming!
There are four weapons, four jewels, four relics, and four magical objects.
And you have one of the four jewels there: the necklace of Moogthar.
Oh... OK.
And you use it to score with girls?
To score with girls?
To seduce them, yeah!
I don't understand.
You're very young, it's true... you're not even ten.
I'm ten and a half!
OK, what's this thing good for?
It turns minerals into powder.
Huh?
A block of stone will turn into sand if the necklace touches it.
Oh, yeah?
But you can only do that once a day... it recharges overnight. So, use it wisely.
Hmm...
OK... I'll keep it as a back-up in case there's suddenly some black ice, and I need sand, so I won't slip.
You really have no respect... People have died to get that necklace.
People die all the time... I'm not going to spend my life crying.
You're a hick with no spirituality. You're a bad influence.
I'm gonna go live over there... there are some caves. And I don't want you following me.

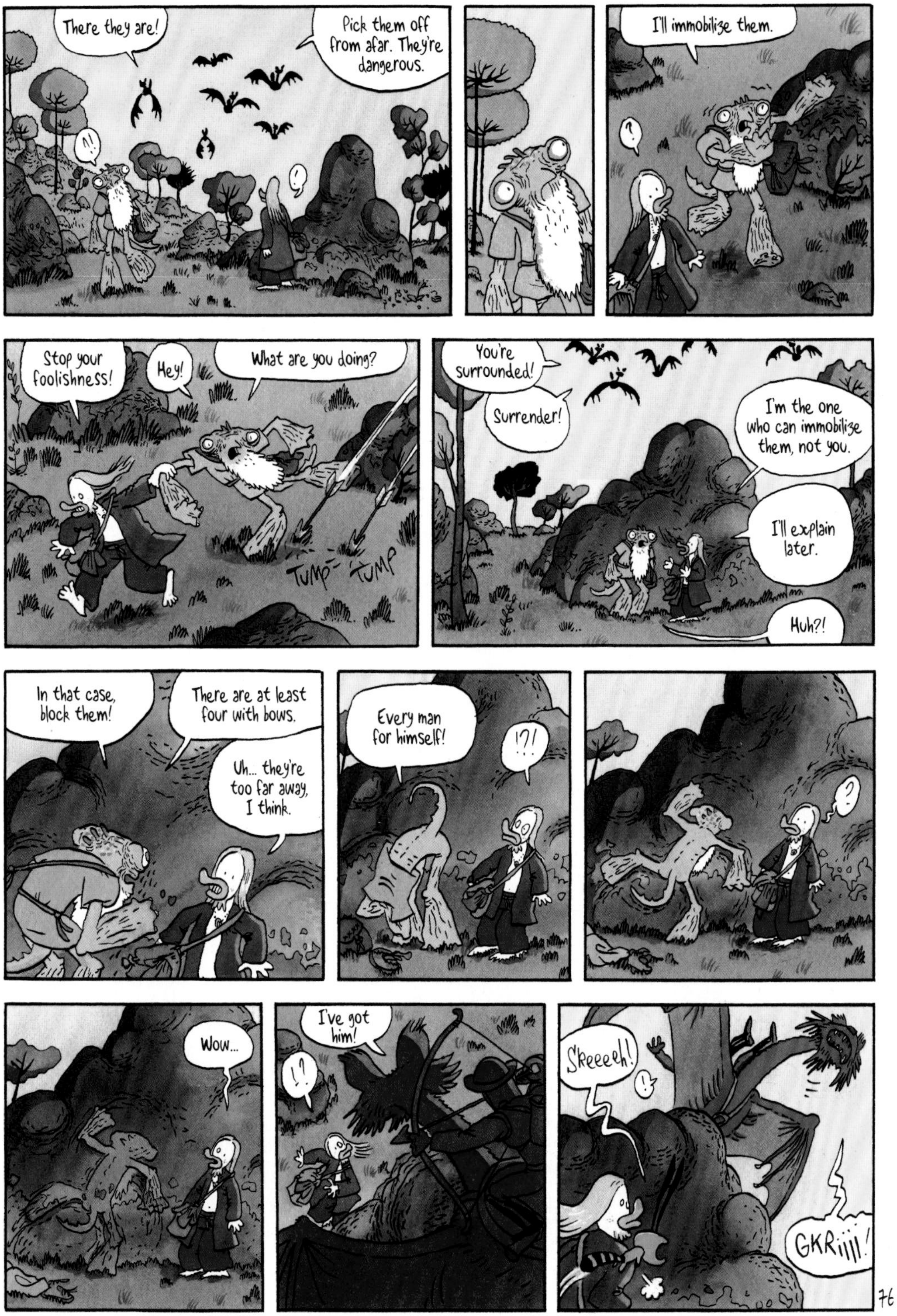
There they are!
Pick them off from afar. They're dangerous.
?!
!
I'll immobilize them.
?
Stop your foolishness!
Hey!
What are you doing?
TUMP TUMP
You're surrounded!
Surrender!
I'm the one who can immobilize them, not you.
I'll explain later.
Huh?!
In that case, block them!
There are at least four with bows.
Uh... they're too far away, I think.
Every man for himself!
!?!
?
Wow...
I've got him!
!?
Skeeeeh!
!
GKRiiiii!
76

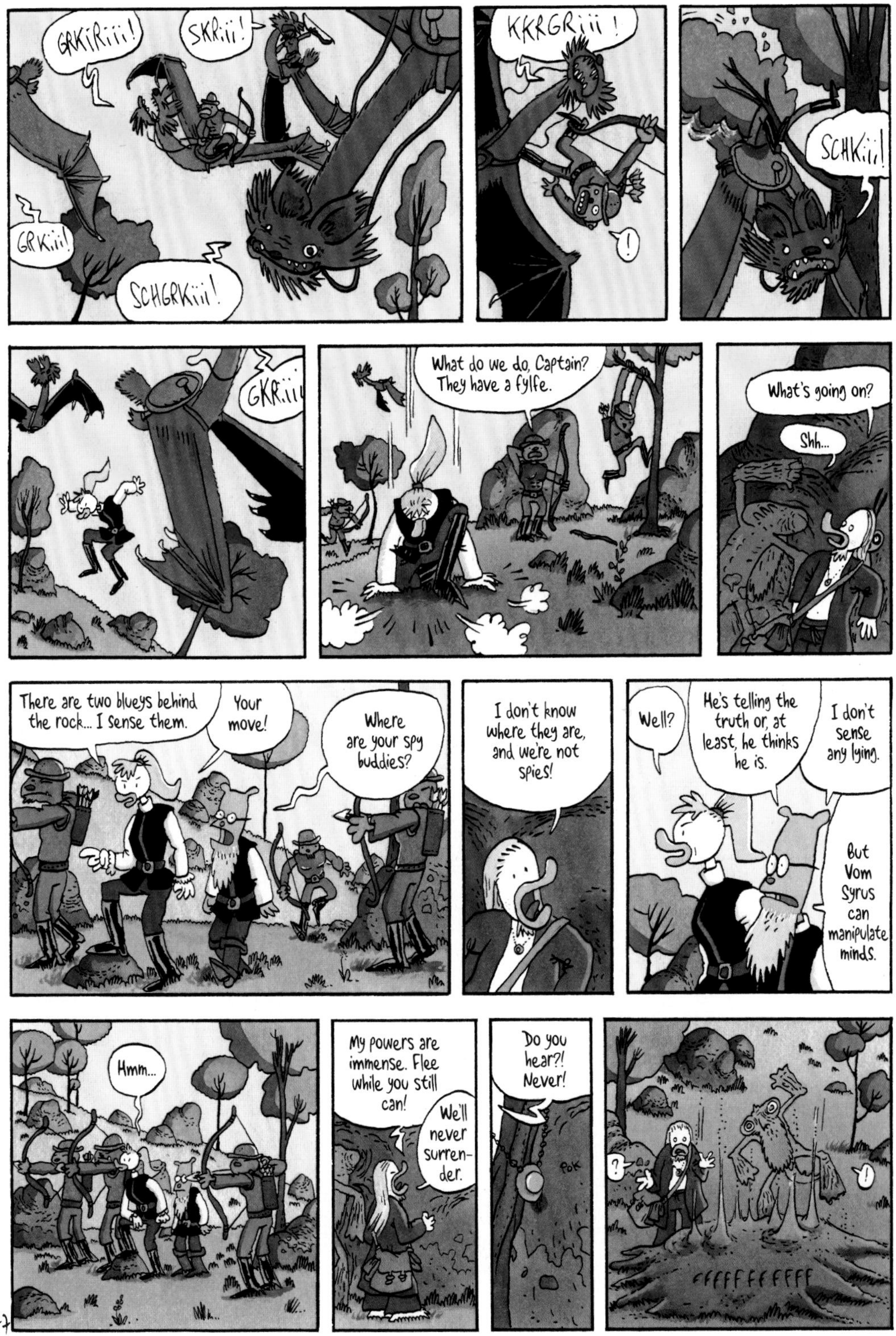
GRKiRiii!
SKRiii!
GRKiii!
SCHGRKiii!
KKRGRiii!
!
SCHKiii!
GKRiii
What do we do, Captain? They have a fylfe.
What's going on?
Shh...
There are two blueys behind the rock... I sense them.
Your move!
Where are your spy buddies?
I don't know where they are, and we're not spies!
Well?
He's telling the truth or, at least, he thinks he is.
I don't sense any lying.
But Vom Syrus can manipulate minds.
Hmm...
My powers are immense. Flee while you still can!
We'll never surrender.
Do you hear?! Never!
POK
?
!
fffffffffff
77

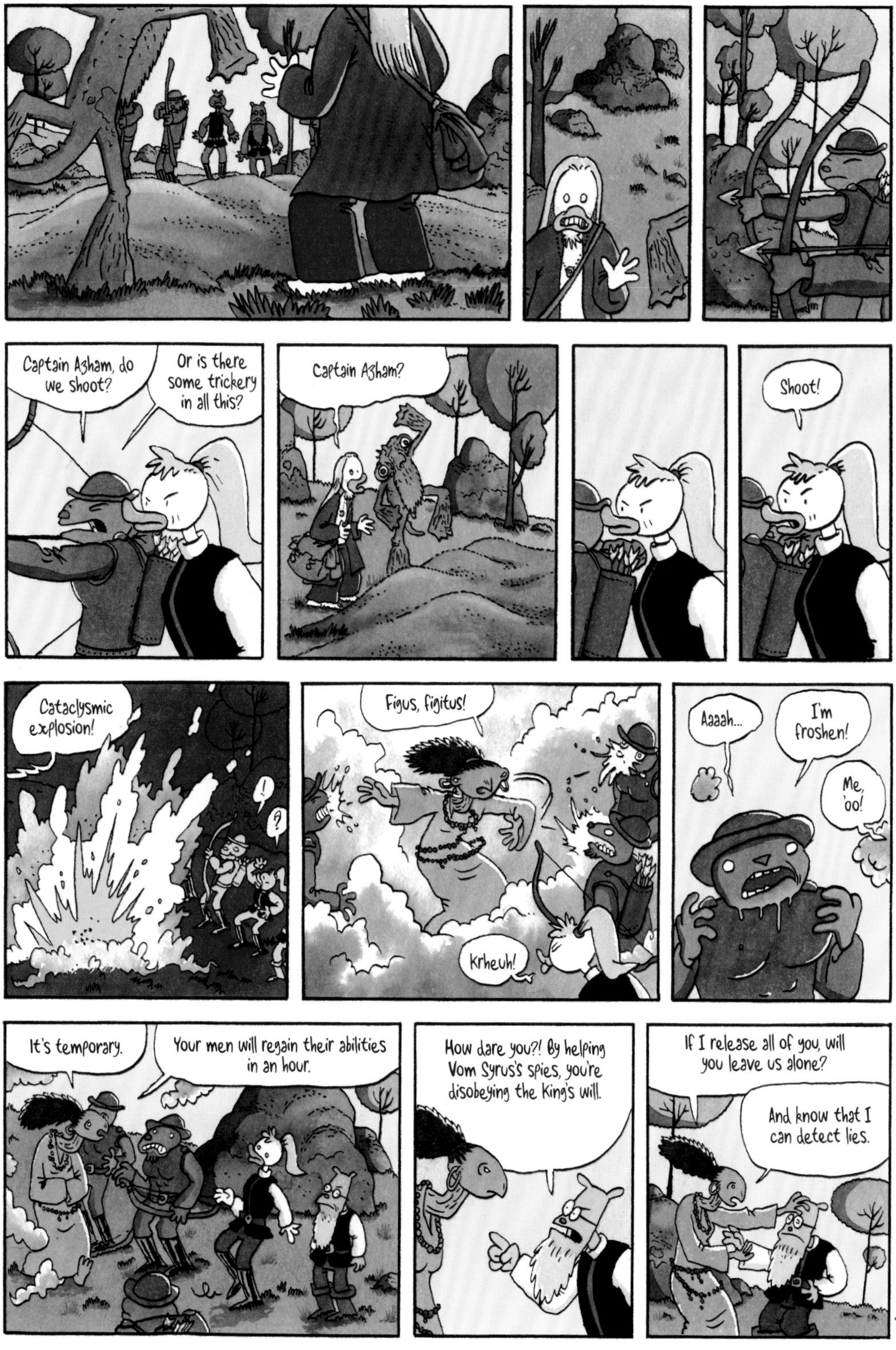
Captain Azham, do we shoot?
Or is there some trickery in all this?
Captain Azham?
Shoot!
Cataclysmic explosion!
!
?
Figus, figitus!
Krheuh!
Aaaah...
I'm froshen!
Me, 'oo!
It's temporary.
Your men will regain their abilities in an hour.
How dare you?! By helping Vom Syrus's spies, you're disobeying the King's will.
If I release all of you, will you leave us alone?
And know that I can detect lies.
78

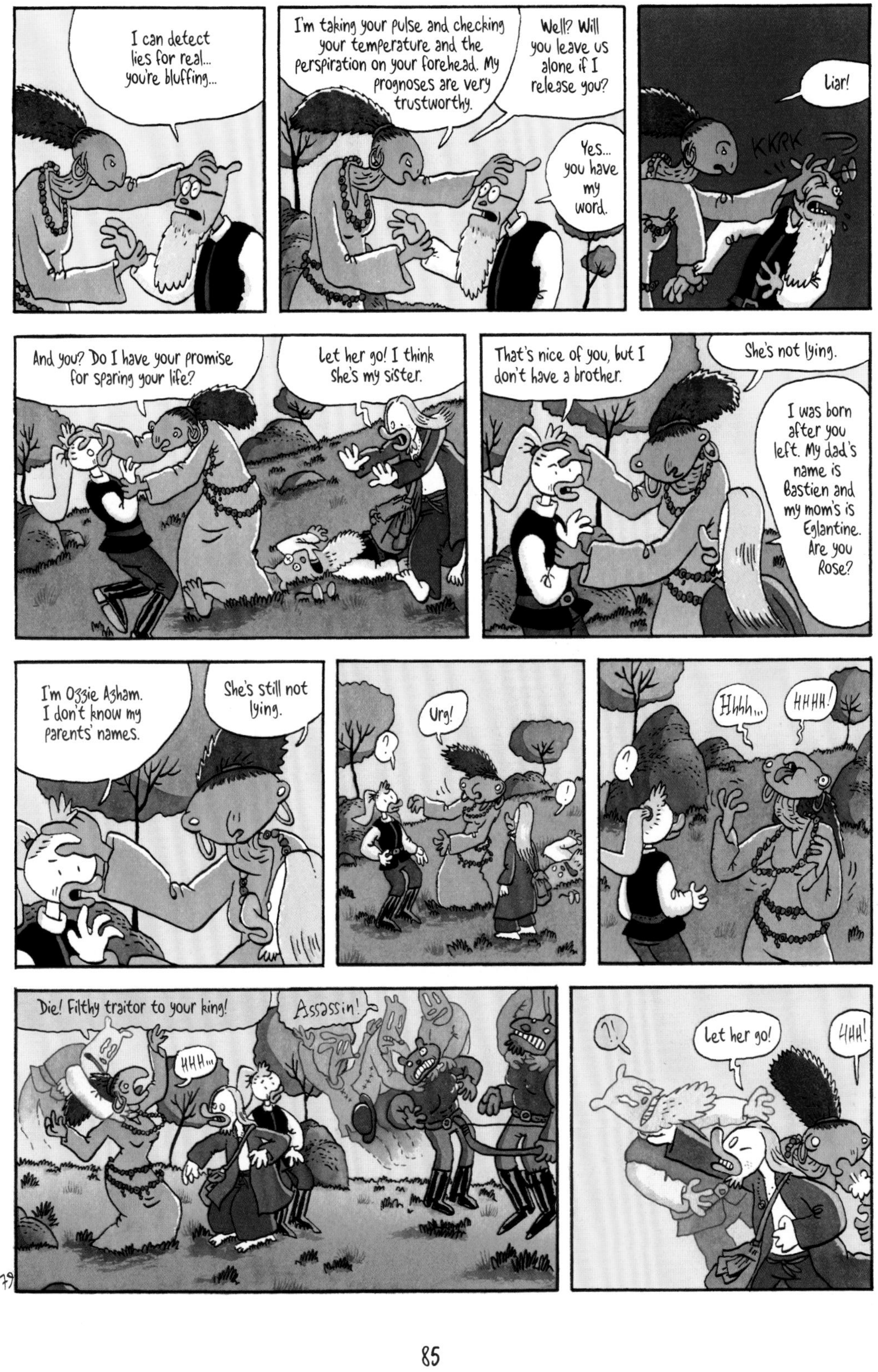
I can detect lies for real... you're bluffing...
I'm taking your pulse and checking your temperature and the perspiration on your forehead. My prognoses are very trustworthy.
Well? Will you leave us alone if I release you?
Yes... you have my word.
Liar!
KKRK
And you? Do I have your promise for sparing your life?
Let her go! I think she's my sister.
That's nice of you, but I don't have a brother.
She's not lying.
I was born after you left. My dad's name is Bastien and my mom's is Eglantine. Are you Rose?
I'm Ozzie Azham. I don't know my parents' names.
She's still not lying.
?
Urg!
!
?
Hhhh...
HHHH!
Die! Filthy traitor to your king!
HHH...
Assassin!
?!
Let her go!
HHH!

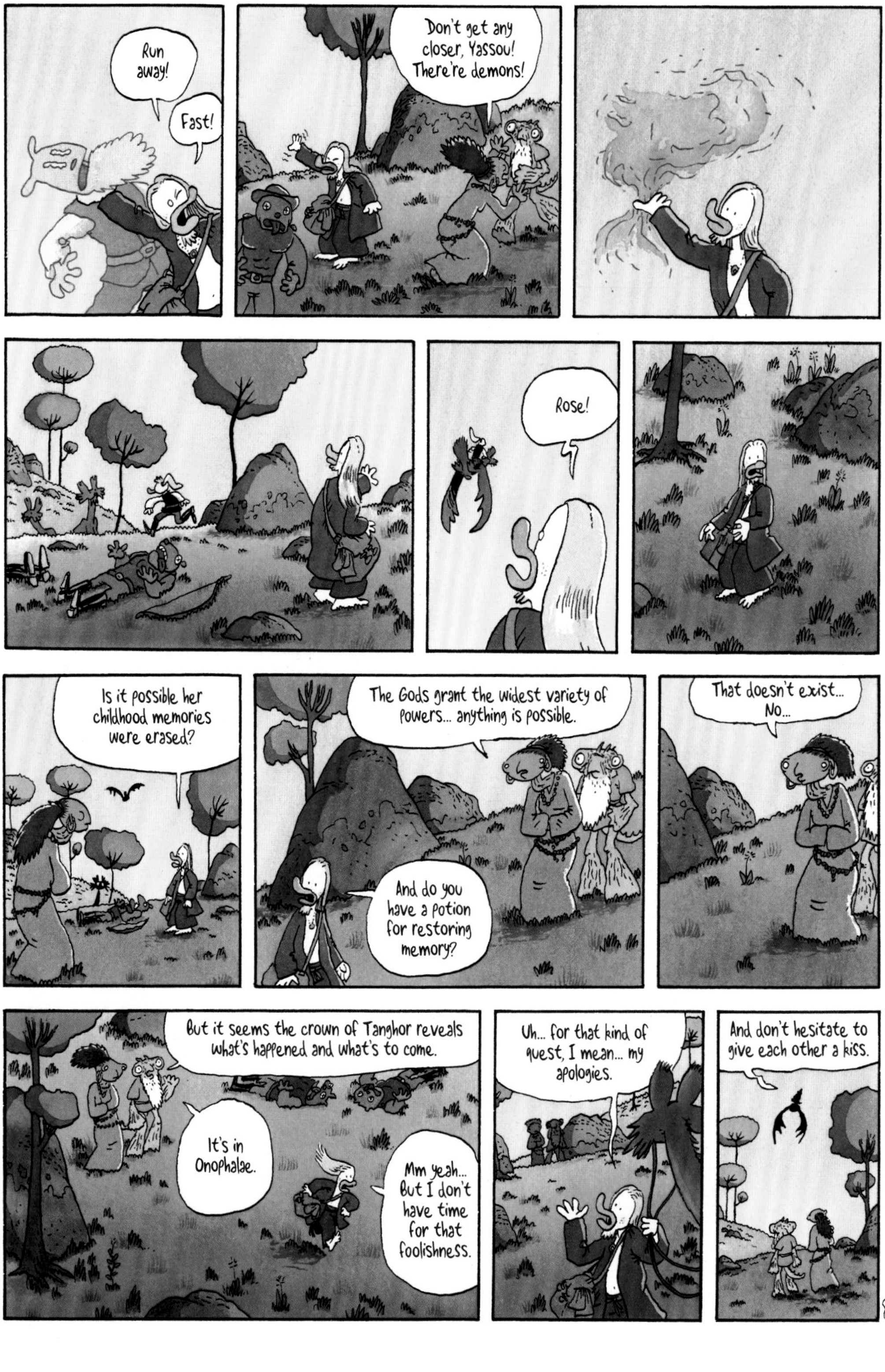
Run away!
Fast!
Don't get any closer, Yassou! There're demons!
Rose!
Is it possible her childhood memories were erased?
The Gods grant the widest variety of powers... anything is possible.
And do you have a potion for restoring memory?
That doesn't exist... No...
But it seems the crown of Tanghor reveals what's happened and what's to come.
It's in Onophalae.
Mm yeah... But I don't have time for that foolishness.
Uh... for that kind of quest, I mean... my apologies.
And don't hesitate to give each other a kiss.

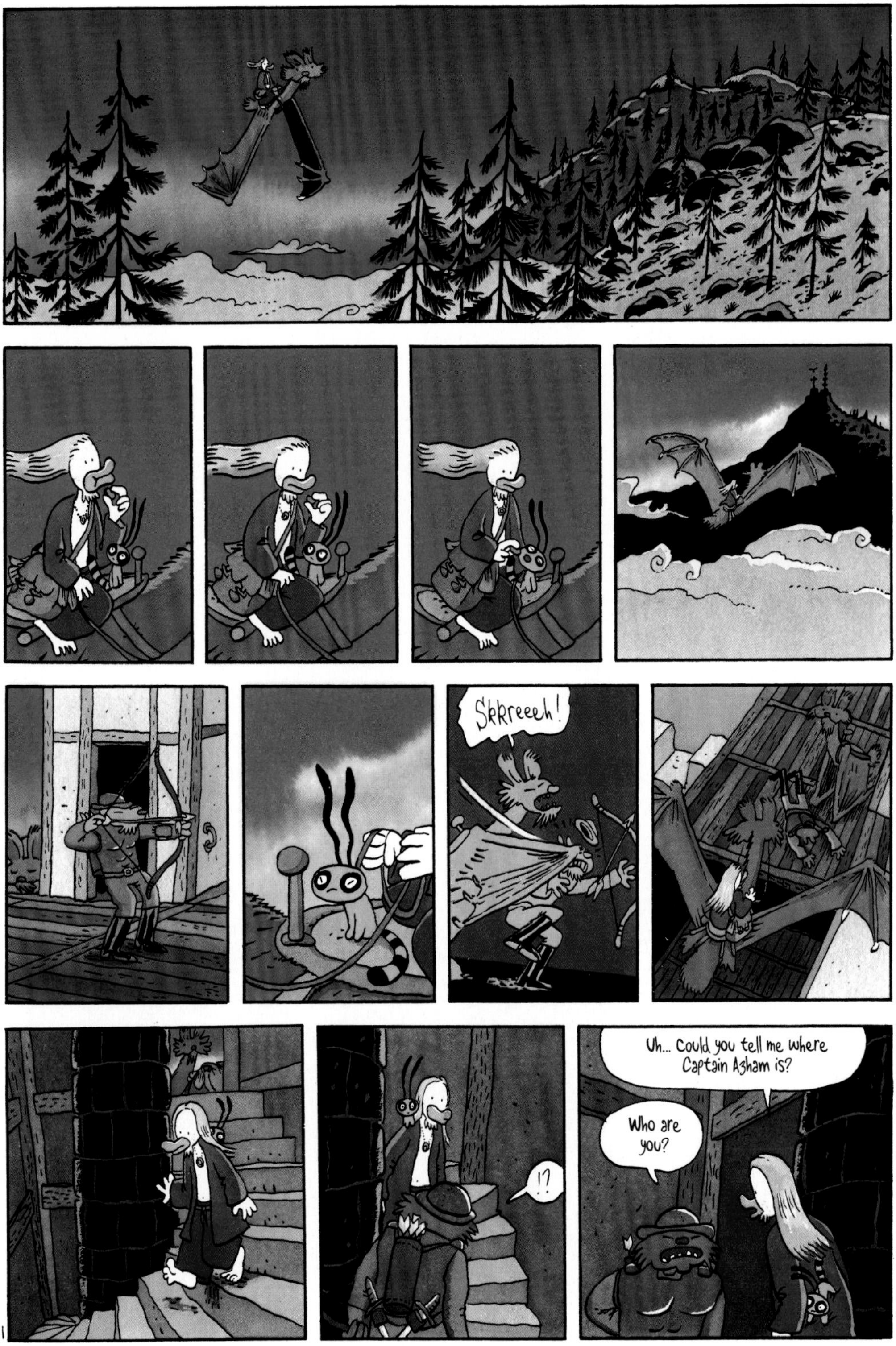
Skreeeh!
!?
Uh... Could you tell me where Captain Azham is?
Who are you?

81

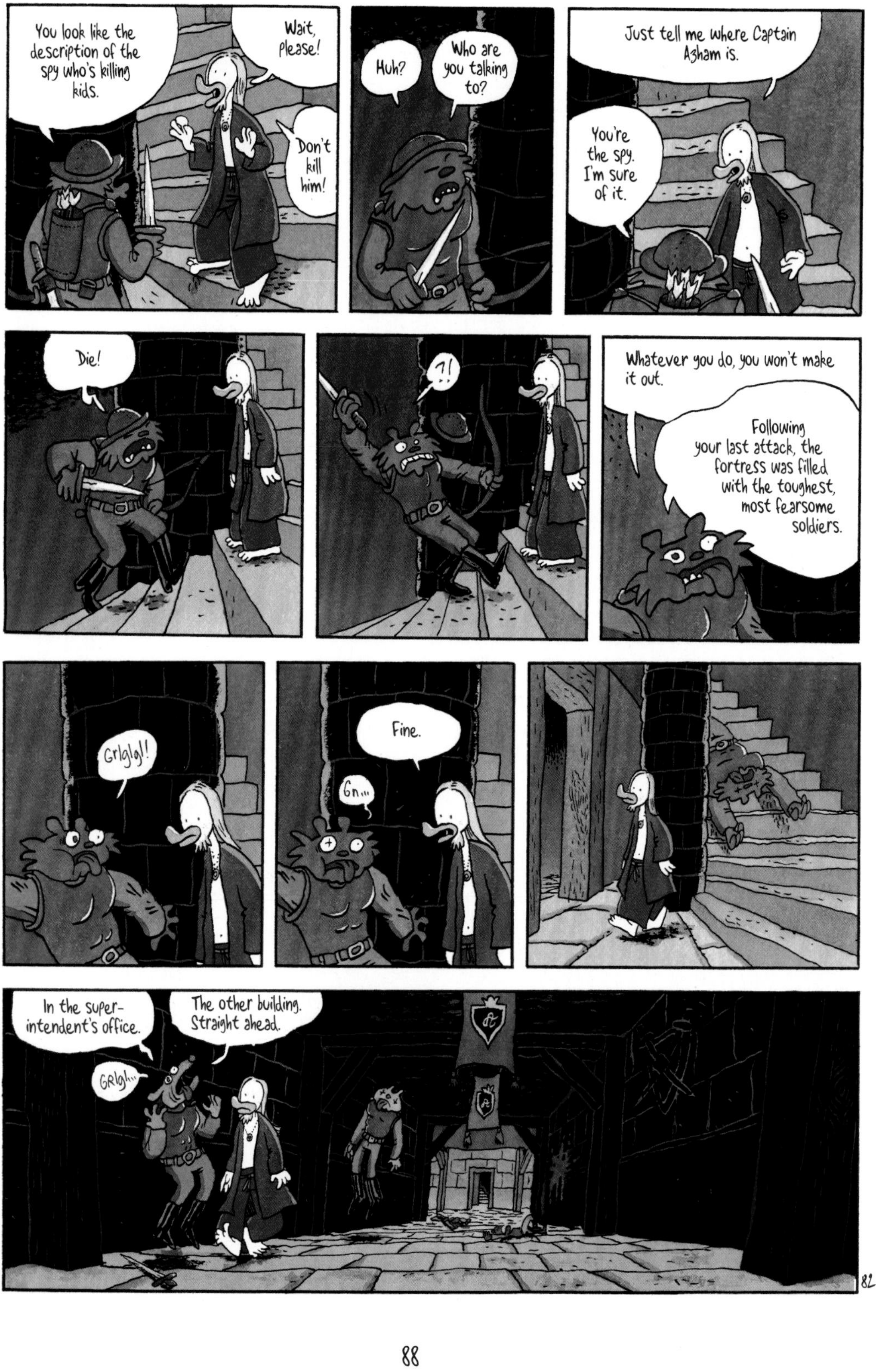
You look like the description of the spy who's killing kids.
Wait, please!
Don't kill him!
Huh?
Who are you talking to?
Just tell me where Captain Azham is.
You're the spy. I'm sure of it.
Die!
?!
Whatever you do, you won't make it out.
Following your last attack, the fortress was filled with the toughest, most fearsome soldiers.
Grlglgl!
Fine.
Gn...
In the super-intendent's office.
The other building. Straight ahead.
GRlgl...
82

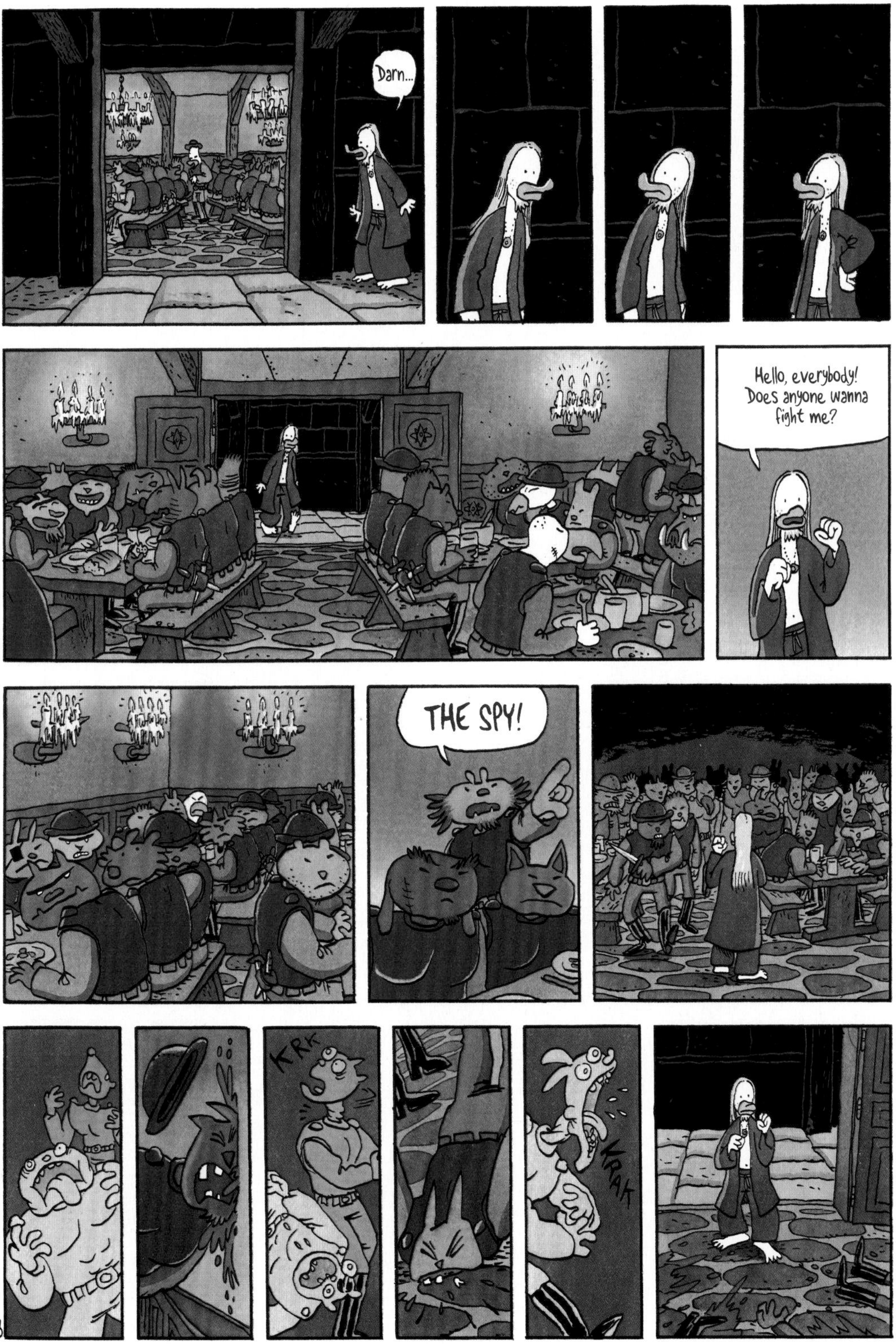
Darn...
Hello, everybody! Does anyone wanna fight me?
THE SPY!
KRK
KRAK

83

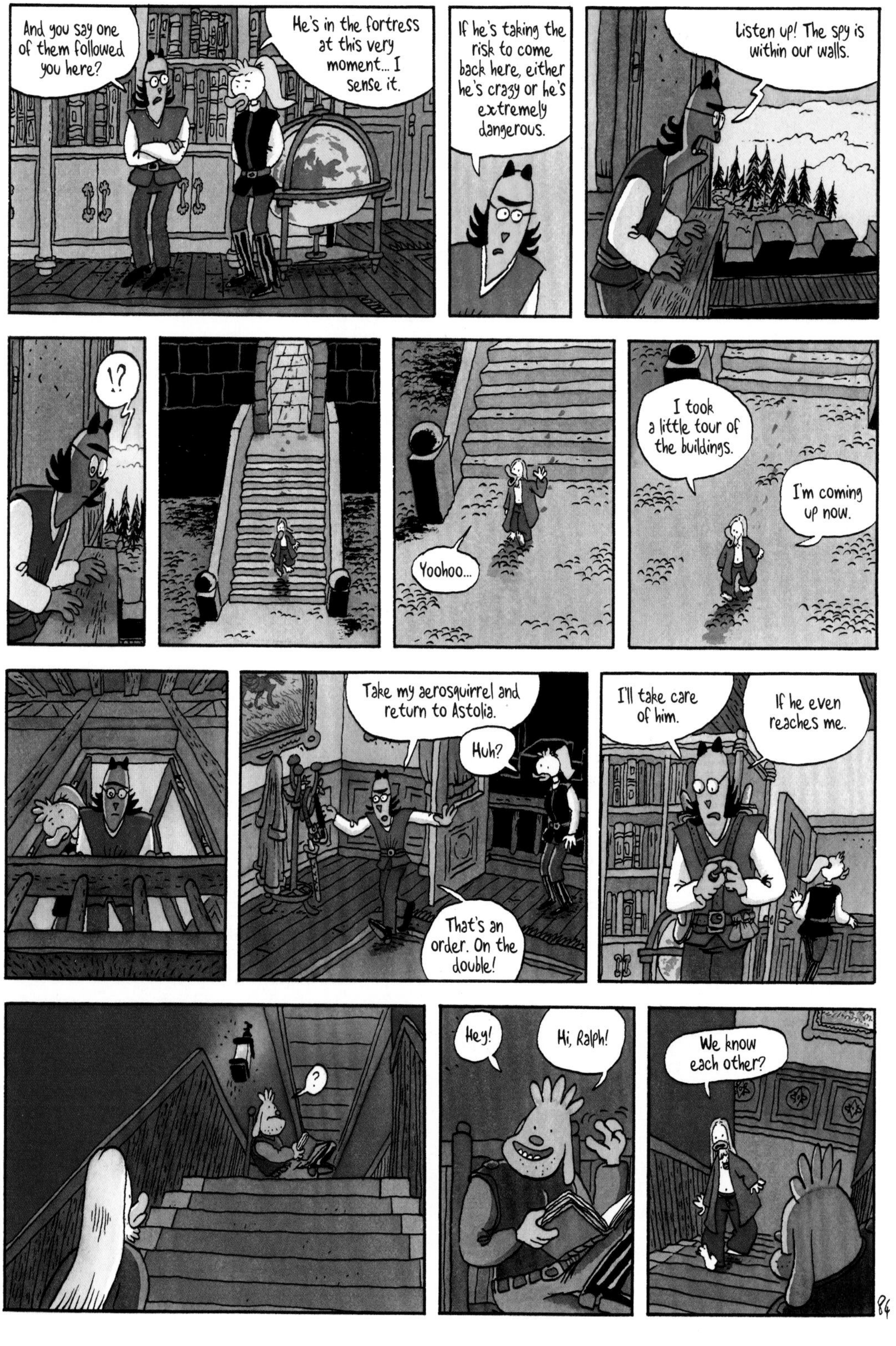
And you say one of them followed you here?
He's in the fortress at this very moment... I sense it.
If he's taking the risk to come back here, either he's crazy or he's extremely dangerous.
Listen up! The spy is within our walls.
!?
Yoohoo...
I took a little tour of the buildings.
I'm coming up now.
Take my aerosquirrel and return to Astolia.
Huh?
That's an order. On the double!
I'll take care of him.
If he even reaches me.
?
Hey!
Hi, Ralph!
We know each other?
84

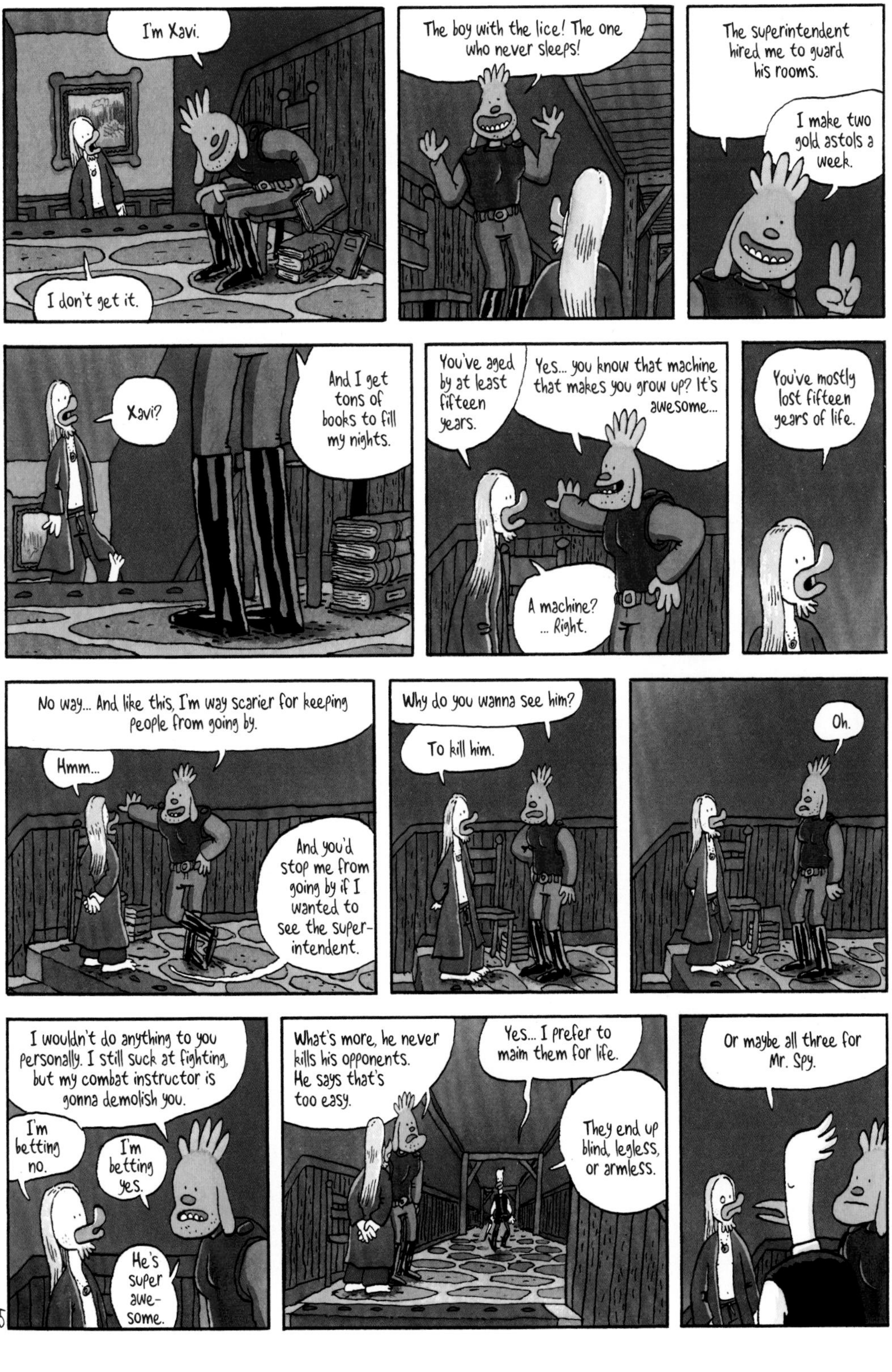
I'm Xavi.
I don't get it.
The boy with the lice! The one who never sleeps!
The superintendent hired me to guard his rooms.
I make two gold astols a week.
Xavi?
And I get tons of books to fill my nights.
You've aged by at least fifteen years.
Yes... you know that machine that makes you grow up? It's awesome...
A machine? ... Right.
You've mostly lost fifteen years of life.
No way... And like this, I'm way scarier for keeping people from going by.
Hmm...
And you'd stop me from going by if I wanted to see the super-intendent.
Why do you wanna see him?
To kill him.
Oh.
I wouldn't do anything to you personally. I still suck at fighting, but my combat instructor is gonna demolish you.
I'm betting no.
I'm betting yes.
He's super awe-some.
What's more, he never kills his opponents. He says that's too easy.
Yes... I prefer to maim them for life.
They end up blind, legless, or armless.
Or maybe all three for Mr. Spy.
85

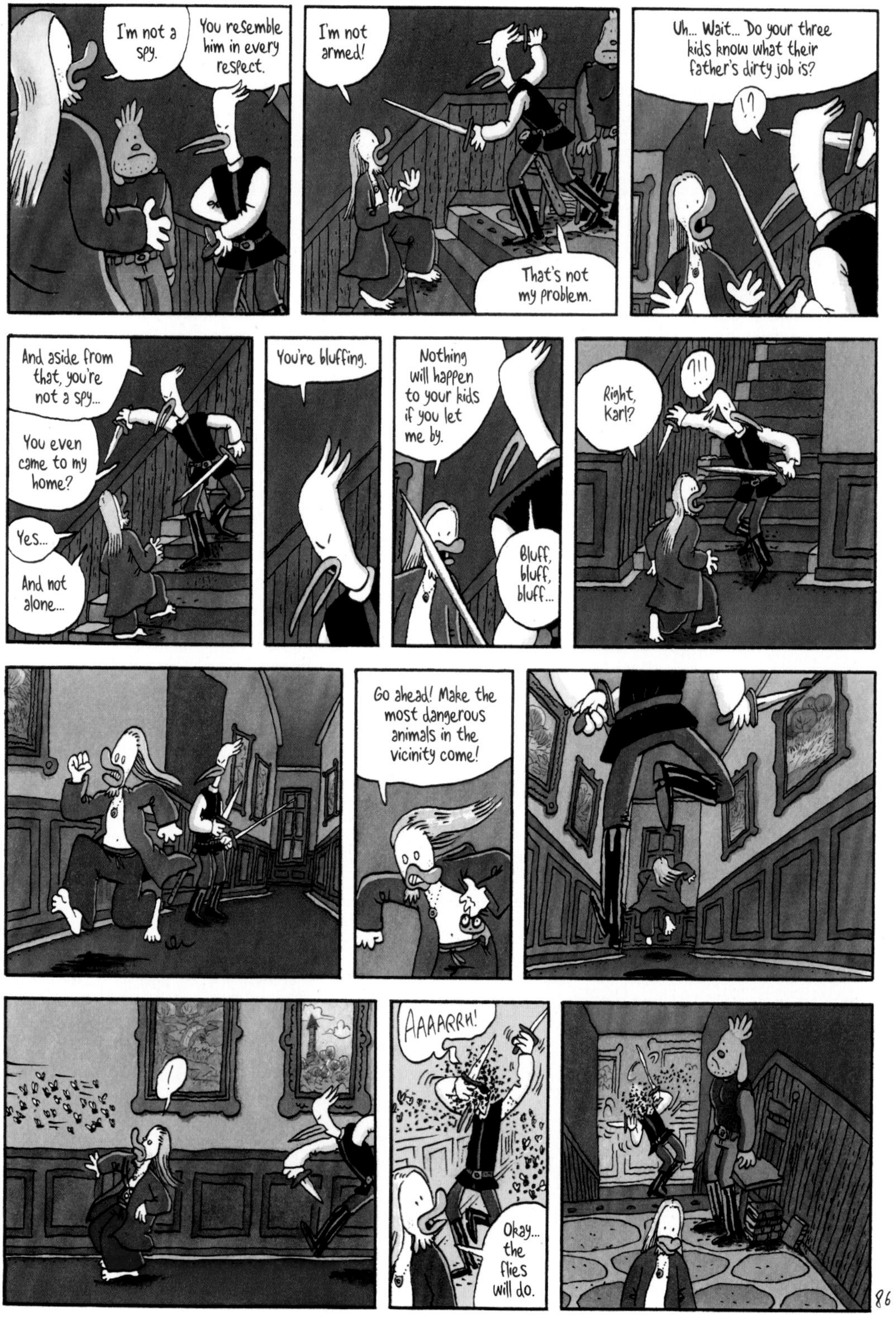
I'm not a spy.
You resemble him in every respect.
I'm not armed!
That's not my problem.
Uh... Wait... Do your three kids know what their father's dirty job is?
!?
And aside from that, you're not a spy...
You even came to my home?
Yes...
And not alone...
You're bluffing.
Nothing will happen to your kids if you let me by.
Bluff, bluff, bluff...
Right, Karl?
?!!
Go ahead! Make the most dangerous animals in the vicinity come!
!
AAAARRH!
Okay... the flies will do.
86

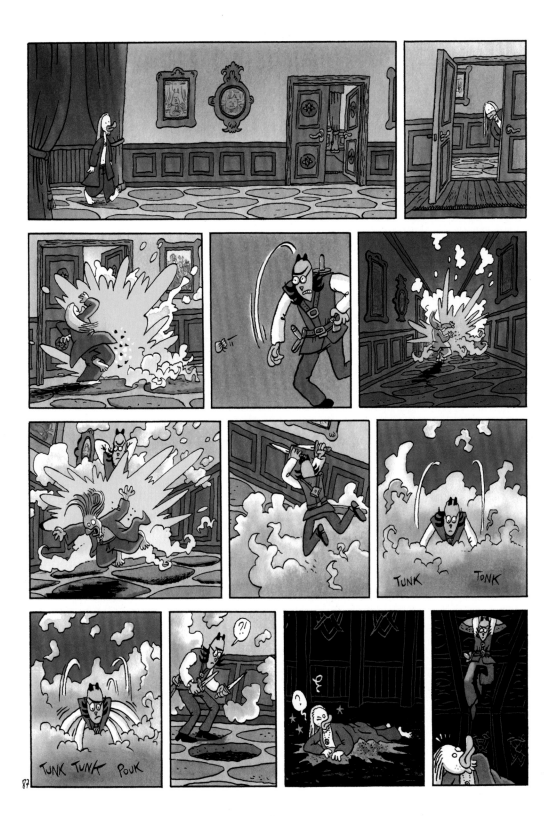

TUNK   TONK

TUNK TUNK POUK

?!

87

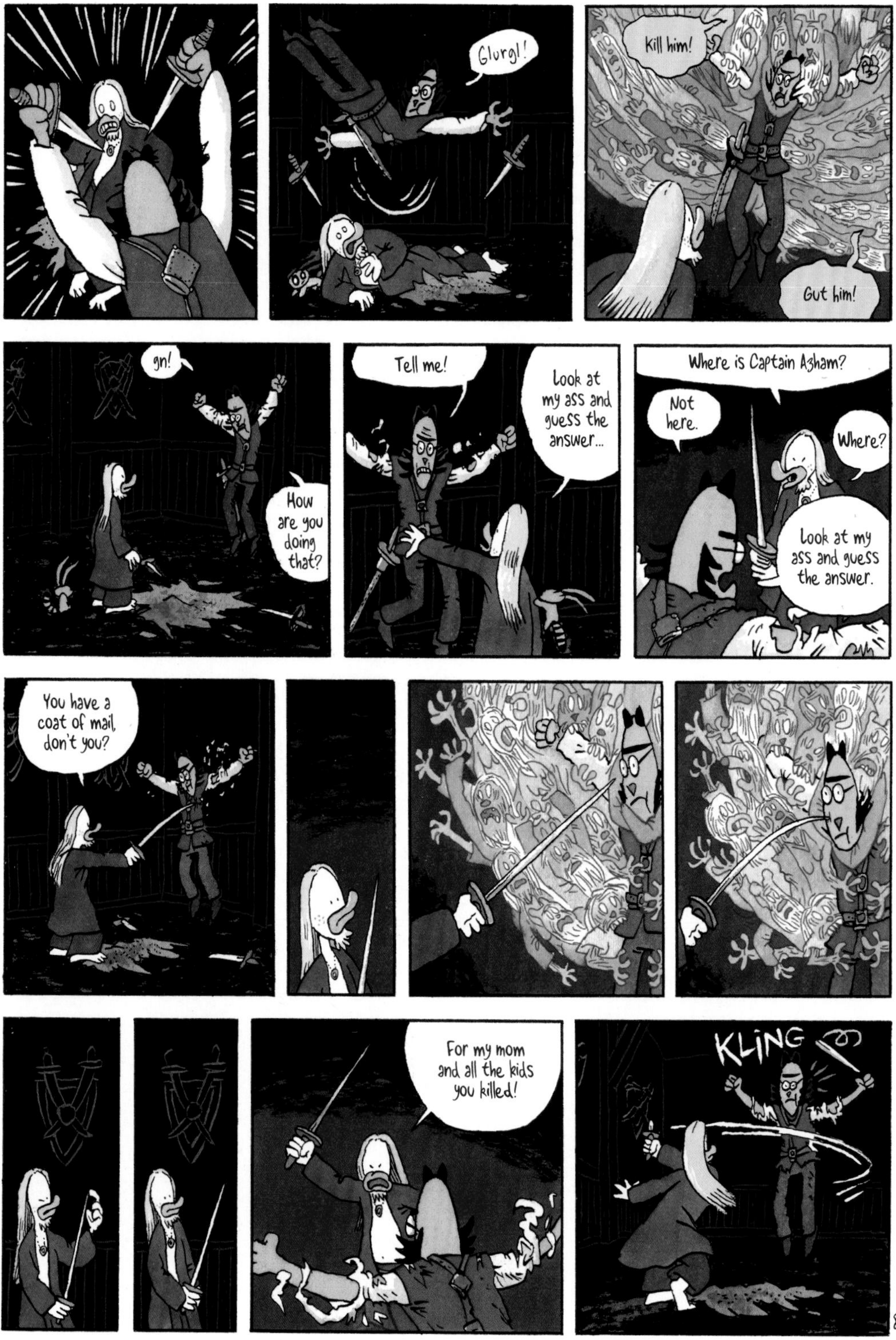
Glurgl!
Kill him!
Gut him!
gn!
How are you doing that?
Tell me!
Look at my ass and guess the answer...
Where is Captain Azham?
Not here.
Where?
Look at my ass and guess the answer.
You have a coat of mail, don't you?
For my mom and all the kids you killed!
KLING

88

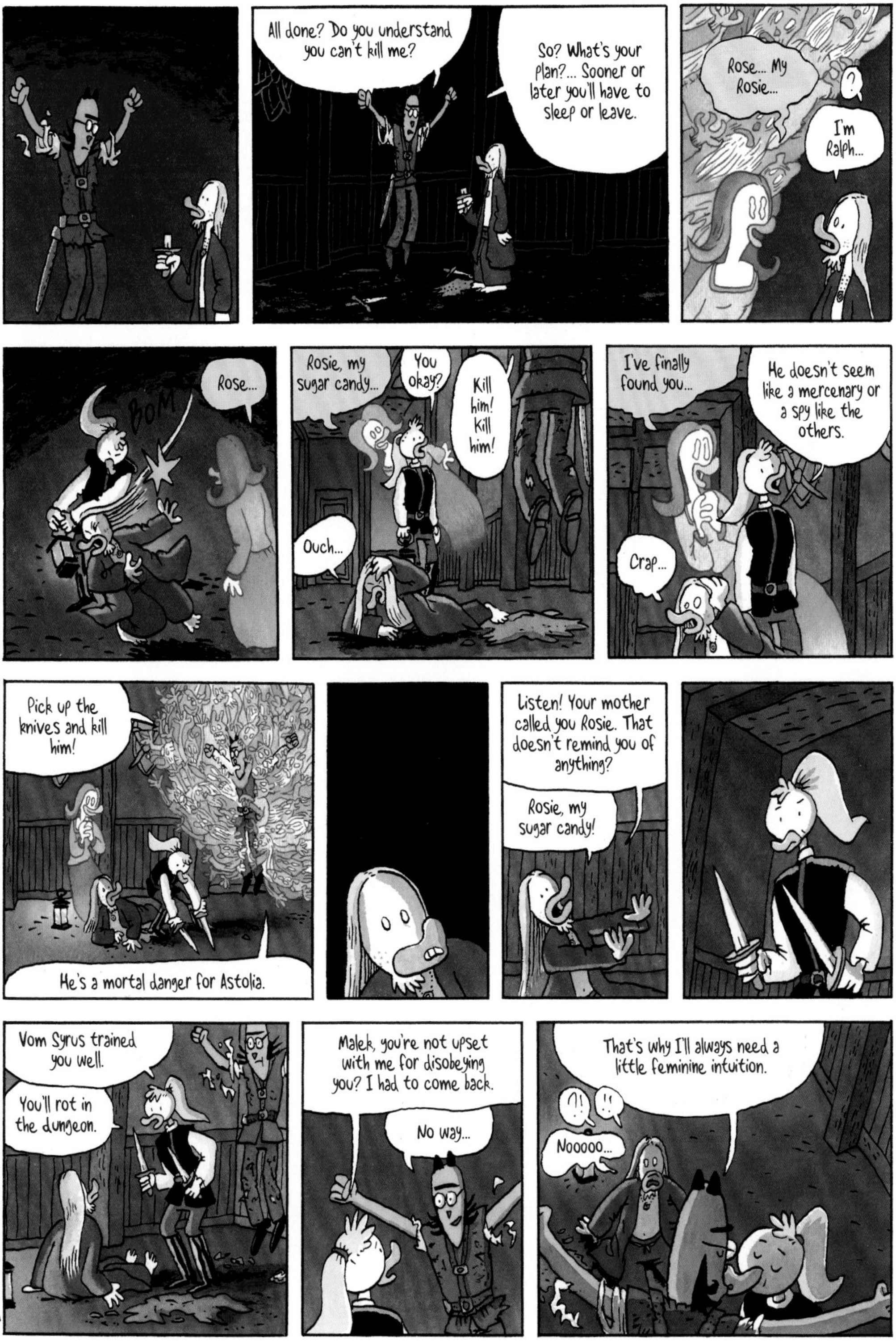
All done? Do you understand you can't kill me?
So? What's your plan?... Sooner or later you'll have to sleep or leave.
Rose... My Rosie...
?
I'm Ralph...
BOM
Rose...
Rosie, my sugar candy...
You okay?
Kill him! Kill him!
Ouch...
I've finally found you...
He doesn't seem like a mercenary or a spy like the others.
Crap...
Pick up the knives and kill him!
He's a mortal danger for Astolia.
Listen! Your mother called you Rosie. That doesn't remind you of anything?
Rosie, my sugar candy!
Vom Syrus trained you well.
You'll rot in the dungeon.
Malek, you're not upset with me for disobeying you? I had to come back.
No way...
That's why I'll always need a little feminine intuition.
?!
!!
Nooooo...

89

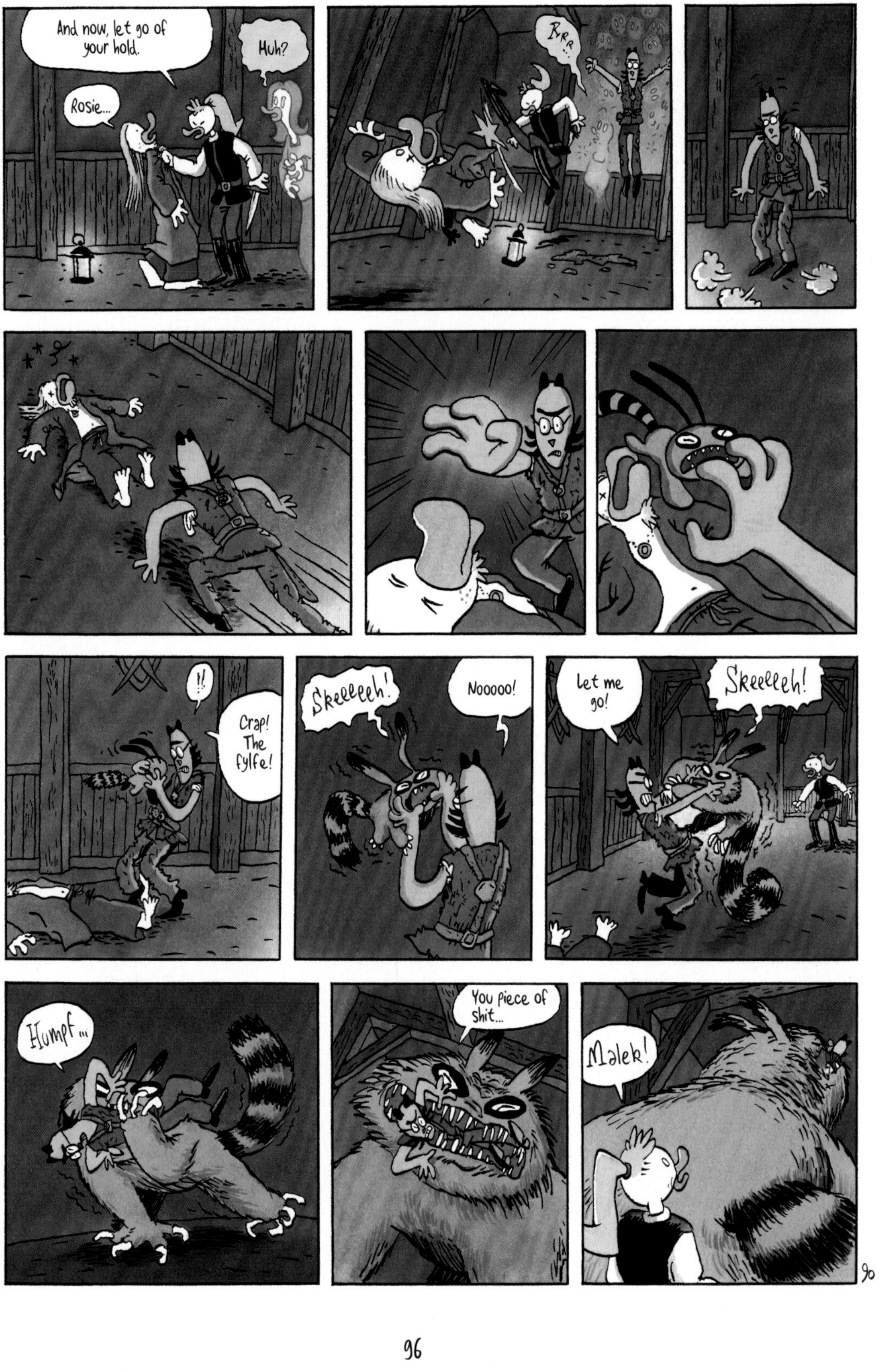
And now, let go of your hold.
Rosie...
Huh?
Rrr...
!!
Crap! The fylfe!
Skeeeeeh!
Nooooo!
Let me go!
Skeeeeeh!
Humpf...
You piece of shit...
Malek!
90

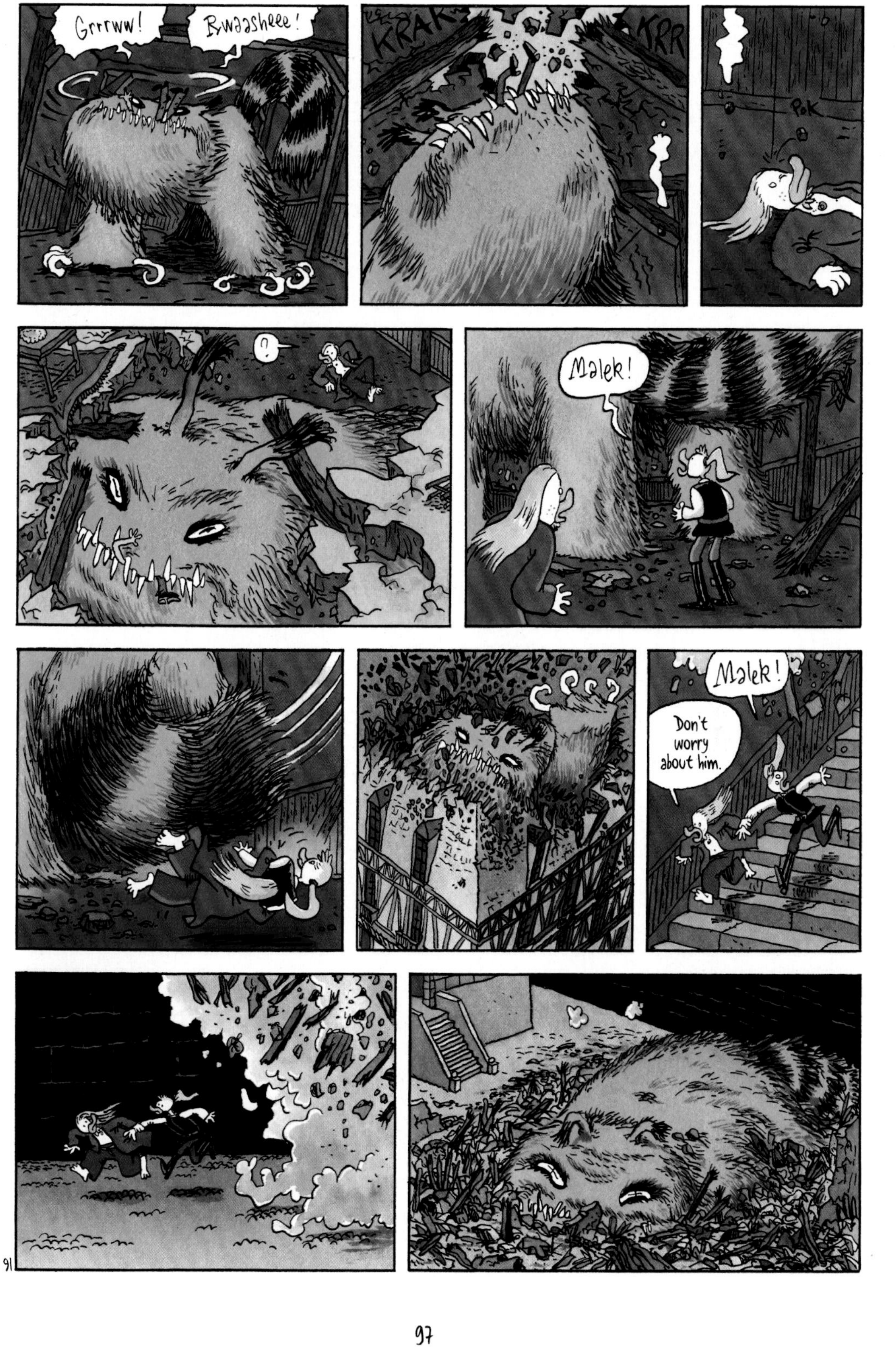
Grrrww!
Bwaasheee!
KRAK
KRR
POK
?
Malek!
Malek!
Don't worry about him.

91

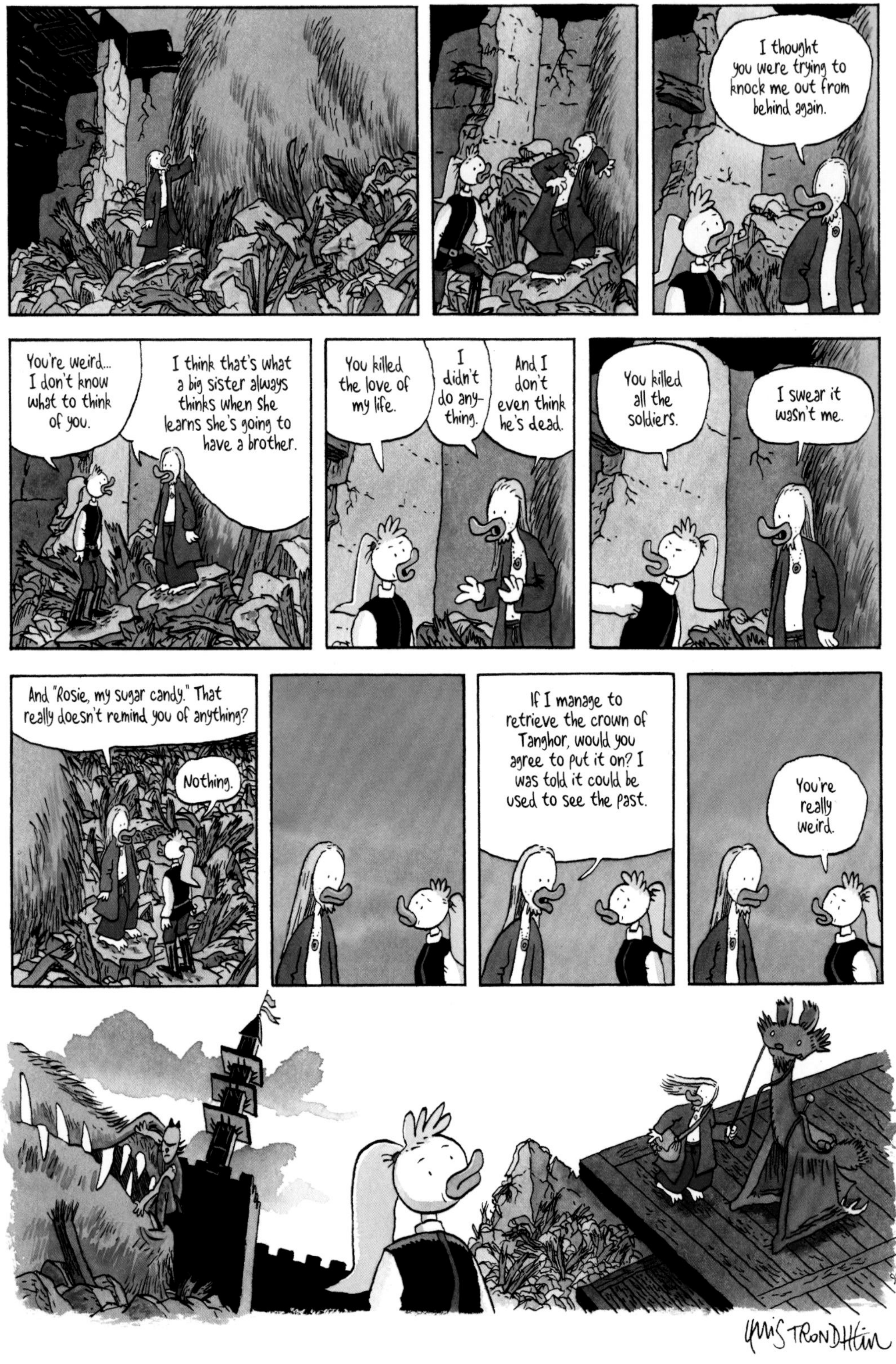
I thought you were trying to knock me out from behind again.
You're weird... I don't know what to think of you.
I think that's what a big sister always thinks when she learns she's going to have a brother.
You killed the love of my life.
I didn't do anything.
And I don't even think he's dead.
You killed all the soldiers.
I swear it wasn't me.
And "Rosie, my sugar candy." That really doesn't remind you of anything?
Nothing.
If I manage to retrieve the crown of Tanghor, would you agree to put it on? I was told it could be used to see the past.
You're really weird.
92
LEWIS TRONDHEIM

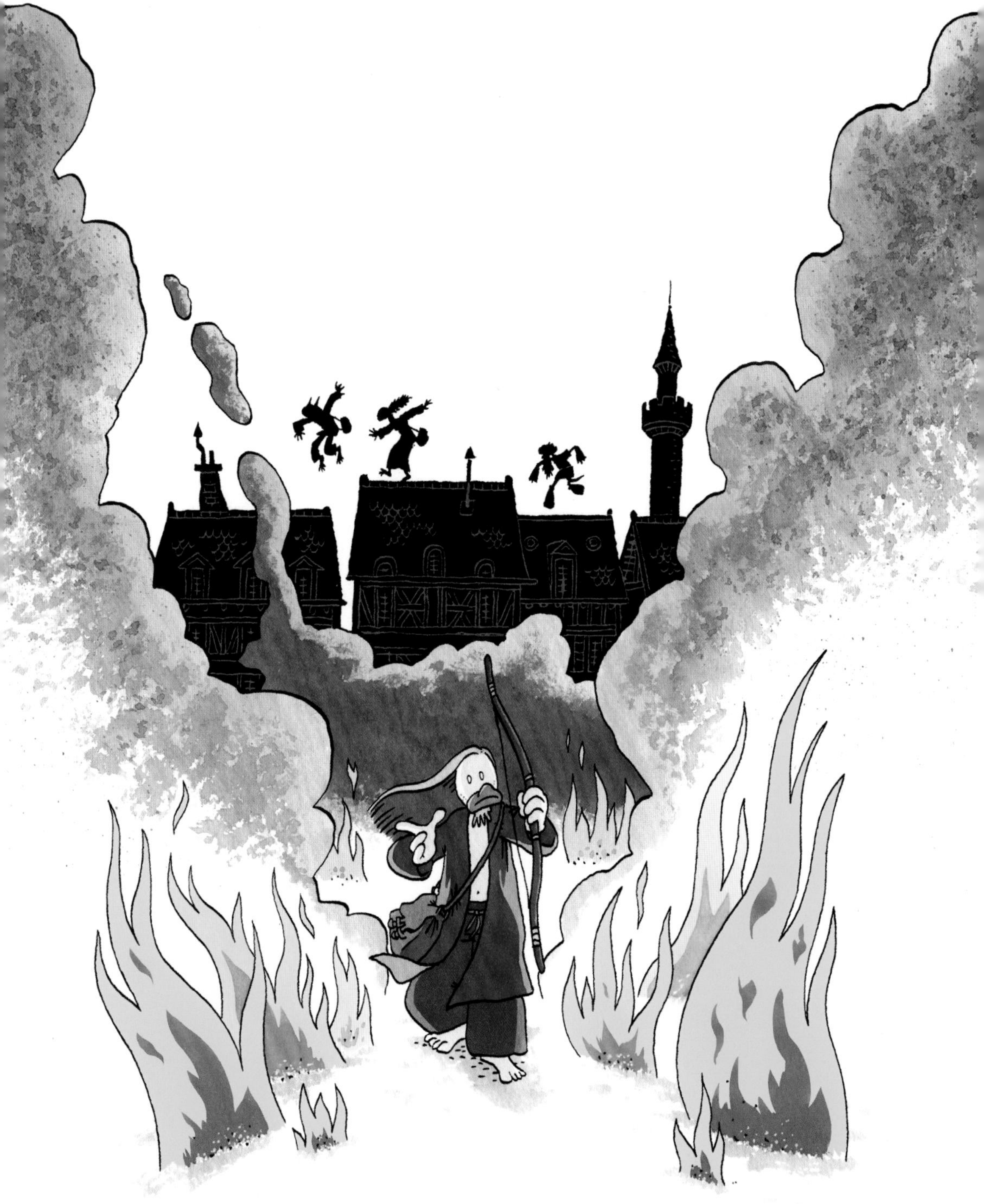

3

Black are the Stars

Story and Art: Lewis Trondheim
Colors: Brigitte Findakly
Translation: Joe Johnson
Lettering: Wilson Ramos Jr.

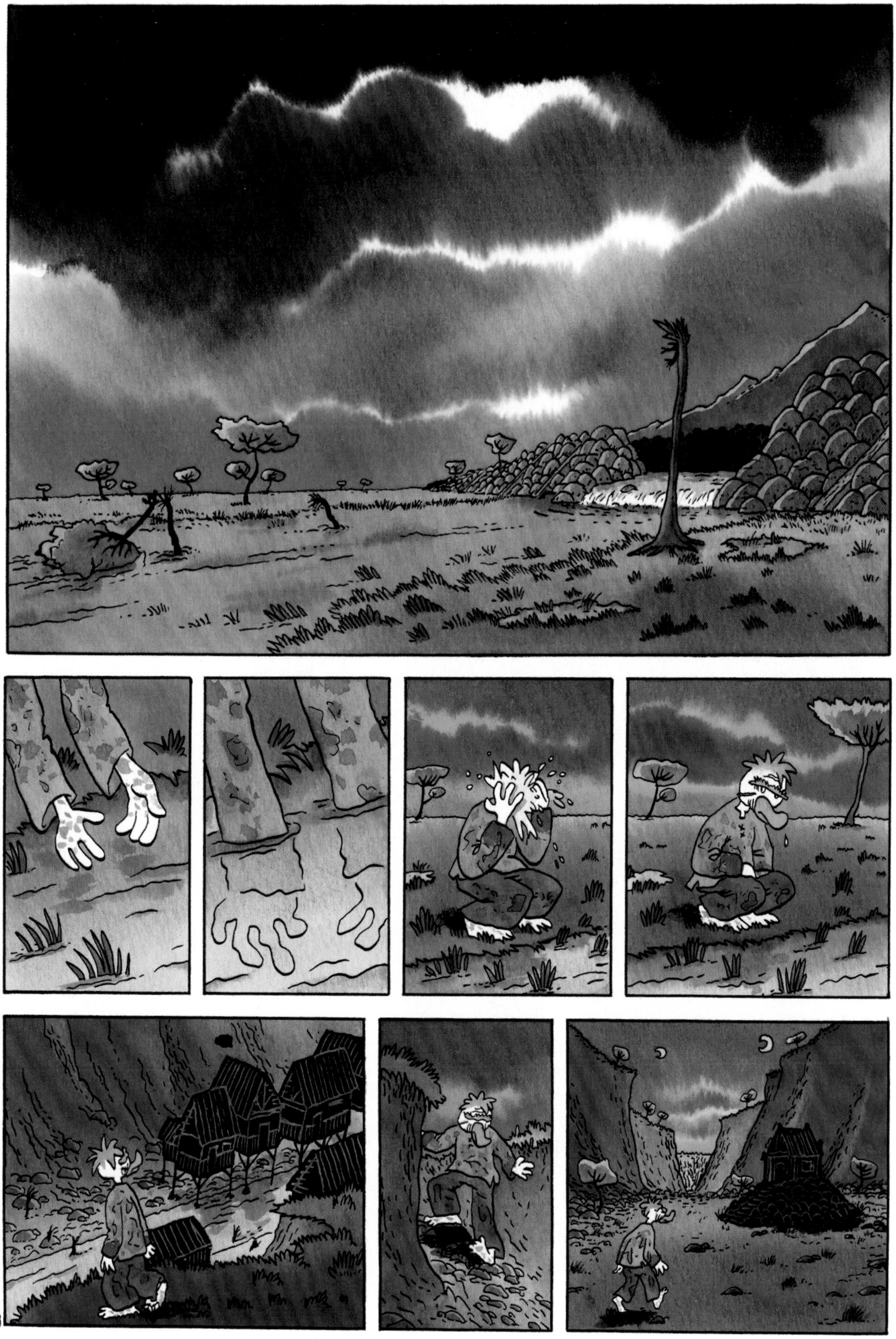

93

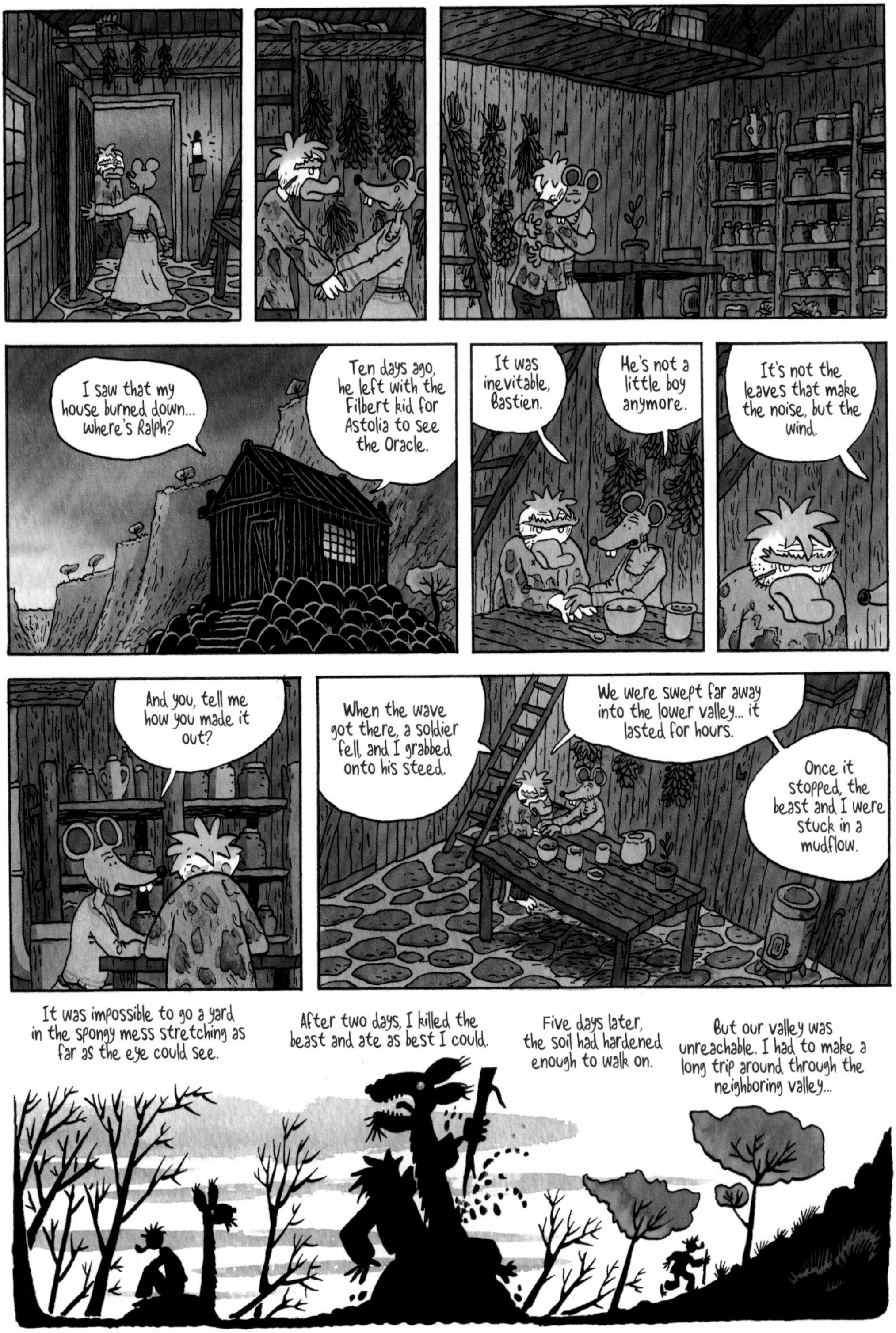
I saw that my house burned down... where's Ralph?
Ten days ago, he left with the Filbert kid for Astolia to see the Oracle.
It was inevitable, Bastien.
He's not a little boy anymore.
It's not the leaves that make the noise, but the wind.
And you, tell me how you made it out?
When the wave got there, a soldier fell, and I grabbed onto his steed.
We were swept far away into the lower valley... it lasted for hours.
Once it stopped, the beast and I were stuck in a mudflow.
It was impossible to go a yard in the spongy mess stretching as far as the eye could see.
After two days, I killed the beast and ate as best I could.
Five days later, the soil had hardened enough to walk on.
But our valley was unreachable. I had to make a long trip around through the neighboring valley...

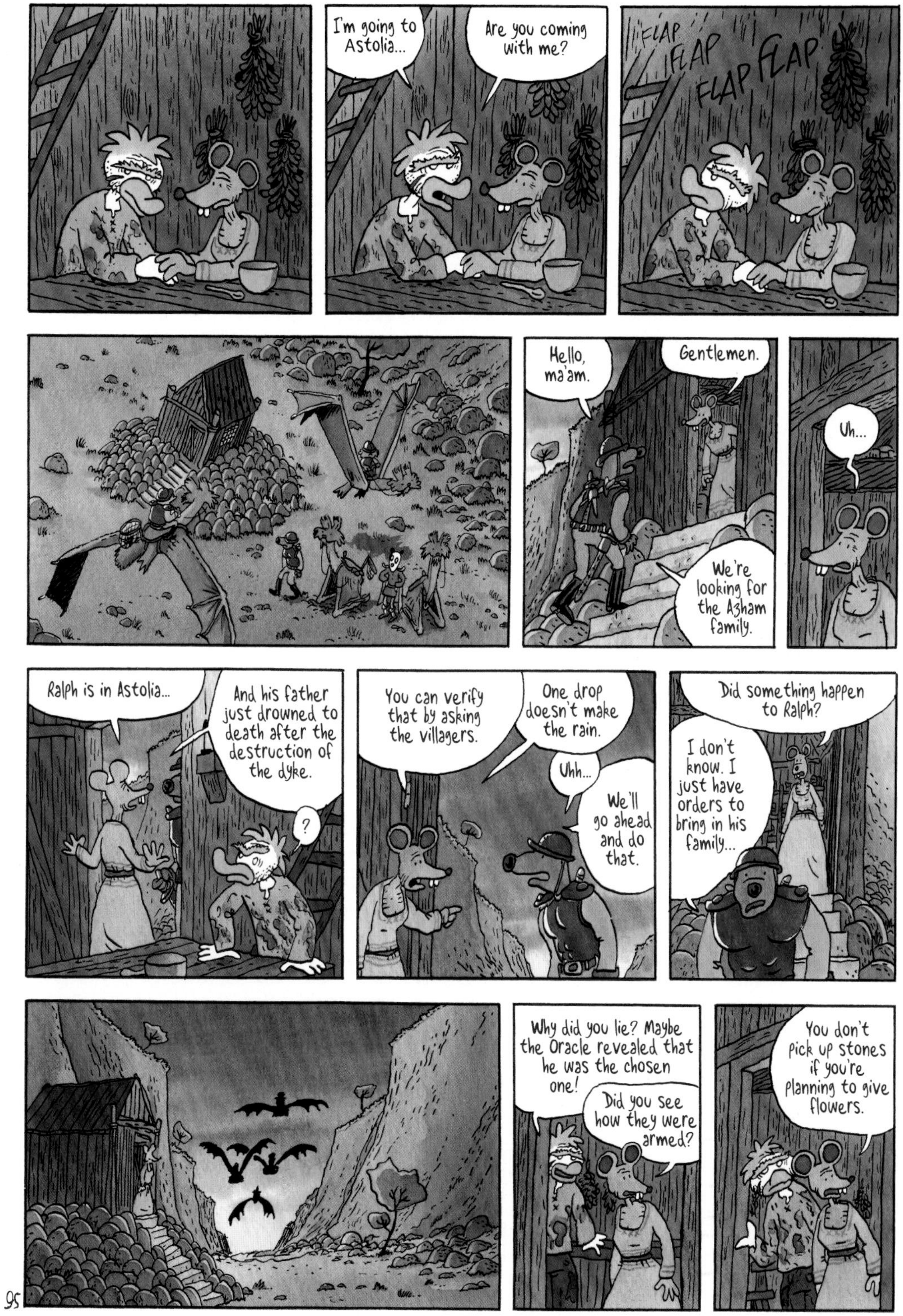
I'm going to Astolia...
Are you coming with me?
FLAP FLAP FLAP FLAP
Hello, ma'am.
Gentlemen.
We're looking for the Azham family.
Uh...
Ralph is in Astolia...
And his father just drowned to death after the destruction of the dyke.
?
You can verify that by asking the villagers.
One drop doesn't make the rain.
Uhh...
We'll go ahead and do that.
Did something happen to Ralph?
I don't know. I just have orders to bring in his family...
Why did you lie? Maybe the Oracle revealed that he was the chosen one!
Did you see how they were armed?
You don't pick up stones if you're planning to give flowers.
95

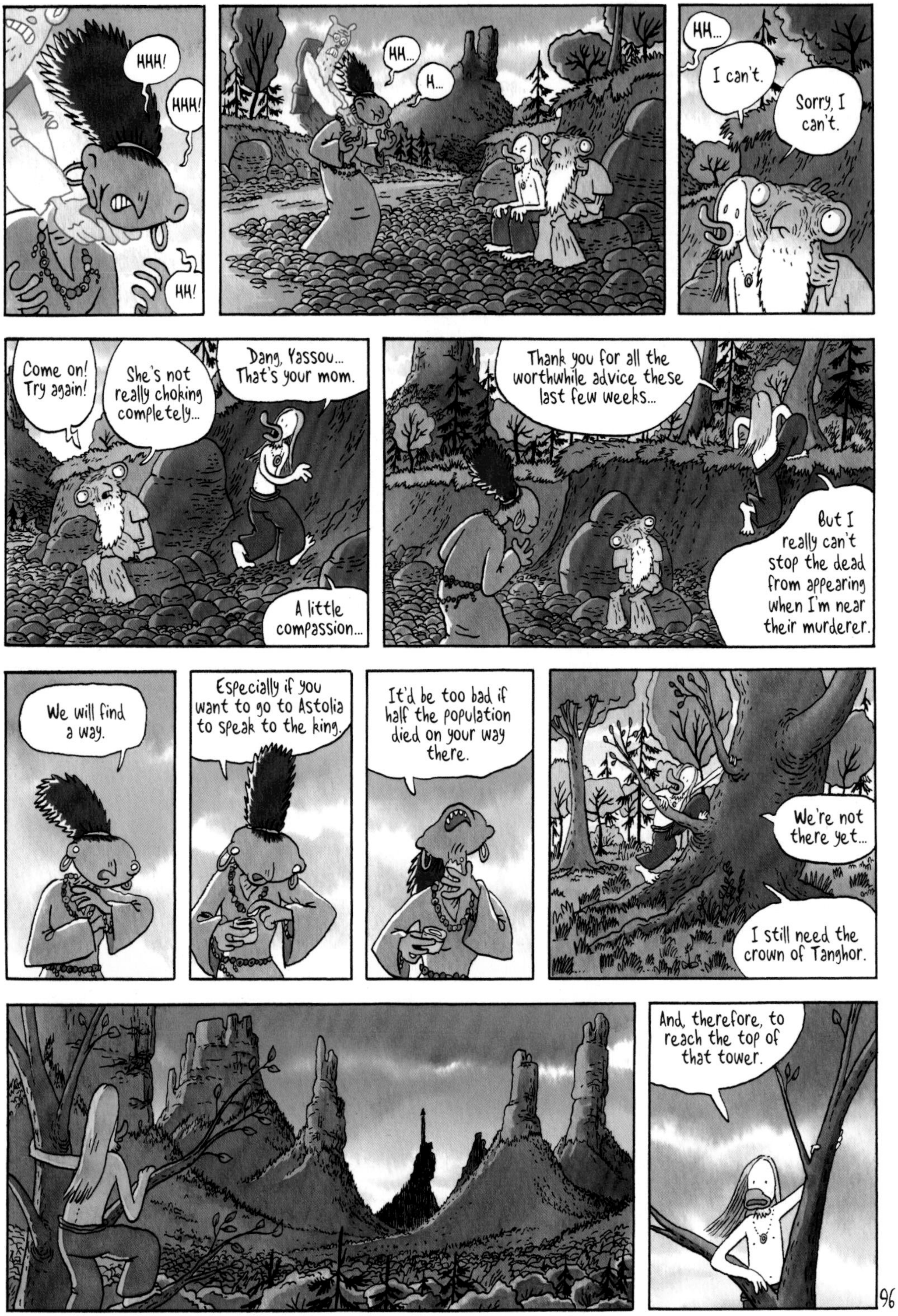
HHH!
HHH!
HH!
HH...
H...
HH...
I can't.
Sorry, I can't.
Come on! Try again!
She's not really choking completely...
Dang, Yassou... That's your mom.
A little compassion...
Thank you for all the worthwhile advice these last few weeks...
But I really can't stop the dead from appearing when I'm near their murderer.
We will find a way.
Especially if you want to go to Astolia to speak to the king.
It'd be too bad if half the population died on your way there.
We're not there yet...
I still need the crown of Tanghor.
And, therefore, to reach the top of that tower.
96

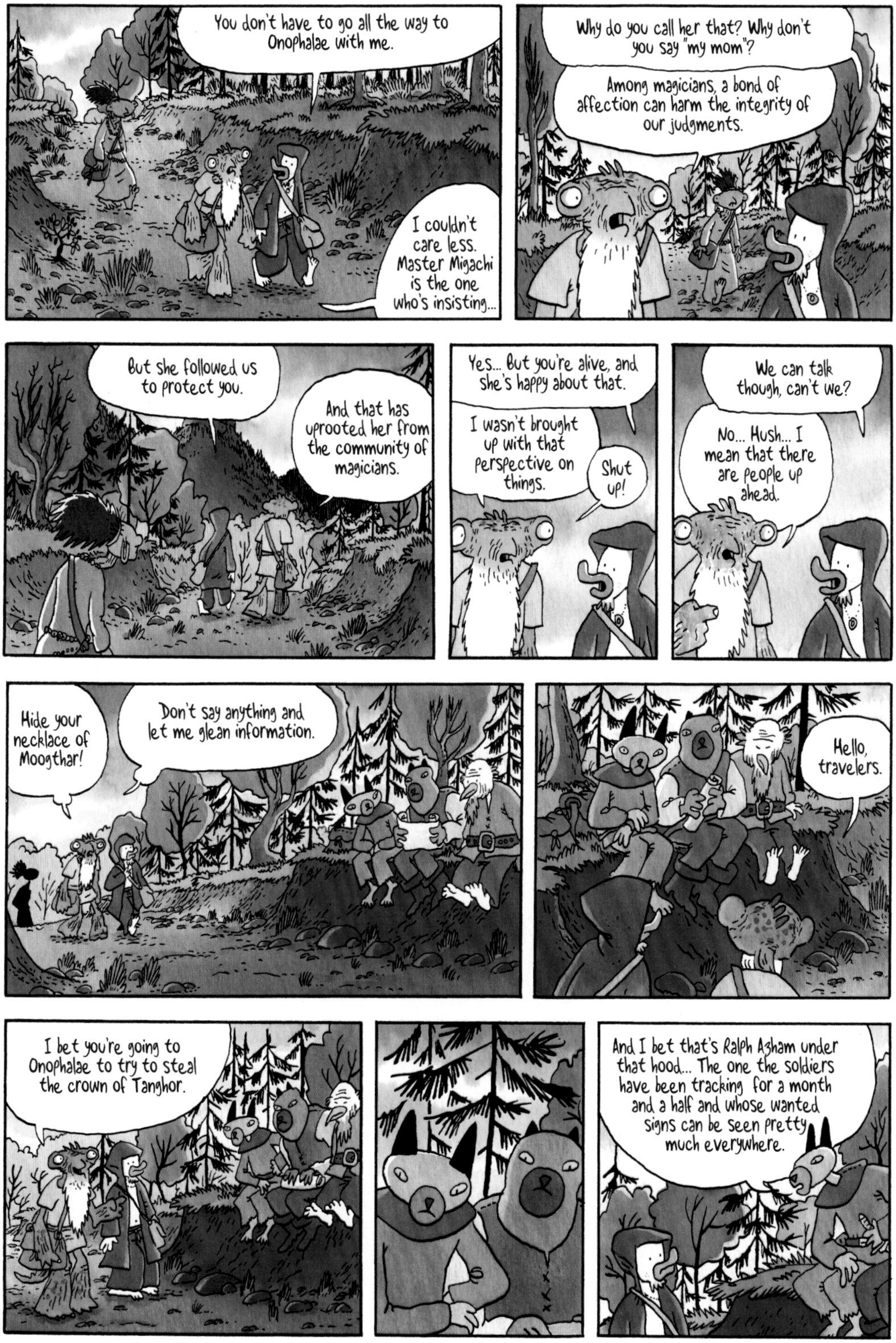
You don't have to go all the way to Onophalae with me.
I couldn't care less. Master Migachi is the one who's insisting...
Why do you call her that? Why don't you say "my mom"?
Among magicians, a bond of affection can harm the integrity of our judgments.
But she followed us to protect you.
And that has uprooted her from the community of magicians.
Yes... But you're alive, and she's happy about that.
I wasn't brought up with that perspective on things.
Shut up!
We can talk though, can't we?
No... Hush... I mean that there are people up ahead.
Hide your necklace of Moogthar!
Don't say anything and let me glean information.
Hello, travelers.
I bet you're going to Onophalae to try to steal the crown of Tanghor.
And I bet that's Ralph Azham under that hood... The one the soldiers have been tracking for a month and a half and whose wanted signs can be seen pretty much everywhere.

97

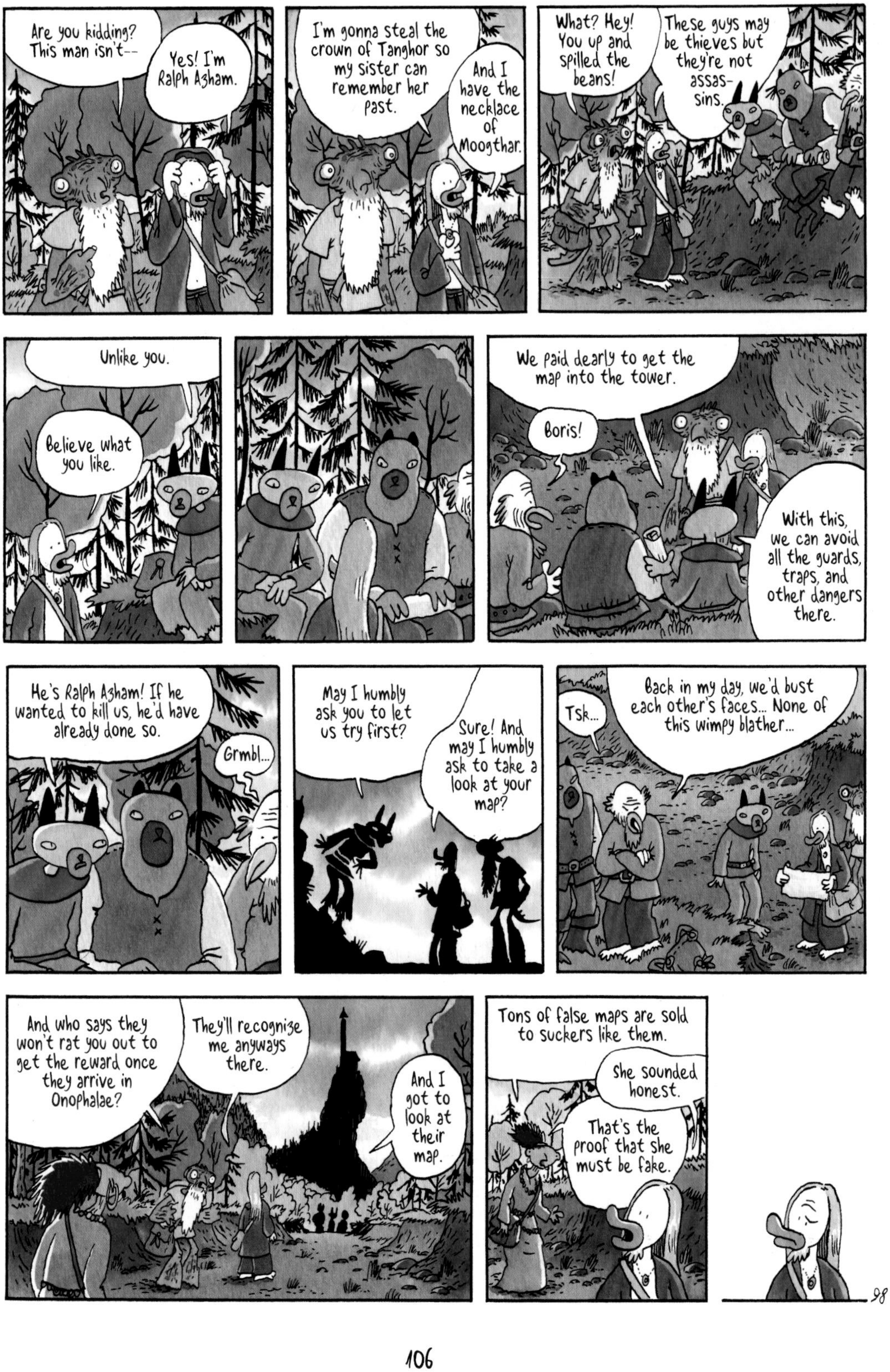
Are you kidding? This man isn't--
Yes! I'm Ralph Azham.
I'm gonna steal the crown of Tanghor so my sister can remember her past.
And I have the necklace of Moogthar.
What? Hey! You up and spilled the beans!
These guys may be thieves but they're not assas-sins.
Unlike you.
Believe what you like.
We paid dearly to get the map into the tower.
Boris!
With this, we can avoid all the guards, traps, and other dangers there.
He's Ralph Azham! If he wanted to kill us, he'd have already done so.
Grmbl...
May I humbly ask you to let us try first?
Sure! And may I humbly ask to take a look at your map?
Tsk...
Back in my day, we'd bust each other's faces... None of this wimpy blather...
And who says they won't rat you out to get the reward once they arrive in Onophalae?
They'll recognize me anyways there.
And I got to look at their map.
Tons of false maps are sold to suckers like them.
She sounded honest.
That's the proof that she must be fake.
98

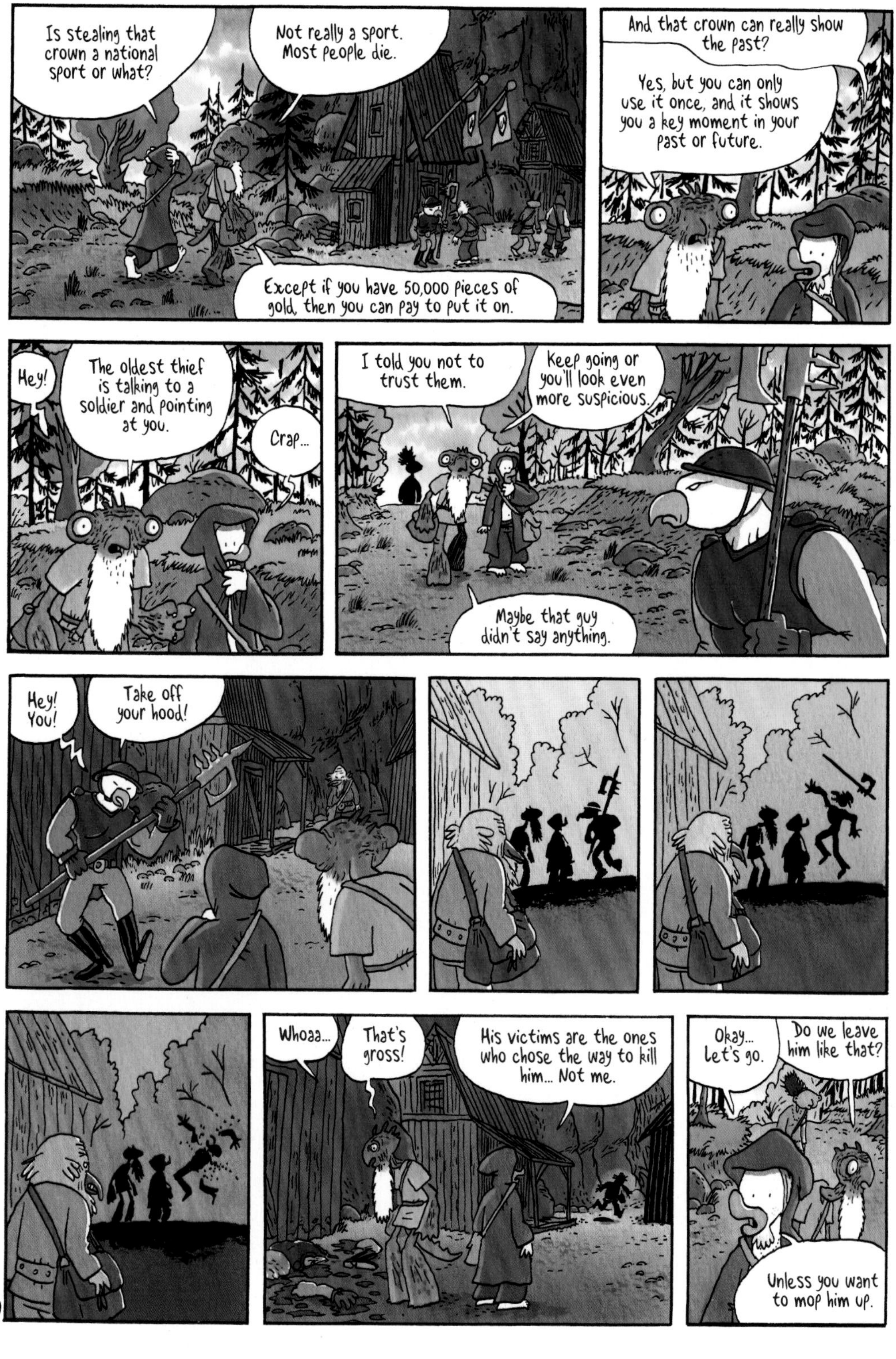

Is stealing that crown a national sport or what?
Not really a sport. Most people die.
Except if you have 50,000 pieces of gold, then you can pay to put it on.
And that crown can really show the past?
Yes, but you can only use it once, and it shows you a key moment in your past or future.
Hey!
The oldest thief is talking to a soldier and pointing at you.
Crap...
I told you not to trust them.
Keep going or you'll look even more suspicious.
Maybe that guy didn't say anything.
Hey! You!
Take off your hood!
Whoaa...
That's gross!
His victims are the ones who chose the way to kill him... Not me.
Okay... Let's go.
Do we leave him like that?
Unless you want to mop him up.

99

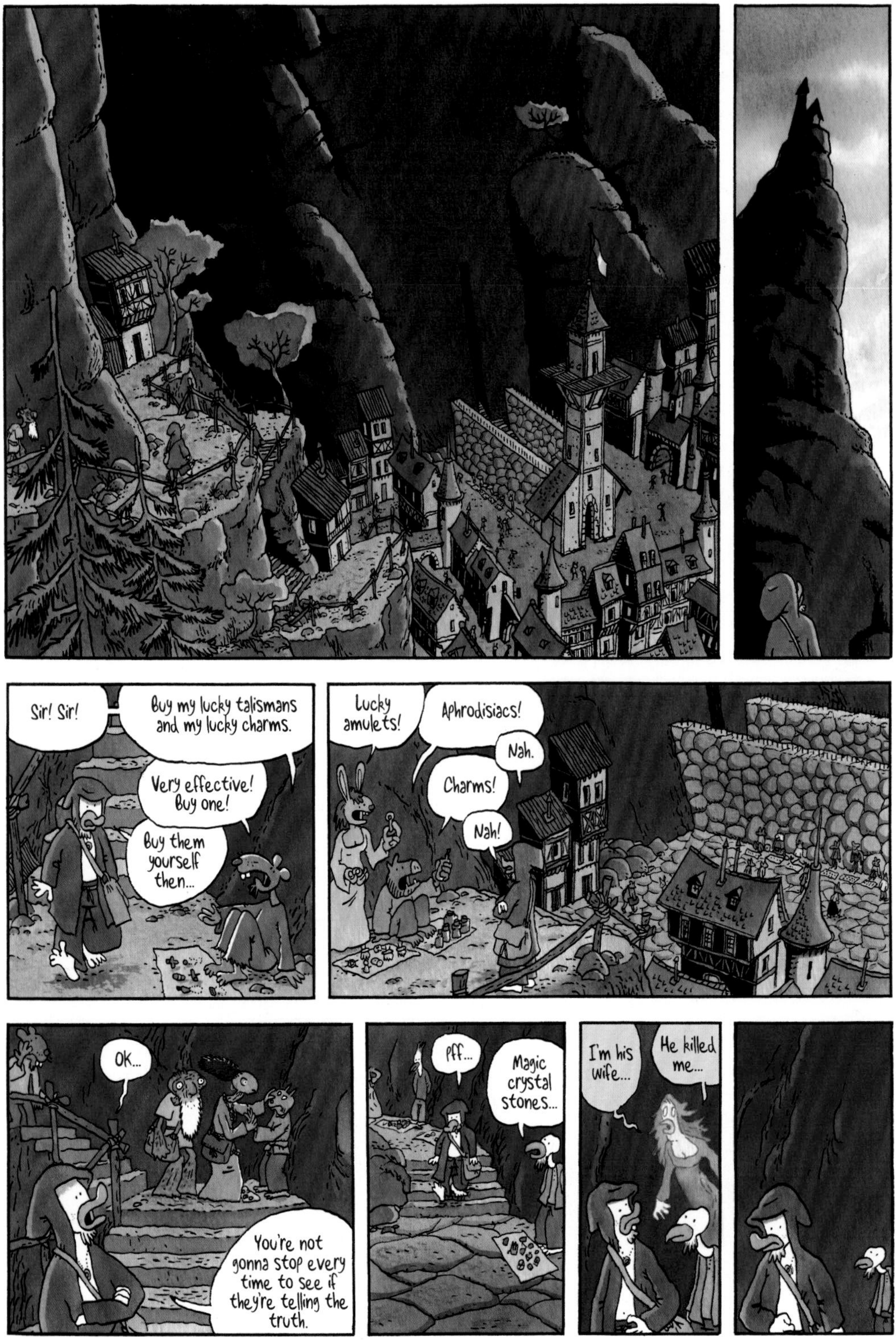
Sir! Sir!
Buy my lucky talismans and my lucky charms.
Very effective! Buy one!
Buy them yourself then...
Lucky amulets!
Aphrodisiacs!
Nah.
Charms!
Nah!
Ok...
You're not gonna stop every time to see if they're telling the truth.
Pff...
Magic crystal stones...
I'm his wife...
He killed me...

100

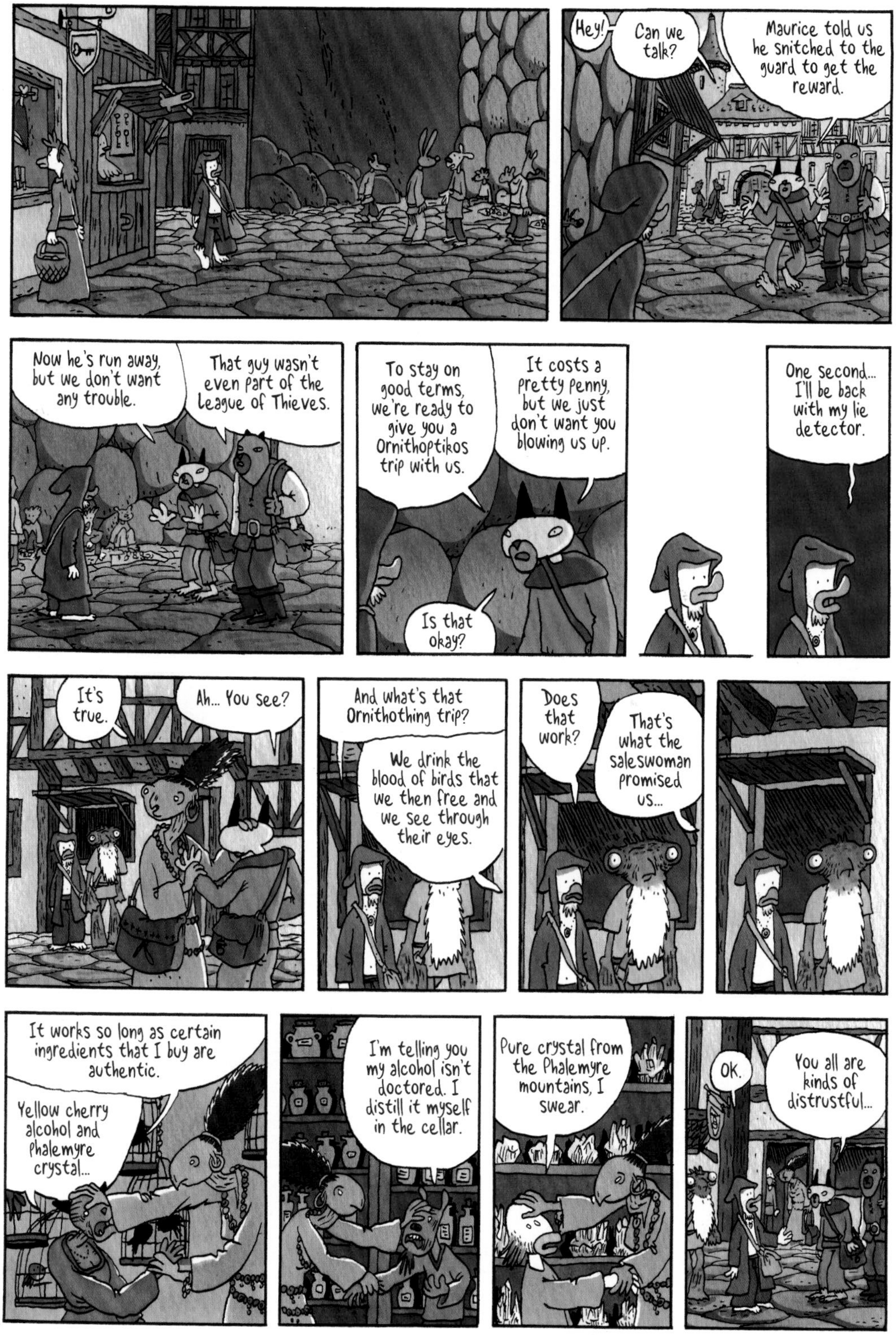
Hey!
Can we talk?
Maurice told us he snitched to the guard to get the reward.
Now he's run away, but we don't want any trouble.
That guy wasn't even part of the League of Thieves.
To stay on good terms, we're ready to give you a Ornithoptikos trip with us.
It costs a pretty penny, but we just don't want you blowing us up.
Is that okay?
One second... I'll be back with my lie detector.
It's true.
Ah... You see?
And what's that Ornithothing trip?
We drink the blood of birds that we then free and we see through their eyes.
Does that work?
That's what the saleswoman promised us...
It works so long as certain ingredients that I buy are authentic.
Yellow cherry alcohol and Phalemyre crystal...
I'm telling you my alcohol isn't doctored. I distill it myself in the cellar.
Pure crystal from the Phalemyre mountains, I swear.
OK.
You all are kinds of distrustful...

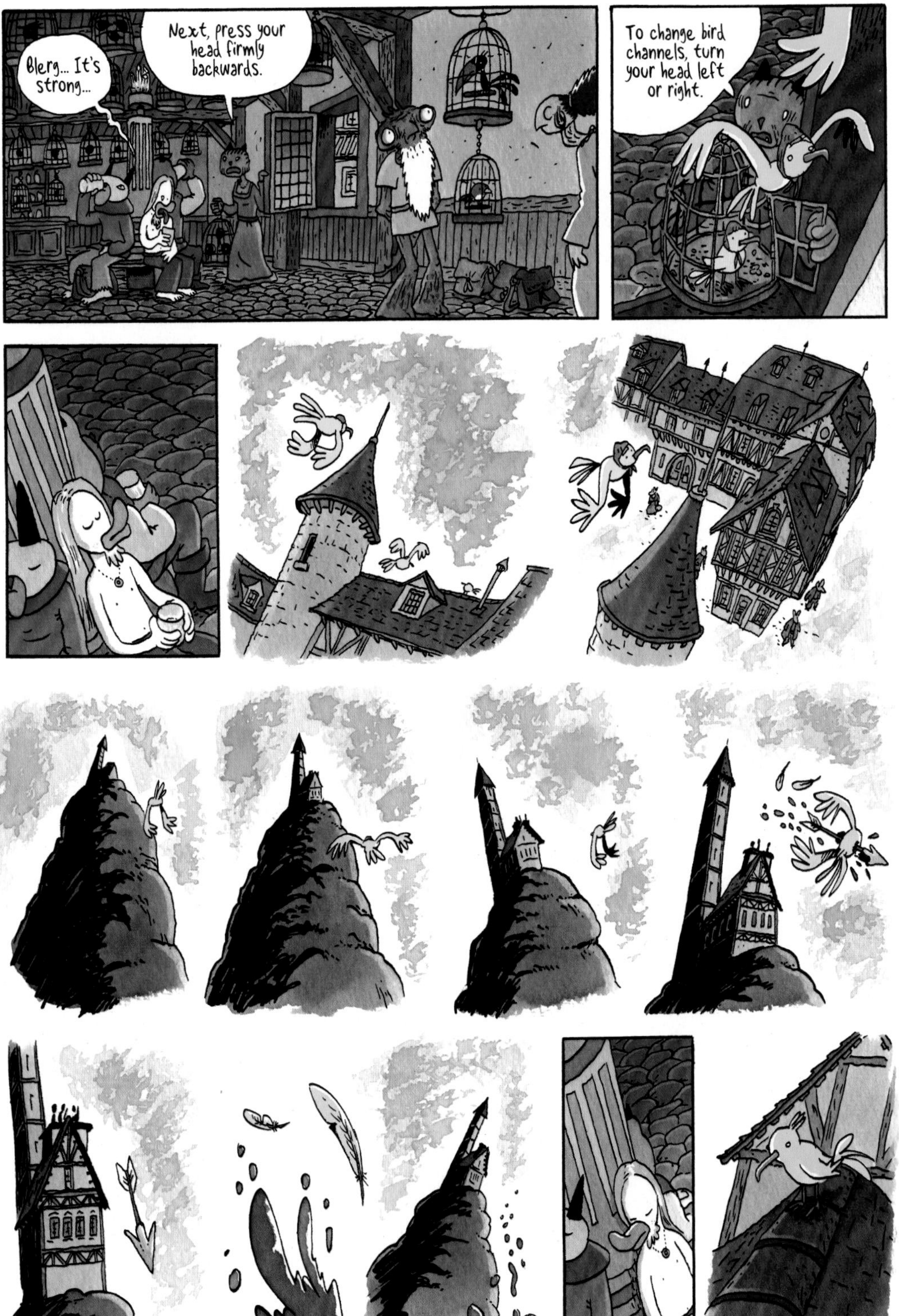
Blerg... It's strong...
Next, press your head firmly backwards.
To change bird channels, turn your head left or right.
lo2

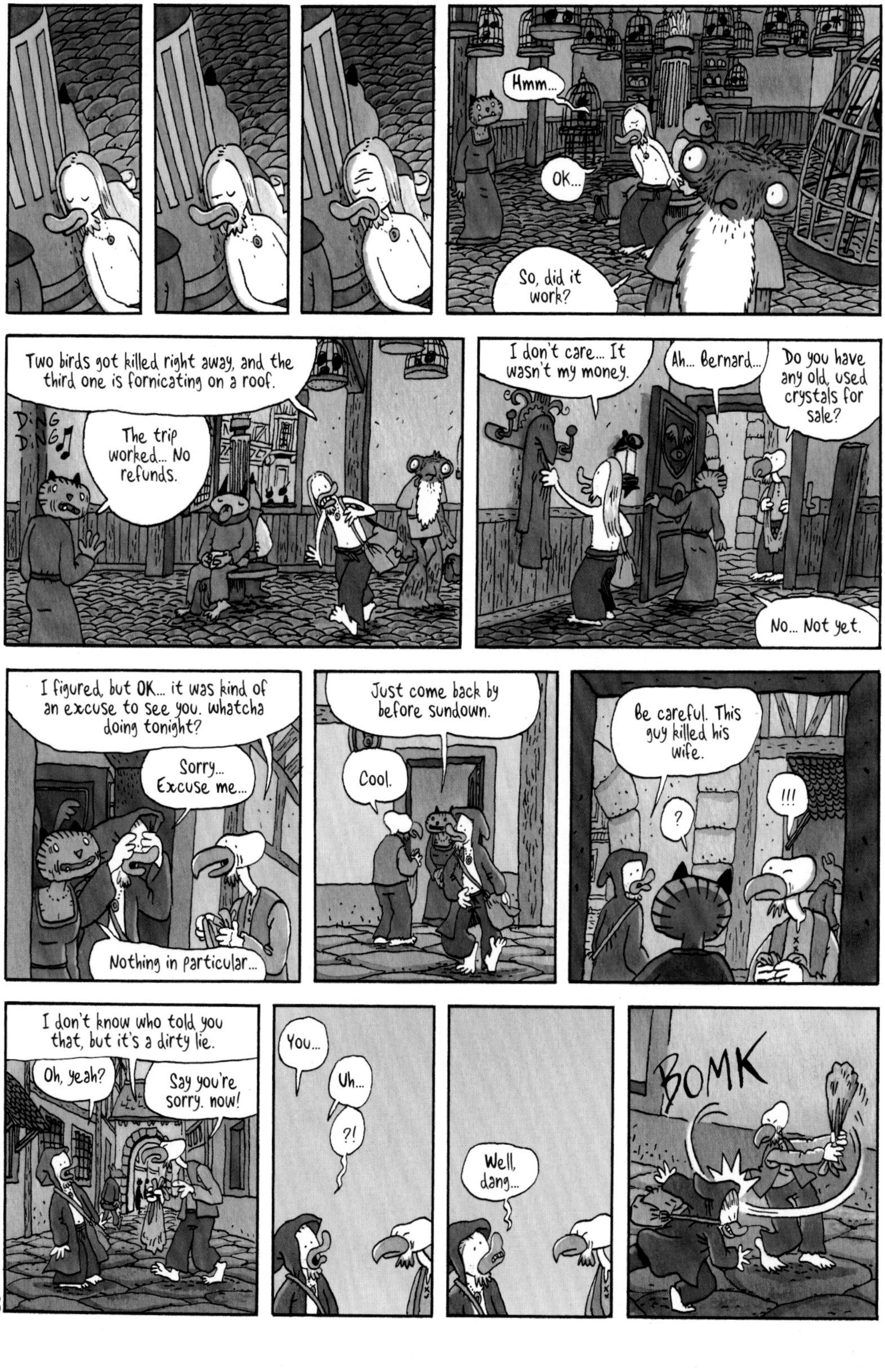
Hmm...
OK...
So, did it work?
Two birds got killed right away, and the third one is fornicating on a roof.
DING DING
The trip worked... No refunds.
I don't care... It wasn't my money.
Ah... Bernard...
Do you have any old, used crystals for sale?
No... Not yet.
I figured, but OK... it was kind of an excuse to see you. Whatcha doing tonight?
Sorry... Excuse me...
Nothing in particular...
Just come back by before sundown.
Cool.
Be careful. This guy killed his wife.
?
!!!
I don't know who told you that, but it's a dirty lie.
Oh, yeah?
Say you're sorry. now!
You...
Uh...
?!
Well, dang...
BOMK

103

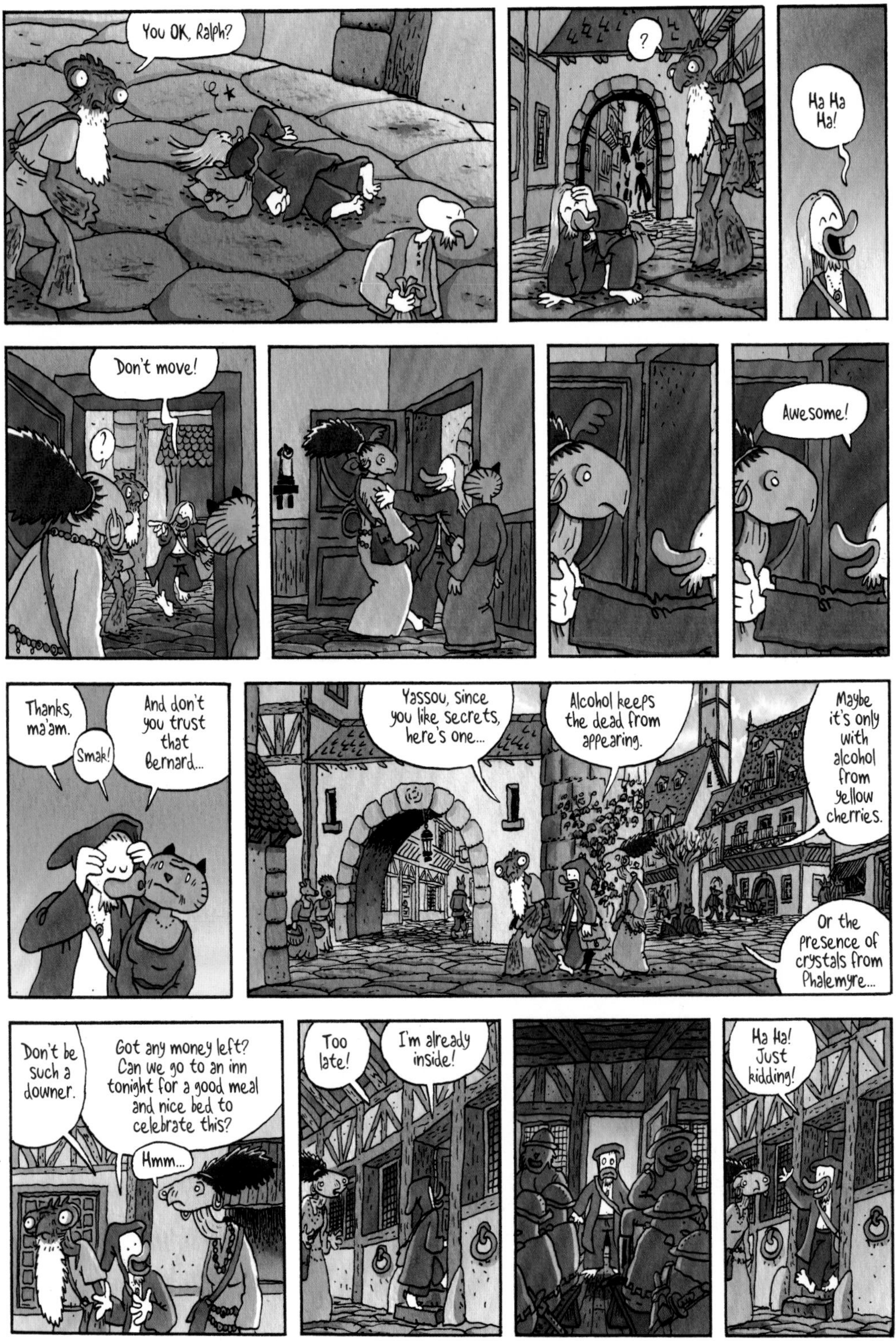
You OK, Ralph?
?
Ha Ha Ha!
Don't move!
?
Awesome!
Thanks, ma'am.
Smak!
And don't you trust that Bernard...
Yassou, since you like secrets, here's one...
Alcohol keeps the dead from appearing.
Maybe it's only with alcohol from yellow cherries.
Or the presence of crystals from Phalemyre...
Don't be such a downer.
Got any money left? Can we go to an inn tonight for a good meal and nice bed to celebrate this?
Hmm...
Too late!
I'm already inside!
Ha Ha! Just kidding!

104

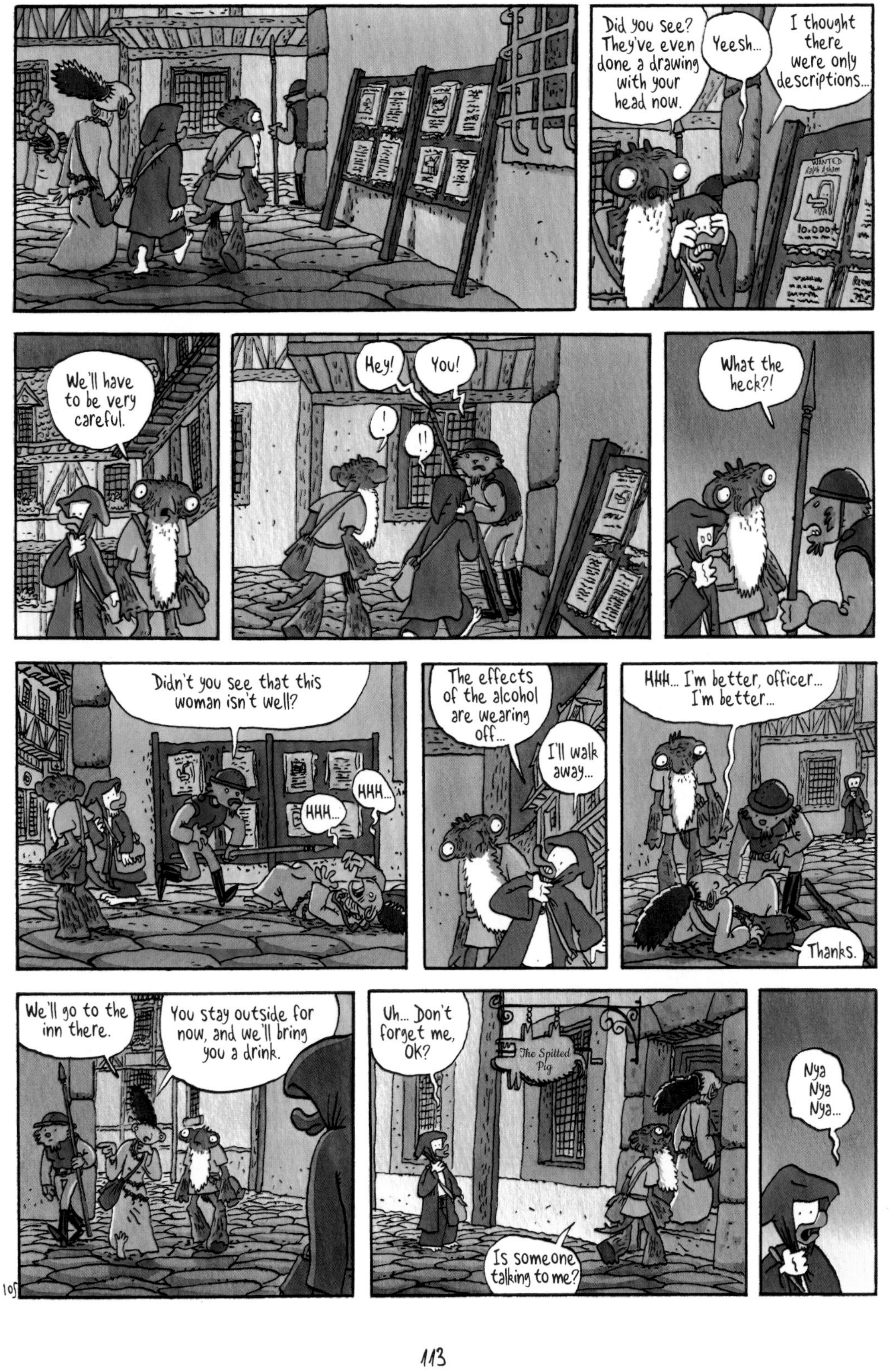
Did you see? They've even done a drawing with your head now.
Yeesh...
I thought there were only descriptions...
WANTED
Ralph Asham
10.000
We'll have to be very careful.
Hey!
You!
!
!!
What the heck?!
Didn't you see that this woman isn't well?
HHH...
HHH...
The effects of the alcohol are wearing off...
I'll walk away...
HHH... I'm better, officer... I'm better...
Thanks.
We'll go to the inn there.
You stay outside for now, and we'll bring you a drink.
Uh... Don't forget me, OK?
The Spitted Pig
Is someone talking to me?
Nya Nya Nya...

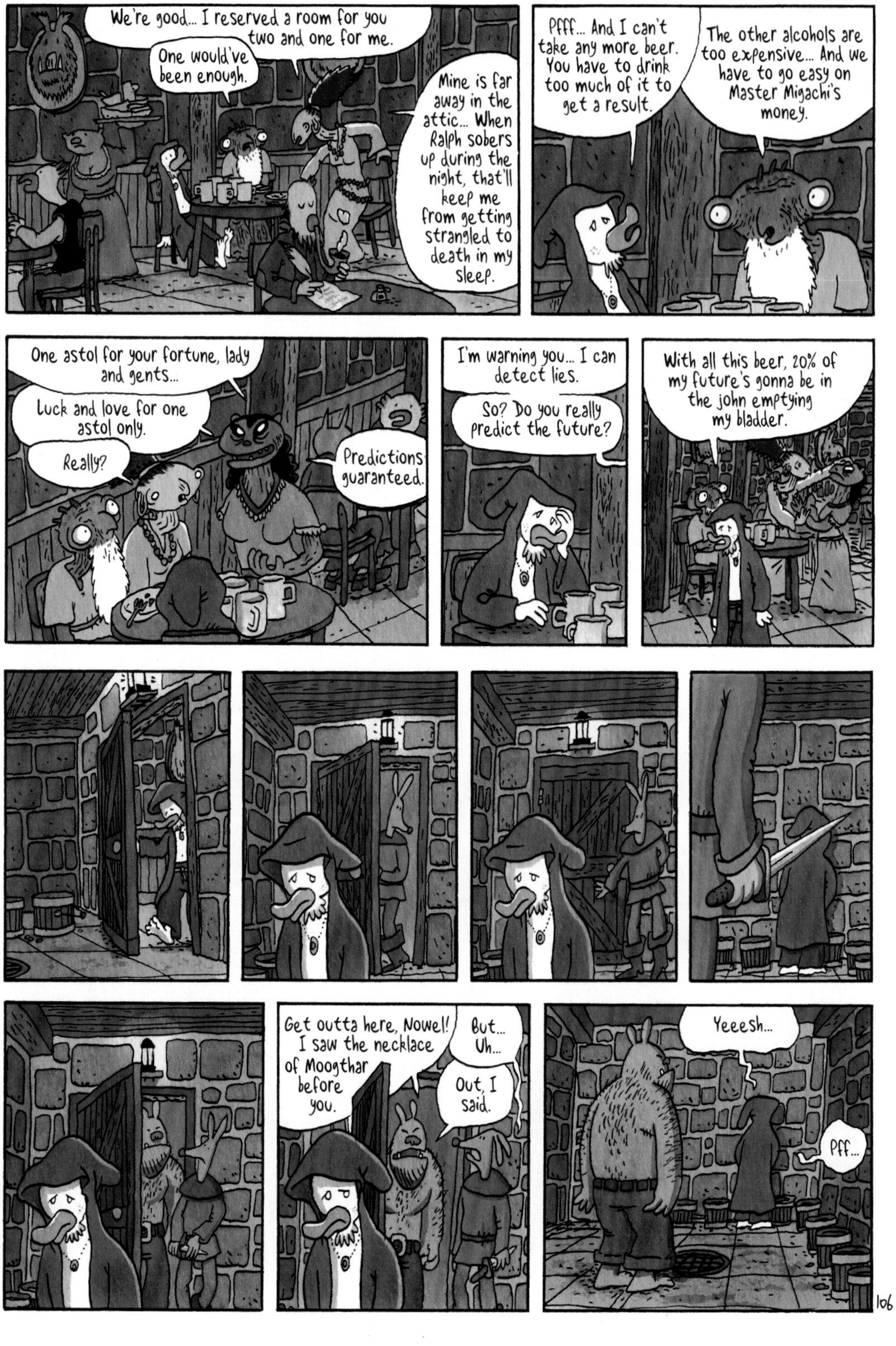
We're good... I reserved a room for you two and one for me.
One would've been enough.
Mine is far away in the attic... When Ralph sobers up during the night, that'll keep me from getting strangled to death in my sleep.
Pfff... And I can't take any more beer. You have to drink too much of it to get a result.
The other alcohols are too expensive... And we have to go easy on Master Migachi's money.
One astol for your fortune, lady and gents...
Luck and love for one astol only.
Really?
Predictions guaranteed.
I'm warning you... I can detect lies.
So? Do you really predict the future?
With all this beer, 20% of my future's gonna be in the john emptying my bladder.
Get outta here, Nowel! I saw the necklace of Moogthar before you.
But... Uh...
Out, I said.
Yeeesh...
Pff...
106

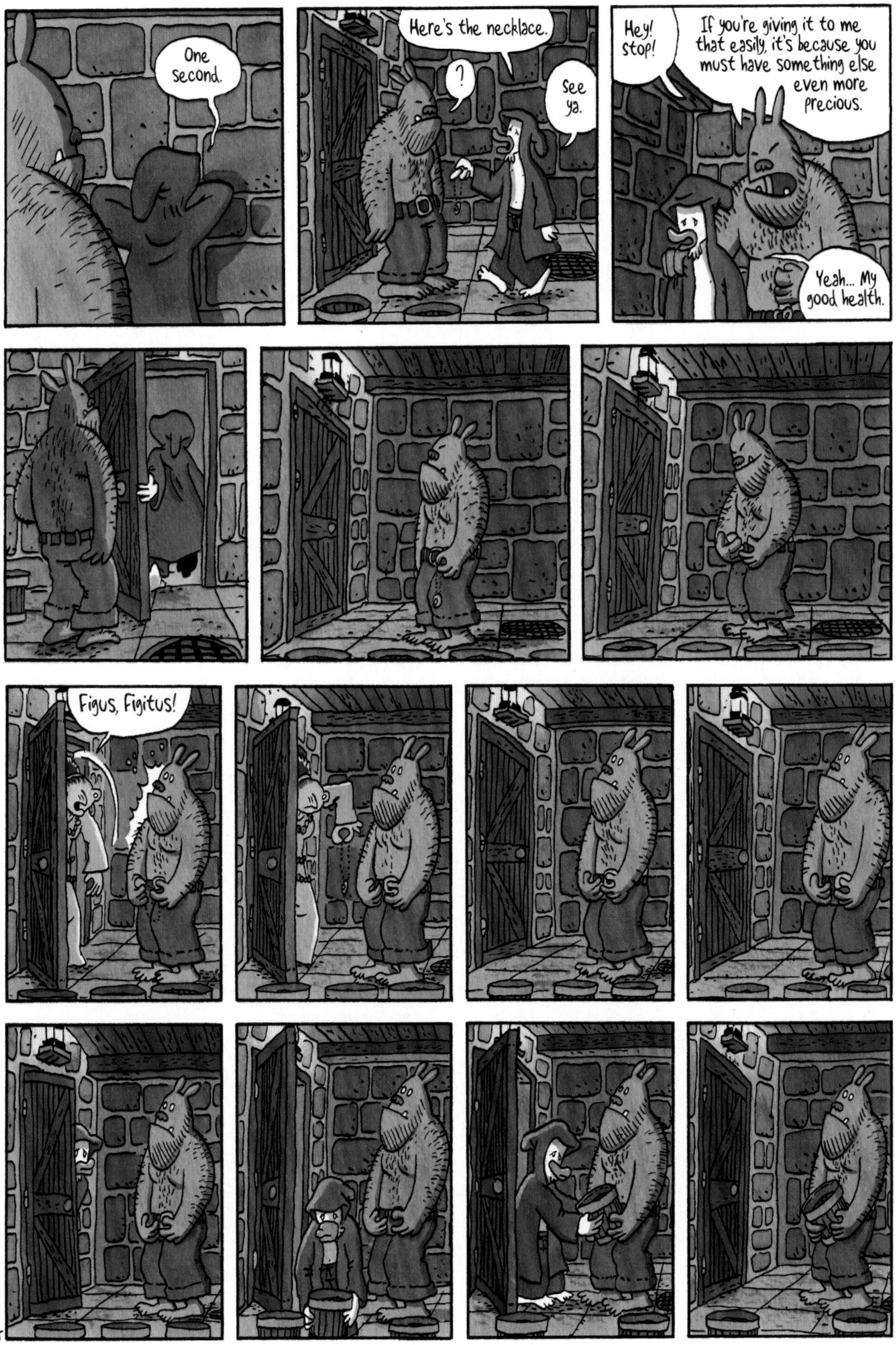
One second.
Here's the necklace.
?
See ya.
Hey! stop!
If you're giving it to me that easily, it's because you must have something else even more precious.
Yeah... My good health.
Figus, Figitus!

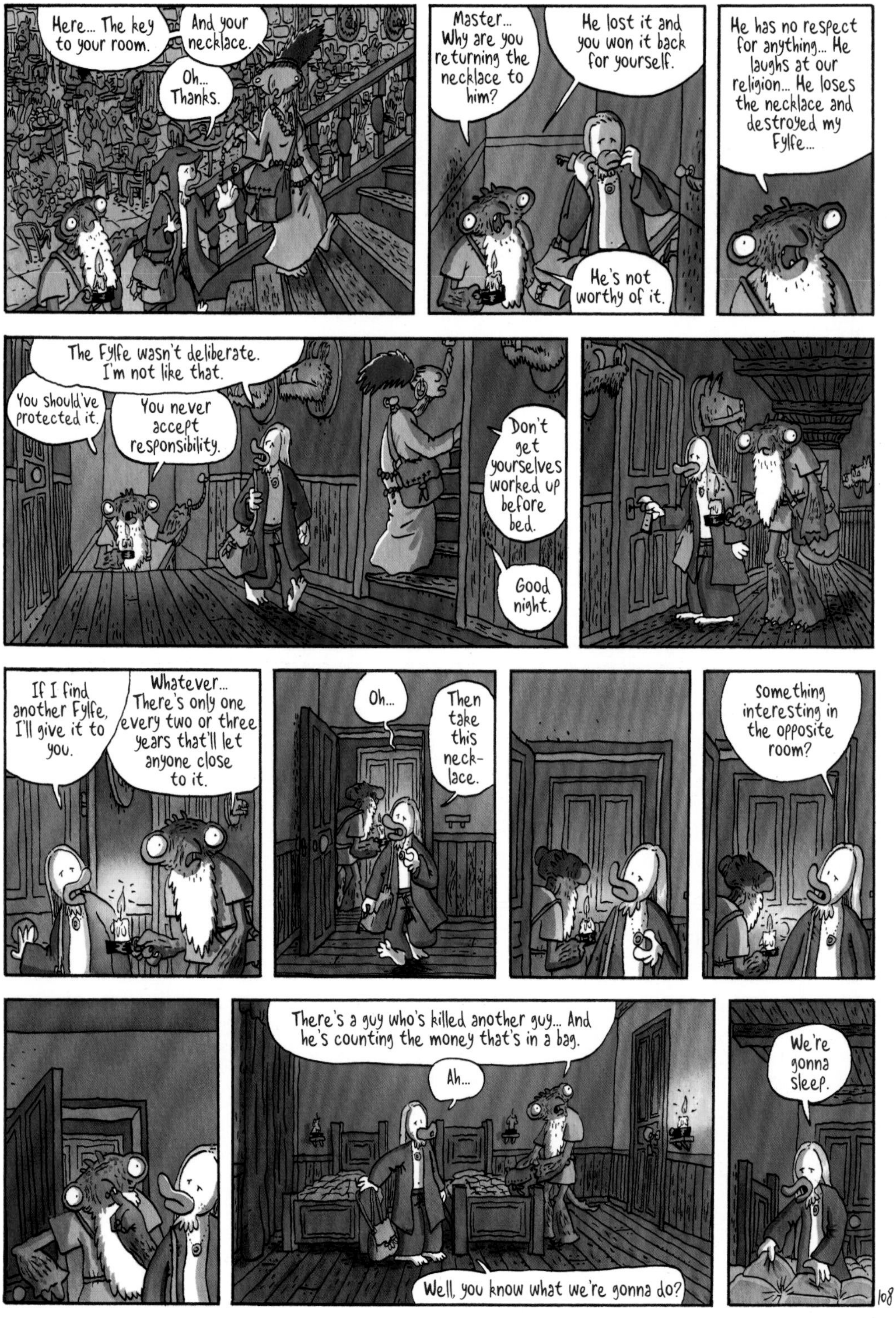
Here... The key to your room.
And your necklace.
Oh... Thanks.
Master... Why are you returning the necklace to him?
He lost it and you won it back for yourself.
He's not worthy of it.
He has no respect for anything... He laughs at our religion... He loses the necklace and destroyed my Fylfe...
The Fylfe wasn't deliberate. I'm not like that.
You should've protected it.
You never accept responsibility.
Don't get yourselves worked up before bed.
Good night.
If I find another Fylfe, I'll give it to you.
Whatever... There's only one every two or three years that'll let anyone close to it.
Oh...
Then take this neck-lace.
something interesting in the opposite room?
There's a guy who's killed another guy... And he's counting the money that's in a bag.
Ah...
Well, you know what we're gonna do?
We're gonna sleep.
108

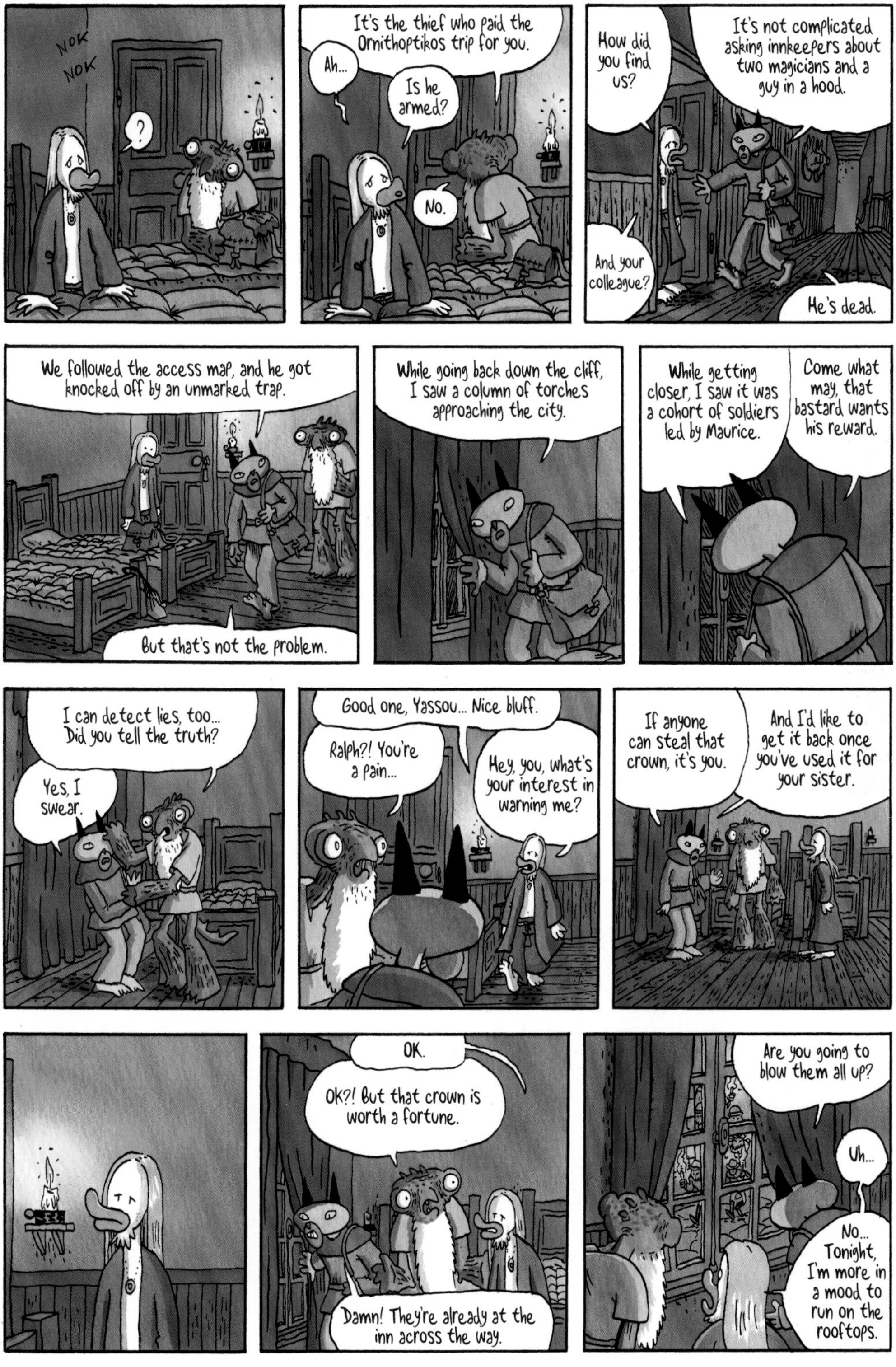
NOK NOK
?
It's the thief who paid the Ornithoptikos trip for you.
Ah...
Is he armed?
No.
How did you find us?
It's not complicated asking innkeepers about two magicians and a guy in a hood.
And your colleague?
He's dead.
We followed the access map, and he got knocked off by an unmarked trap.
But that's not the problem.
While going back down the cliff, I saw a column of torches approaching the city.
While getting closer, I saw it was a cohort of soldiers led by Maurice.
Come what may, that bastard wants his reward.
I can detect lies, too... Did you tell the truth?
Yes, I swear.
Good one, Yassou... Nice bluff.
Ralph?! You're a pain...
Hey, you, what's your interest in warning me?
If anyone can steal that crown, it's you.
And I'd like to get it back once you've used it for your sister.
OK.
OK?! But that crown is worth a fortune.
Damn! They're already at the inn across the way.
Are you going to blow them all up?
Uh...
No... Tonight, I'm more in a mood to run on the rooftops.

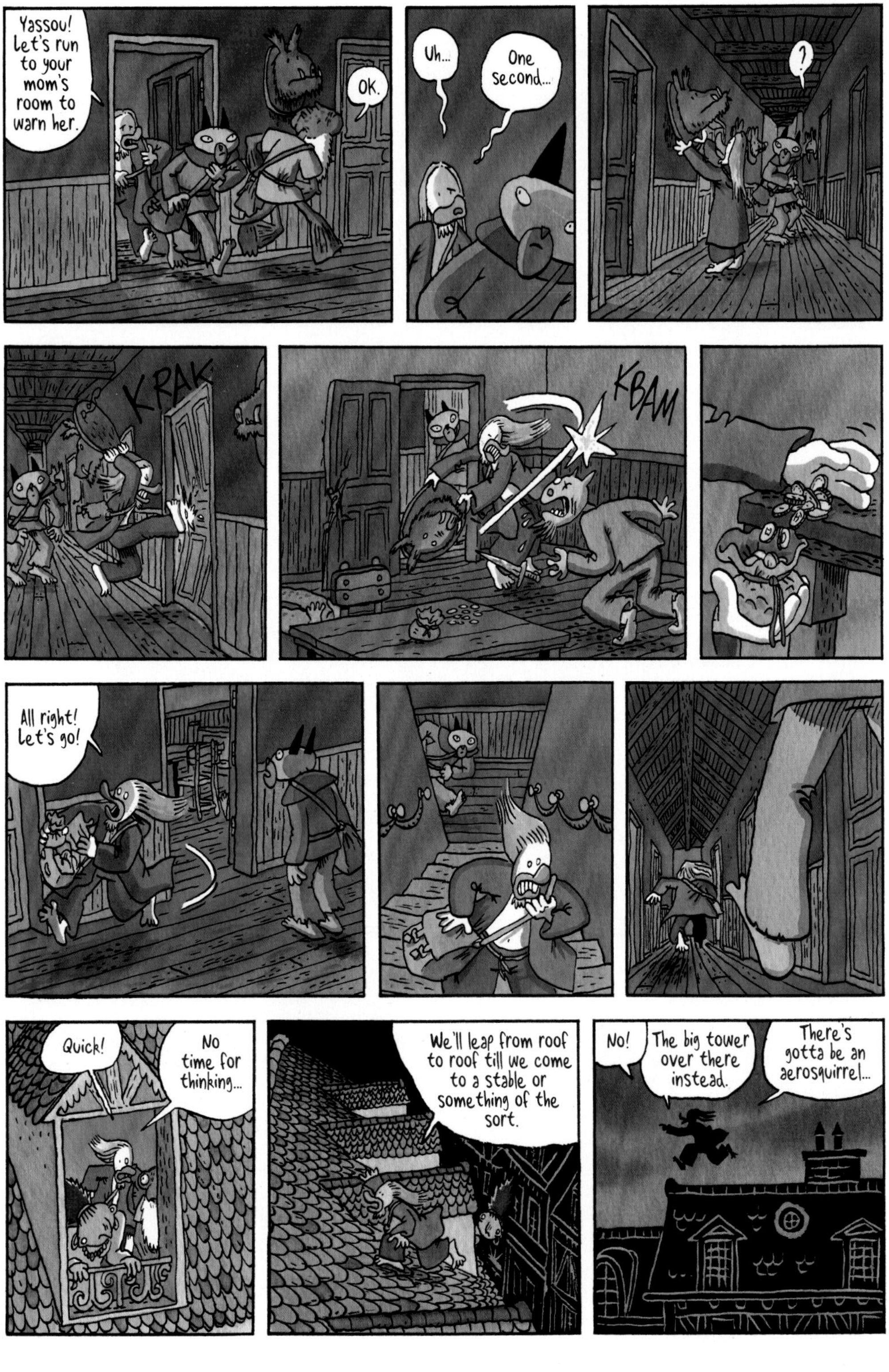
Yassou! Let's run to your mom's room to warn her.
OK.
Uh...
One second...
?
KRAK
KBAM
All right! Let's go!
Quick!
No time for thinking...
We'll leap from roof to roof till we come to a stable or something of the sort.
No!
The big tower over there instead.
There's gotta be an aerosquirrel...
110

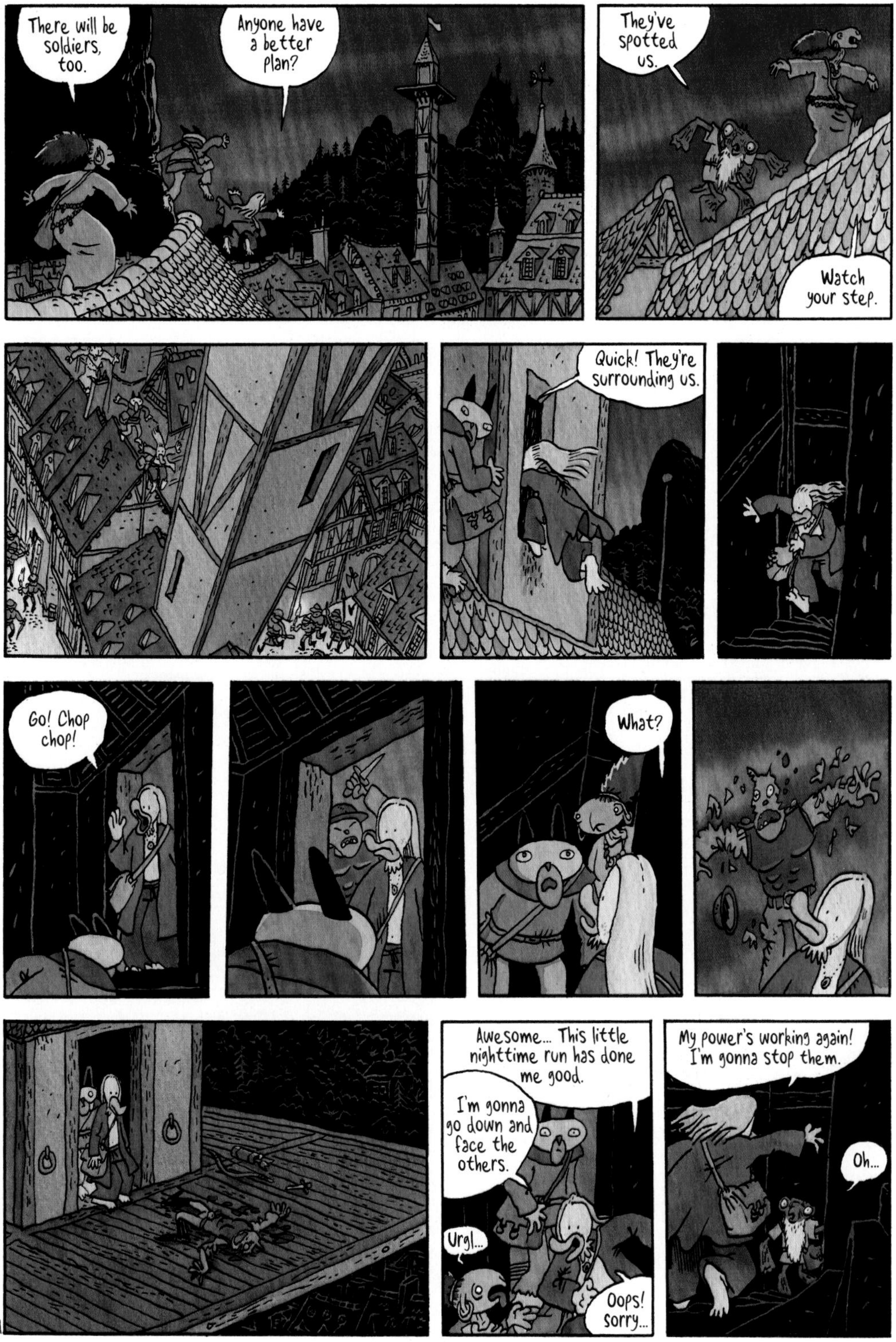
There will be soldiers, too.
Anyone have a better plan?
They've spotted us.
Watch your step.
Quick! They're surrounding us.
Go! Chop chop!
What?
Awesome... This little nighttime run has done me good.
I'm gonna go down and face the others.
Urgl...
Oops! sorry...
My power's working again! I'm gonna stop them.
Oh...

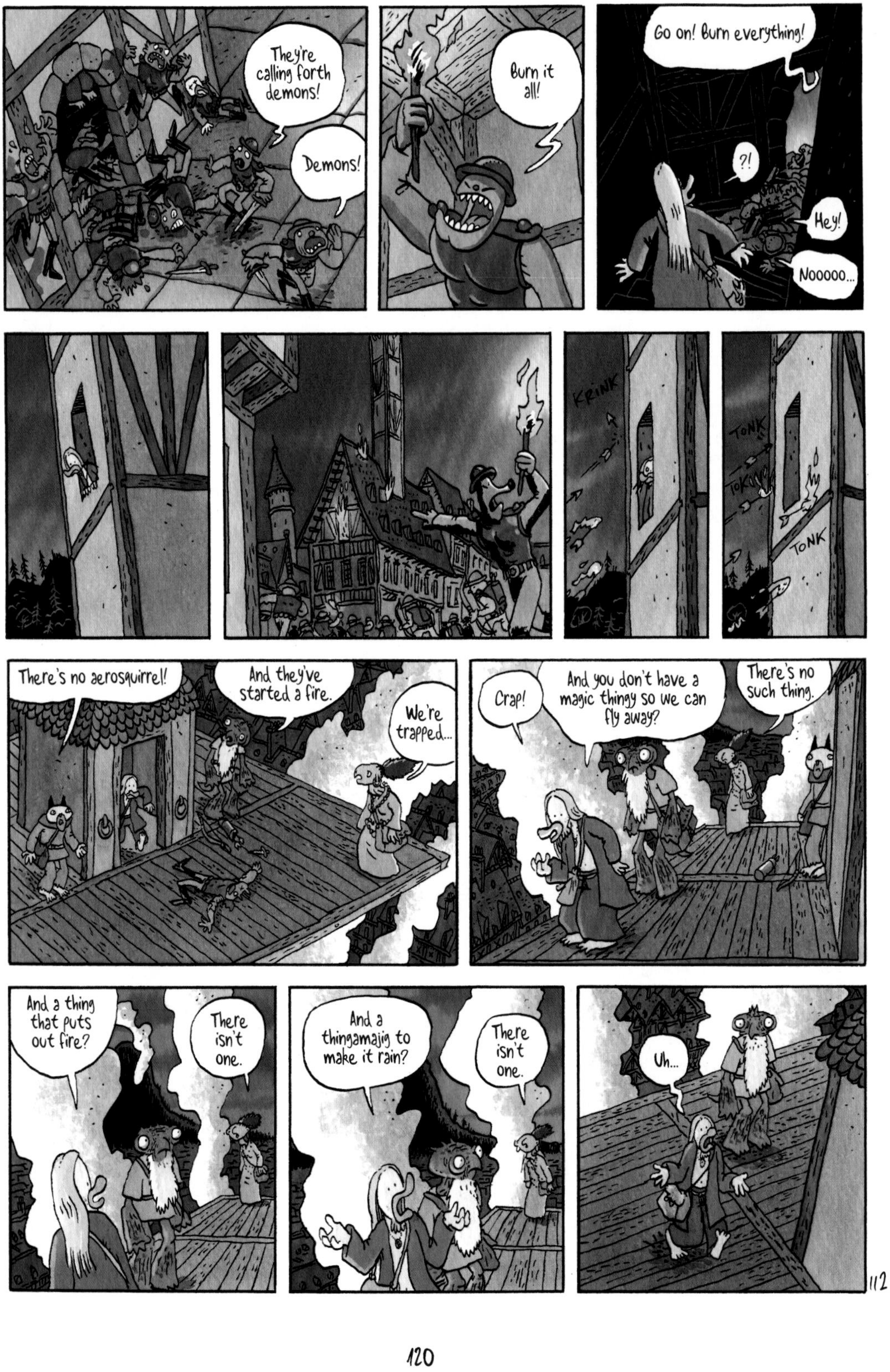
They're calling forth demons!
Demons!
Burn it all!
Go on! Burn everything!
?!
Hey!
Nooooo...
KRINK
TONK
TOK
TONK
There's no aerosquirrel!
And they've started a fire.
We're trapped...
Crap!
And you don't have a magic thingy so we can fly away?
There's no such thing.
And a thing that puts out fire?
There isn't one.
And a thingamajig to make it rain?
There isn't one.
Uh...

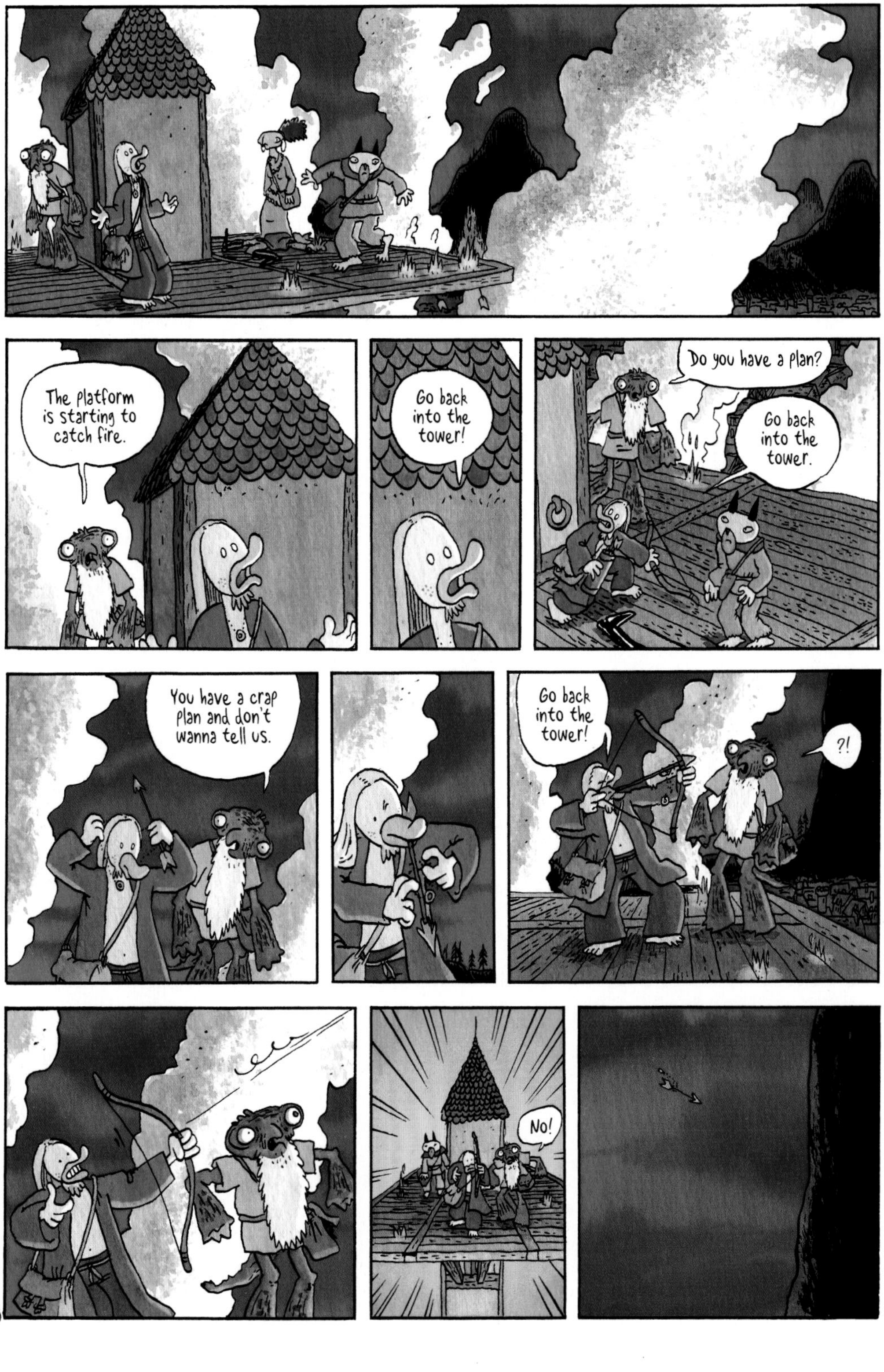
The platform is starting to catch fire.
Go back into the tower!
Do you have a plan?
Go back into the tower.
You have a crap plan and don't wanna tell us.
Go back into the tower!
?!
No!

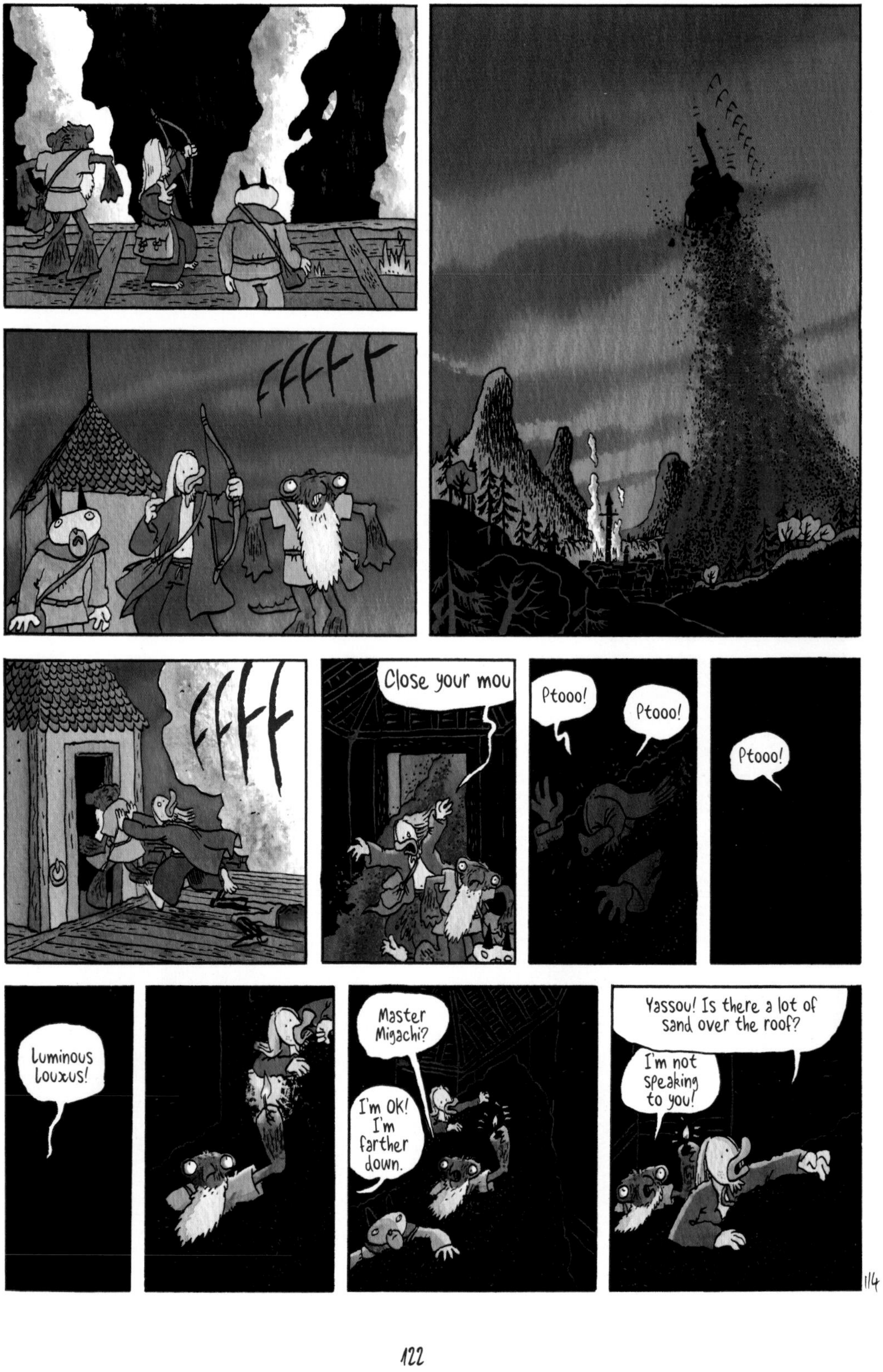
FFFFFF
FFFFF
FFFF
Close your mou
Ptooo!
Ptooo!
Ptooo!
Luminous Louxus!
Master Migachi?
I'm OK! I'm farther down.
Yassou! Is there a lot of sand over the roof?
I'm not speaking to you!
114

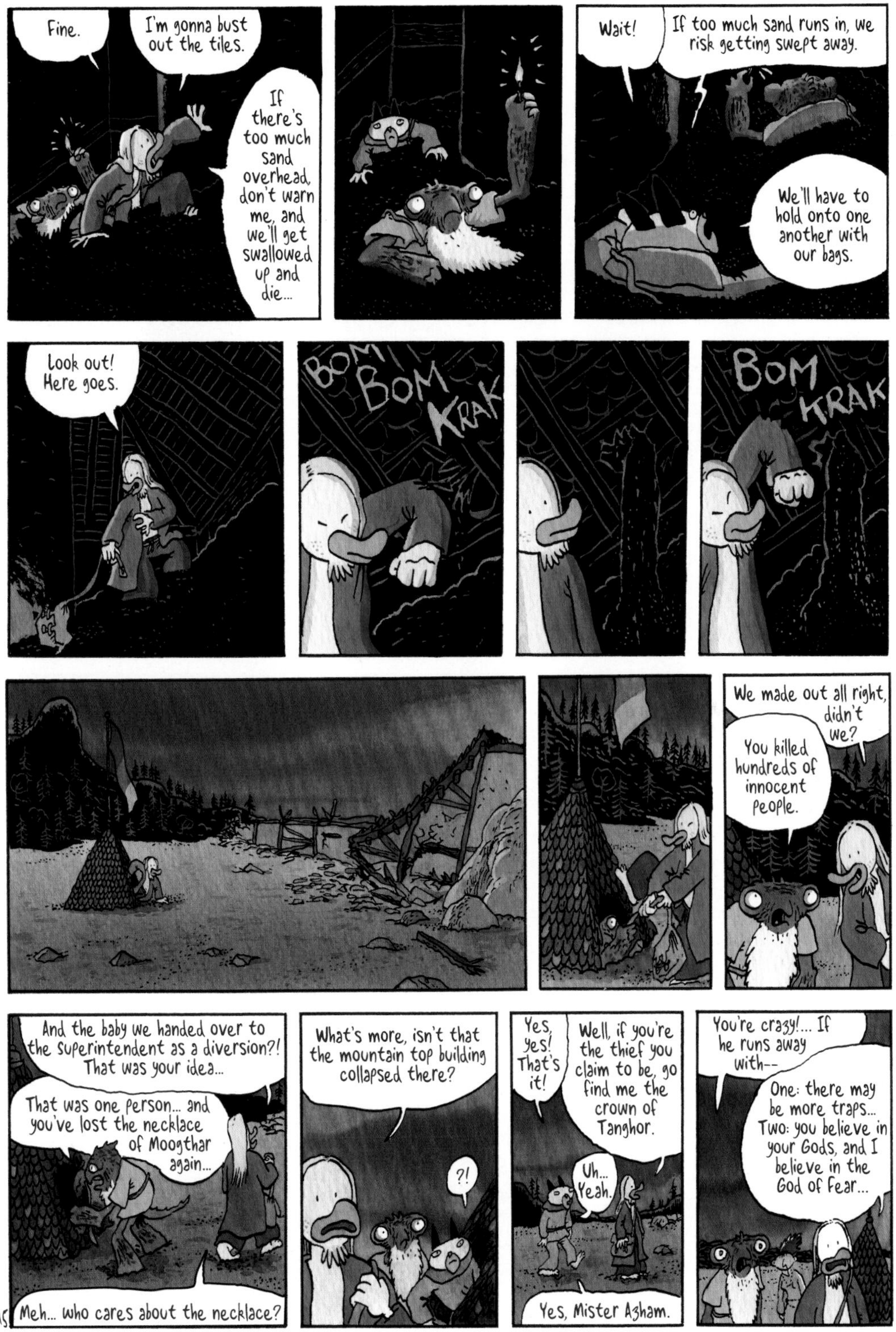

Fine.
I'm gonna bust out the tiles.
If there's too much sand overhead, don't warn me, and we'll get swallowed up and die...
Wait!
If too much sand runs in, we risk getting swept away.
We'll have to hold onto one another with our bags.
Look out! Here goes.
BOM BOM KRAK
BOM KRAK
We made out all right, didn't we?
You killed hundreds of innocent people.
And the baby we handed over to the superintendent as a diversion?! That was your idea...
That was one person... and you've lost the necklace of Moogthar again...
Meh... who cares about the necklace?
What's more, isn't that the mountain top building collapsed there?
?!
Yes, yes! That's it!
Well, if you're the thief you claim to be, go find me the crown of Tanghor.
Uh... Yeah.
Yes, Mister Azham.
You're crazy!... If he runs away with--
One: there may be more traps... Two: you believe in your Gods, and I believe in the God of Fear...

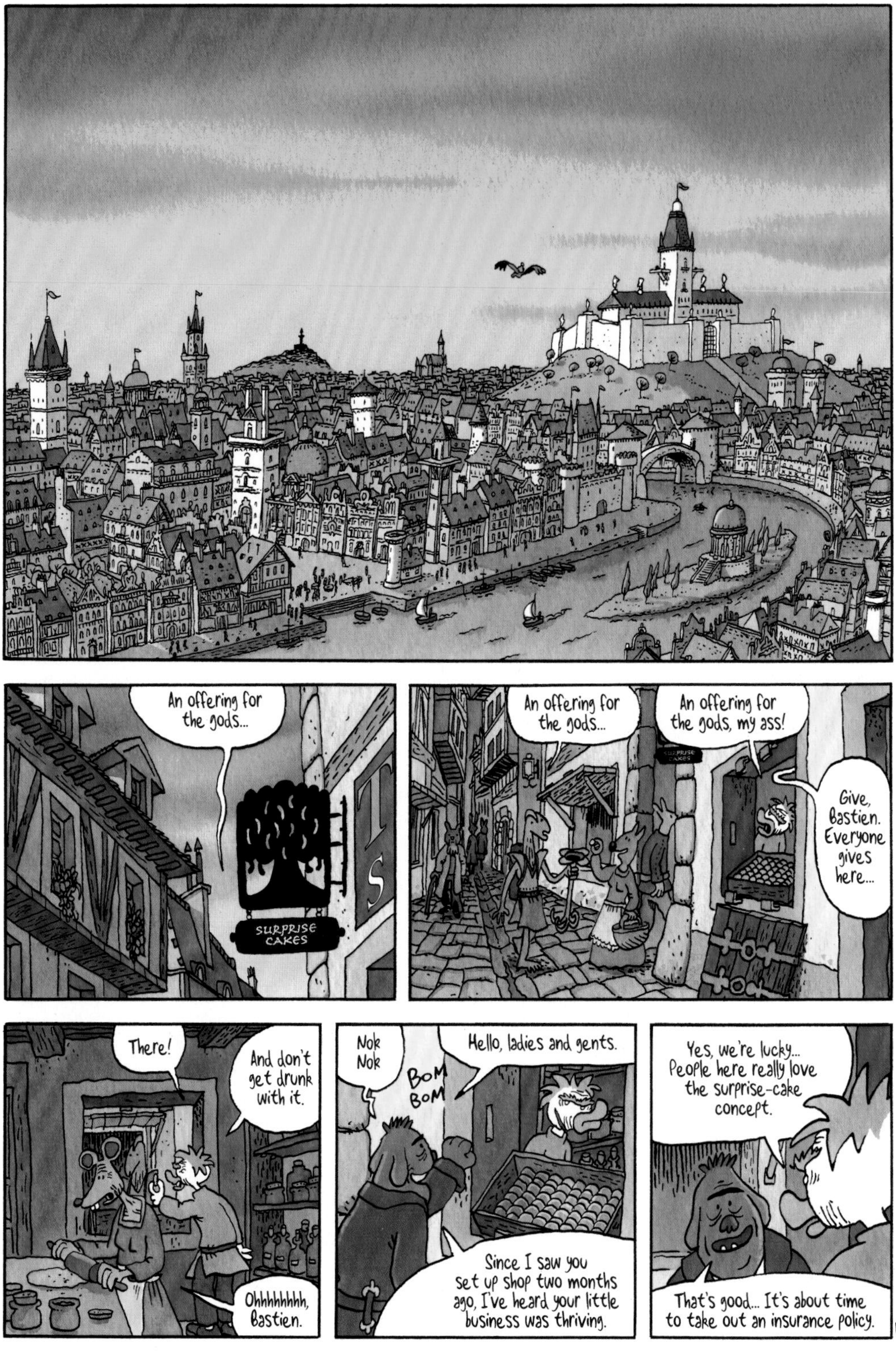
SURPRISE CAKES
An offering for the gods...
An offering for the gods...
An offering for the gods, my ass!
SURPRISE CAKES
Give, Bastien. Everyone gives here...
There!
And don't get drunk with it.
Ohhhhhhhh, Bastien.
Nok Nok
BOM BOM
Hello, ladies and gents.
Since I saw you set up shop two months ago, I've heard your little business was thriving.
Yes, we're lucky... People here really love the surprise-cake concept.
That's good... It's about time to take out an insurance policy.

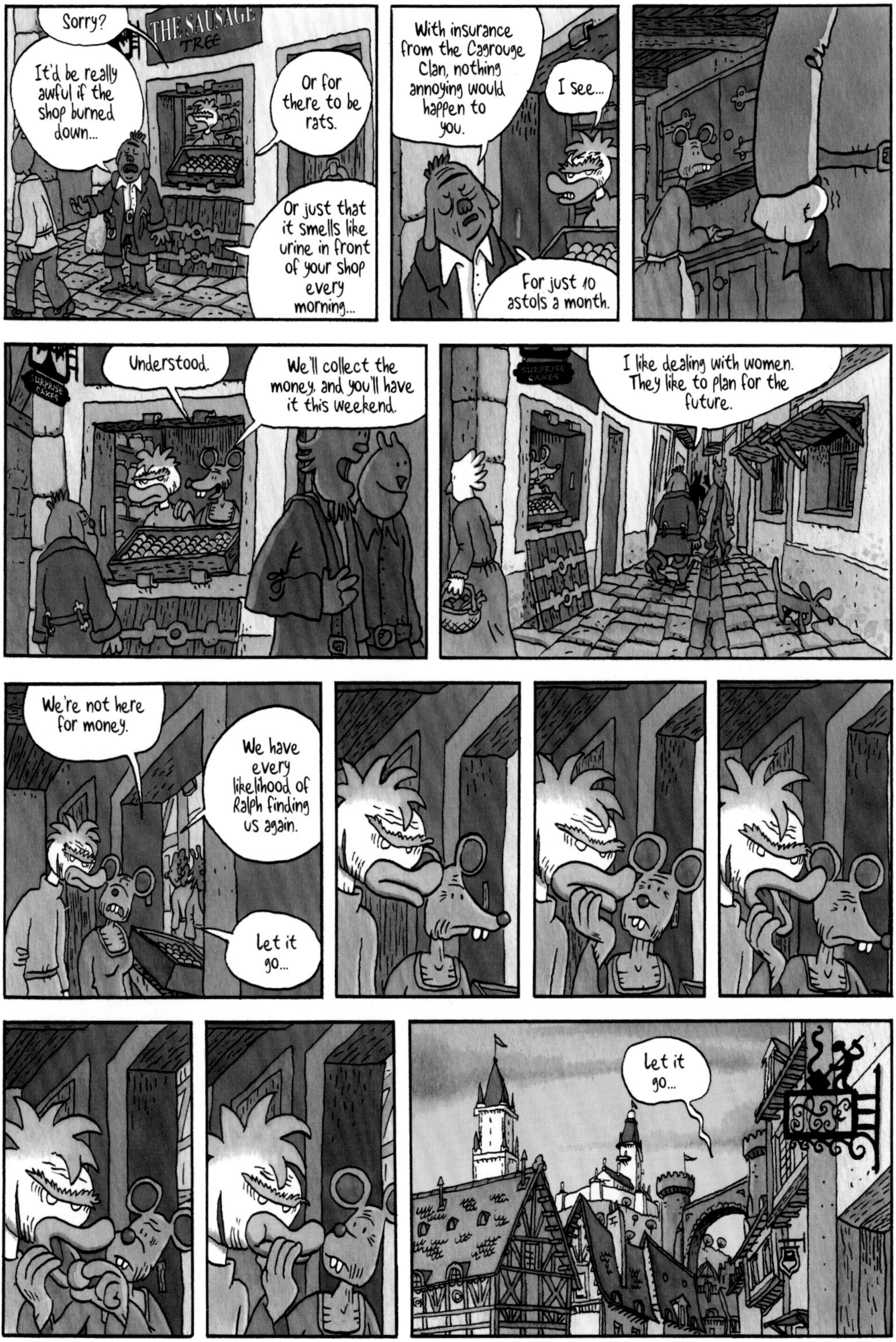
THE SAUSAGE TREE
Sorry?
It'd be really awful if the shop burned down...
Or for there to be rats.
Or just that it smells like urine in front of your shop every morning...
With insurance from the Cagrouge Clan, nothing annoying would happen to you.
I see...
For just 10 astols a month.
SURPRISE CAKES
Understood.
We'll collect the money, and you'll have it this weekend.
SURPRISE CAKES
I like dealing with women. They like to plan for the future.
We're not here for money.
We have every likelihood of Ralph finding us again.
Let it go...
Let it go...
117

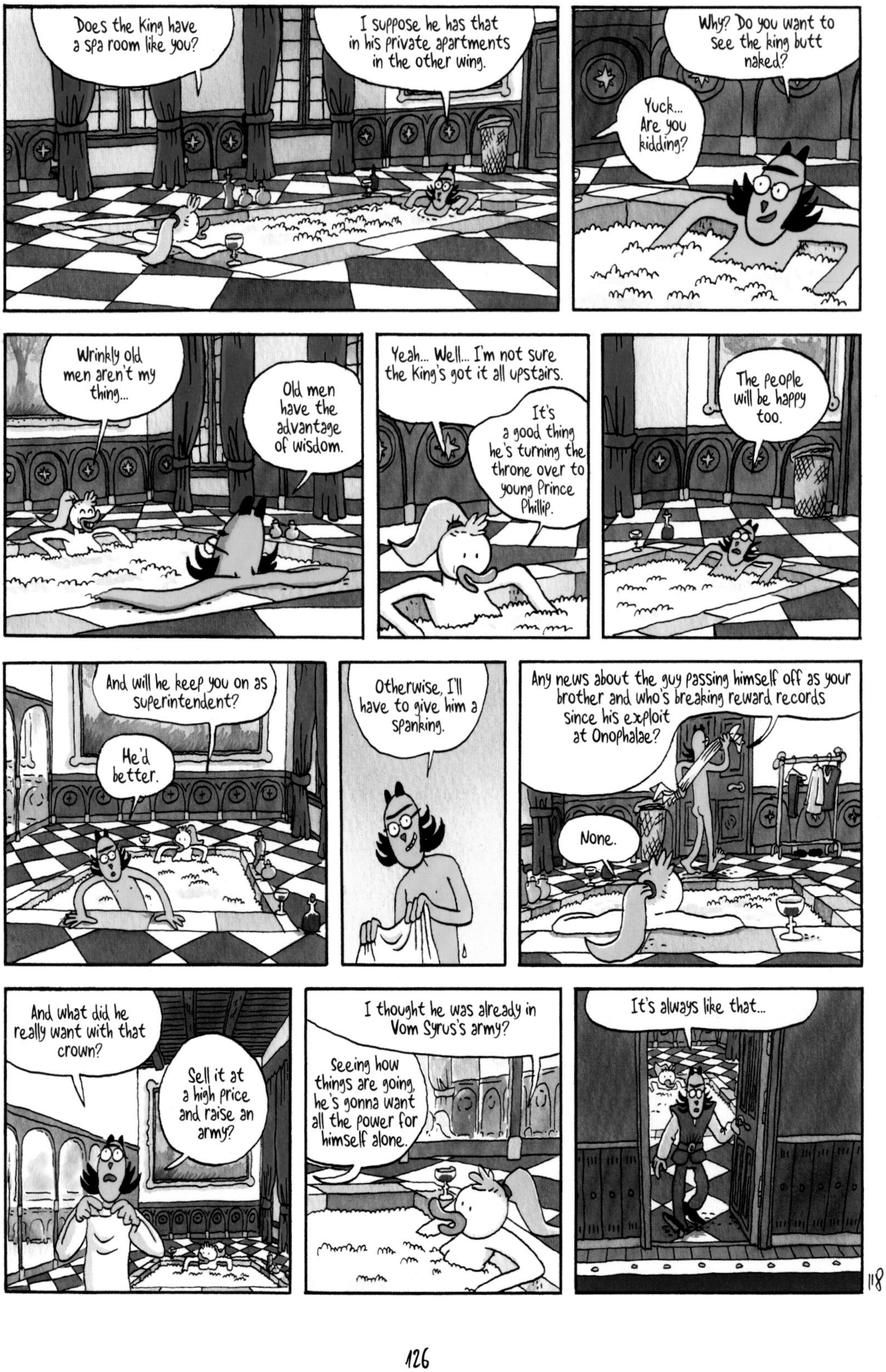
Does the King have a spa room like you?
I suppose he has that in his private apartments in the other wing.
Why? Do you want to see the king butt naked?
Yuck... Are you kidding?
Wrinkly old men aren't my thing...
Old men have the advantage of wisdom.
Yeah... Well... I'm not sure the King's got it all upstairs.
It's a good thing he's turning the throne over to young Prince Phillip.
The people will be happy too.
And will he keep you on as superintendent?
He'd better.
Otherwise, I'll have to give him a spanking.
Any news about the guy passing himself off as your brother and who's breaking reward records since his exploit at Onophalae?
None.
And what did he really want with that crown?
Sell it at a high price and raise an army?
I thought he was already in Vom Syrus's army?
Seeing how things are going, he's gonna want all the power for himself alone.
It's always like that...
118

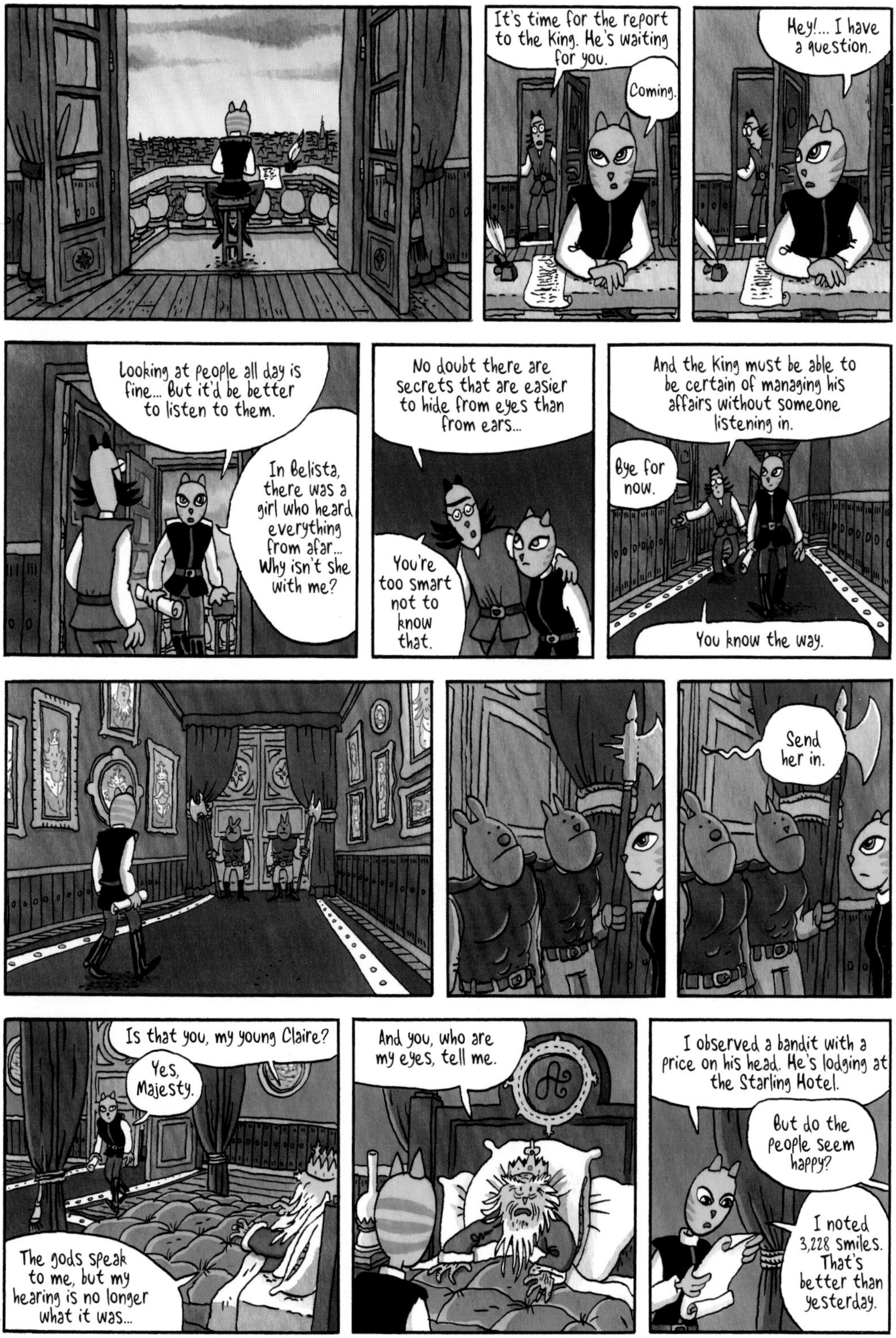
It's time for the report to the King. He's waiting for you.
Coming.
Hey!... I have a question.
Looking at people all day is fine... But it'd be better to listen to them.
In Belista, there was a girl who heard everything from afar... Why isn't she with me?
No doubt there are secrets that are easier to hide from eyes than from ears...
You're too smart not to know that.
And the King must be able to be certain of managing his affairs without someone listening in.
Bye for now.
You know the way.
Send her in.
Is that you, my young Claire?
Yes, Majesty.
The gods speak to me, but my hearing is no longer what it was...
And you, who are my eyes, tell me.
I observed a bandit with a price on his head. He's lodging at the Starling Hotel.
But do the people seem happy?
I noted 3,228 smiles. That's better than yesterday.
119

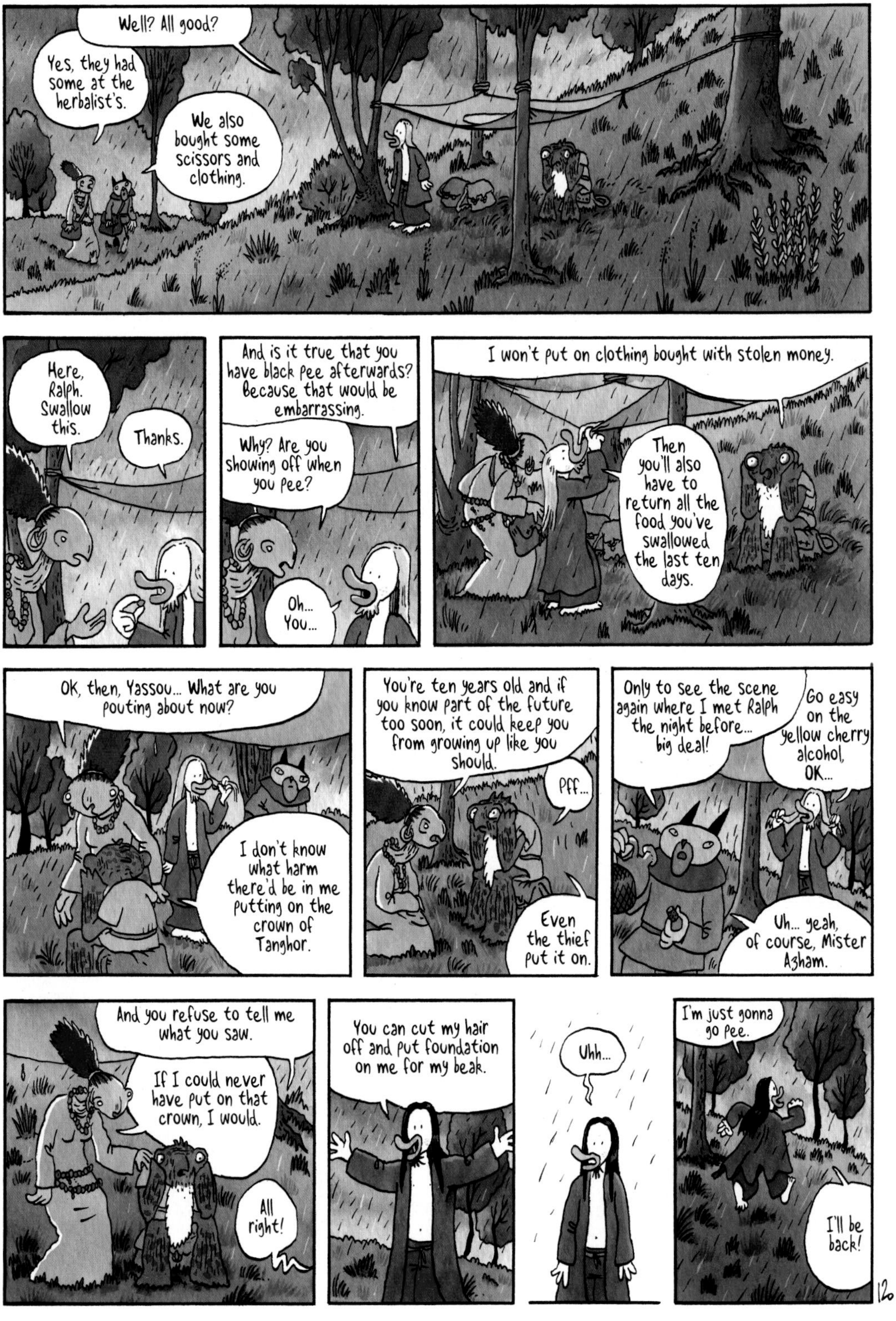
Well? All good?
Yes, they had some at the herbalist's.
We also bought some scissors and clothing.
Here, Ralph. Swallow this.
Thanks.
And is it true that you have black pee afterwards? Because that would be embarrassing.
Why? Are you showing off when you pee?
Oh... You...
I won't put on clothing bought with stolen money.
Then you'll also have to return all the food you've swallowed the last ten days.
OK, then, Yassou... What are you pouting about now?
I don't know what harm there'd be in me putting on the crown of Tanghor.
You're ten years old and if you know part of the future too soon, it could keep you from growing up like you should.
Pff...
Even the thief put it on.
Only to see the scene again where I met Ralph the night before... big deal!
Go easy on the yellow cherry alcohol, OK...
Uh... yeah, of course, Mister Azham.
And you refuse to tell me what you saw.
If I could never have put on that crown, I would.
All right!
You can cut my hair off and put foundation on me for my beak.
Uhh...
I'm just gonna go pee.
I'll be back!
12

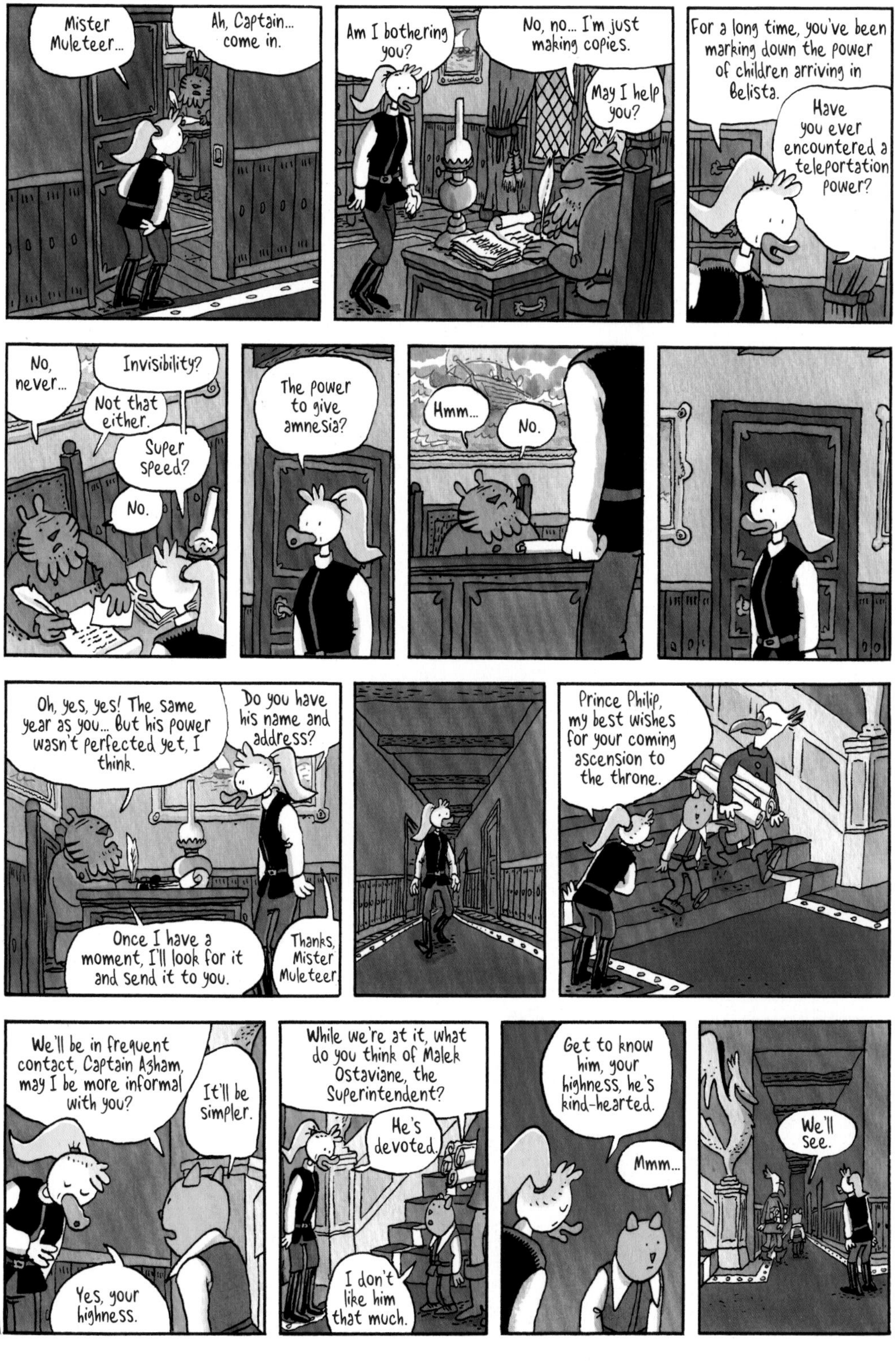
Mister Muleteer...
Ah, Captain... come in.
Am I bothering you?
No, no... I'm just making copies.
May I help you?
For a long time, you've been marking down the power of children arriving in Belista.
Have you ever encountered a teleportation power?
No, never...
Invisibility?
Not that either.
Super speed?
No.
The power to give amnesia?
Hmm...
No.
Oh, yes, yes! The same year as you... But his power wasn't perfected yet, I think.
Do you have his name and address?
Once I have a moment, I'll look for it and send it to you.
Thanks, Mister Muleteer.
Prince Philip, my best wishes for your coming ascension to the throne.
We'll be in frequent contact, Captain Azham, may I be more informal with you?
It'll be simpler.
Yes, your highness.
While we're at it, what do you think of Malek Ostaviane, the Superintendent?
He's devoted.
I don't like him that much.
Get to know him, your highness, he's kind-hearted.
Mmm...
We'll see.
121

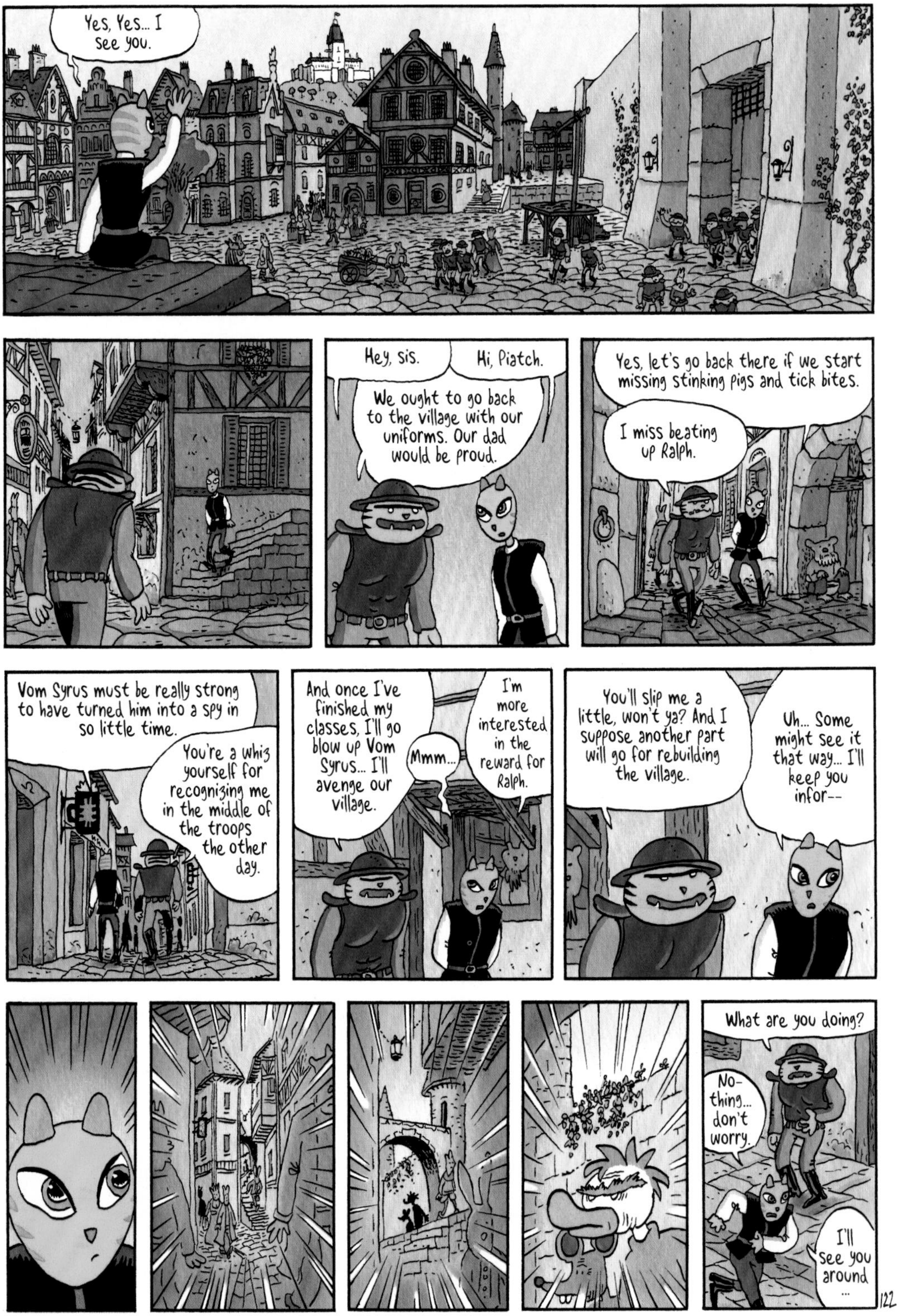
Yes, Yes... I see you.
Hey, sis.
Hi, Piatch.
We ought to go back to the village with our uniforms. Our dad would be proud.
Yes, let's go back there if we start missing stinking pigs and tick bites.
I miss beating up Ralph.
Vom Syrus must be really strong to have turned him into a spy in so little time.
You're a whiz yourself for recognizing me in the middle of the troops the other day.
And once I've finished my classes, I'll go blow up Vom Syrus... I'll avenge our village.
Mmm...
I'm more interested in the reward for Ralph.
You'll slip me a little, won't ya? And I suppose another part will go for rebuilding the village.
Uh... Some might see it that way... I'll keep you infor--
What are you doing?
No-thing... don't worry.
I'll see you around ...
122

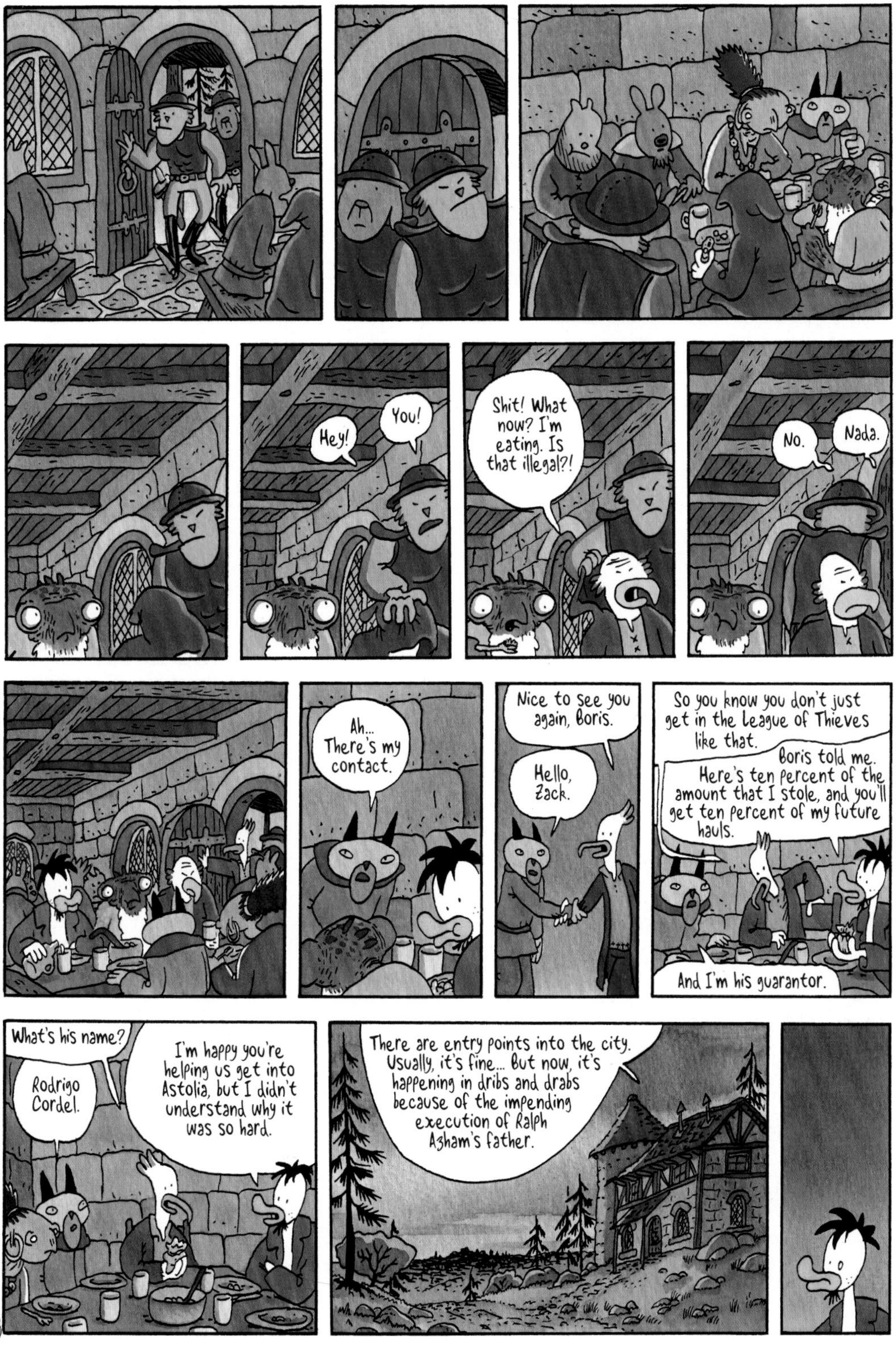
Hey!
You!
Shit! What now? I'm eating. Is that illegal?!
No.
Nada.
Ah... There's my contact.
Nice to see you again, Boris.
Hello, Zack.
So you know you don't just get in the League of Thieves like that.
Boris told me. Here's ten percent of the amount that I stole, and you'll get ten percent of my future hauls.
And I'm his guarantor.
What's his name?
Rodrigo Cordel.
I'm happy you're helping us get into Astolia, but I didn't understand why it was so hard.
There are entry points into the city. Usually, it's fine... But now, it's happening in dribs and drabs because of the impending execution of Ralph Azham's father.

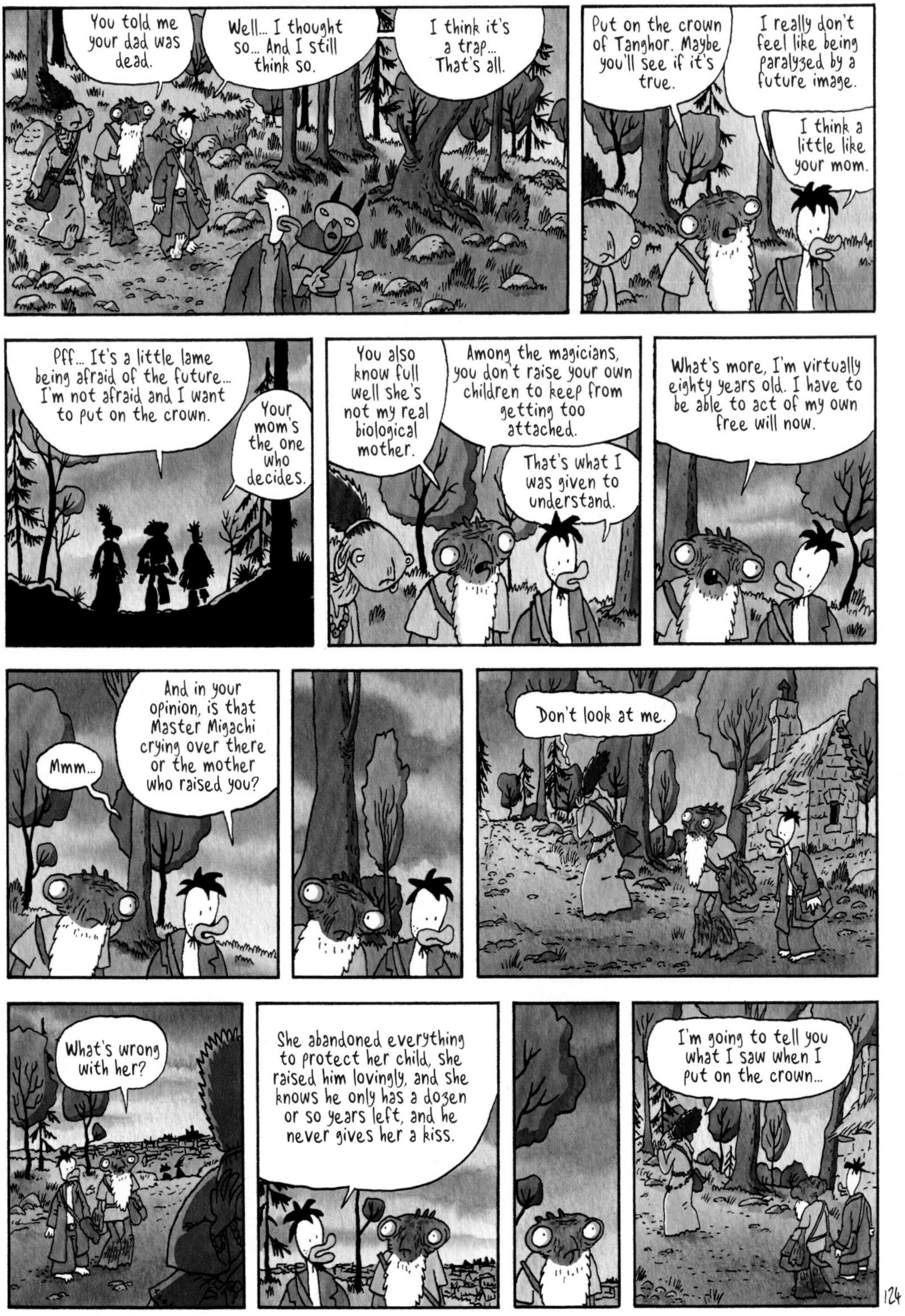
You told me your dad was dead.
Well... I thought so... And I still think so.
I think it's a trap... That's all.
Put on the crown of Tanghor. Maybe you'll see if it's true.
I really don't feel like being paralyzed by a future image.
I think a little like your mom.
Pff... It's a little lame being afraid of the future... I'm not afraid and I want to put on the crown.
Your mom's the one who decides.
You also know full well she's not my real biological mother.
Among the magicians, you don't raise your own children to keep from getting too attached.
That's what I was given to understand.
What's more, I'm virtually eighty years old. I have to be able to act of my own free will now.
Mmm...
And in your opinion, is that Master Migachi crying over there or the mother who raised you?
Don't look at me.
What's wrong with her?
She abandoned everything to protect her child, she raised him lovingly, and she knows he only has a dozen or so years left, and he never gives her a kiss.
I'm going to tell you what I saw when I put on the crown...
124

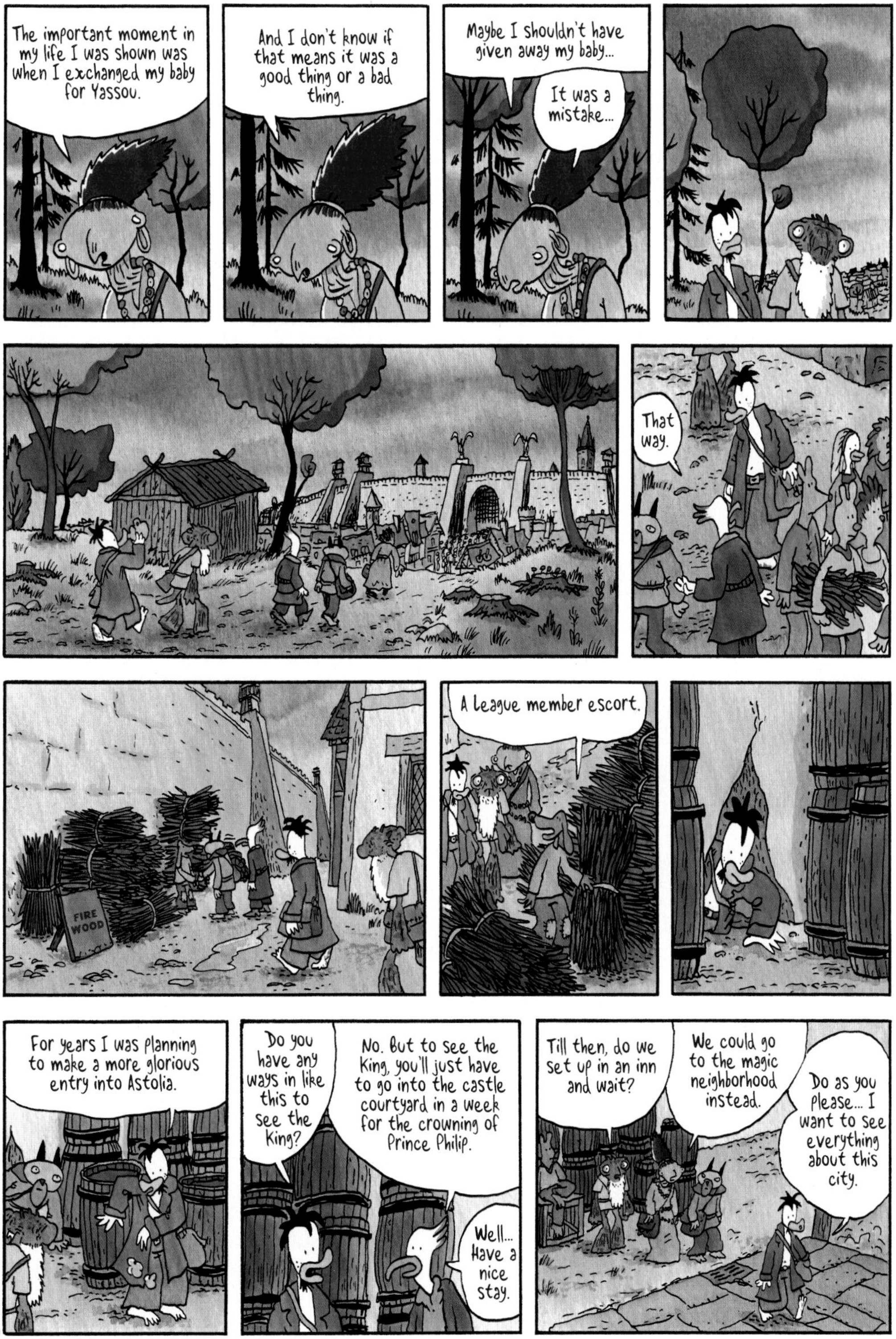

The important moment in my life I was shown was when I exchanged my baby for Yassou.
And I don't know if that means it was a good thing or a bad thing.
Maybe I shouldn't have given away my baby...
It was a mistake...
That way.
FIRE WOOD
A League member escort.
For years I was planning to make a more glorious entry into Astolia.
Do you have any ways in like this to see the King?
No. But to see the King, you'll just have to go into the castle courtyard in a week for the crowning of Prince Philip.
Well... Have a nice stay.
Till then, do we set up in an inn and wait?
We could go to the magic neighborhood instead.
Do as you please... I want to see everything about this city.

125

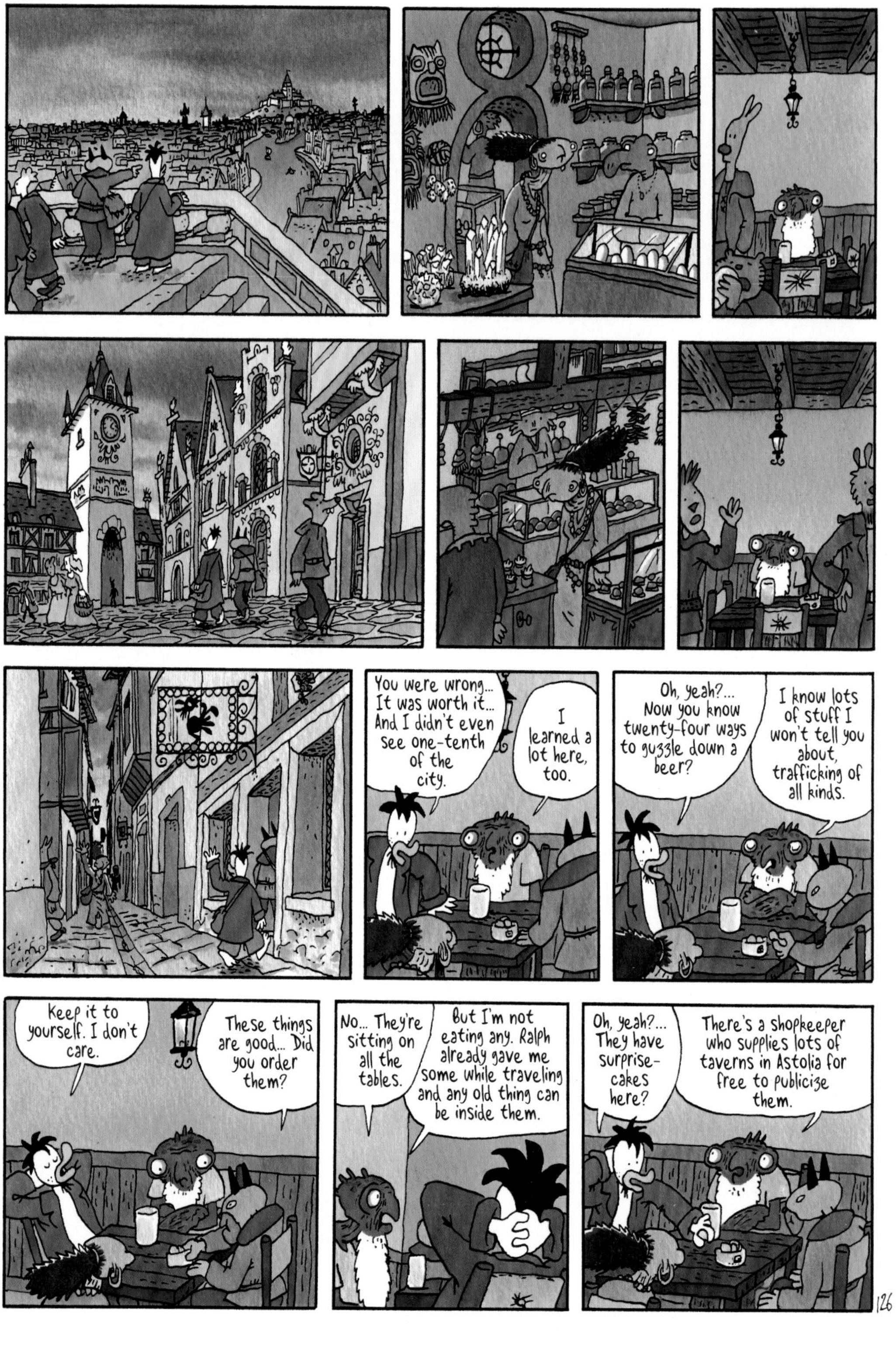
You were wrong... It was worth it... And I didn't even see one-tenth of the city.
I learned a lot here, too.
Oh, yeah?... Now you know twenty-four ways to guzzle down a beer?
I know lots of stuff I won't tell you about, trafficking of all kinds.
Keep it to yourself. I don't care.
These things are good... Did you order them?
No... They're sitting on all the tables.
But I'm not eating any. Ralph already gave me some while traveling and any old thing can be inside them.
Oh, yeah?... They have surprise-cakes here?
There's a shopkeeper who supplies lots of taverns in Astolia for free to publicize them.
126

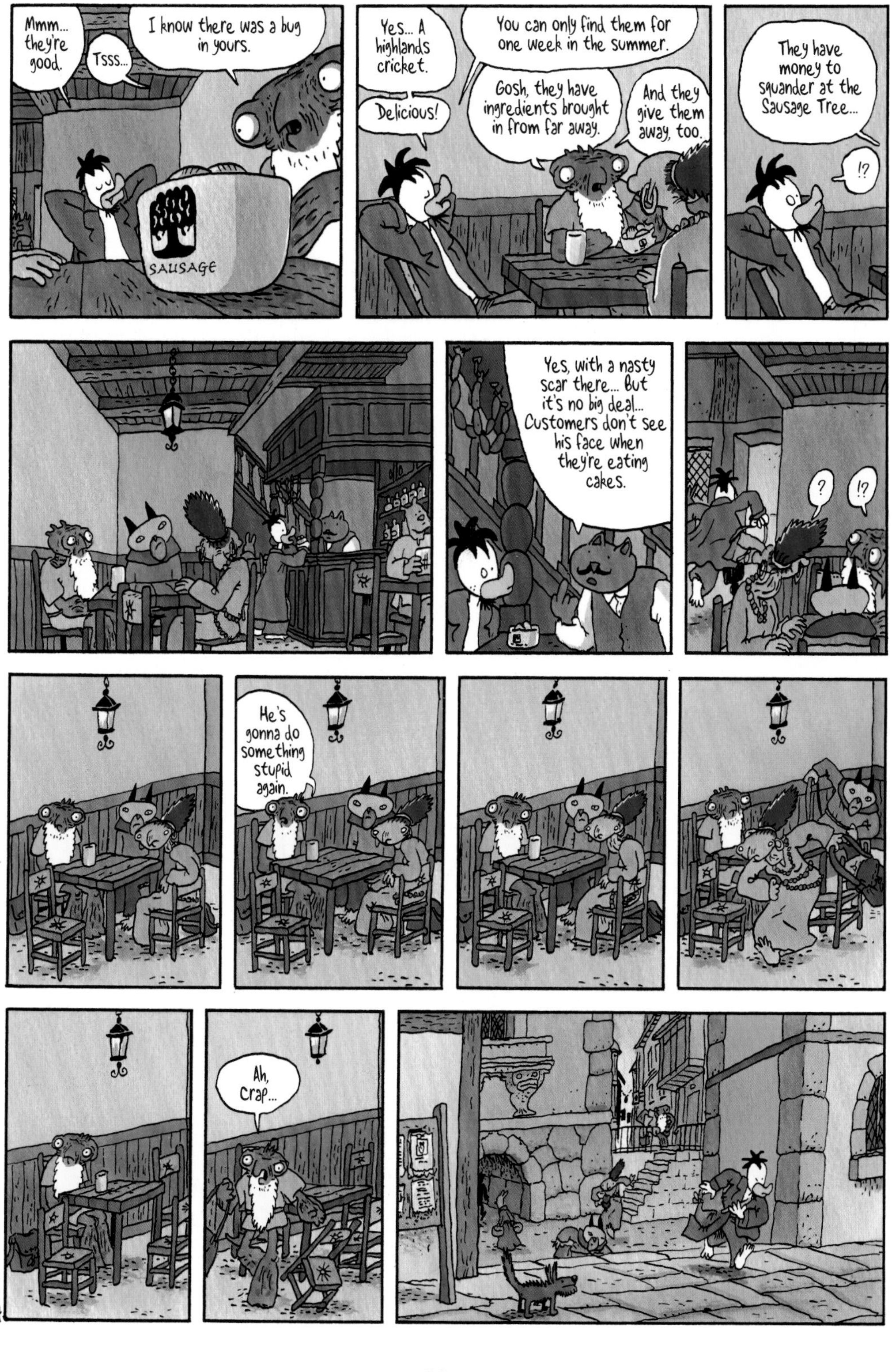
Mmm... they're good.
Tsss...
I know there was a bug in yours.
SAUSAGE
Yes... A highlands cricket.
Delicious!
You can only find them for one week in the summer.
Gosh, they have ingredients brought in from far away.
And they give them away, too.
They have money to squander at the Sausage Tree...
!?
Yes, with a nasty scar there... But it's no big deal... Customers don't see his face when they're eating cakes.
?
!?
He's gonna do something stupid again.
Ah, crap...

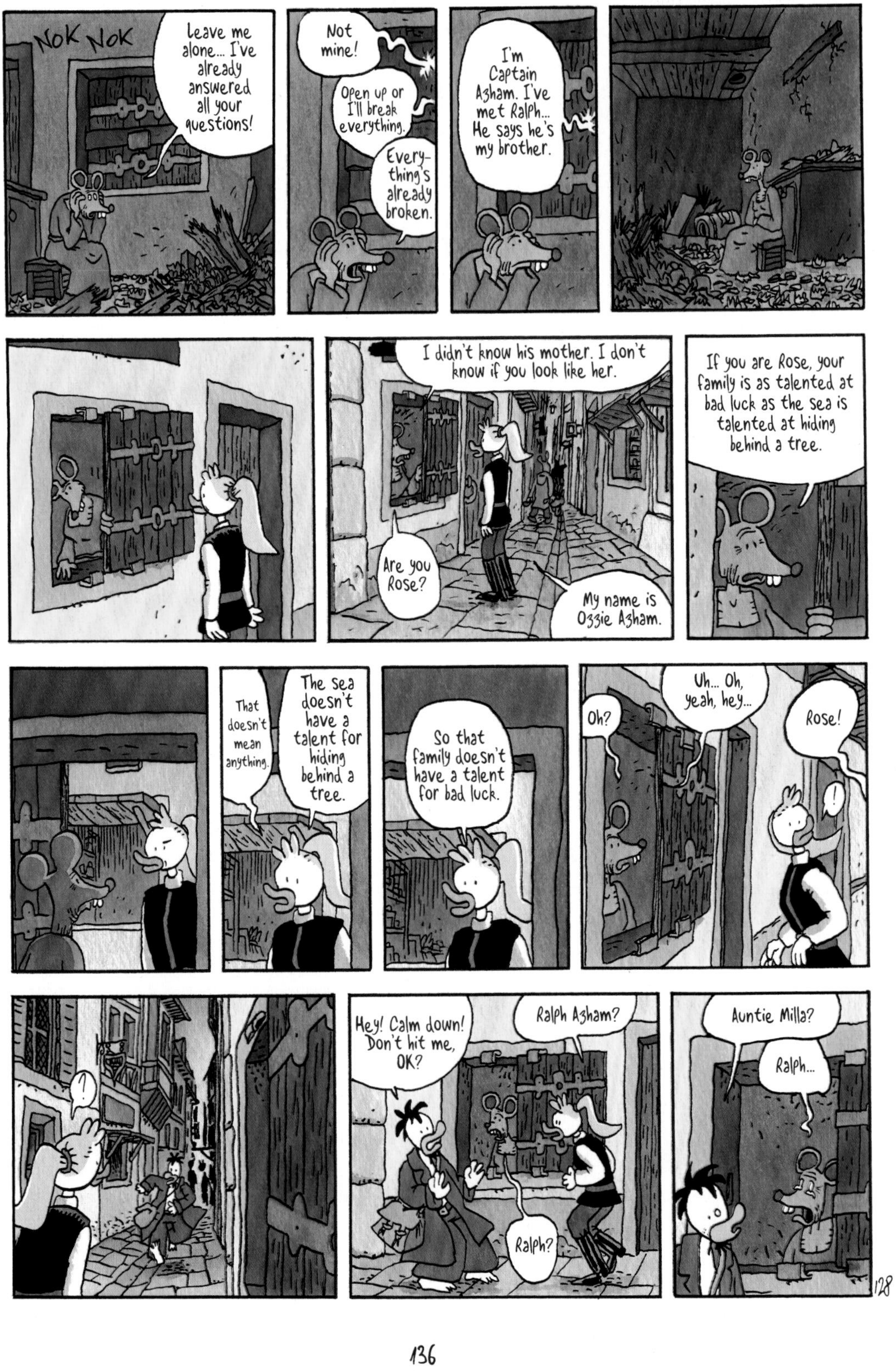
NOK NOK
Leave me alone... I've already answered all your questions!
Not mine!
Open up or I'll break everything.
Every-thing's already broken.
I'm Captain Azham. I've met Ralph... He says he's my brother.
I didn't know his mother. I don't know if you look like her.
Are you Rose?
My name is Ozzie Azham.
If you are Rose, your family is as talented at bad luck as the sea is talented at hiding behind a tree.
That doesn't mean anything.
The sea doesn't have a talent for hiding behind a tree.
So that family doesn't have a talent for bad luck.
Oh?
Uh... Oh, yeah, hey...
Rose!
!
?
Hey! Calm down! Don't hit me, OK?
Ralph Azham?
Ralph?
Auntie Milla?
Ralph...

128

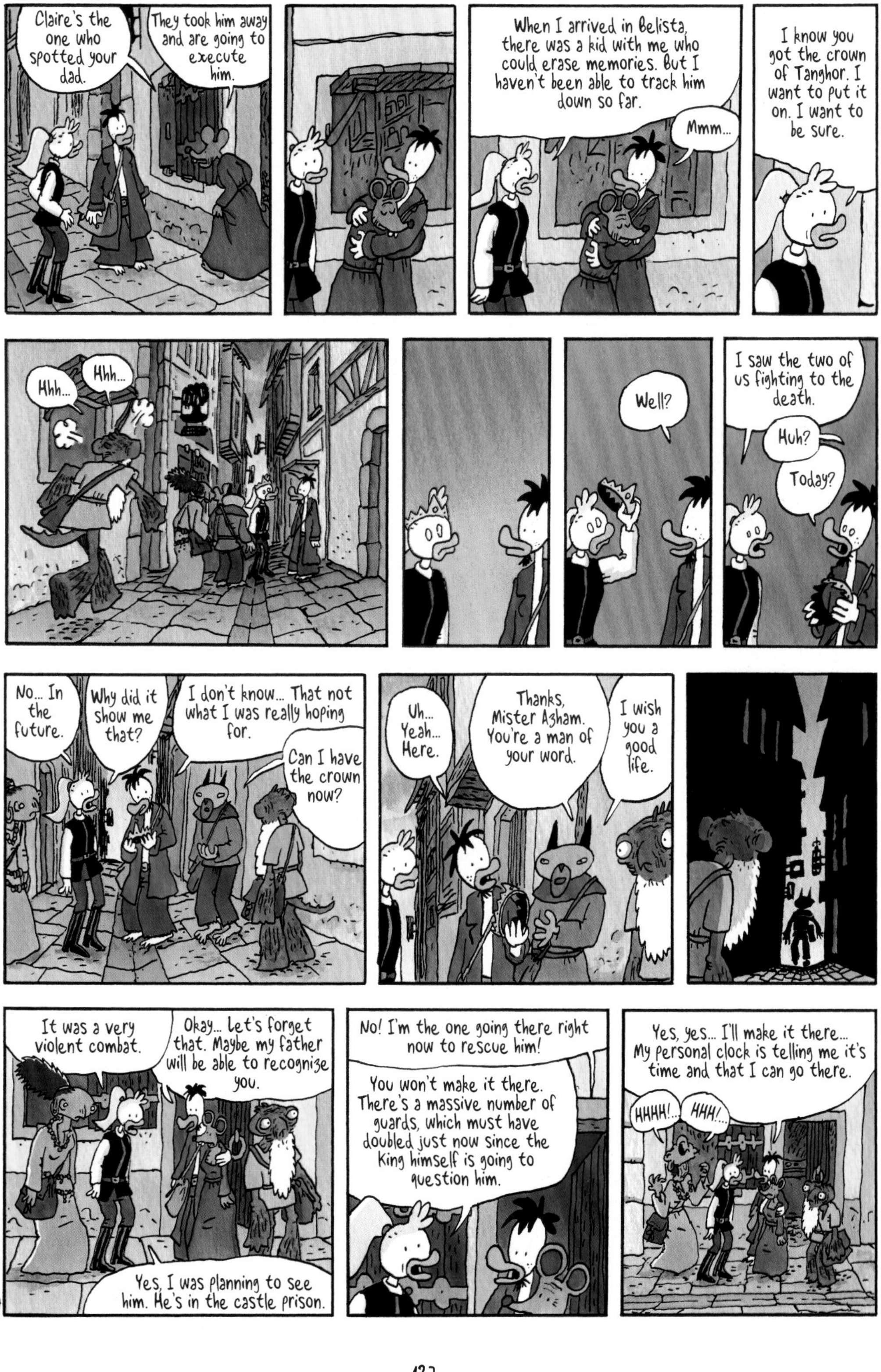
Claire's the one who spotted your dad.
They took him away and are going to execute him.
When I arrived in Belista, there was a kid with me who could erase memories. But I haven't been able to track him down so far.
Mmm...
I know you got the crown of Tanghor. I want to put it on. I want to be sure.
Hhh...
Hhh...
Well?
I saw the two of us fighting to the death.
Huh?
Today?
No... In the future.
Why did it show me that?
I don't know... That not what I was really hoping for.
Can I have the crown now?
Uh... Yeah... Here.
Thanks, Mister Azham. You're a man of your word.
I wish you a good life.
It was a very violent combat.
Okay... Let's forget that. Maybe my father will be able to recognize you.
Yes, I was planning to see him. He's in the castle prison.
No! I'm the one going there right now to rescue him!
You won't make it there. There's a massive number of guards, which must have doubled just now since the King himself is going to question him.
Yes, yes... I'll make it there... My personal clock is telling me it's time and that I can go there.
HHHH!...
HHH!...

129

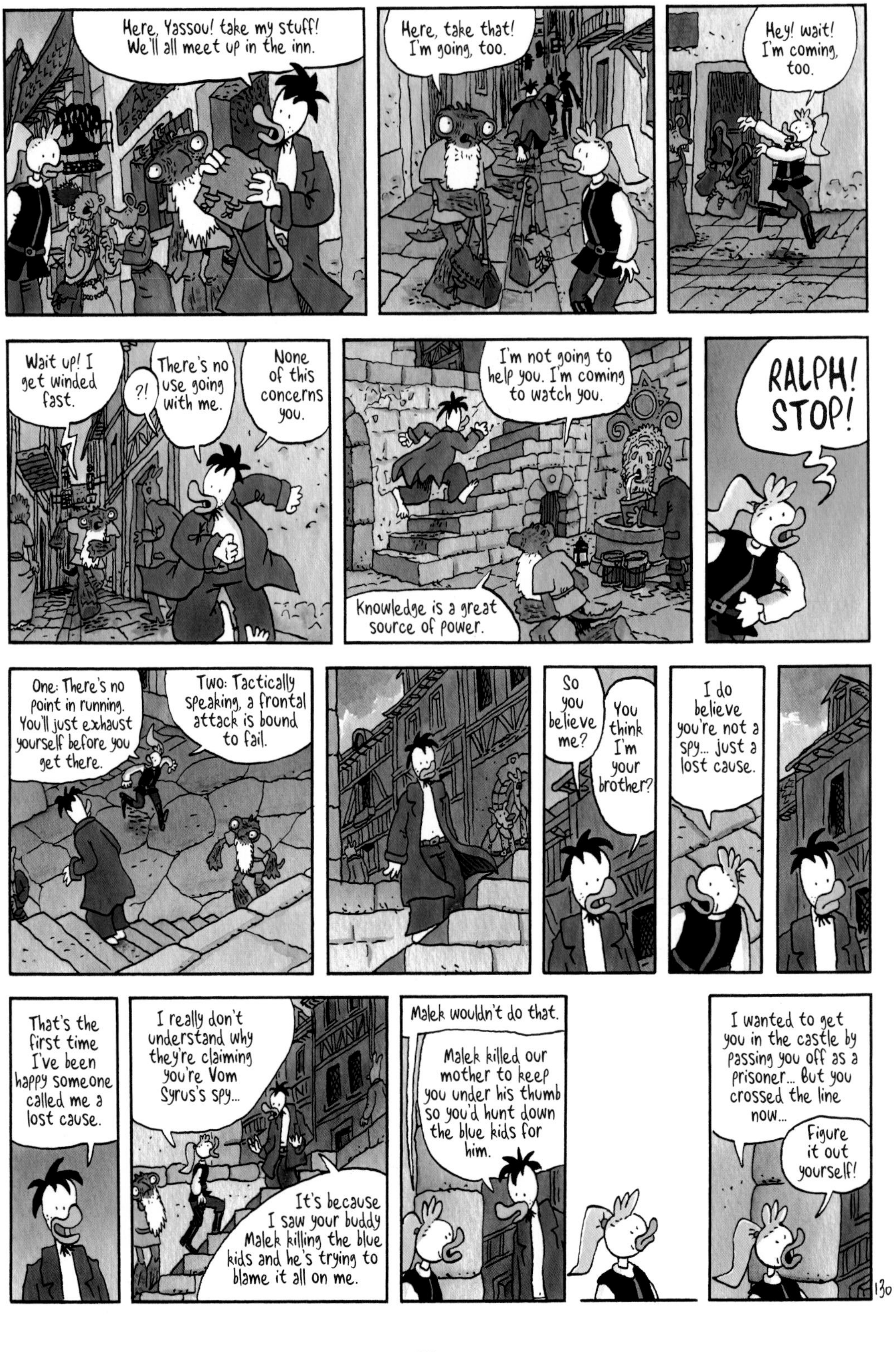
Here, Yassou! take my stuff! We'll all meet up in the inn.
Here, take that! I'm going, too.
Hey! wait! I'm coming, too.
Wait up! I get winded fast.
?!
There's no use going with me.
None of this concerns you.
I'm not going to help you. I'm coming to watch you.
Knowledge is a great source of power.
RALPH! STOP!
One: There's no point in running. You'll just exhaust yourself before you get there.
Two: Tactically speaking, a frontal attack is bound to fail.
So you believe me?
You think I'm your brother?
I do believe you're not a spy... just a lost cause.
That's the first time I've been happy someone called me a lost cause.
I really don't understand why they're claiming you're Vom Syrus's spy...
It's because I saw your buddy Malek killing the blue kids and he's trying to blame it all on me.
Malek wouldn't do that.
Malek killed our mother to keep you under his thumb so you'd hunt down the blue kids for him.
I wanted to get you in the castle by passing you off as a prisoner... But you crossed the line now...
Figure it out yourself!
130

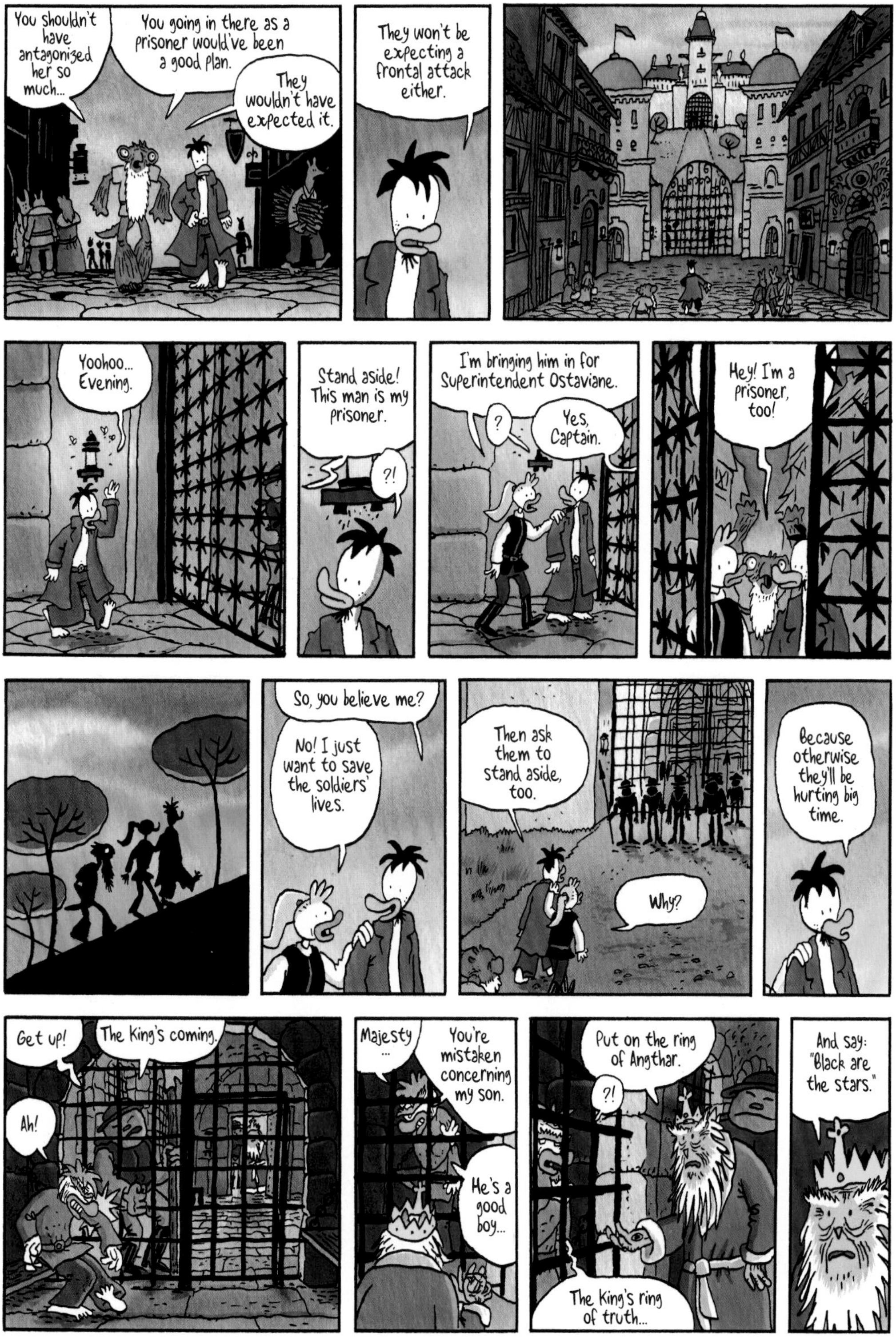
You shouldn't have antagonized her so much...
You going in there as a prisoner would've been a good plan.
They wouldn't have expected it.
They won't be expecting a frontal attack either.
Yoohoo... Evening.
Stand aside! This man is my prisoner.
?!
I'm bringing him in for Superintendent Ostaviane.
?
Yes, Captain.
Hey! I'm a prisoner, too!
So, you believe me?
No! I just want to save the soldiers' lives.
Then ask them to stand aside, too.
Why?
Because otherwise they'll be hurting big time.
Get up!
The King's coming.
Ah!
Majesty ...
You're mistaken concerning my son.
He's a good boy...
Put on the ring of Angthar.
?!
The King's ring of truth...
And say: "Black are the stars."
131

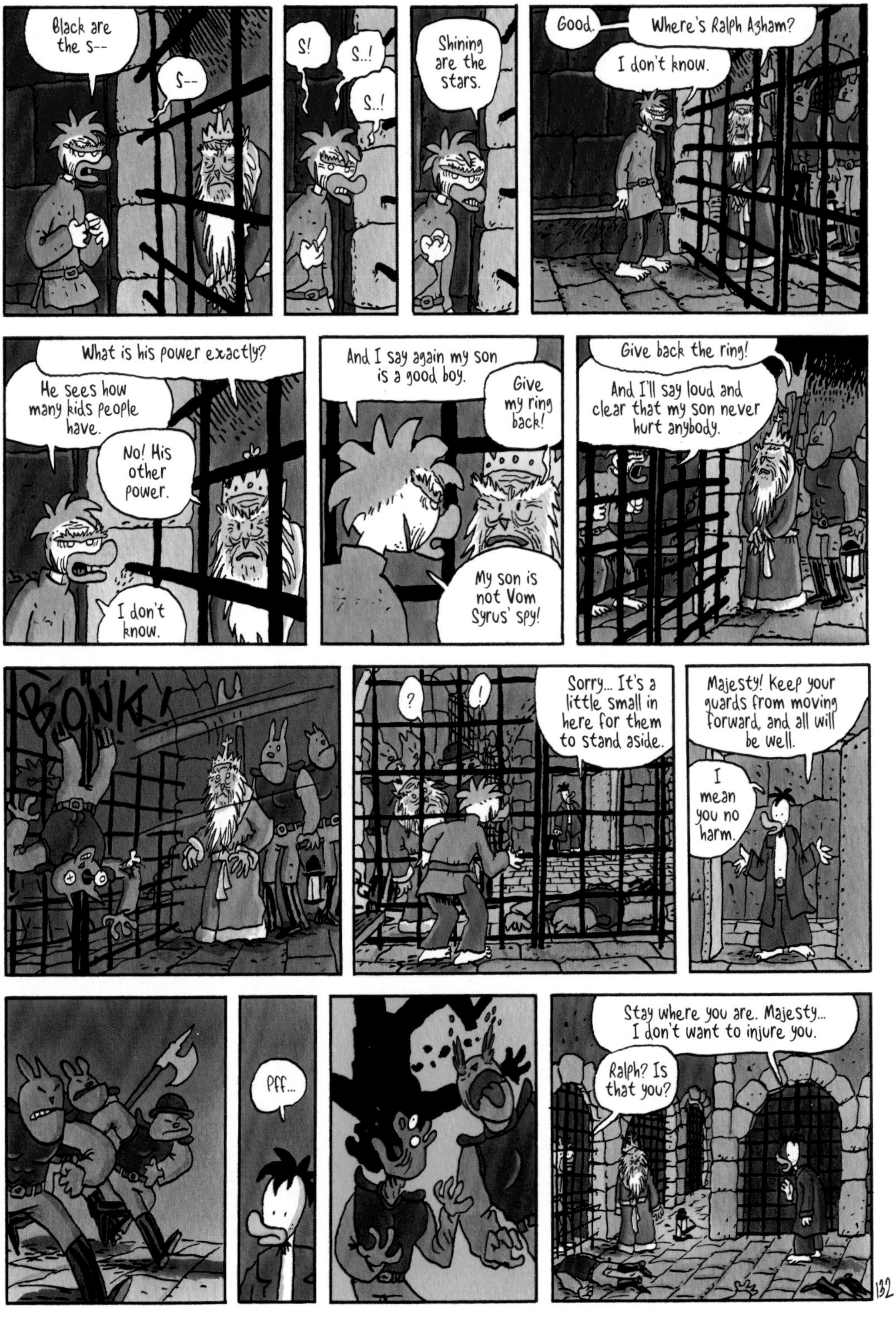
Black are the s--
S--
S!
S..!
S..!
Shining are the stars.
Good.
Where's Ralph Azham?
I don't know.
What is his power exactly?
He sees how many kids people have.
No! His other power.
I don't know.
And I say again my son is a good boy.
Give my ring back!
My son is not Vom Syrus' spy!
Give back the ring!
And I'll say loud and clear that my son never hurt anybody.
BONK!
?
!
Sorry... It's a little small in here for them to stand aside.
Majesty! Keep your guards from moving forward, and all will be well.
I mean you no harm.
Pff...
Stay where you are. Majesty... I don't want to injure you.
Ralph? Is that you?
132

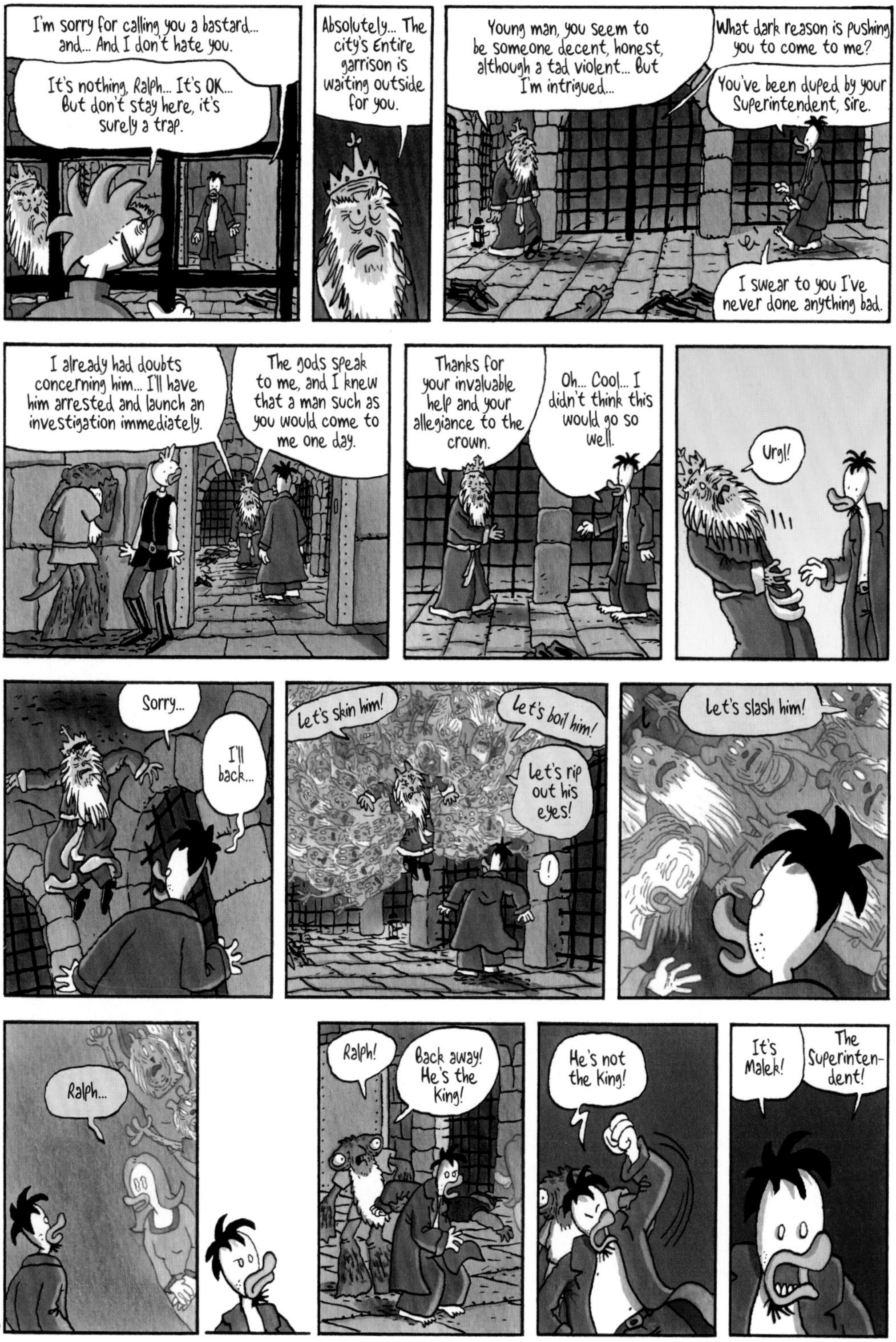
I'm sorry for calling you a bastard... and... And I don't hate you.
It's nothing, Ralph... It's OK... But don't stay here, it's surely a trap.
Absolutely... The city's Entire garrison is waiting outside for you.
Young man, you seem to be someone decent, honest, although a tad violent... But I'm intrigued...
What dark reason is pushing you to come to me?
You've been duped by your Superintendent, Sire.
I swear to you I've never done anything bad.
I already had doubts concerning him... I'll have him arrested and launch an investigation immediately.
The gods speak to me, and I knew that a man such as you would come to me one day.
Thanks for your invaluable help and your allegiance to the crown.
Oh... Cool... I didn't think this would go so well.
Urgl!
Sorry...
I'll back...
Let's skin him!
Let's boil him!
Let's rip out his eyes!
!
Let's slash him!
Ralph...
Ralph!
Back away! He's the King!
He's not the King!
It's Malek!
The Superintendent!

133

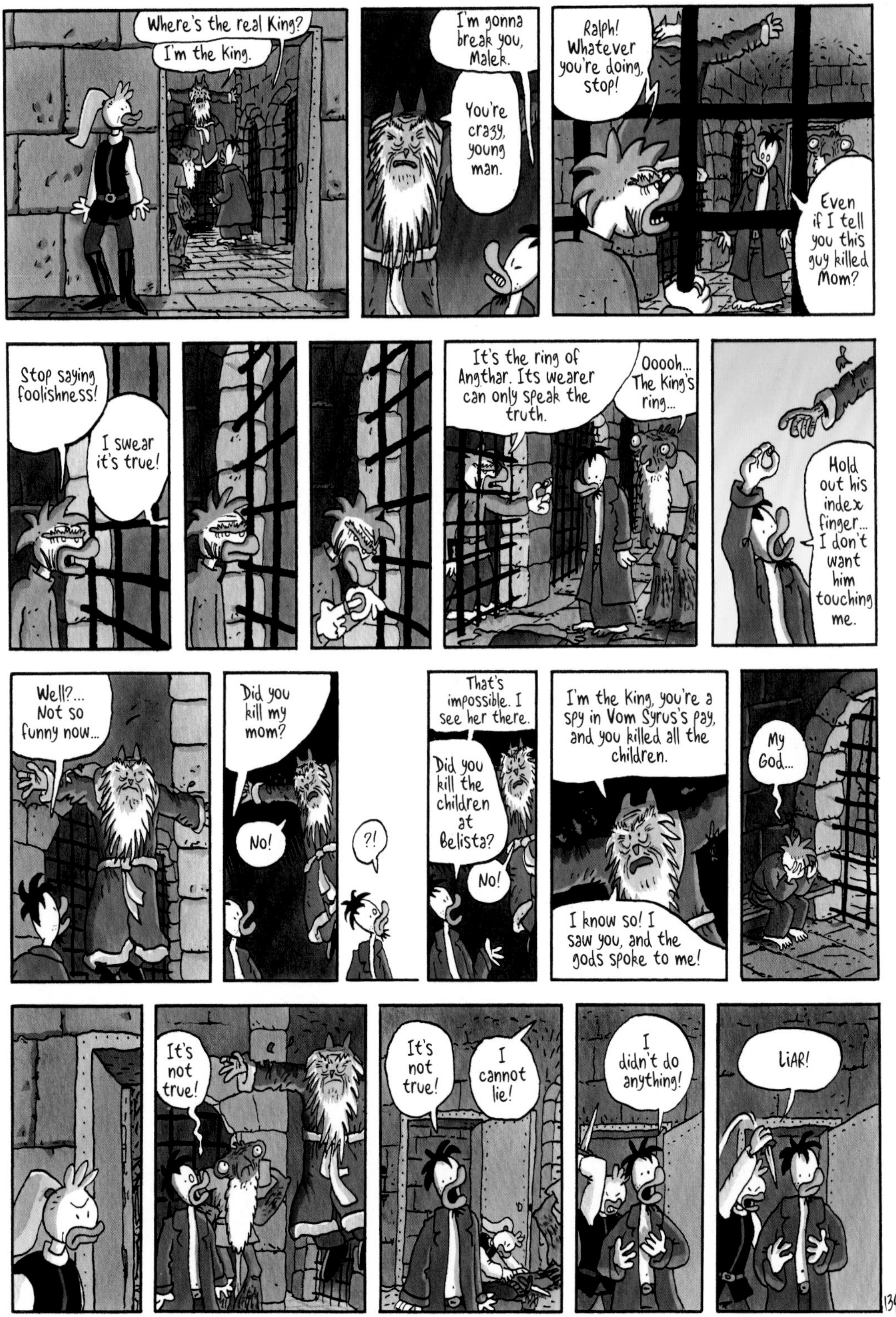

Where's the real King?
I'm the King.
I'm gonna break you, Malek.
You're crazy, young man.
Ralph! Whatever you're doing, stop!
Even if I tell you this guy killed Mom?
Stop saying foolishness!
I swear it's true!
It's the ring of Angthar. Its wearer can only speak the truth.
Ooooh... The King's ring...
Hold out his index finger... I don't want him touching me.
Well?... Not so funny now...
Did you kill my mom?
No!
?!
That's impossible. I see her there.
Did you kill the children at Belista?
No!
I'm the King, you're a spy in Vom Syrus's pay, and you killed all the children.
I know so! I saw you, and the gods spoke to me!
My God...
It's not true!
It's not true!
I cannot lie!
I didn't do anything!
LiAR!
134

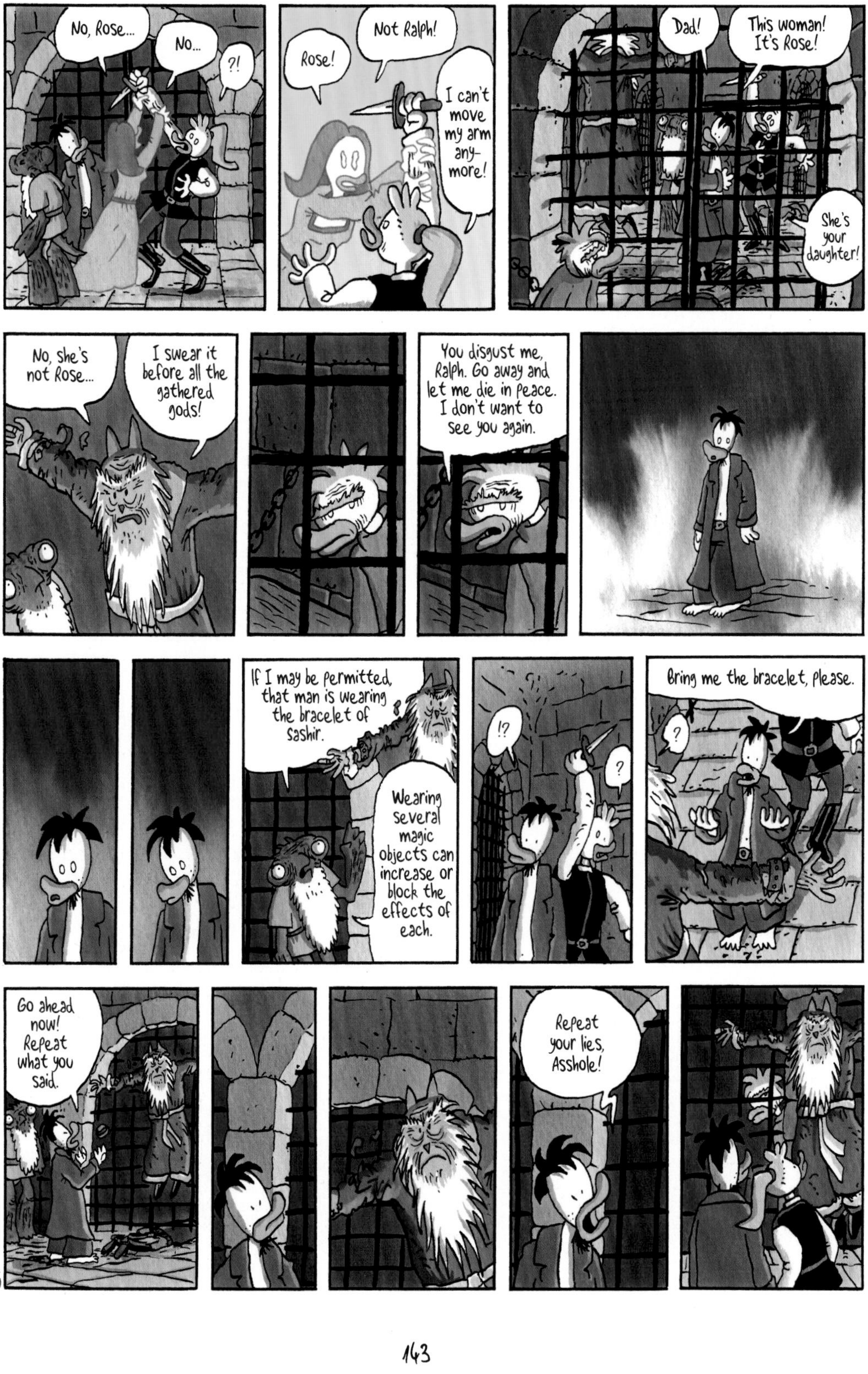
No, Rose...
No...
?!
Rose!
Not Ralph!
I can't move my arm any-more!
Dad!
This woman! It's Rose!
She's your daughter!
No, she's not Rose...
I swear it before all the gathered gods!
You disgust me, Ralph. Go away and let me die in peace. I don't want to see you again.
If I may be permitted, that man is wearing the bracelet of Sashir.
Wearing several magic objects can increase or block the effects of each.
!?
?
Bring me the bracelet, please.
?
Go ahead now! Repeat what you said.
Repeat your lies, Asshole!
135

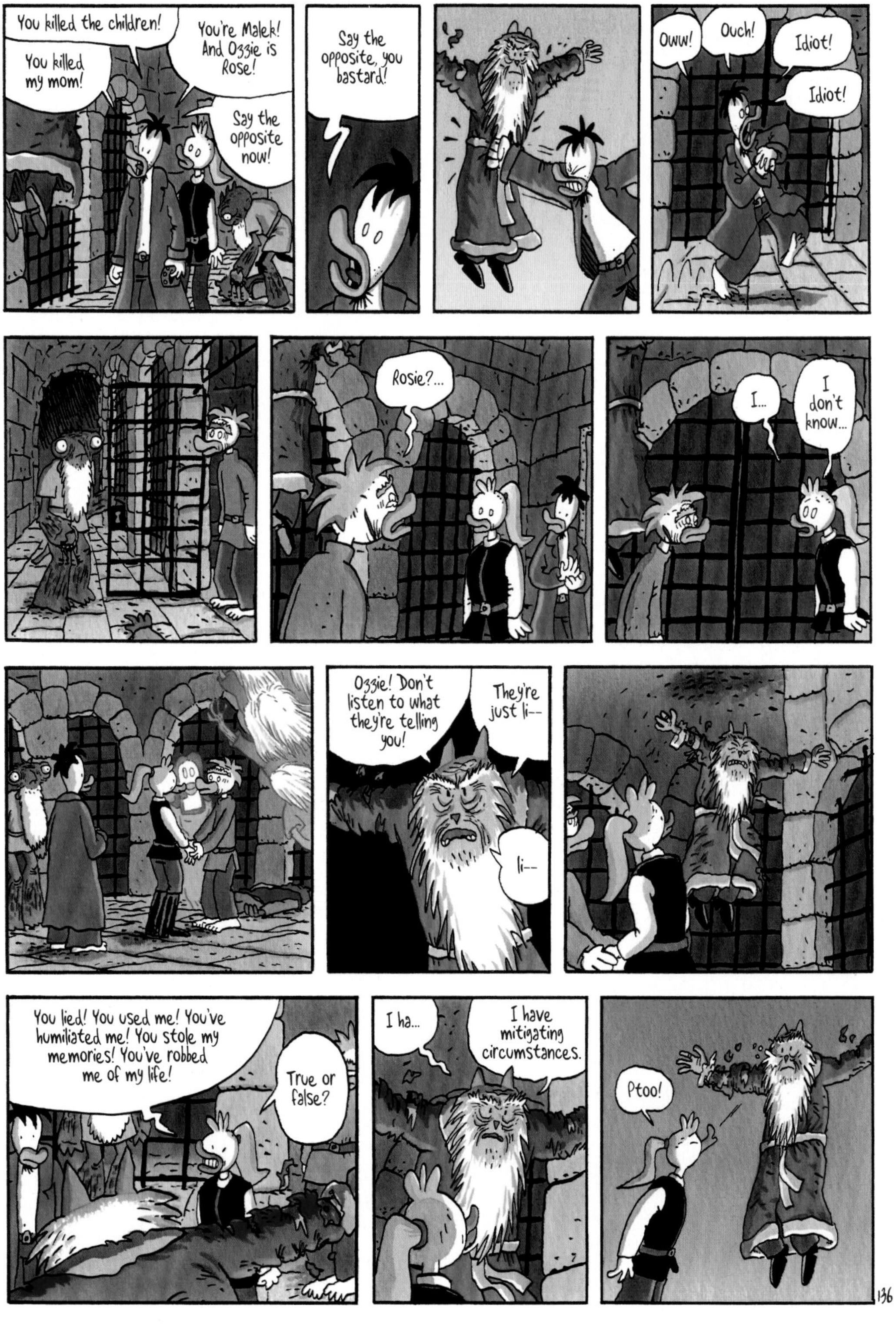
You killed the children!
You killed my mom!
You're Malek! And Ozzie is Rose!
Say the opposite now!
Say the opposite, you bastard!
Oww!
Ouch!
Idiot!
Idiot!
Rosie?...
I...
I don't know...
Ozzie! Don't listen to what they're telling you!
They're just li--
li--
You lied! You used me! You've humiliated me! You stole my memories! You've robbed me of my life!
True or false?
I ha...
I have mitigating circumstances.
Ptoo!
136

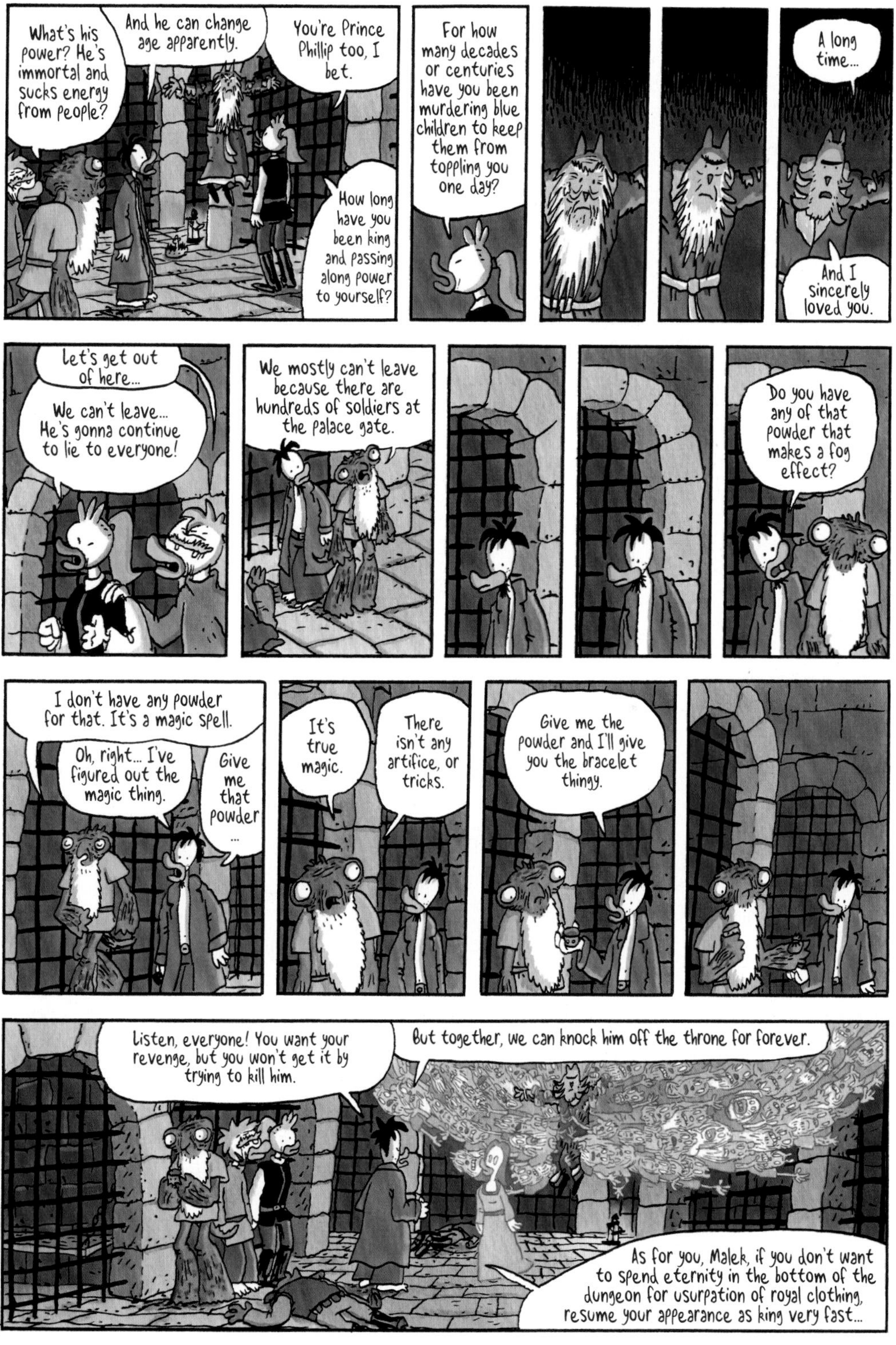
What's his power? He's immortal and sucks energy from people?
And he can change age apparently.
You're Prince Phillip too, I bet.
How long have you been king and passing along power to yourself?
For how many decades or centuries have you been murdering blue children to keep them from toppling you one day?
A long time...
And I sincerely loved you.
Let's get out of here...
We can't leave... He's gonna continue to lie to everyone!
We mostly can't leave because there are hundreds of soldiers at the palace gate.
Do you have any of that powder that makes a fog effect?
I don't have any powder for that. It's a magic spell.
Oh, right... I've figured out the magic thing.
Give me that powder...
It's true magic.
There isn't any artifice, or tricks.
Give me the powder and I'll give you the bracelet thingy.
Listen, everyone! You want your revenge, but you won't get it by trying to kill him.
But together, we can knock him off the throne for forever.
As for you, Malek, if you don't want to spend eternity in the bottom of the dungeon for usurpation of royal clothing, resume your appearance as king very fast...

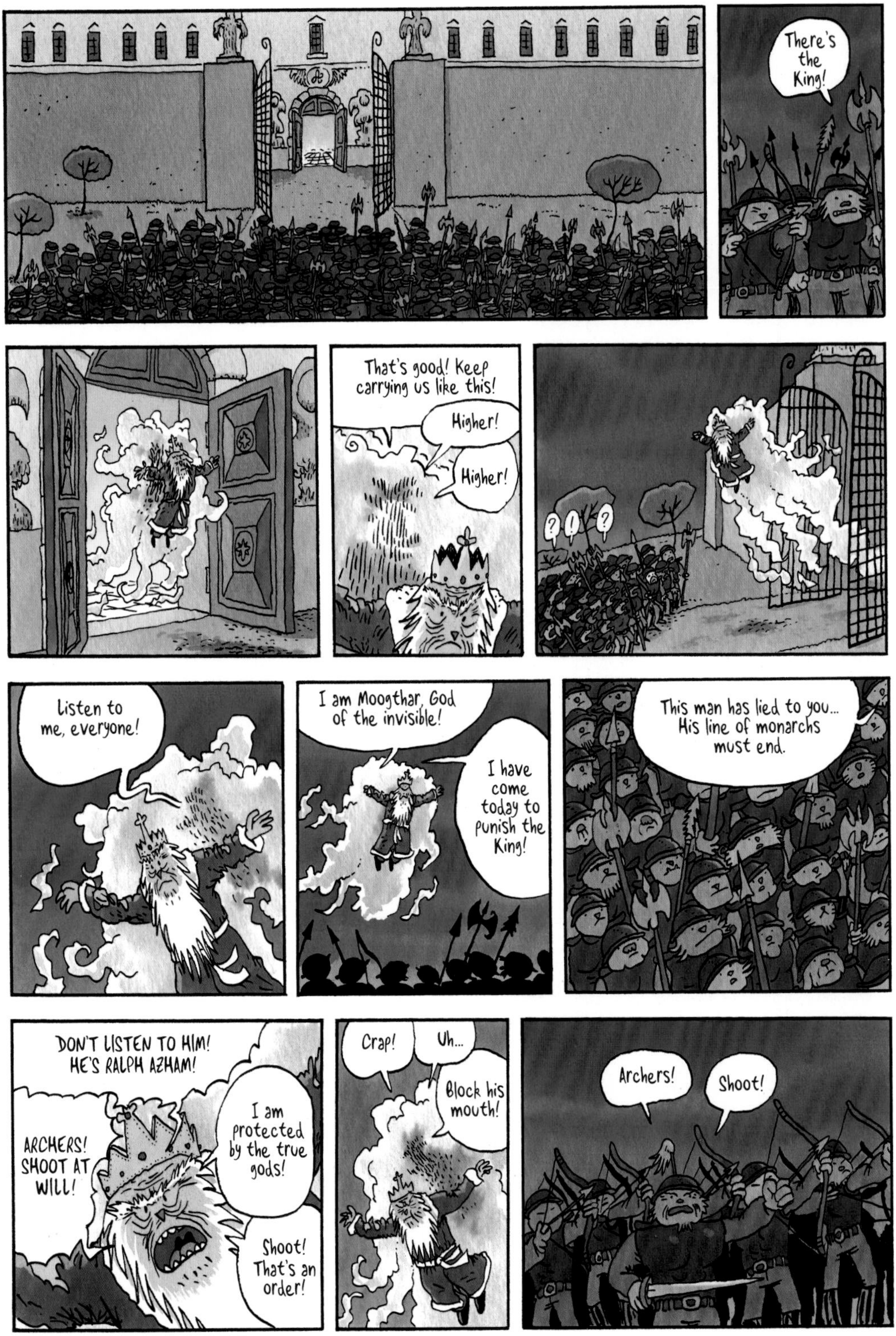
There's the King!
That's good! Keep carrying us like this!
Higher!
Higher!
? ! ?
Listen to me, everyone!
I am Moogthar, God of the invisible!
I have come today to punish the King!
This man has lied to you... His line of monarchs must end.
DON'T LISTEN TO HIM! HE'S RALPH AZHAM!
ARCHERS! SHOOT AT WILL!
I am protected by the true gods!
Shoot! That's an order!
Crap!
Uh...
Block his mouth!
Archers!
Shoot!

138

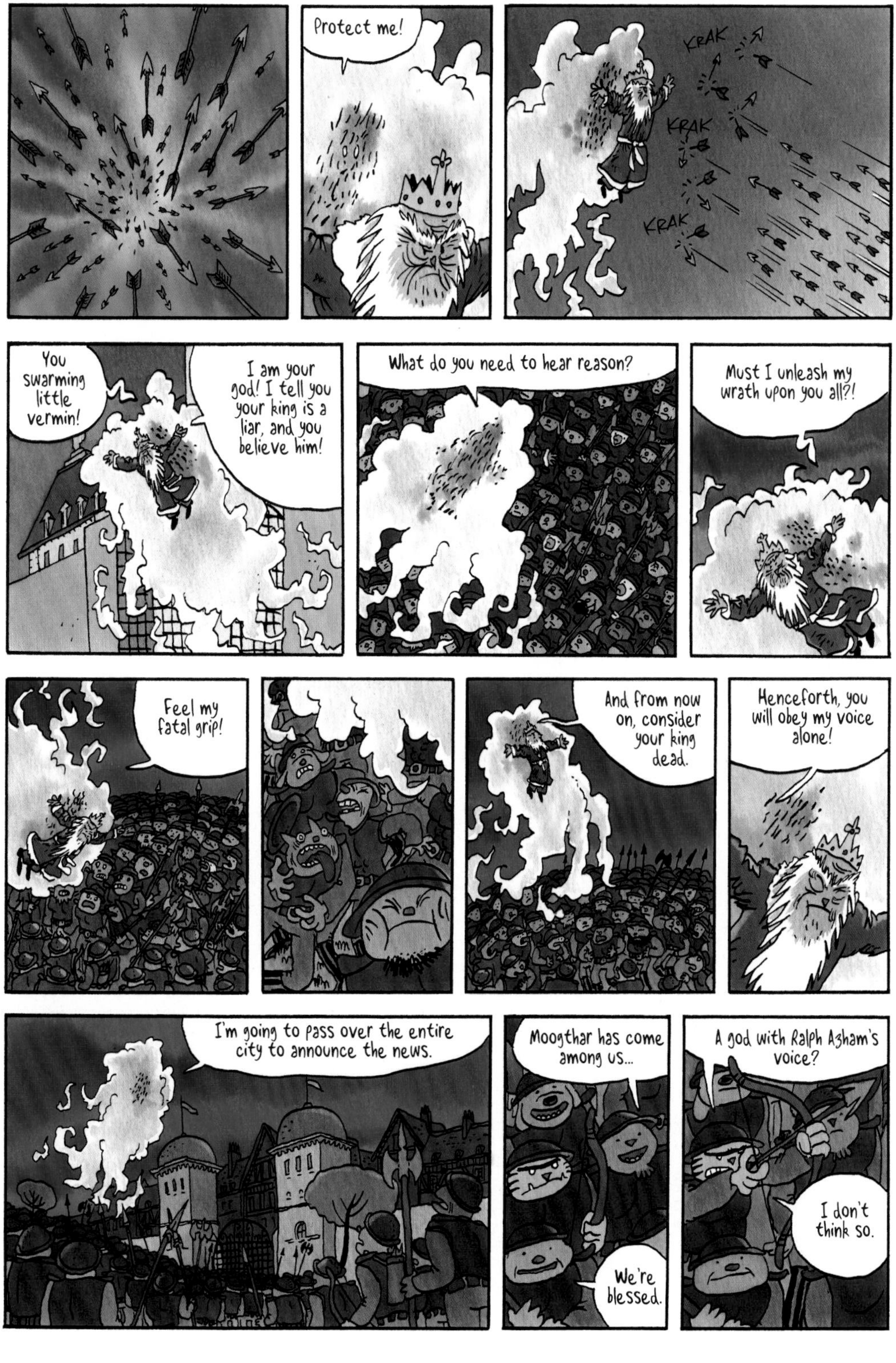
Protect me!
KRAK
KRAK
KRAK
You swarming little vermin!
I am your god! I tell you your king is a liar, and you believe him!
What do you need to hear reason?
Must I unleash my wrath upon you all?!
Feel my fatal grip!
And from now on, consider your king dead.
Henceforth, you will obey my voice alone!
I'm going to pass over the entire city to announce the news.
Moogthar has come among us...
We're blessed.
A god with Ralph Azham's voice?
I don't think so.
179

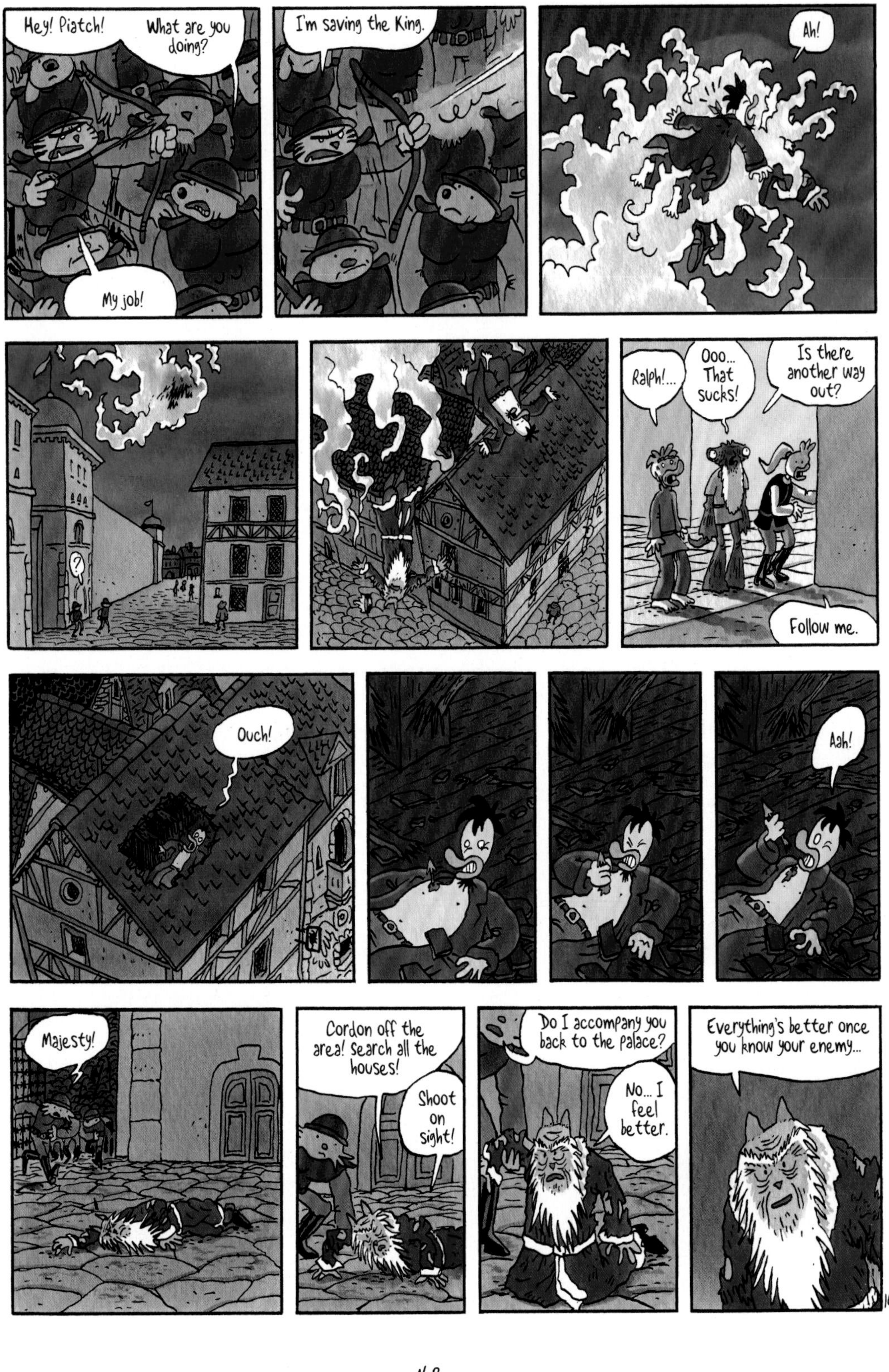
Hey! Piatch!
What are you doing?
My job!
I'm saving the King.
Ah!
Ralph!...
Ooo... That sucks!
Is there another way out?
Follow me.
Ouch!
Aah!
Majesty!
Cordon off the area! Search all the houses!
Shoot on sight!
Do I accompany you back to the palace?
No... I feel better.
Everything's better once you know your enemy...
140

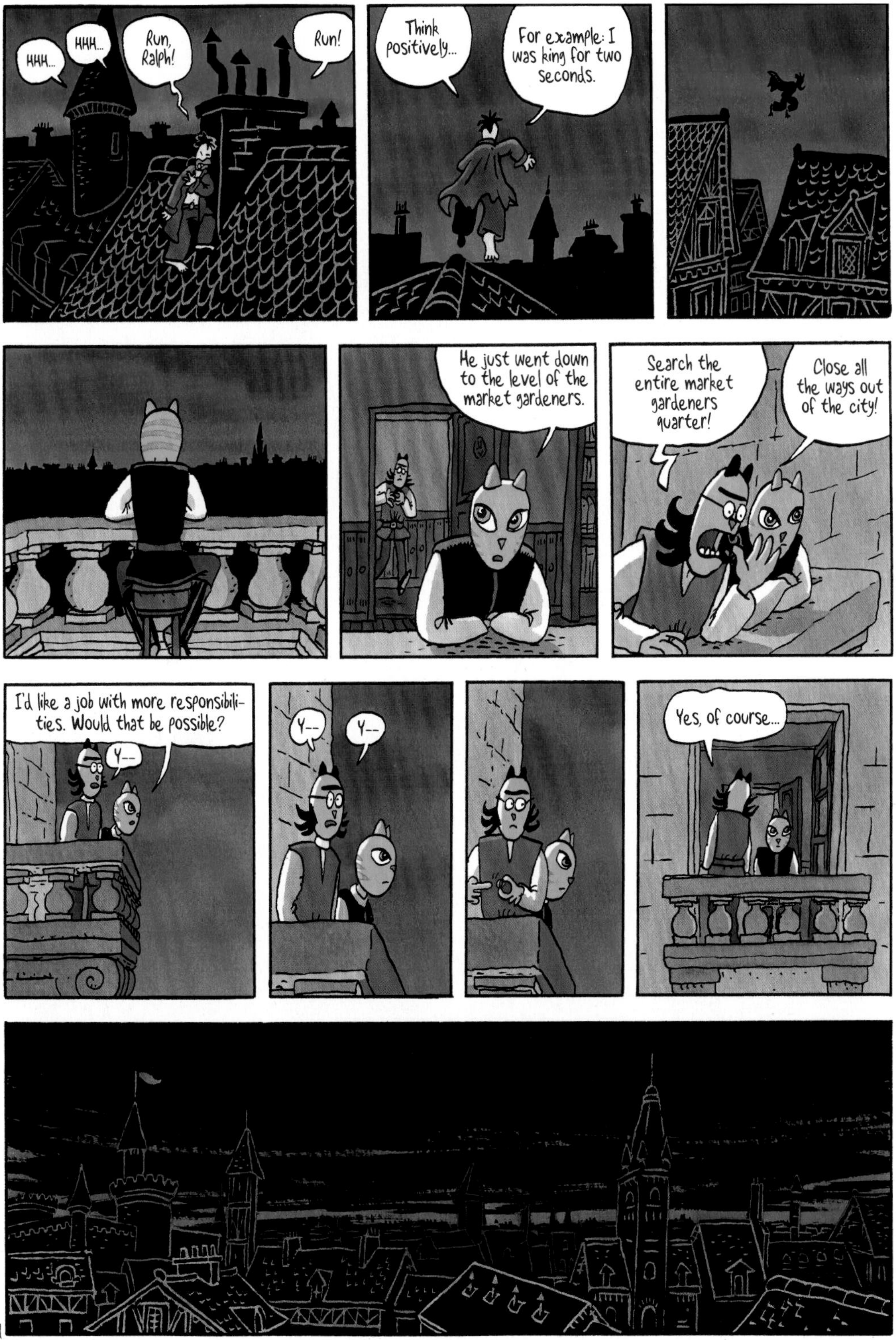
HHH...
HHH...
Run, Ralph!
Run!
Think positively...
For example: I was king for two seconds.
He just went down to the level of the market gardeners.
Search the entire market gardeners quarter!
Close all the ways out of the city!
I'd like a job with more responsibili-ties. Would that be possible?
Y--
Y--
Y--
Yes, of course...
141

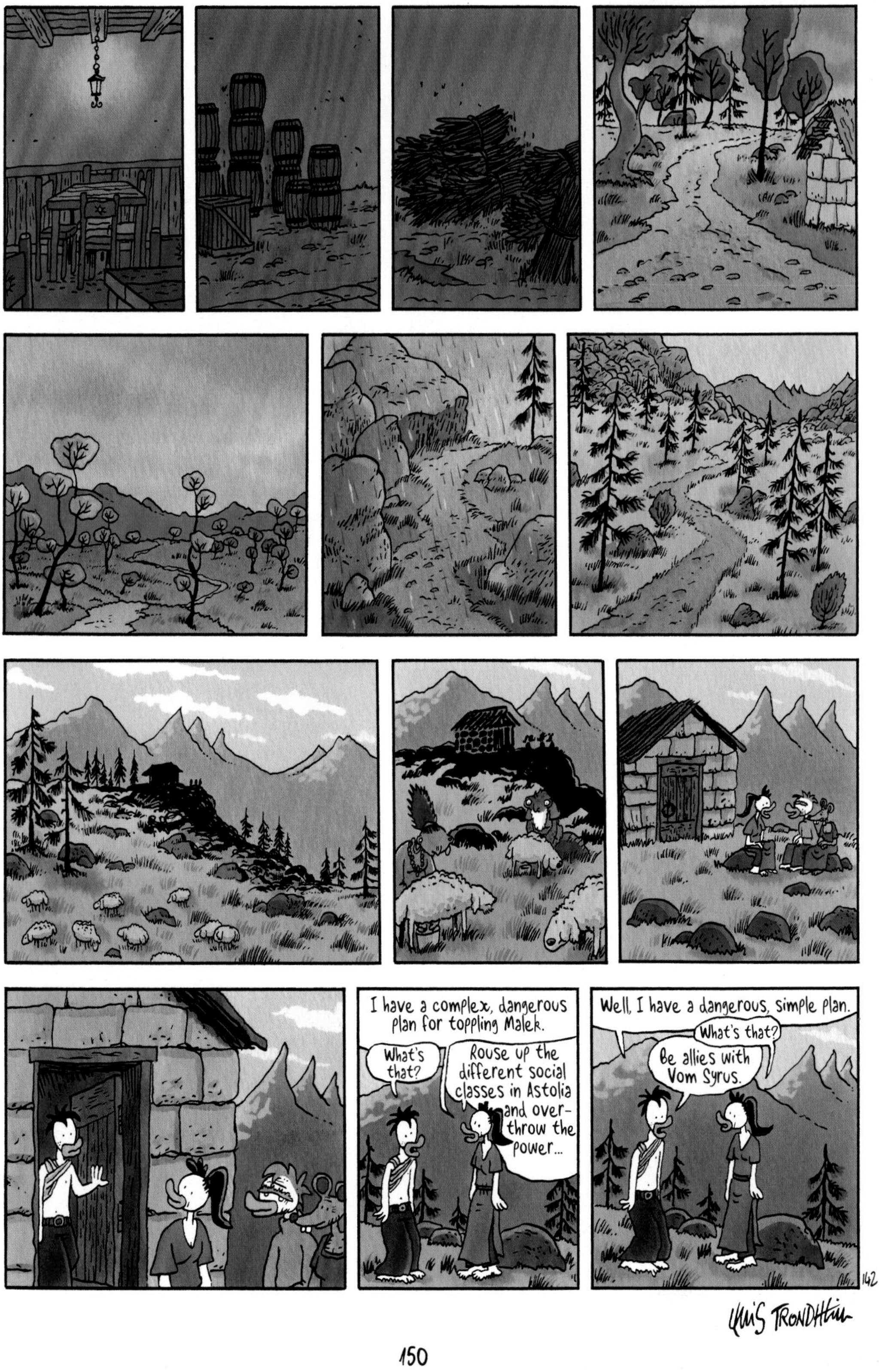
I have a complex, dangerous plan for toppling Malek.
What's that?
Rouse up the different social classes in Astolia and overthrow the power...
Well, I have a dangerous, simple plan.
What's that?
Be allies with Vom Syrus.
142
Lewis Trondheim

SUPER GENIUS

CONTACT INFO: EMAIL: salicrup@papercutz.com · WEB: supergeniuscomics.com
FANMAIL: Super Genius, 160 Broadway, Suite 700, East Wing, New York, NY 10038

What's Super Genius?
A really, really, smart person. It's also the name of this imprint from Papercutz, those clever folks dedicated to publishing great graphic novels for all ages. As the Editor-in-Chief of Papercutz, I passionately love putting together graphic novels that everyone can enjoy. Graphic novels such as THE ATTACK OF THE STUFF by Jim Benton, GILLBERT by Art Baltazar, SCHOOL FOR EXTRATERRESTRIAL GIRLS by Jeremy Whitley and Jamie Noguchi, THE SMURFS by Peyo, THE QUEEN'S FAVORITE WITCH by Ben Dickson and Rachael Smith, ASTERIX by René Goscinny and Albert Uderzo, and many more, including THE FLY by Lewis Trondheim. But I love all kinds of comics and in order to publish graphic novels for older audiences we (Papercutz publisher Terry Nantier and me) decided to launch the Super Genius imprint.

Who's a Super Genius?
While the name "Super Genius" is tongue-in-cheek and over-the-top, we have published some exceptional material, such as: WWE SUPERSTARS—Hey, don't laugh! We had none other than the great Mick Foley give us his unique take on his fellow superstars.

A true sports entertainment legend writing about what he knows best. NEIL GAIMAN'S LADY JUSTICE, MR. HERO, and TEKNOPHAGE—a whole universe of amazing characters conceived by Neil Gaiman. TALES FROM THE CRYPT—a new take on the classic horror comic. TRISH TRASH, ROLLERGIRL OF MARS—Talk about high concept! This series presented the sports entertainment aspect of the roller derby with a sci-fi twist (almost a mad mash-up of the two previous Super Genius series) by Jessica Abel. HIGH MOON—a werewolf Western by David Gallaher and Steve Ellis. THE JOE SHUSTER STORY—an innovative comics biography of the creators of Superman, by Julian Voloj and Thomas Campi. VINCENT—a coming of age comic featuring anthropomorphic gaming and comics fans, by Vitor Cafaggi. THE WENDY PROJECT—a girl dealing with a terrible tragedy with a Peter Pan twist, by Melissa Jane Osborne and Veronica Fish. THE CHILDREN OF CAPTAIN GRANT—Alexis Nesme's beautifully painted anthropomorphic adaptation of Jules Verne's classic tale. Whether you like these graphic novels or not, you have to agree they represent a wide range of wild concepts! Which brings us to Lewis Trondheim…

Who is Lewis Trondheim?

Born in 1964 in Fontainebleau, France, as Laurent Chabosy, he grew up to become the prolific cartoonist Lewis Trondheim. He's one of the founders of L'Association which turned comics publishing on its head. From wordless strips such as THE FLY (recently a North American edition was published by Papercutz) and Mr. O to the darkly tongue-in-cheek loving spoof of heroic fantasy Dungeon (American editions published by NBM) which he co-writes with Joann Sfar to comics he writes that are illustrated by others such as Maggie Garrison and Infinity 8, his breadth of contributions to comics is staggering. He's also known for McConey's Rabbit, A.L.I.E.E.E.N., and the MONSTER series (North American edition published by Papercutz), among other kids' graphic novels and he also heads the imprint called "Shampooing," which among other titles produces MAGICAL HISTORY TOUR (also published by Papercutz in English), for one

Self-portrait of Lewis Trondheim

of France's largest publishing companies. Both THE FLY and his Kaput and Zösky have been made into animated cartoons. There just seems to be no end to this cartoonist's creative output. Which now brings us to RALPH AZHAM…

Who is RALPH AZHAM?

As a comics fan, I simply can't get enough of Lewis Trondheim's work, no matter how prolific he may be—I always want more. Unfortunately, I don't speak or read French, so I'm dependent upon his work being translated into English. In 2001 when Fantagraphics said they were going to publish THE FLY (as Buzz Buzz) in a small announcement in the back of Approximate Continuum Comics (a wonderful biographical graphic novel by Trondheim) I was excited, and when they published the first volume of Ralph Azham, I could wait for the rest of that series.

So I waited.

And waited.

And waited. Until now. My wait is over. Finally, Papercutz published THE FLY and Super Genius is publishing RALPH AZHAM. Nothing against Fantagraphics—they're one of the greatest graphic novel publishers in the world. Not everything turns out as we hope. There are several Papercutz series I still wish we were publishing, but for various heart-breaking reasons it's not to be (although I still hope we do). This Super Genius volume of Ralph Azham includes the first Fantagraphics volume (the first story in this book) with the excellent translation by the late, great Kim Thompson, who was also co-publisher at Fantagraphics, as well as the next two volumes published for the first time in North America.

Personally, these stories have been well worth the wait. And even publishing three stories in one volume has an unexpected benefit as well. Sometime Trondheim will introduce an important plot point that doesn't pay off until many pages later, often in the next story. Having the stories together in one book makes it a bit easier to understand and enjoy when that happens.

If all goes well, we'll soon be back with the next three volumes in RALPH AZHAM #2 "The Land of the Blue Demons." If we're really lucky, we may even be able to publish more graphic novels by Lewis Trondheim in the future.

Thanks,

JIM

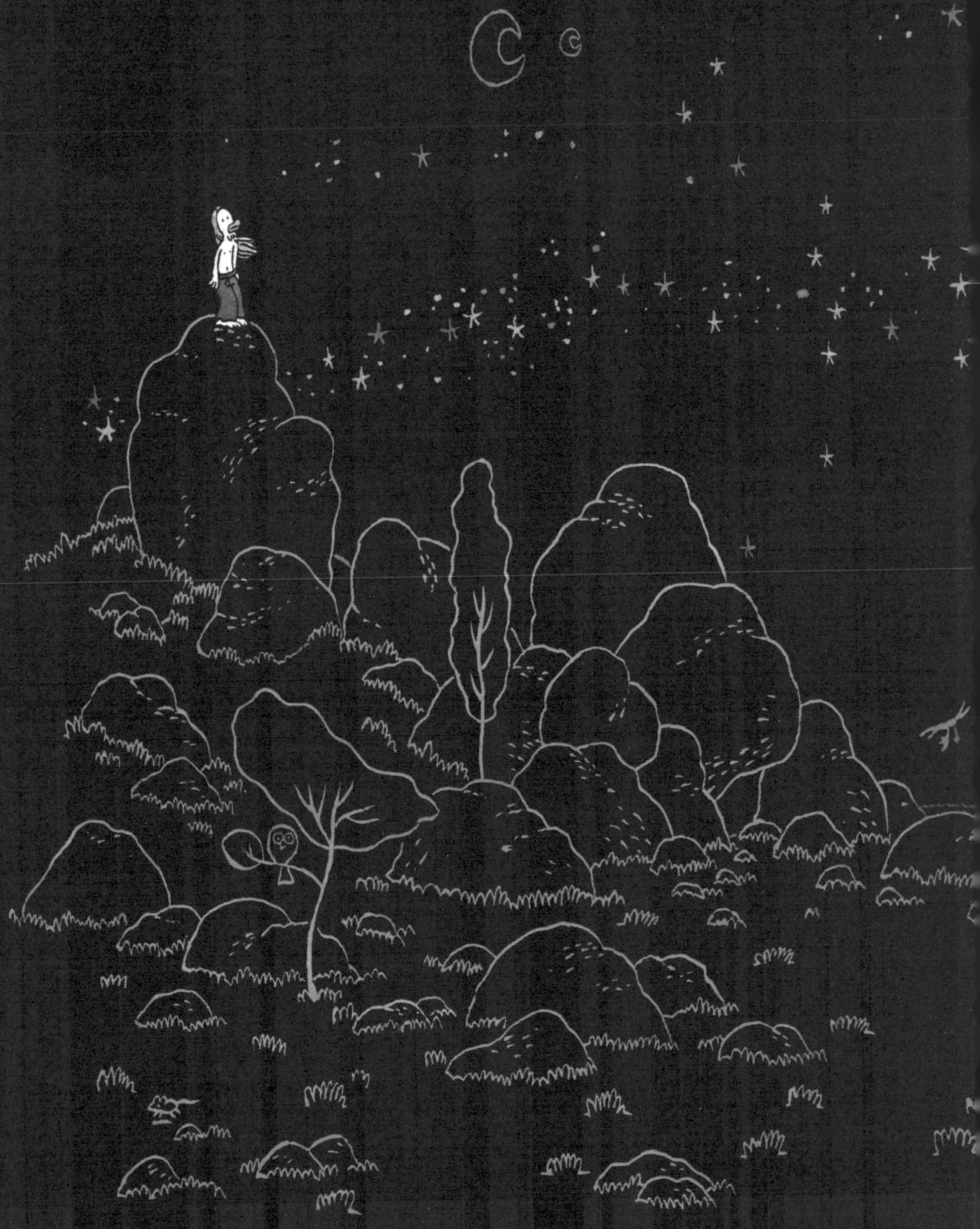